Time to Play the Game

By

Tim Jousma

I dedicate this book to my wife Vanessa, whose patience and love helped bring this project to fruition. From the bottom of my heart, thank you.

To Izaak, Ashley, and Luke, my children. I dedicate this to you as well. As George McFly would say, you can accomplish anything if you put your mind into it. If a guy like me can write a book, you three can do anything.

And to anyone who thought I could never accomplish anything like this, I got two words for ya...

SUCK IT!

THE PREVIOUS WEEK

Phil McKnight walked into the foyer of the Spring Arbor Hotel and Apartments and approached the counter. The attendant lifted her head and smirked.

"Can I help you?" she asked.

"Is that all I get Mel?"

Melanie VanderVeen scowled. "You're lucky I don't call security."

"What did I do?"

"You helped my ex-husband spy on me when I had hired you to get information on him."

"Hey, what can you do? Sorry. How have you been?"

"I don't want to shoot the breeze with you. What do you want?"

"I have business with one of the residents here."

"Name?"

"Desmond DiSalvo."

"Mr. DiSalvo doesn't accept visitors."

Phil pulled out his Private Investigator license. "I'm not visiting. I'm here on business."

"You whip out a badge you probably got from the back of a magazine and you expect me to act? There's the door. Don't let it smack you on the way out."

Phil sighed. "I should have expected this. I'm sorry I hurt your feelings. If there's anything I can do to make up..."

"All I want is a VIP invitation to your funeral. I'll forgive you then."

Phil paused then left. What to do? he thought. He saw the walkway that connected the Spring Harbor with the Brisbane Grand Hotel a couple blocks to his left and the Grand Rapids Arena a block to his right and got an idea. He ran till he reached the Brisbane Grand Hotel. He entered the front door and ran to the stairway heading to the second floor and the entrance to the walkway. He darted through the maze until he was in the Spring Arbor again. He found an elevator and got in.

Damn. The floors of the apartments, which were on the top five floors, were accessed by key card only preventing everyone but the folks who lived there to reach those floors. He took the elevator to the highest floor he could reach and got out. He looked around. A maid walked past pushing a cleaning cart. Phil stopped her.

"Excuse me, ma'am?"

"Yes?" the woman replied.

"I live on the penthouse level on the top floor and I seem to have forgotten my elevator key. I was wondering if you could help me out."

"You'll have to go to the front desk for that."

"Between you and me, we know that woman at the counter is a bitch. I don't like dealing with her. I was thinking I could make it worth your while to help me out," he said, pulling some money from his wallet.

The maid spotted the money and grinned. "Yeah. That woman does have a certain air about her. Follow me."

She headed back with Phil to the elevator. When the doors opened, she took out her card key and activated the top floor. He took out a hundred dollars and handed it to her.

"Thank you. What's your name?"

"Talinda. And make sure you forget that name if you get caught," she said, stepping out.

Phil smiled as the doors closed. The elevator rose up and in moments reached the top floor. The doors opened. He stepped out and scanned the area.

Desmond's room would be at the end of the hallway to his left. He strolled towards the door, trying to appear calmer then he felt. He brushed his hands against his suit coat, wiping the sweat from them. Phil stopped in front of Desmond's door and knocked.

No reply. He knocked again hoping deep down that all this wasn't in vain.

He heard the click of a gun behind him and stopped, lowering his hand.

"What's your business?" a man asked.

Phil smiled. "Based on my latest tax returns not much. How bout yours?"

Phil shot his leg back and landed his foot in the man's groin. He turned and punched the man on the jaw. The man tumbled to the ground, his gun flying across the hallway. Phil pulled out his gun from his holster and leveled it at the man's head.

"How many more of you are up here?" Phil asked.

The man smiled despite the pain. "The odds aren't in your favor pal I can tell you that much."

"As a wise man once said, never tell me the odds."

Phil kicked the man in the head, knocking him out. He heard footsteps coming from the elevator bank and looked around for an escape. The door to the stairs beckoned to him from the end of the hallway on his left. He ran for the door, kicked it open and bolted down the stairs.

A few floors from the ground floor he heard something that made him cringe. More people were coming up to greet him. He opened the door to the floor he was on and ran inside.

The direction sign for the walkway got his attention. He headed for the arena. There was a hockey game in a couple hours and if he were lucky, he'd be able to mingle with the crowd and lose these men.

About halfway across the runway, armed guards came running towards him from the direction of the arena. He stopped and turned round. The guards who were chasing him from the hotel boxed him in. He was trapped. He looked out the window of the walkway onto Fulton Street. A semi-truck ambled towards him. He smiled and raised his gun.

Three shots shattered the glass, sending it onto the road below. The men rushed him. Phil hopped onto the ledge and eyed the truck. The jump had to be perfect or else he'd be a speed bump for that massive hunk of metal.

Now. He jumped, landing on the trailer. Once the truck drove under the walkway, he fired off a couple shots at the walkway in order to scatter the men inside. Once the truck was a safe distance away, he pulled out his cell phone and dialed.

"Hello?"

"Hey Laura. Guess where I am?"

A pause. "Do I want to know?"

Darrell Sampson was in trouble. He burst through his apartment door locking it behind him. He leaned against it breathing hard, thinking about the shit storm he was in. He grabbed his bag off his shoulder with his shaky hand and reached inside pulling out a flash drive.

He'd overheard what Wilcox said was on this thing. Man, his brother would ring his neck now cause of his need to quench his curiosity at all costs. He knew the type of guy that Wilcox worked for. He'd heard and even witnessed on a couple occasions what Wilcox and the people he worked for could do. Yet here he was, stolen flash drive in hand, his life all but forfeit. Well, if he was going to die anyway he might as well see what all the fuss was about. He walked back to his bedroom closing the curtains along the way.

Heading into his bedroom, he moved the dresser to block the door. He headed to the bedroom window and closed the curtains. This precaution was probably all for naught but as long as he was breathing, he had to do whatever he could to protect himself. And in the movies, at least locking the doors and closing the curtains would keep the bad guys out. When he felt as comfortable as he could he pulled his laptop out of his bag and set it up on his desk. Firing it on, he slipped the flash drive into the USB port. Once ready, he opened the file on the flash drive.

He started reading. His fingers trembled, shaking with excitement. Times, places, people, money, it was all there. If he could just find a way to profit from this.

A noise from his living room startled him. He reached into his bag pulling out his gun. He rose from his chair and slowly stepped toward the bedroom door taking the flash drive from the computers USB port and slipped it in his pocket.

Someone on the other side started banging against the door. Darrell shook in fear watching the door come loose and his dresser creep closer with each slam. After about the fifth slam the door flew open. A bald man in his late forties walked through the door dressed completely in black. He held a gun that to Darrell looked as if it could blow a hole in an aircraft carrier.

"Who are you?" Darrell stammered.

"You know why I'm here. Where's the flash drive?"

"I don't know where it's at."

The man smiled. "I don't believe you."

"It's not here."

The man leveled his gun at Darrell's head. "I'm gonna ask you one more time. Where's the flash drive?"

Darrell raised his gun. "I said I don't know."

"Put that water pistol away boy. You ain't scaring me."

"I'm sorry," Darrell said, pulling the trigger.

It was as if he could see the bullet floating in the air straight into the man's forehead. The man in black stumbled, looking at him as if he didn't expect him to actually pull the trigger then fell to the floor dead.

Holy crap! Darrell thought. He ran to his desk and packed his laptop into his backpack. More noises came from the living room. Darrell ran to the window, ripped open the curtain, and opened it. Four guys with guns came storming into his apartment building. Once he saw them inside, he climbed out and fell to the ground. Darrell ran off toward his car.

****

Annie Walker knew the man in the gray t-shirt was following her. She smiled, thinking about how his ego would be shattered if he knew he wasn't as smooth as he thought. She had places to go so she couldn't keep this charade up for much longer. Her destination was just up ahead, the parking garage on Pearl Street. She had a thought that made her smile. Annie stood an elegant six two, her brown hair flowing from under a beret. A pair of dark sunglasses hid her eyes. Her shapely figure was framed in a beautiful low cut dress. If her beauty were a disease, she'd **be lethal. And it was that lethalness she'd use to her advantage.**

As she passed by a coffee shop, she pretended to stumble. Annie paused, placing the palm of her hand on her ankle gently tugging the silk stalking up her thigh. With a flash of modesty, as if suddenly realizing how much leg she was showing, she quickly pulled down her skirt. Annie had to get this guy to think with the head in his pants and one way to do that was with one of her favorite weapons, her innocent girl act. She gave him enough of an image to last him many a lonely night then headed to the parking garage.

The man in the gray t-shirt followed her into the garage. From his surveillance earlier, he knew her car was on the second level. He went to the stairs and took them up to the next floor. He spotted her car on the other side of the garage. The place echoed with his footsteps. He was glad no one would be around to see what he had to do. He headed toward her car.

He reached her car yet she wasn't there. Something was wrong. He turned around.

Before he could react, Annie's car door opened and a pair of hands reached out and pulled him into her car. A roll of duct tape quickly covered his mouth and a pair of handcuffs secured his hands. Annie straddled the man and stared into his eyes.

"You know it's awfully rude to sneak up on someone like you've been doing. Now when I take the tape off you're going to answer a couple questions. If you're cooperative, then maybe I'll be nice to you. If not, I think you know enough of my reputation to know what I can do. Are we going to have any problems?"

The man shook his head no. Annie smiled, taking the tape off his mouth.

"Now, why are you following me?"

The man laughed. "You know, in any other situation this could be quite sexy."

Annie smiled. "Wrong answer."

She reached into the front seat and pulled out a box. It appeared to be a common flip top box containing a pair of eyeglasses. She flipped it open and pulled out a long needle. Closing the box, she waved the needle in the man's face.

"This will hurt."

She put the tape back across the man's mouth. His cockiness disappeared the moment the needle appeared in front of him. She placed the tip of the needle on his bicep. With a mischievous smile, she shoved the needle into his arm. The tape stifled most of his scream but she could still feel the agony coursing through his body. It sent a shiver of excitement through her spine. After pulling out the needle, she pulled out the tape from his mouth again.

"Let's start this again. Why are you following me?"

The man took a couple deep breaths. "It was your boyfriend George. He thinks you know."

"Know what?"

"Know what he's been doing."

"Humor me. What has he been doing?"

"If you don't know….."

She stabbed the man in the arm again, this time letting his screams fill the car. Pulling the needle out of his arm, she waved the bloody piece of steel in front of his eyes.

"I have all day and many more parts of the body to explore. Quit toying with me."

After a couple breaths the man responded, "He's been stealing money from Xander. He thought you knew and were going to inform Xander and have him killed."

Annie smiled. "After all this, I'm going to do just that."

She took the needle and shoved it in his ear severing his brain stem, killing him instantly. She hopped into the front seat of her car, started it up, and pulled out. She got to the first floor of the garage, pulled out her electronic pass, and exited through the monthly parking lane. She took a right heading toward Division Street. At the stop light, she pulled out her cell phone. She had Xander on speed dial.

"Hello?"

"Xander, its Annie. I have some news for you."

"What's that?"

"Georgie boy has been stealing some money from you. I can assume what you want me to do to him correct?"

A pause. "Yeah. Head over to Great Lakes Bank for me first as we planned. Then take care of George for me. Call me when you're done."

"Talk to you later."

Annie hung up the phone. After she disposed of the mess in the back seat, she'd have to have a sit down with George. The sooner the better.

****

Richard Wilcox sat at the red light impatiently waiting for it to change. His impatience had been brought on by the news that the Sampson kid had escaped. How some dumb kid in his mid-twenties could get past trained armed guards was beyond him. But no situation had only one solution. If there was something his Father always taught him, always have a plan B.

The light turned green just as his cell phone rang. He took out his phone as he stepped on the gas.

"Hello?"

"It's Xander. I'm hearing some reports that your plan didn't work out as planned in regards to that Sampson kid. Is that true?"

"It is. But you know me Xander. I have a plan B."

"Will this be another plan of yours that ends in failure too?"

"Xander…"

"Don't start. You're riding my last nerve here. I entrust you with something of a private nature, a flash drive with information that in the wrong hands can cause a lot of people trouble, and you end up losing it."

"Like I was trying to say Xander, yes plan A failed. But I have a plan B."

"And what is plan B?"

"I'm traveling to his office now. If the news from the past week is any indication, he'll jump at the money I'm going to offer him."

A pause. "This had better work."

****

The dog lay curled on the floor, asleep. Curtis Banfield approached it with a large steak in his hand. As he got closer, the dog's nose started sniffing and its head rose, anticipating its treat. Curtis stopped.

"Come on boy," he said.

The dog rose and stared at the steak. Curtis waved the snack in the air once, twice, and on the third swing, he threw it. The massive dog jumped as far as its chain allowed. The steak landed in its mouth and the dog clamped onto its meal. Curtis knelt down and petted the dog.

"Why the hell do you keep that mean ass dog here Curtis? He don't like no one but you."

"Well, Thomas, a man has to know whom he can trust. This guy only loves me and his friends. And you ain't one of them."

Curtis turned and surveyed the room. His gang was waiting for him. The three men waiting were the best criminals the state of Michigan had to offer. Curtis walked to his chair, built like a throne, and faced them as the king he felt he was.

"Well, boys, we got some work to do today. The shipment happens early tomorrow morning. But we got a problem."

"What now?" asked Derrick.

"The route needs to be changed. Someone got some advanced word about it and told the bacon."

"Who's the snitch?"

"Don't know, don't care. However, it's still going down. We just have to change the plans a little. Derrick, I want you and Thomas to go and pick up the delivery. I know it don't seem like much but it's quite important. Smelly Boy, you're coming with me."

"Why do you have to keep calling me that?" Smelly Boy asked.

"Cause you're the only cracker I know who got picked out of a lineup based on his nasty ass." The other's laughed.

Curtis rose. "Thomas, I want to talk to you a sec. The rest of you get to work."

The men got up and began to leave. Curtis walked over to Thomas.

"It's important that you and Derrick go out and pick up that delivery for tomorrow. I wouldn't send anyone I didn't trust. Besides, the pay's good."

"All right. I just don't want a crap job," Thomas said.

Curtis smiled. "You're the best man I've ever met. Besides my dog."

****

The coffee was thick and had the smell of rotting wood. Yet to Phil McKnight, it was the perfect medicine for his insomnia. He took a sip and shivered as the punishing liquid traveled down his throat.

It appeared to be the start of another red-letter day for a low-level private eye. The only cases that seemed to come his way were from some wife who suspected that their husband's overtime at work meant he must be cheating. Most of the time their suspicions proved correct and Phil gave the information he accumulated to the woman's attorney. However after dealing with some of these basket cases that had long ago gotten drunk off the pleasure money gives you from marrying wealthy, he'd meet with their husbands and inform them of their wives' actions saying that for a price he'd give them an alibi. So for a business that depended on positive word of mouth he had a reputation for being a dick that was a dick.

Phil walked over to the filing cabinet, adjusted his tie, and took out the one thing inside, a Robert Ludlum novel. He turned his head and glanced at the mirror that his wife Laura thought would look nice in his office. Black suit and tie, the beginnings of wrinkles spreading across his face, and eyes that looked like they hadn't seen sleep in a few months time. He walked over to his desk and sat down, shoving aside the bills the city of Grand Rapids gave him for the damage he made on the crosswalk over Fulton Street. Phil took a quick glance at a picture on his desk of his son Ty. He smiled at the little face that beamed back at him. Then he opened the book and continued where he left off.

A knock on his office door jolted him. Business, he thought. Or the landlord.

"Come in," Phil yelled, putting the book in a drawer.

The door opened and a man dressed like a weasel in a suit walked inside. Phil rose from his desk.

"Can I help you?" Phil asked.

"You're Phil McKnight?"

"That I am. And you are?"

"My name is Richard Wilcox. You a Tarantino fan or something?"

"No. I'm more of a Blues Brother's man. What brings you here?"

"You come in high regard from people who know people."

"I'm touched. Please take a seat. My time is money and this mindless chatter is putting me in the hole."

Richard laughed, taking the seat across from Phil. "I understand."

"You want some coffee?" Phil asked.

Richard peered into Phil's cup. "Uh, no."

Phil paused. "Well then, what brings you to my office?"

"I have a problem. I own a small business that deals mostly in computers. An employee of mine who I thought I could trust ended up running off with a flash drive containing information from the computer of a very important man in this state."

Phil took a sip from his coffee. "Guy have some good porn on it or something?"

"I take my business seriously sir."

"I'm sure you do. Please forgive my moment of levity. Continue."

"The person who owns that computer with the missing flash drive will be picking it up tomorrow. I'm willing to pay you anything to get it back."

"What's so important about it?" Phil asked.

"I don't care what's important about it. I just want my customer to get it back."

A pause. "Tell me about the employee."

Richard made a little movement with his mouth that made him look more like a weasel as he talked. "I didn't know him that well personally. He was kind of a loner. But I tell you, he was magic with computers. I'm probably more upset that I'm losing such a great employee than I am with catching a thief."

"What's his name?"

Richard pulled out an envelope and handed it to Phil. "This is all the paperwork I have on him. His name is Darrell Sampson. His address is there along with his social security number."

"Do you have a DNA sample? Don't answer. Just being silly. I can do this. But it's going to cost you."

"I realize that. I'm willing to pay you anything. I have to get this flash drive back anyway I can. I also need you to bring Darrell to me as well."

Phil leaned back in his chair a moment. "Sounds illegal."

"The term illegal is all in how you look at things."

Phil looked at the man, thinking of the total of the bill from the city and decided he would add another ten percent to that figure. "Anything illegal is going to cost you. Ten thousand should just about do it."

Richard smiled. "I understand."

He pulled out his wallet and counted out ten thousand dollars in cash. As each one hundred dollar bill slapped down on his desk, Phil cursed himself for not asking for more.

"If that's not enough, call me at this number." He handed Phil his card. "If it gets messy, I'll give you more to clean it up."

"You must want this thing back pretty bad."

The weasel leaned over the desk and with his stare, drilled holes in Phil's eyes. "Eager? Try numb with fear. A man has to keep his reputation you know. One bad incident like this and I'm ruined."

"Well, if you want to have any chance of keeping that reputation, I'll need to get to work." Phil rose from his desk.

Richard, Weasel Man as Phil thought of him now, rose from his chair. "Remember; bring him to me along with the flash drive. In fact, the quicker you do it, the bigger your bonus."

With that, the man turned and left. Phil turned his head so he wouldn't be tempted to see if Richard had a tail.

"I've got a job," he said to himself.

Phil rose from his desk and walked over to the filing cabinet. He opened a drawer, pulling out a metal lock box. He walked over and placed it on the desk, opening it. Inside was his gun, plenty of ammo, and his holster. He couldn't quite pinpoint why he mistrusted the Weasel. Something in his head told him to bring along some protection. But as long as he needed the cash to pay off the city for the damage he made he had to take this job.

He put on the holster. It had been a long time since he'd used it. It felt good being on him again. He put his gun in the holster and walked over to mirror. He stared at himself and posed. With a face like this, I could be in pictures. He headed for the door to leave. With the cash Richard left him, he'd feel better if it was safely stashed away in the bank.

Phil's cell phone rang. He answered on the second ring. "Hello?"

"Hello Phil."

Phil cringed. I have to get caller ID on this phone. "Hi Laura. How are you?"

"You forgot to call your son this morning."

"Now is not the best time."

"Are you in the middle of a chapter? Should I tell him you can't speak with him cause your book is so interesting?"

The woman had a way to make words feel like knives. "I have no problem talking to Ty but believe it or not I have a job."

"From the size of your pay check I was beginning to wonder."

"Stop that. Just put him on the phone."

There was a rustling as the phone changed hands. "Hi Daddy."

"Hey little man. How are you?"

"I'm playing with the car Grandma got me."

"Cool. I'll see ya tonight little man. Please put Mommy back on the phone."

"Bye."

The phone rustled. "Phil?"

"What? Want to yell at me some more?"

Laura sighed. "I was harsh. I'm sorry. I'm starting that job at Senator Wilson's today and I'm a little nervous. I just wish you would keep your word with Ty, that's all."

Phil hung his head and sighed. "You're right. You don't have to be all in my face and stuff though."

"I know things have been rough lately with your lack of work and having to pay off the damage you made. We'll get through this like we always do."

Phil smiled. "What would I do without you? Thanks baby."

"You're welcome."

"Bye."

Phil shook his head. I'll never understand that woman, he thought.

****

Laura heard the doorbell and turned to her son. "You ready to see Cora?"

"Yeah."

Laura walked Ty to the door and opened it. Cora met her there with a smile.

"Hey bay-be. Come on over and give Cora some sugar. Boy, you growin like a weed."

Ty ran over and gave her a hug. "I played with my new car at the park yesterday."

She smiled. "Why don't you get your toys together so you can play with them at my house."

"Cool." Ty turned and headed for his bedroom.

Cora turned to Laura. "Girl, you got somethin heavy weighin on your mind?"

Laura smiled. Cora had been Ty's nanny for a couple years now and she felt like a part of the family. "I'm ok. I'm just tired."

"Oh please. Now you know you can't hide nothin from me."

"I'm fine. I've got that new job at Senator Wilson's estate today and I'm just nervous starting there with it being a high profile job and all."

"Mmph. Politicians. I'd never trust one of them lyin dogs." She put her hand on Laura's shoulder. "You're a strong woman and sometimes it seems like you don't even realize it. You've gone through much more than I have when I was your age. I know you got it in you."

"Thank you. I needed that." Laura turned to see Ty running back from his room. "Have a good time at Cora's and listen to her, you hear me?"

"Yes Mom," he said.

The boy grabbed Cora's hand. "Let's go," he said.

"He must have got that mouth from his Daddy," Cora laughed.

****

Phil pulled his car into the bank parking lot. He found the space he wanted and parked, pulling out his last bit of change for the meter.

Time to make a deposit, he thought. Only a fool would carry around five thousand dollars in cash. He opened the door to the bank and cursed. On today of all days, when he only had a quarter for the parking meter, the line had to be longer than the Great Wall of China. He walked over to the end of the line and started waiting. In front of him was a little old lady just as mad as he was.

"I hate this," Phil said.

The old woman turned around and smiled. "You should have seen it before you got here. I was thirty three then." They both laughed.

The sound of the gun shocked them all. Phil forced the old woman down so she wouldn't get hurt. He turned and spotted a woman with a sawed off shotgun.

The woman, knowing she had everyone's attention began to speak. "I'm not here to rob this place. I'm looking for a man who works here. His name is Dawson Layfield. If he comes forward, then you all will be free to go about your business. Otherwise I'm going to have to start killing someone every ten minutes."

11:00 AM-12:00 PM

"With the election only five months away, speculation is running high on whether or not Governor Davis Creston will be successful in his forth bid for the office. Governor Creston has been the most popular Governor in state history. However, Democrats have upped their efforts this election year in a bid to oust the man who's beaten them at every turn. I'm Clarissa Day. Back to you in the studio."

Nathan Gibraltar turned off the replay of last night's news broadcast online in disgust. He had someone looking to kill him and Governor Davis Creston was looking towards his second term. Nathan wondered about the sanity of the voters if a geriatric old fool like Davis Creston stood in high regard while true political geniuses like himself sat in political obscurity. The only reason Nathan had accepted the Lt. Governorship in the first place was that he didn't think Davis would run for his second term. He thought this position would be a quick stepping-stone to future greatness. Instead, he sits here, languishing in oblivion, making speeches at the opening of farm shows that didn't even give him a sound bite on the local news.

His Chief of Staff Steven Alexander Falcone walked into the room to go over his itinerary for the day. "Good morning Nathan. How are things this morning?"

"My assistant along with a friend of hers kept me up for most of the night."

Steven laughed. "You have a hell of a job. You ready for your trip today?"

Nathan moaned. "Oh man. And let me guess where."

"Your favorite place. Grand Rapids. They're rededicating the statue of one of their town fathers, Otis Brisbane."

"I see. Go there; suffer through some stupid ceremony, than we get some Brisbane money for the campaign this fall."

"It starts at three."

"I know when it starts. Question is how long do I have to be there?"

"About an hour and a half at the max."

Nathan smiled. "Good. Then I can have some drinks before I get there so I can be in a good mood. Get my speechwriter on the phone. I have a masterpiece to create."

"Will do. Also, we've had your security bumped up as well. We've received a credible threat that you're old friend Robert is back in town."

Nathan shook his head. "The plans we've discussed will be in place, correct? If we have to deal with him it has to be done right."

"Nathan, I have it covered. He will not be a threat to you. What more do I have to do to prove my loyalty?"

Nathan laughed. "Forgive me. As my wife would gladly tell you I can be quite a bastard."

****

"You have three more minutes Dawson," the woman yelled. "You won't end up making me kill one of your customers, will you?"

Phil glanced around at each door for its nameplate, trying to find out where this Dawson person's office she was looking for. He spotted Dawson's nameplate on a door.

"Hey lady," Phil yelled, "why don't you try his office instead of killing people while he sits in there like a coward?"

"Good idea. Why didn't I think of that? Wait a minute, it's because I want his sniveling, donut eating posterior to come out here and beg for his life."

"Hey, shut up man. Don't get her angry," someone yelled.

"What did he do?" Phil asked, ignoring the person.

"One more minute Dawson."

Dawson, if he was in there, wasn't coming out. The seconds ticked by much faster than the crowd wanted them to. People hoped they wouldn't be the first to be killed. Finally, it was 11:10 a.m.

The woman forced a frail old man to his feet. She turned and looked at the security monitor. "Here's one for you Dawson."

The woman raised her shotgun. Phil, making sure he wasn't spotted, took out a guns.

"Put that away," the old woman whispered.

"Just get back and stay low."

Phil jumped to his feet and shot the gun out of the woman's hand. The old man dove to the ground and crawled away as fast he could. Phil approached the woman, gun raised.

"I think it's time to stop this nonsense, wouldn't you agree?"

The woman looked at him and smiled. "Great shot."

"Comes with practice."

The door to Dawson Layfield's office opened. He poked his head out. Dawson spotted Phil and stepped out.

Before Phil could react, the woman lowered her hand in Dawson's direction. Phil heard a snap and a thump. He saw Dawson, knife in his throat, blood spraying out like a garden hose.

The crowd panicked. The woman used this as her chance to run. Phil followed her in pursuit.

****

Darrell stepped off the bus and ran over to his friend's apartment building. The trip had taken longer than he'd expected and his paranoia, already jacked up to levels he thought impossible, was ready to boil over. He reached the lobby of the apartment building. On the wall to his right were the buzzer buttons for the apartments, meant to keep out unnecessary people but generally ignored by its residents. He scanned the buttons looking for his friend Marty's apartment number. Once he found it, he pressed the button.

"You better be home," Darrell muttered.

After a moment of silence, a beep spat out from the speaker. "Who is it?"

"It's Darrell. Let me in."

A buzz and Darrell ran into the building. He raced to the top floor, apartment seven C. Marty had the door open.

"What's going on Darrell?"

Darrell pushed Marty inside. He turned and locked the door. He grabbed his friend by the arm and dragged him to the bedroom.

"What the hell are you doing?" Marty yelled.

"Close your curtains."

Darrell put the backpack on the bed, taking out the laptop and flash drive. "What's this? What the hell is wrong with you?" Marty asked.

"It was that thing I told you about the other night. That flash drive I stole from work."

"Shit. Why are you bothering me with this nonsense?"

"Don't say nothing till you see what's on here."

Darrell turned on his laptop and began showing him the secrets the flash drive held.

****

Derrick pulled into the gas station and parked next to a pump. He got out of the car and took off the gas cap. He grabbed the nozzle, punched the button for the cheapest gas, and started pumping. Thomas rolled down the window.

"How long does it take to get there?" Thomas asked.

"Eight hours there and eight back. We should be back in town around three in the morning."

"Damn. I'll enjoy the payday but damn. Sitting on my ass for that long."

"A man's gotta do, know what I mean. I love driving. Hell, I used to be a cab driver. My advice, head inside, buy lots of caffeine. Get some of them little pills too. Makes driving fun."

Thomas laughed. "I didn't know you were a pill head."

"Oh yeah. You know those aspirin sleeping pills things? Take about fifteen to twenty of them and you start seeing shit."

"Damn. I need to party with you more often."

The gas nozzle stopped. Derrick pulled it out and put it back on the pump.

"I'm heading in to pay. Want anything?"

"With the drive we got, load us up on shit to keep us up."

****

Phil sat against the wall outside the bank. The woman had escaped. What a hell of a way to start the day.

The cops finally arrived along with an ambulance for the late Mr. Layfield. Phil stood up as one of the police cars stopped in front of him. Phil had to smile.

"Detective Campbell, is that you?"

"You bet yer ass."

Detective Stone Campbell stepped out of his unmarked car. He'd been Phil's only real friend in the police department since he'd set up shop.

Stone straightened his shirt and walked over to shake Phil's hand. "What the hell happened in there?"

Phil sighed. "Some strange woman came in with some rigged up shotgun demanding to see Dawson Layfield. Threatened to kill a person every ten minutes if he didn't come out. I was able to get the gun out of her hands, which made Mr. Layfield feel safe. That's when she was able to get a knife in his throat, straight out the back of his neck. She had a rig on her arm or something. The crowd went nuts. She ran out of the building. I tried to chase after her but with the crowd as freaked out as they were she ended up getting away."

"Is her gun still in the building?"

"Yeah. She's even on the security camera. She made no attempt to hide her identity. That chick had some balls."

Stone laughed. "That's a girl after my own heart. So, Phil my boy. What's been keeping you busy?"

"I got hired on a case this morning. Looking for some kid named Darrell Sampson because he…"

"What was that name?" Stone interrupted.

"Darrell Sampson."

Stone shook his head. "There was a homicide today at his house. And he's missing."

"His boss said he ran off with a flash drive owned by a big shot. Do you have an address on him you can give me?"

"That I do. Your cell phone still work?"

"It will a lot more if you can help find that kid."

Stone laughed. "You're a trip. I gotta get inside to check out that mess. See ya later. And thanks for the statement."

****

The gunman pulled up next to the curb and shut off his car. He had to find that Sampson kid. If he couldn't find him, then maybe he can find one of his friends and force them to tell him where the kid was. He had to find that flash drive the kid stole, no matter whose life needed to be taken in the process.

He picked up his cell phone and dialed. "I found the building Mr. Wilcox."

"What's the word?" Richard replied.

"I'm in front of the Old Warehouse Apartments. What you want me to do?"

A pause. "Find that jerk off friend of his, Marty, and do whatever it takes to find Darrell."

The gunman smiled. "No problem."

****

Annie Walker sat in a booth at her favorite coffee house a few blocks from the bank waiting for her guest. She sipped her tea, letting her active mind rest for a minute or two. She picked up a packet of honey crystals on her left, opened it, and poured the contents into her drink.

The clanging bell announced another customer and Annie knew it would be George. After finding out the length of his betrayal, it wasn't going to be difficult to take him out of the picture. Besides, this whole lovey dovey act was getting old. If he only knew who her true love was...

George came up behind her and put his hand on her shoulder. "Hello Annie."

She kept her gaze on her tea. "Have a seat."

He stepped over and sat in the booth across from her. "What is it? You seem upset."

She took a breath and lifted her head. "I'm fine."

"Were you able to get the job done?" he asked.

She sipped her tea. "Yeah."

"And Layfield..."

"Is out of the picture. I took care of him."

George sat back and sighed, content. "That ought to make Xander happy."

"I'm sure it will."

"You really do seem upset. What's wrong?"

"Nothing."

George offered out his hand. "Come here."

She put her hand in his. He caressed it. She hid her revulsion behind a dreamy smile.

"You are my angel. I love you so much. Without you, I'm an incomplete man."

"I have to get going. Xander has more work for me."

"Oh you tease. When will I see you again?"

"Oh, I don't know. Call me tomorrow," she smiled. "Do you want the rest of my tea?"

"Sure. I ordered a drink when I came in but it looks like it won't be here any time soon."

She picked up the cup. Without him seeing, she slipped a small pill from her pocket and dropped it into the tea. She rose, handing him the cup.

"I'll call you," he said.

"I'm sure you will."

She turned and walked out of the coffee shop. She'd miss him but he'd served his purpose.

****

Phil pulled into the parking lot of a convenience store about two blocks from Darrell's house. He wanted to see if anyone in the neighborhood knew him and whether he'd been seen recently. Basically, the type of work he hated doing, talking to people. He got out of his car and walked to the store entrance. A cool, air-conditioned breeze pulled him inside. He walked up and down the aisles looking for something to buy.

Ahh, chips, pop, and an English muffin. A single man's healthy, nutritious breakfast. He brought everything to the counter for the cashier to ring up.

"How's it going?" Phil asked.

"Not bad. You?" the cashier replied, his disinterest as obvious as polio.

"I'm cool. How long you work here?"

The cashier thought about it a moment. "About three years. Before I met my wife."

"Would you recognize a person if I showed you a picture?"

"You a cop or something?"

"Something like that, yeah."

Phil pulled the picture out of his pocket and showed it to the cashier. The cashier looked at it a moment then smiled.

"It's that little punk Darrell Sampson," the cashier said.

"Have you seen him lately?"

"He was in earlier. Bought a candy bar. He was heading to his friend Marty's house."

"Where does his friend live?"

"Does it matter?"

"This is a criminal investigation. Everything is relevant."

The cashier wrote an address on a slip of paper and handed it to Phil. "Marty and I used to party back in the day."

Phil paused, stifling a laugh. "Was he alone or with someone?"

"That kid? Alone."

Phil smiled. "Not a ladies' man, huh?"

"That'd be him."

"Can you tell me anything else about him?"

"I'm a cashier, not his biographer."

Phil smiled. He handed the cashier ten bucks for his purchase.

"Keep the change," Phil said.

****

Marty pushed Darrell again. "Get the hell out of my house!"

"Marty, come on. I need your help."

"With what you got, I ain't doing shit. Do you think I want to die?"

"I don't want to die myself," Darrell said. "I didn't know what would be on that flash drive when I took it."

"Ignorance is ignorance and I refuse to die for yours."

Marty pushed him out of the bedroom. Darrell zipped up his backpack.

"Marty, please. I have no one here to help me. "

"What do you expect? I work in a factory for God's sake. I don't want anything to do with this. "

Someone pounded on the front door. Both men froze, glaring toward the entrance. Darrell walked into the kitchen, pulled out his gun, and put the backpack in the bottom cupboard.

"What do we do? " Marty whispered.

"I think we have to improvise. "

****

The place looked like a ghost town, minus the tumbleweed and horses. Phil turned off his car and stepped out, taking in the foul air of the nearby factories. The wrong side of the tracks. His kind of town.

He walked to the entrance of the apartment building and pressed a bunch of the buttons at once. Some of the apartment dwellers answered over the intercom, some buzzed the door, not caring who could be there. Phil opened it and walked inside.

Phil reached the top of the stairs and sensed something was wrong. He pulled his gun out of the holster and approached Marty's door. Or what was left of it. He heard screaming from inside the apartment and decided he had to help. He stepped through.

****

The man dragged Marty out of the closet, his gun at Marty's head. Darrell stared, unable to act.

"Where is it Darrell? You just gonna let your friend die like this?"

The orbs of Darrell's eyes widened to the size of saucers. "Don't touch him."

The man laughed. "What're you gonna do about it? I know you got your shot in earlier on Johnson but guess what? He was a pussy. Now do me a favor and tell me where the flash drive is or your pal gets it."

Darrell didn't answer. The man pulled the trigger, killing Marty. His friend slumped to the floor, the remaining insides of his head spilling onto the carpet. The man looked at the mess and smiled. Then he raised his gun at Darrell.

A shot rang out. Darrell stared at the man, not knowing what had just happened. A growing red stain appeared on his shirt. The man looked down, shocked. He turned toward the source of the shot and fell next to Marty.

What the hell is this? Darrell thought. Some guy dressed in a ratty old suit walked into the room, gun raised. He had to run. But he had nowhere to go. The man approached him.

"You Darrell Sampson?" the man asked.

Darrell stared, not knowing how to react. How does he know my name? How could he know it?

"Please don't kill me," Darrell said.

"If I wanted to I would have already."

"Who are you?" Darrell asked.

The man held out his hand. "Phil McKnight. Let's get out of here before more of his friends show up."

"Where are you taking me?" Darrell asked.

"Back to my office. I'm a private detective. I was hired by your former boss to get something back that you stole."

"I ain't going nowhere. He wants me dead." Darrell raised his gun.

"Why would he do that?"

"Why would he send someone to kill me and my friend? Because of what's on the flash drive"

"What are you talking about? What could be so important about a damn flash drive?"

"It's not anything you'd understand. The information stored on it is like dynamite."

"What kind of information?"

"I'd have to show you."

"I'm sure you do. We'll head to my office and I'll give Mr. Wilcox a call."

"You work for him and yet you won't kill me? You're full of it."

"If you want this resolved in your favor in any way then tell me something now or else I collect my fee from Mr. Wilcox."

Darrell hesitated. "I don't know."

Phil took out his cell phone. "I'll call him now."

Darrell lowered the gun. "Don't. I'll show you what it has at your office. What I've been able to get off it that is."

"Huh?"

"That's all I can explain without being able to show you. You'll understand when you see it."

Phil put his finger in Darrell's face. "It'd better have something. That's all I'm saying. Now get that damn gun out of my face," Phil said, slapping the gun away.

"What about Marty?"

"We'll leave that for the police."

Before they left, Darrell stepped into the kitchen and took out his backpack. He put his gun inside, zipped it up, and ran to catch up with Phil.

****

Mr. Gibraltar read over the text of his proposed speech for the rededication ceremony in disgust. He couldn't believe the ineptitude of his speechwriters. How could inarticulate drivel like this garbage get the attention of the people who needed to hear this most, the media?

The opening of his study door caught his attention. "What?" he asked.

"Honey, we have to talk," Eva, his wife, said.

"You have my attention," he said without turning from the speech.

Eva took a breath. "Little Alex has gotten in trouble in school again. He broke a girl's leg."

"And?"

"Didn't you hear me?"

Mr. Gibraltar closed his eyes and sighed. "I'm working, all right? Take care of it."

"But Nathan, This is the third time he's hurt someone. He's out of control." Eva said.

Mr. Gibraltar stood up from his desk, gazing at his wife with a lazy smile on his face. He walked over to her.

"We have two wonderful sons. They are the apples of my eye. If anyone decides when Alex has a problem, it will be me."

Mr. Gibraltar pulled Eva into his office and closed the door. Moments later, pounding and screaming could be heard from the room.

Clarissa Day strode across the newsroom floor towards Stu's office. She waved to some of her co-workers on her way. Stu had called her to his office for a promisingly good story. It'd better not be another puff piece, she thought. I've had enough of those.

Clarissa came as close to stardom as this local station would allow her. She had been billed as a star reporter based on her looks alone but after three long years, she had earned the respect she had wanted from her peers. She had earned it, only to find out that that respect wasn't worth the effort she had made. Everywhere she turned, she'd either get asked to make a story about a despicable human being in order for them to get some good press or she'd be ask to sit on a story that, if the public were made aware, would lose someone high up their precious jobs or worse. She thought that the ideals and ethics they teach reporters in school were products of an era that may never have existed. At least the money's good, she surmised.

She burst through the office door. Stu looked up at her and smiled. He motioned toward a chair across from him.

"Take a seat."

Clarissa did so with no response. Stu passed a folder across his desk.

"An interesting item came up on the police scanner. Bank robbery. Inside is some information on the unnamed gun woman and the private eye that took her down, or tried to actually. This should be simple for you," he said, sarcasm dripping like a leaky faucet.

"For what do I owe this pleasure?" she asked, returning the sarcasm.

"That piece you did on Governor Creston. He called the station manager and said you're the only reporter he wants to deal with from this station. You got quite a coupe."

"Good things happen to people with integrity."

Stu smirked. "Sure. How's old Davis anyway?"

"I wouldn't want to play poker against him. He knows how to keep on a good game face."

"Why's that?"

"Nathan Gibraltar. The man gives him one continuous headache. I'm surprised he's keeping him on the ticket for the election."

"What's Nathan doing that's so bad?" Stu asked, turning his to his computer.

"Nathan's a chameleon. He's done a masterful job at keeping his personal problems out of the news. My opinion, he's just plain evil."

"Well, we don't base the news on your opinions now do we? Get the story done. There may be two other stations there by now."

Clarissa picked up the folder, got up, and left the office. She had to get her crew together to head to the bank. She did not like being assigned a simple, rookie story like this but getting out of that idiot Stu's office would make it worth it.

****

The phone in Xander's pocket buzzed, tickling his chest. He took it out of his suit and turned it on.

"Yes?"

"It's Richard. Reilly took care of Darrell's friend. Unfortunately, someone popped Reilly before he could get Darrell and the flash drive."

Xander leaned back in his chair and sighed. Not again, he thought. How could he have given so much responsibility to someone clearly not ready for the job? He ran his left hand through his thick blond hair.

"Your people are failing me, Wilcox."

"Xander…"

"No. I don't need an excuse. Work over who you need to in order to find this kid. I need this taken care of in the next few hours, not days. I'm not going to have some prepubescent dumb ass screwing up my plans. Get the job done or I'll find someone who can."

Xander turned off his phone. What a mess. He thought about what he would end up having to do but he didn't like it. He dialed a number on his phone. After a couple rings…

"Yes sir."

"I need the car to Grand Rapids within the hour."

"Yes sir."

Xander hung up the phone. I hate traveling, he thought. At least I have a driver.

****

Curtis rang Melissa Hunter's doorbell. He stood alone in the hallway, Smelly Boy waiting outside in the car. This job was too personal for the boss to let just anybody handle. When it came for the praise, he wanted to be the one in line to get it.

The door opened as far as the chain lock allowed. "Can I help you?" she asked.

"Melissa Hunter home?"

"Yeah?"

"I'm here on behalf of a friend. Your secret friend as you called him. May I come in?"

Silence. Then the door shut long enough for the woman to take off the chain. She opened the door and escorted Curtis inside.

"Why did he send you?" she asked.

Curtis didn't respond for a moment, taking in the sight of this beautiful woman. A smile crept on his face.

"You are more beautiful than he said."

"What are you here for?"

"My boss cared a lot for you. He wanted nothing in the world more than to see you happy. However, you had to leave him. Why?"

"He didn't love me. He wanted a toy he could control and when I wouldn't play his games, he got mad. I think you need to leave."

Curtis smiled. "A beautiful woman like you should be careful who she trusts because making friends with the wrong people can put a man like me in your house."

Curtis shut the door.

****

Phil walked through the door to his office, dragging Darrell behind him. He tossed him onto the chair by his desk next to his computer. Phil turned it on.

"Get that damn thing hooked up and show me what you have," Phil said.

"No offense but your computer looks like it was made in the 90's. Let me get my laptop out."

Darrell placed the backpack on the table and took out his laptop. As he pulled it out, he spotted his gun. He grinned, closing the bag.

"Set it up," Phil said.

Darrell turned on the computer. It took about a minute to warm up. He inserted the flash drive into the USB port, clicked the icon on the screen, and opened up the file.

"Here it is," Darrell said. "Read'em and weep."

Darrell rose, grabbing his backpack. Phil sat down in the chair and began the files Darrell brought up. Darrell watched him, making sure Phil wasn't paying attention to him. His hand slipped into the bag, his fingers stroking the destructive piece of metal inside. When he was sure Phil wasn't looking, he yanked out the gun, dropped the backpack to the floor, and leveled the weapon at Phil.

"I have to leave," he said.

Phil looked up and shook his head. "What the hell do you think you're doing?"

"I have no idea who you are for one and two, you said it yourself. You want to bring me back to Wilcox. I can't allow you to do that."

"You're willing to shoot me over what's on this thing?"

"No. I'm willing to shoot you for putting me in danger."

Phil thought a moment. "In order for you to be safe, you're willing to use violence.

Sounds kind of backwards to me."

"Quit with the jokes. I want to leave."

"You're being foolish. Don't leave until I've read what's on here. If you still want to leave when I'm done, what can I say. You have the gun. But if something important is on here, then you'll need some protection. I'm going to do the right thing, not try, and milk a dry cow if ya know what I mean," Phil said.

"You're nothing but a sleazy private dick willing to solve your case no matter how it gets solved and you have the nerve to lecture me?"

"I happen to be the best sleazy private dick thank you very much. However, I will not do anything that I know is wrong just to get the job done. That's not how I work. Most of the time."

"Forgive me for not believing you. I got to get going."

An electronic beep stopped the tense conversation. It was Phil's cell phone.

"I have to answer that," he said.

"Go ahead. Any sudden moves, you die."

Phil reached inside his suit coat slowly and grabbed his cell phone. He brushed up against his gun as he took the phone out. He showed the phone to Darrell, smiling as he turned it on.

"Hello?"

"Hello. Is this Phil McKnight?" a female voice asked.

"Yes. Can I help you?"

"My name is Clarissa Day from News 12. I was wondering if I could take a couple minutes of your time for an interview about the bank robbery you witnessed today."

"I'm kind of busy now. Is there some other time we can do it?"

"Is one thirty ok?"

"Sure. Meet me at my office. You have the address?"

"That I do. I'll be there."

"Goodbye."

Phil shut off the phone and slowly put it back in his pocket. As he pulled his hand out, he grabbed hold of his gun and whipped it out of the holster. He dived, shooting at the wall behind Darrell's head.

"Now if you don't mind," Phil said while standing, "I'd like this nonsense to be over with. I got business to do you know."

Darrell stared at Phil. "I can't let you get me killed," he said.

"I won't. Otherwise, you'd already be dead. Now put the gun down before you hurt someone."

Darrell paused. Phil thought for a moment that he might fire the gun but sighed in relief when Darrell lowered it, handing the gun to him.

"Thank you," Phil said. "I'll let you have it back if you change your mind."

****

Annie Walker pulled the flower to her face and inhaled its fragrant smell. She smiled, the smell being the only happy part in her day. She put the flower down next to the tombstone.

She walked further into the cemetery, not sure why a cemetery made her feel at peace. She wanted nothing more than to live a long, happy, peaceful life. Yet how did she end up here? She never sat back as child and imagined that she'd be living the life of a killer. Not that she ever wanted to be the type of woman who would grow up to be a housewife, having children, and rubbing the back of the man who would be the one to go out and earn the money for the family. However, a certain security came with that which she lacked in her life that was worth more than all the money she could steal in the world.

She read the names on the tombstones, trying to picture what sort of people were buried six feet under her. Were they good people? Bad people? Were they still thought of by the living?

She wouldn't be. If you really sat back and thought about it, not many people, including celebrities and other people of that caliber would be remembered for very long after they died. Someone's great-great-great-great-grandfather could be remembered more than the first screen heartthrob in Hollywood, Rudolph Valentino. That's the thing about time. It was a son of a bitch.

Her cell phone rang, breaking her distracted mood. She pulled it out of her purse and put it to her ear.

"Hello," she said.

"Expecting me?"

"Xander, it's nice to hear from you."

He laughed. "You almost sounded sincere."

"What do you have to tell me?" Annie asked.

"Why are you always in a rush?"

"I'm only in a rush with you cause your jobs always bring me lots of money so the sooner I can get to them the better."

"Good girl. You took care of that boyfriend of yours?"

Annie paused, looking at the grass. "Yeah, I did."

"Good. I can't have people stealing from me. I'm glad to know who I can trust."

"I know who butters my bread. And I took care of Layfield for you. But there may be a problem."

Xander paused. "Oh?"

"A man shot the gun I brought out of my hand. I had to take care of that fat slug Layfield with a knife."

"At least you got it done. I'll see if the police have anything substantial in terms of evidence and make sure it promptly disappears. Anyway, down to business. I need you to be at the Concord parking garage at two o'clock to deal with some people I've had problems with. You'll find a car at the Hungry Horse grocery store parking lot on 28th and Clyde Park with the license plate number TWS 432. Instructions will be in the car. I don't think I have to tell you what to do with those instructions once you memorize them. "

"I know the drill."

"Ciao babe."

Xander hung up. Annie folded up her phone and put it back in her purse. Yeah, she didn't like that she had to kill George. But Xander was right. Business is business. If you don't play by the rules, you lose the game.

****

Governor Davis Creston sat at his desk reading over the paperwork of the day sipping a cup of tea. His schedule as of late made it hard for him to get a full day's work in but he tried his best to get as much done as he could. He considered this a tedious but important function of his job. Why else was he elected to office?

The phone rang. The Governor set his papers down and picked it up.

"Hello?"

"It's Audrey."

"Good afternoon my dear."

"Eva just called me. He beat her again."

Davis leaned back in his chair and sighed. "How bad?"

"She threw up a little blood if that's any indication."

"Is she going to the hospital?"

"No. She doesn't want to get Nathan in trouble."

"Damn it. Is he going to have to kill her for her to get the point?

"Davis!"

"I'm not trying to be insensitive. I just find it hard to comprehend her reasoning for staying with that monster."

"It's not as black and white as you think. She can't break up with him like a high school crush. She has her husband's career to think about as well as yours I might add."

Governor Creston pounded his desk. "How can you say that?"

"It's true Davis and you know it. If she goes to the hospital and goes on record with what Nathan's done to her she'll not only ruin her husband, she'll ruin you. You have the election to worry about."

"We are not having this conversation. Get Dr. Benn over to help her now."

"I will. Also, I'm going to be out of town for the rest of the day. I have a women's conference at Luther College in Grand Rapids."

"Have a good day my dear."

Governor Creston hung up the phone. He looked around his office. Why did this have to happen? He believed in the golden rule of doing unto others as you'd have them do unto you. The idea of conning someone into doing things your way, all this counterproductive political maneuvering, was against his idea on how to live life. He was the last of a dying breed. Successful politicians these days were the ones who knew how to play the game. You couldn't be honest and do this job anymore.

Governor Creston touched the intercom button for his secretary. After a moment, she responded.

"Yes Governor?"

"I'm going to be out of my office for a while."

"And when will you be returning?"

"About an hour. I have to pay a visit to an old friend."

Governor Creston rose from his desk and left his office. I think it's time I try to solve my problem before the voters fire me, he thought.

****

Nathan picked up the phone in his study. "Hello?" he asked.

"I got some unexpected news for you," Steven said.

"What's that?"

"Dawson Layfield was killed in Grand Rapids this morning."

Nathan smiled. "You brought some joy to my day. Never thought I'd say that but it's true."

"All right," Steven said. "Keep working on that speech. It needs to be Gettysburg Address good."

"Then send me some people who know how to put coherent thoughts together."

"There are only so many people who want to work with such an unimportant person in your position, sad to say."

"That's why you work for me. Find those people and get rid of the morons we have currently employed."

Nathan hung up the phone. He heard a soft moan in the bedroom. He stood up and walked to the door, opening it. His wife lay on the floor, her vomit soaking in the expensive carpet he'd had installed two months earlier.

"You soiled my carpet like an animal. What's wrong with you?"

He walked over and kicked her in the ribs. Her petite body flew, landing against the wall. She got on all fours and made a dash for the bathroom. She closed the door and locked it.

"I don't care if you go in there," Nathan said. "If you think you can hide, you've got another thing coming my dear."

Eva burst into a fresh round of tears. Nathan smiled. He turned and left the room, hoping the maid was still downstairs so the mess could be cleaned up.

He stopped for a moment and looked at himself in the mirror. After a moment of observation, he smiled. Damn, I still got it.

****

One of Richard Wilcox's thugs looked through his binoculars again and smiled. He couldn't believe it. That little son of a bitch was sitting in Phil's office. He picked up his cell phone and dialed his boss.

"Hello?"

"Richard, it's me. I spotted McKnight in his office with that little punk Sampson."

A pause. "You got to be kidding. He hasn't contacted me yet."

"What do you want me to do?"

"If they leave there and Phil doesn't contact me, kill them and grab the flash drive. If Phil calls, I'll give you with the all clear signal. Got that?"

"Why can't I just go in now and get it?"

"Why? I'll give that private eye a chance. Have a little patience and call me if anything changes."

Wilcox's thug hung up the phone. He picked up his binoculars and looked inside Phil's office again. He hoped beyond anything that Phil wouldn't call Wilcox.

****

Robert lay on the roof of the building in the heart of downtown Grand Rapids. He gripped his freshly assembled sniper rifle. The sniper rifle that he hoped would end Nathan Gibraltar's sad little life.

Most people who would hear of his reasoning for doing this would call him selfish, delusional, anything they could think of to make him out to be a bad guy. It's always the assumption on people's part that the members of the lower middle class to just plain poor folk were criminals and delinquents. They didn't take time out of their lives to listen to people's stories.

No matter how bad Nathan is he'd still come out the hero in the end, which made Robert consider dropping everything. However, he reasoned that if Nathan could turn his life into hell, then there would be someone else out there whom he'd do it to as well if he chose to do nothing about it.

He had been married to a beautiful woman who felt the need to share her love with men other than him. One of those men was Nathan Gibraltar. When he found out Nathan was screwing his wife, he called him up and threatened to call the press and tell them about the affair. Nathan laughed, telling him to do whatever he had to do.

One week later, a car hit his wife. The police ruled it a homicide. A driver ran over her like a speed bump and sped away before anyone could get the license plate. They never found the driver. Never made an effort to find them in fact. The night after her funeral, a note was pinned to his front door. It said all that was needed about the whole messed in a few short words. 'That's what you get when you mess with me.' What kind of man would do that?

A demented man who knew how to cover his ass in every way. The arrogance of Nathan was appalling. And the fact that he was getting away with things like that while being one step away from the Governor's mansion left him numb.

He aimed the rifle to the ground below. He tested out the scope, scanning around for the stage in front of the statue. Nathan will be right there, he thought. One pull on the trigger and boom, he's gone. He pulled the rifle back and laid it on the roof. It was going to be a long time waiting for three o'clock to come. It would be worth the wait though.

His cell phone rang. He pulled it out. "Hello?" he asked.

"I spotted one of Wilcox's boys by McKnight's office. What do you want me to do?"

"Do what you do best Lydia. Wait till the scumbag makes a move then smoke him. I don't want him hurting my little brother."

****

Curtis sat in the passenger seat with his cell phone in his hand. Smelly Boy looked out the window, the boredom he felt barely being controlled.

"Pick up the damn phone," Curtis fumed.

"Why the hell do you need to talk to Thomas now?" Smelly Boy asked.

"Does it really matter? Maybe I want to talk about what I did to your Ma last night. You need to keep your mouth shut before somethin happens."

Curtis stayed on the phone for a few more rings before hanging up. Stupid fuck, he thought. Curtis put the phone back in his pocket and closed his eyes.

"What we doing next?" Smelly Boy asked.

Curtis sighed and stretched. "We wait."

"What?"

"You ask too many questions boy. Shut the fuck up."

****

Lydia picked up her binoculars and stared at Wilcox's man in the car on the street below. There he sat; gripping the steering wheel like it was someone's throat. He'd better not think of doing what I think he's contemplating, she thought. She knew this thug by reputation and knew what he could do to someone like Robert's brother Darrell. She picked up her cell phone and called Robert again.

"Yeah?" he asked.

"Call it women's intuition but I think that man watching Darrell is getting quite antsy."

"What do you mean?"

"I mean that if his steering wheel were human, he'd be getting the electric chair. I have a bad feeling about that guy."

"Do you think there's a chance he'll hurt Darrell?"

"Wilcox may be a moron but he knows enough to hire dangerous people to do his dirty work."

"Then do what you have to do to save my brother."

"I will."

Lydia hung up the phone. There were times where Robert thought with his emotions. Thinking like that would get him killed.

****

"I can't believe what I read," Phil said.

"I told you."

Phil stood up, heading for the coffee machine. "Is that all the files on there?"

"That's all I could get off it."

"There's more?" Phil asked, pouring a cup of old coffee.

"Yeah. There's a file that has a security code on it that I can't crack."

Phil's phone rang. He took a sip of the coffee, winced, and picked up the phone.

"Hello?"

"Phil, its Richard. How are things going?"

"Good," Phil said, putting the coffee on the desk.

"Just wondering if you got any leads on Darrell?"

Phil paused. "I have some promising leads, yeah. I'll have this taken care of before tomorrow."

"All right. See you soon."

Phil hung up the phone. He felt a migraine coming on thanks to all this nonsense. Having Richard call now sure didn't help his head. He rubbed his temples, hoping he could get rid of some of the pain.

"We're in danger," Phil said.

****

The gunman's phone rang. "Yeah?"

"Take them out. If you forget that flash drive, don't expect to live."

The phone went dead. That's all he needed to hear. The gunman took the keys out of the ignition and got out of the car. He walked to the trunk and opened it. There ya go, he thought, the smile growing on his face like a flower in bloom. He pulled out a shotgun and headed across the street toward Phil's office.

****

Lydia walked down the last set of stairs thankful that she would be seeing some action. All of this preparation by Robert made her quite eager to do something, anything.

Lydia walked to the front of the building. She reached the window and looked out at the gunman.

Damn. She watched as he walked across the street with a shotgun. This wasn't going to end pretty.

She took her weapon of choice from her pocket. She'd always been curious about tribes of Africa and Asia and the weapons they used. The weapon that fascinated her most was the blowgun.

Her blowgun wasn't fancy but it got the job done. She'd gotten its usage down to a science. One time she'd actually been able to blow a dart through the middle of a moving target, something she was proud of. Her target now would also be moving, but due to many years of fast food joints and gallons of cheap alcohol, he was enough of a target for a deaf, dumb, and blind person to hit from three hundred yards.

She grabbed one of her special darts. The tip was dipped in the deadliest Cyanide she'd ever had the fortune of buying. She waited for the man to make a move.

She watched as the door of Phil's office opened and Darrell and Phil stepped outside. The brute stopped Phil and Darrell in their tracks. Darrell looked like he was a three year old being caught breaking a dish in the kitchen. Phil stood his ground, looking like an actor in a western.

The gunman raised his gun and aimed it at Darrell. Phil reached into his jacket and pulled out his weapon. She put the blowgun to her mouth.

She took a deep breath and watched. Watched as the gunman pulled the trigger, shooting Darrell in the chest. Watched as Phil dove for cover, blasting away at air. She blew out the dart. It landed right where she wanted, in the gun man's neck. Time to make a quick exit.

****

It felt like a bee had stung him. He put his hand on his neck and felt the dart. What the…? he thought. He pulled the dart out, examining it.

That's when his body began shutting down. His legs wobbled and he slumped to the ground. The gunman tried to take in a breath but couldn't, as if his lungs decided not to work.

His body began shaking. He realized he was going to die. He wouldn't get the chance to die like a real man, taking a bullet in the head or anything like that. He was going to die like someone stranded on an island with the locals out for his head. Damn.

Before he sunk into blackness, he saw Phil approach. Phil looked like he was staring at an animal run over by a semi. His body convulsed some more. Just as death covered him like a thick winter blanket, he swore he smelled almonds.

The restaurant mirrored a picture of a bistro that could be on a tiny street in Italy. Davis walked through the doors and found an empty table near the back. The candle on his table was out so he switched it with a candle from another table. A waitress approached to take his order.

"Governor. Welcome back. What can I get you today?"

"I told you to call me by my name Elsie."

She smiled. "I know. But you're the Governor so I want to be formal."

"I don't have much time today. How about some spaghetti?"

"Anything else?"

"If my wife were here I'd ask for a diet soda. Since she's on her way to Grand Rapids I'll splurge with a glass of your best wine."

"I won't tell her."

"Thank you," Governor Creston smiled. "Before you go, is Tony back there?"

"Yeah. He's doing the books today and he's kinda pissed."

"With as much money as this place makes I would be too. Can you send him out here? Tell him the Governor needs to speak with his advisor."

Elsie smiled and headed to the kitchen. Davis grabbed a spoon and absently tapped it on the table. The kitchen door opened a minute later and Tony Palermo walked out, heading toward Davis. The Governor stood and shook his hand.

"I was about ready to vote for your opponent. Where you been keeping yourself?"

"Old folks homes, elementary schools, the usual campaign stops. Got time to talk?"

"Official government business. You got me intrigued. Anything for you my friend."

Tony sat across from Davis. He moved the candle to the next table.

"Hey, I like that candle."

"You'll have to forgive me. Cigarettes killed my lungs. Can't stand the smoke. Now, what can I help you with?" Tony asked.

"My Lt. Governor. I made the wrong choice picking him and I don't know what to do now."

Tony rubbed his chin. "Why didn't you come to me earlier before you picked the guy?"

"Henry Halford resigned at the last moment and I had to pick someone fast. I looked at all the data my advisors gave me and saw that Nathan could be an asset. I wasn't aware of his baggage."

Tony smirked. "If you're gonna follow any of my advice then you need to get rid of your advisors. You're a hit with the public because you play it honest. The people hired to advise you though are some of the dirtiest people in the game. When this election's over and you still have your job, fire those pricks. And Nathan Gibraltar..."

Tony shook his head and looked down at the floor. Davis waited for his friend to respond.

"What about Nathan Gibraltar?" Davis asked.

"What dirt do you have on the guy?"

"The man's a wife beater. That's the only thing I know for sure. The rest is conjecture. If any of this got out though I'd be ruined."

Tony balled his hands in fists and hit the table. "What's the problem?" Davis asked.

"Nothing I wanna concern you with. Look, I know how elections work. If you drop Nathan now it'll make you look weak to the voters. Keep him on until you get reelected. Then dump his ass like a rotten pot roast."

"I have the feeling you know more about Nathan than you're letting on."

"Stupid people tend to know things they shouldn't," Tony smiled.

Elsie came over with Davis' order. Tony rose from the chair.

"Look, I gotta get back to work. You need me for anything you know where I'm at. I'm always here for you."

Tony turned and went back to the kitchen. Davis picked up his fork and attacked the food on his plate. Tony knew something about Nathan Gibraltar that he wasn't sharing. One day he would have to find out what that something was but for the moment, the only thing he'd get from Tony was his plate of spaghetti.

****

"My brother's dead?"

"I did everything I could. I killed the man who shot him," Lydia replied.

Robert leaned back against the edge of the roof. Darrell was dead. He was alone. He knew somehow that Nathan Gibraltar was somehow involved in this. A tear flowed down his cheek. Then another. Then another. Before he could stop, he was crying.

"Robert, you there baby?"

"I'm here." He wiped his eyes and took a deep breath, stifling the tears.

"Did you need anything from me?"

"No. This is all up to me now."

Robert hung up the phone. He put it in his gun case. There was no point talking to anyone now. Nathan had done everything he could to him without having someone put a bullet in his own head. Now, if everything went as planned...

****

Derrick brought his tray to the table and sat down. He grabbed the saltshaker and shook a liberal amount onto his fries.

"Aren't you going to hurt some organ with all that?" Thomas asked.

"My philosophy with life is to enjoy it while you can cause you may get shot in the head when you're not looking."

Thomas shrugged, taking a bite from his burger. "Do you think the new route will be ok or not? I don't need a bullet in my happy ass."

Derrick nodded, taking the wrapper off his burger. "We did our work, man. That route is all but assured to be safe when it moves."

"But why did the route have to change so suddenly?"

Derrick took a drink from his soda. "We've been sent on a wild goose chase. If there really were a problem with the original route, they wouldn't send people like us out at the last minute. There's too much money involved. I don't know how or why but they're dicking us around."

Thomas took a bite from his fries. "That don't make sense either way. I know it seems silly us finding a new route and all but it also wouldn't make sense sending us out for nothing."

"Something big is going down, man. I mean..., it's like we're being tested you know?"

"In what way?"

Derrick took a bite from his burger. "It's almost like we're all getting some sort of job review. The ones screwing up will be sifted out while the others go on to bigger things."

Thomas smiled. "What do you think will happen to Curtis and Smelly Boy?"

Derrick smiled. "I wouldn't want to be them, that's for sure."

****

Nathan placed the folder with the speech into his briefcase and closed it, snapping the locks. He turned and walked to the door of his office, stopping in front of the mirror. He adjusted his tie, smiling when everything was perfect. He left the room, closing the door behind him.

His wife sat on a chair in the hallway. Her hair was a mess, looking like a large fan had whipped it around. He walked up to her.

"Will everything be all right when I'm gone?"

Eva kept her eyes on the carpet. "Yes."

"It distresses me that Alex's behavior is what it is. That ends up reflecting poorly on me. However, I know my boy. He'll get through this like Nathan Jr."

Eva nodded her head.

"I'm glad you see things my way," Nathan said. "I don't think either of us wants another episode like this morning."

Nathan turned and left. He walked to the end of the hallway and took the stairs to ground level. His entourage waited for him by the door.

Nathan walked up to his chief of staff. "The speech is ready."

"Good. Grand Rapids is a swing city. It could go either way at election time."

Nathan opened the door and walked outside, heading for the limo. His entourage followed at his heels, almost like a group of teenage girls mobbing the newest Hollywood heartthrob. Nathan reached his limo and got in, followed by Steven.

"What's the security at the event?" Nathan asked.

"It's moderate to light just like I told you this morning. What more should you expect?"

Nathan bristled. "Don't talk to me like that. You work for me, remember?"

"Don't worry about things. Everything is taken care of."

Nathan leaned over to Steven. "You'd better begin treating this job seriously. You never know when I might get a promotion."

Steven stared him down then smiled. Nathan pressed the button on the intercom.

"Let's get this show on the road." Nathan leaned back in the seat, taking advantage of the liquor bottles stacked in the mini fridge next to him.

****

Phil gazed out the window, watching as the last ambulance drove off. He closed the curtain, not wanting to think about what had happened. He walked over to his desk and grabbed his coffee cup, getting the courage to have another cup of his toxic gourmet. He swirled the liquid around inside the cup, observing that the texture was almost gravy like.

"You want a cup?" Phil asked.

"No thanks. It's hard enough breathing as is."

Darrell rubbed his chest. He leaned back and took a deep breath, as much as his shocked ribcage would allow. By his feet was Phil's bulletproof vest.

"Did you thank that police officer for me?" Darrell asked.

"Yeah. Ol' Stoner's always ready to help a friend. He's running our files as homicides so we can have an hour or two to snoop around in peace in quiet. I just hope our time's productive."

"So where do we go from here?"

Phil sat on his desk, wincing as he took another sip. "Wilcox wanted us dead. That says to me he's kinda desperate to get that flash drive back which tells me that the stuff I saw is true. Since it will take Wilcox will take a while to realize that we're alive, I want to find out why he did it. Then maybe we can find out who's making him desperate enough to do this cause something tells me someone else is pulling his strings. You have to tell me what you did for Wilcox. I don't see him being the kind of guy who could run a legitimate business on his own."

Darrell smiled, careful not to laugh. "No, that little bastard can barely run his car, much less a business. I'm a self-employed computer expert, which means that, with the right amount of cash, I'll do anything you want with a computer if you know what I mean. He's hired me for a few jobs hacking into various banks withdrawing large amounts of cash."

"Damn. And I have trouble turning mine on some days. How did you come into contact with the flash drive?"

"The other day, he stops by my place with a computer in his trunk along with the flash drive asking me to fix it for a friend. I took the cash he offered and started working on it. Curiosity struck me so when I had a chance to read what was on the flash drive, I knew I could sell the thing to the right person for the right price."

"That you do," Phil said.

"Look, the bank transactions that you saw, I know how we can find out more of where they originated from and who they were paid to and why. Then maybe we can find out what's ultimately going on and who's responsible for this."

"How do you propose to do that? Wait, I think I have an idea."

Phil went to his desk and picked up the phone. He dialed a number.

"Hello? Let me speak to English Bob."

****

Richard grabbed the bottle of antacid and took a generous swallow of the comforting liquid. He rubbed the sweat off his forehead.

Where was his man? He hadn't heard from him in about a half hour now and he was getting worried. He knew that as each second ticked on, he was one second closer to death. Before he knew it, Xander would be here. He didn't know what he would say or do when he showed up so he wouldn't try to be on Xander's bad side. He had at least fifteen minutes to think of something to keep his job. Or his life.

Now he had to wait. Waiting felt like sharp knives jabbing into his belly. Waiting meant you had time to ponder every mistake you've made. Mistakes couldn't be made when someone like Xander employed you.

His phone rang, startling him from his thoughts. He picked it up from his desk and answered it.

"Hello?"

"I'm hearing a strange report that two people were killed in front of Phil McKnight's office. Can you explain that?"

Richard felt a lump in his throat. "Xander, I didn't, uh, hear that news."

"I figured. What kind of business are you running for me over there? I need someone intelligent and responsible to handle things and all I get is some jerk off who likes to sniff some snow on special occasions and party with his boyfriends on the weekends."

"Damn it Xander! My life…"

"Is my business Richard. I don't care if you like to play cowboy with the local fairies in town. All I care about is you keeping a dick out of your mouth long enough to do your job right. Do you understand?"

Richard gripped the phone like a vice. "Yes."

Xander hung up. Self-righteous bastard, he thought as he slammed the phone into the receiver. Richard picked up a three hole punch on his desk and threw it at the wall. He stood up and started pacing; trying to keep his shaking hands to his sides.

****

The knock came on the door. Phil rose from his desk and headed toward the entrance. He opened it, gasping as a beautiful woman stood in the doorway.

"I hope I can help you," Phil said.

"My name is Clarissa Day from News 12. I'm looking for Phil McKnight."

"You found him. Come on in," Phil beamed.

Clarissa walked in with her crew. They set up a makeshift set with lights, boom mikes, and other amenities. Phil escorted her to a chair across from his desk. Darrell kept quiet in the background.

"Thank you for accepting the interview," Clarissa said.

"No problem. It gives me a break from my day."

"And what a day you've had so far."

"Right you are. As of a half hour ago, I was listed as dead."

"Huh…"

"You don't want to know right yet. Maybe I'll tell you later."

"I see. Let's get ourselves seated so we can get started. I'll start off with the questions."

The make due set was ready. Phil took his seat behind his desk. Clarissa swiveled her chair to face him. Clarissa looked at her cameraman.

"We all set?" she asked.

She received nods of approval from her boys. She turned to Phil and put her game face on. The light on the camera turned on and it was show time.

"How difficult was it to stop the murderer?"

Phil leaned back in his chair and stroked his chin. "It wasn't all that hard. When you're dealing with someone who's had no experience doing that sort of thing it becomes quite easy taking care of them."

"Can you describe the perpetrator?"

"Six feet, six two, blond hair, nice body. The kind of woman every man would notice."

"Can you tell us what happened in detail?

"Well, I went into the bank to make a deposit. I was standing in line and out of nowhere, this gun toting crazy broad walks in demanding to see someone named Dawson Layfield."

****

Dawson Layfield. The name clicked in Darrell's head. He got up from his chair, being shushed by one of Clarissa's crew. He grabbed his backpack and sidestepped back to his chair.

He unzipped it and took out his laptop. After sticking the flash drive into the laptop's USB port, he began searching through the files, remembering he'd seen the name Dawson Layfield somewhere. The click, clacking of the keyboard was loud enough to get the attention of the soundman until Darrell stopped.

"Phil?"

Phil turned in annoyance. "What is it?"

"Dawson Layfield. His name is on the flash drive."

"What? Tell me what you got?"

"There are some bank transactions here with his name on them."

"Why should we think Layfield did anything wrong?"

"Your average teller is not going to be allowed to do these kinds of transactions. Only someone high up in the bank could approve something this big."

Phil rubbed his chin in thought. "If that's true, then we got some bigger fish to fry. Damn, I wished I asked for more money. Let's talk more about this when English Bob gets here."

"You're the private eye," Darrell acquiesced, taking a seat. Phil turned back to Clarissa.

****

Xander took a sip of vodka. He stared out the window, a stern look on his face. He hated Grand Rapids.

He had to take care of Wilcox's errors. There was no two ways about it. That meant finding out what that private eye McKnight knew and where that blasted flash drive was.

He took out his cell phone and dialed a number. If he could trust anyone to rectify this situation, it would be Ray.

"Hello?" Ray answered.

"Is that all you're going to say to an old friend?"

"Xander, nice to hear from you."

"I need some help."

"With what?"

"Wilcox."

"Ah. I've been expecting this call for a while."

"The job is simple. I want to see his dead body when I walk into his office."

"I'm about five minutes from there. He'll be dead before the top of the hour."

****

A knock came on Phil's office door. Phil excused himself and went to answer it. He smiled when he saw the man behind the door.

"English Bob, you son of a bitch."

The two men hugged. English Bob looked like the typical white trash male. He wore denim shorts, a t-shirt, his last few hairs clung for life on his head. He stroked his van dyke as he surveyed the room.

"What kind of party you got here?" English Bob asked.

"I'm doing an interview with the local news station about a bank robbery I was witness to. The man you want to see is over there," said Phil, pointing to Darrell.

"Gotcha. Get back to the pretty lady and I'll get down to business."

English Bob walked over to Darrell and started talking shop. Phil went back to his seat and resumed the interview with Clarissa.

"Sorry about that," Phil said.

"Big case you working on?"

"Getting bigger by the minute."

"Care to talk about it? Off the record of course."

Phil sat for a moment in thought. "It's just a simple case of stolen money."

"Ooh, sounds sexy. I need to hear. Anything that can entertain me until the Gibraltar speech at three I'll most certainly enjoy."

****

A car pulled into the parking lot of a dilapidated building. Pathetic, Ray thought. A little bit of paint and some items that were made in this century would have kept this place inconspicuous. But that lazy piece of trash Wilcox used his cash to fulfill his sick ass desires. Well, as an investor in this business, I think it's time for a hostile takeover.

Ray walked through the doors of the dilapidated shack and headed for the counter. No one there. He drummed his fingers on the counter, looking around the place. All he saw were computers that were barely able to perform multiplication. He gazed in disgust at some of the artifacts of technology.

He heard a noise, a low wail coming from the back of the store. He pulled out his gun and headed for the back office, the sound of the wailing getting louder. He waited a moment, took a deep breath, and opened the door.

Richard, who was sitting at his desk, raised his head. Sweat covered his dirty little face. Some unknown kid was on the floor, naked and unconscious. Ray walked over to the kid, raised his gun, and shot him in the head. Richard leaped out of his chair and backed into a corner.

"Please don't kill me." Richard wailed.

"Now why would I go and do that?" Ray taunted.

"Why are you doing this to me? I did everything Xander wanted me to do."

"That's not for me to say one way or the other," he said.

"I can pay you."

"You wouldn't have enough."

Ray shot him. Richard fell to the floor, blood flowing from the new hole in his chest.

"Pathetic bastard."

****

Curtis watched as the little hatchback pulled onto their level of the parking garage and coasted for an empty space. The driver found a spot and parked the car. The driver got out. Curtis fell instantly in lust.

Looking like she just walked off the set of a fashion runway, the woman walked to her trunk and opened it up. She bent over to search for something inside, sending Curtis and Smelly Boy into a wave of prepubescent glee.

"Don't you just love how the Lord made women?" Curtis smiled.

The woman pulled out a briefcase from the trunk and looked around. She appeared lost. She looked around for help then spotted them in the car. Smelly Boy turned to

Curtis.

"Let me have this," Smelly Boy said.

The woman walked up to the driver's side window. Smelly Boy rolled it down.

"Can you boys help me? I'm late for an appointment and I need some directions."

"Where do you need to go?" Smelly Boy asked.

"Grand Rapids Municipal Bank. Do you know where it's at?"

"Yeah, I can tell you how to get there," Curtis said.

"Thank you," said the woman.

She pulled a pen and pad of paper from her briefcase. Before she began writing, she clicked the pen. There was a snap. Smelly Boy put his hand to his neck and turned to Curtis. Blood flowed from Smelly Boy's neck, a small metal spike protruding from between his hand. Curtis scrambled for his gun but stopped when he heard the woman laugh.

"Get out of the car sunshine," she said, her own gun aimed at his head.

Curtis complied. The woman motioned for Curtis to go to the hatchback. He walked over and waited for further instruction. The lady opened the backdoor and shoved Curtis inside.

"Sit in the middle seat," she said.

He followed the order. Once in the right spot, metal clamps snapped over his hands and his feet. The woman looked at Curtis.

"You know, you're kind of cute."

2:00 PM-3:00 PM

The bushes were the perfect spot. The man saw the old woman and the boy playing in the woman's back yard. The kid ran around the fenced in yard, exerting energy like a tiny combustible engine. The woman looked on the boy's activities and smiled.

The man pulled out a walkie-talkie and pressed a button, signaling his partner back in the car.

"Echo three to echo seven, over."

"Yeah. I'm here."

"Where have you been?"

"Taking a leak. What's your status?" the man in the car replied

"I spotted the woman and the boy. We'll be ready to execute our plan later. I'll be back in the car in a minute. Get the engine started."

The man shut off his radio. When he turned and looked up, he almost wet himself. A Rottweiler stared at him, drool coming from its snarling mouth. The dog took a step toward him.

"Good boy," he said.

The man backed up slow. The dog followed him step for step. He reached for the knife on his left thigh, careful not to give the dog a reason to attack. It's now or never, he thought. He faked a lunge toward the dog. The dog pounced, ready to have this man for breakfast. The man gripped the knife with both hands and, as the dog was overhead, sliced through the dog's throat. After a sudden yelp, the dog fell to the ground, blood draining from its neck. The man got up and ran for the car.

The car sat idling on the corner. The man signaled the driver to open the trunk.

Once opened, the man walked over and unloaded the equipment he was wearing and tossed it in a metal box. He tossed his gear into the box and closed the box. He glanced around, seeing if any neighbors were getting curious. Satisfied they were being ignored, he went to the passenger side and got in.

"So what the hell took you so long?" the driver asked.

"I ran into a mean old bitch. Let's go."

****

"I want to help you with your case," Clarissa told Phil.

"I wouldn't consider it. Remember, Darrell over there got shot in the chest. Wouldn't want that to happen to a celebrity."

"I can get my hands dirty with the best of them. Let me give you my cell phone number anyway and if you need my help, I'll be there for you."

"Looks like I can't say no. If something comes along I'll call you."

Phil and Clarissa shook hands. She helped her crew finish packing and left. When they left, Phil went over for another cup of coffee, wondering why he drank the sludge.

"Holy Schmoly! The file is open." English Bob yelled.

"What's on it?"

English Bob addressed the audience in his head. "The secret file that, thanks to the skills of myself and this little squirt here has revealed five locations in town."

"So?" Phil said.

"So, one of these locations is the place where all these transactions are coming from. Once we get someone talking we'll be able to find out who's receiving the money and why."

"You think we can get people to talk?" Darrell asked.

"Phil and I can be pretty persuasive if we have to be. Now I do believe that the Spanish Moon would be better suited to getting this operation underway," English

Bob said. "So if you don't mind let's say we head over to my place."

"As long as you're buying," Phil said.

"I wouldn't have it any other way. Besides, I'm sure you don't even have the money to pay."

****

Ray heard his cell phone and pulled it from his pocket. He flipped it open.

"How are things?" Xander asked.

"Better now that Richard's dead. He fucked up bad, man. He had at least two instances where he could've had the flash drive and he didn't take advantage of it."

"What plans have you put into place?"

"Some friends in high places say McKnight and Sampson are both dead which I have reason to believe is bullshit. They're around this town somewhere so I sent everyone I could to find them."

"When Richard told me he was hiring that private eye, I did a little work on him and found out some of his favorite hangouts in Grand Rapids. I'll email you those locations. I'm not looking for you to kill him but it is imperative you get that flash drive back."

"If I may ask, what's on the flash drive anyway?"

"Without getting into specifics, it has the locations of the money people we're using for a little operation we're doing tomorrow that'll make us a lot of money. I have a tracking device built into the flash drive that once opened we'll be able to get a lock on its location but I want the item retrieved before anyone can get a chance to see any of it."

"Gotcha. I'll get to work."

****

The shock of electricity shot through Curtis' body, making him spasm. The woman up front smiled as the metal restraints held him in place. Why does she want me alive? he thought. Thankfully, the electricity stopped.

"We have matters to discuss," the woman said.

Curtis caught his breath. "It must really be important."

"My boss has a job for you to do. He wants you to do a little security work for someone important."

Curtis gawked. "That's all? You couldn't just ask?"

"A woman shouldn't have to ask."

She pushed the button. Curtis screamed in agony.

"Next time you say something stupid, I may forget to take my hand off the button."

"Ok, ok. What's the plan?"

"It's a little sniper duty. There's a gentleman who has plans on killing a politician today and it will be your job to make sure he doesn't succeed."

"If that's what you wanted why go through all this?"

"I'm a tease." She smiled, pressing the button.

The hatchback pulled to a stop. The woman turned the engine off and got out of the car. She opened the door to the back seat and got in next to Curtis.

"You know your role, correct?"

"Yeah," he said. "I'd be a fool if I didn't."

"If you try anything when I release you, you're dead."

"Listen, you don't have to tell me twice. I'm down with your plan."

The woman pressed the button releasing the restraints. Curtis rubbed his sore hands and legs. The woman got out of the car. Curtis followed.

"You will find a blue ribbon tied on a telephone pole in front of the office where you will set up. In a garbage can two feet from the entrance you will find a flower box."

"Let me guess what's inside."

The woman took something from her pocket. "Put this in your ear."

Curtis grabbed the earpiece and put it in. "I'll be monitoring you through this. If you fuck up, I'll know," she said.

"I get the picture."

"Then get to work." The woman walked past Curtis and got back in the car.

****

The advance team for Nathan Gibraltar went through the final inspection of the area. Not that they expected any trouble but you had to be careful, the times being what they were.

Norman Scofield headed to the last building needing inspection. His last stop was a building owned by Gerrie Simmons, a local real estate agent. He had met him on a previous engagement and found him to be a likeable enough guy.

He walked up to the building and stepped inside. The air-conditioned hallway was a lifesaver what with the dark suits they wore. He walked back to Gerrie's office.

The door stood ajar. That's odd, he thought. He tipped the door open with his foot. Empty. Where the hell is Gerrie? He pulled out his gun and walked inside.

He spotted something on the floor. It looked like drops of blood. What is going on here? he thought.

The slamming of the door shocked him. He turned, his gun leveled, ready to fire.

Walter Cisco stood smiling, twirling an ink pen in his hand. Norman lowered his gun.

"What the hell did you do that for?" he asked. "You scared the crap out of me," Norman said.

"Sorry about that. Just trying to finish my job."

"Why are you working my list? I'm not complaining but…"

"Consider it a favor done. I was just on my way out. Maybe we can grab a bite before Gibraltar gets here."

"In a sec. Did you catch this here?" he asked, pointing to the drops of blood.

Walter shook his head. "I didn't see that."

He walked over and inspected it along with Norman. "Let's check the rest of the office," Walter said.

Norman headed for the back, followed by Walter. They checked every square inch, looking for something out of the ordinary. They got to the back. One last door. Norman got on one side of the door with Walter on the other.

"You open it," Walter said.

Norman put his hand on the knob and turned. The body inside forced it open the rest of the way. Norman jumped back in surprise.

"I got to get on the radio," he said.

Walter put his hand on Norman's shoulder. "I wouldn't do that if I were you."

"Why?"

"Because I killed him."

Norman stood, stunned. "What…"

"Let me explain."

"You killed someone and you want to have a chin wag?"

"You got two options. You can walk out of here, forget this, and end up a much richer man, or I kill you. Your choice."

"What are you doing this for?"

"I'm a cog in the machine of life you could say. Or, I've been paid a butt load of money to do one little thing for a very powerful man."

Norman couldn't speak. He couldn't decide how best to react. He didn't have to.

Someone from behind jammed a knife in his neck.

****

Phil, English Bob, and Darrell walked into the ladies' room of The Spanish Moon at the same time, which had struck some of the more sober customers as odd before they went back to their drinks. English Bob went to the middle stall, which had an out of order sign on it, and kicked the door open. He flushed the toilet. A hidden door behind the toilet revealed itself. Darrell looked as if he were about to say something. English Bob raised his hand.

"Maybe I'm not the most original guy around," English Bob said. "Sue me."

English Bob stepped into the room behind the toilet. Phil and Darrell followed him in.

The office, for lack of a better term, was a large room with every amenity a person could ask for. Sophisticated computer equipment lined the walls along with various other gadgets that would make a man dance like a teenage girl at a boy band concert. English Bob took Darrell over to one of his computer terminals and hooked up the flash drive.

"All right, the plan is this. I'll get us the addresses and some info of the inhabitants of the buildings we're going to be visiting. Then we'll split up and find out all we can."

"Are we going to be doing anything illegal?" Darrell asked.

"Illegal is such a vague term these days," mused English Bob.

"What gear we gonna take?" Phil asked.

English Bob smiled. He pressed a button on the console and another portion of the wall opened up. Costumes and weapons of all kinds hung on racks, ready for immediate use.

"Wait a minute," Darrell said. "What the hell is the plan?"

Phil said, "We'll get the list of financial institutions in town from the flash drive. We'll visit these places to find out who's in control of the money and what it's being used for. At that point we'll take our information to the authorities."

"And how do you propose getting people to talk?" Darrell said.

"We use these." English Bob pulled out a box from a shelf. He reached in and tossed Darrell something he never thought he'd possess. A badge.

"These are legal, if you make them look legal," English Bob said. "Give it a quick flash and most people won't question you. Just try to keep your game face on or you could be in trouble. Understood?"

Darrell nodded. "Then let's get the hell out of here and get working," Phil said.

****

"Any reflections?" Ron Peters asked the cameraman.

"It's fine."

"This ought to give them bastards something to talk about at the station."

"I don't think they give a flyin flip personally. They just needed someone to cover the thing since Clarissa Day got assigned another story this afternoon."

"I know. I'm trying to remain positive here."

The cameraman laughed. "You're the first one. Enjoy the life while you can."

"So when is Nathan Gibraltar supposed to get here?" Ron asked his producer in the truck through the microphone.

"Any minute now. Stay alert," came the reply over his earpiece.

"How long is this ceremony expected to go Scott?" Ron asked the cameraman.

"As long as those scumbags have wind in their lungs. That's a lot of air. I remember this one event…"

"They're here," the producer said in Ron's earpiece.

Ron looked and pointed out the motorcade for the cameraman. Scott whipped the camera around and got a shot of the limo's pulling up by the staging area. Ron abstractedly began straightening himself up, wanting his time on camera to be perfect.

****

Curtis walked up to the man inside the hallway. In his hand he carried a carton that to anyone else appeared to be a carton of roses.

"Are you…" Curtis asked.

"Yeah," the man said. "Bout damn time you made it. I went through a lot to clear this space."

"Hey, I'm just the hired help."

"Follow me. And never mind the bodies."

The man led him to the staircase and ascended the stairs to a barren room. "This is it. She'll tell you what to do next. And don't fuck up."

"She doesn't seem like the kind of gal you want to piss off."

The man walked downstairs without a reply. Curtis gave the man a rude gesture when he made sure the man wasn't looking. Then he noticed a piece of the wall by the stairway exit fall to the floor. He walked up and examined it. It was a bullet hole. He didn't want to know from where. Curtis got to work setting up the gun.

****

The secretary at the local CPA looked at him with a turn of her head. "Can I help you?"

"Howdy ma'am. I just want to ask a couple questions," English Bob said, flashing the badge.

She glared at him without responding. "Who may I ask is in charge here?" English Bob asked.

"That would be Woodward Johnston," she replied, her tone cold enough to freeze a boiling pot of water. "He's in a meeting at the moment."

"Well, I don't want to interrupt his schedule but I have a couple questions that need answering immediately. I promise you that my questions will not be too much of a dereliction of his time."

The secretary hesitated. "I said he's in a meeting."

"Can my friend Mr. Franklin change your mind?" he asked.

She hesitated then snatched the money from English Bob's hand. "Oh, all right. But make it quick."

The secretary got on the phone and rang her boss.

A minute later Mr. Johnston walked up to the front. "What in God's name is going on here?"

English Bob flashed the badge. "I have a couple questions to ask then I'll let you get back to work."

"Well I hope so," Mr. Johnston said, glaring at his secretary. She ignored her boss by doing some busy work on her computer.

English Bob took out a printed copy of the money transactions from the flash drive and handed it to Mr. Johnston. "Have you seen this transaction before?"

Mr. Johnston took the paper and examined it. "Why would I tell you anything about this?"

"You mean you've seen this before?"

"What do I mean? I mean that if I told just anyone my customer's transactions without a court order, I'd be out of business."

English Bob took the paper from Mr. Johnston's hand. "Would you give a guess as to what financial establishment handled this transaction?"

"It didn't come from here. Now leave and never come back. I do not service rude people, even if they are officers of the law," he said.

****

Nathan took one last swallow of vodka. "That should make for a good speech," he said.

His chief of staff smiled. "It will make it an antacid day for me if you're not careful."

"Truth be told, last time I spoke in the Senate chamber, I was half in the bag on some good bourbon. Don't worry. I'll be fine. I've been doing this before you had your first keg party."

"There's not that tremendous difference in our ages Nathan."

"I know, but come on. I'm a professional. I wouldn't do anything that would jeopardize my career, old chap."

Steven shrugged. "Speaking of that, we do have something to talk about."

"What is it?"

"There's someone that's come forward claiming that you've beaten your wife."

Nathan stared at him, a smile plastered on his face. "They're wrong of course."

"All right. However, more of these are coming out. What are you doing that would make all these people come forward like this?"

Nathan glowered. "Greed. Or whatever else a person would hate about a person with means. That's what people don't see about us upper class in society. We do all the hard work to get to our position and people who do nothing and work for nothing do what they can to take you down."

"That's a nice speech but what does that do for this situation?"

"Let me guess. They want money?"

"Of course."

"Give it to them. What little they take I'll make back in a matter of minutes."

"Again, that is true. However, what's going to happen when someone comes along who doesn't want to be paid off?"

Nathan looked at the ground a moment. "Then you leave them to me."

****

Phil walked up to the secretary and flashed his badge. The thick metal badge fell out of his wallet and landed on her desk.

"Can I help you, um, officer?"

Phil picked up the badge, embarrassed. "Sorry about that. I need to speak to your boss."

"That's impossible without an appointment."

"This is something I have to insist upon. I am a private investigator and I need to ask him a few questions involving a case I'm working on."

"If you're a private eye then I'm Princess Leia. Now if you please..." she shooed him out of the office.

Phil sighed and left. Heading back to his car, he took out his cell phone and dialed up English Bob.

"Hello?"

"It's Phil. Any luck?"

"Nope. The guy here was a pompous jerk. How about your end?"

"I never even saw the guy. I fumbled my introduction and landed my sorry ass outside."

"Was the secretary a guy or something?"

"I just hit a brick wall, that's all. No need to bust my balls about it."

"You need that info man. The kid is driving right?"

"Yeah."

"Then I have a suggestion for you."

"What's that?"

"Scare the hell out of them, my friend. Bust up in there with your gun out and demand answers."

Phil shook his head. "Why should I do that? We're already treading the waters into illegality here."

"You know what I'm talking about. This is Grand Rapids. You want some info and this guy has it. What have you got to lose?"

Phil looked back at the entrance of the building. "I don't know why I'm listening but I'll call you back if I get anything."

Phil turned off the phone. He headed back to the office door and entered the building again.

The secretary rolled her eyes. "I thought I told you…"

Phil walked past her, taking his gun from its holster. He kicked the office door open.

Terrance Millhouse, who had the build of a piece of straw, sat behind his desk, going over some information with a client on the phone. He looked up at Phil.

"I'll have to call you back," he said to the client. He placed the phone back in the cradle. "May I help you?"

Phil walked over and sat on Terrance's desk. "I'm a private investigator. I have a question for you."

"Maybe it's just me, but couldn't you have been a little more polite when you entered?"

"Your secretary prevented a proper introduction."

"Take a seat. And Monica," he said, "there's nothing to worry about. I was actually expecting this."

Phil sat in a chair, taking out the computer printout from his jacket pocket. "I have an off shore bank account that I need some info on." He handed the paper to Terrance.

Terrance glanced it over. "It's an account in the Cayman Islands."

"Do you know whose account this is?"

"People put their money in those types of accounts so they can remain anonymous. But there is one thing I can do for you."

Phil sat back in the chair. Terrance typed something into the computer, he found what he wanted, grabbed a pen, and wrote something on the printout.

"There is the PO box of the holder of that account," he said, passing Phil the paper.

"Do you have a name for me?"

"Yeah. And since I value my life and the life of my family I won't tell you."

Phil nodded. "Thank you for your help."

"What is your name by the way?"

"Phil McKnight."

"Next time you need your taxes done, I'll do them half priced."

Phil shook his head and walked out of the office.

****

Ferrell Denton waddled up to the hot dog stand and pulled money out of his pocket. He looked at the menu on the side and made his choice.

"Give me five chili dogs please."

"Whoa boy, think you can handle that?"

Ferrell looked at him. "I wouldn't ask if I couldn't. Give me the dogs."

The vendor shrugged and made the hot dogs for him. He liberally spread on the chili, noticing the man's longing glance at the fattening addition to the normal hot dog. He passed it to him. Ferrell clutched them like a lost treasure and walked off into the crowd.

It was his moment to shine. He had to be one of the few people on Earth to be the authority on a subject. He knew more about Otis Brisbane than anyone else. Not that many would care but to be the top in something meant a lot. The only thing this knowledge didn't bring him was a woman but they weren't much of a logical species anyway.

He weaved his way through the crowd and found his way to the entrance to the back stage area. The security guard let him pass. He'd already had a run in with him and if he knew what was best, he'd keep to himself. He went to a metal folding chair next to the stage entrance and sat down, intent on finishing his food. The stage manager walked up, knowing he'd be in for a hassle with him.

"Mr. Denton, I have to know how long your speech is going to run."

Ferrell took a bite. "Mmmmpphmm."

"Can you repeat yourself?"

Ferrell swallowed his food. "I said I'll be done when I'm done. When will you people leave me alone?"

"When you give us an exact time to your speech."

"Listen, and you will listen. This will probably be the only time when these people hear about the life and times of the great Mr. Brisbane and I'm not going to miss my chance."

"Like anyone gives a fuck about..."

"Then why would they bring me here? Answer that tough guy."

The stage manager paused, letting the anger subside. "When you signed the contract to be here today, you were obliged to give a time for how long your speech was to be."

"All right. You want a time? Five hours, that's the time of my speech. Now let me finish with my pre-speech snack."

The stage manager threw his hands up and walked away, defeated. Ferrell attacked the hot dog as if it had just committed a crime against his mother.

****

The doors to the limos opened almost simultaneously, men dressed in expensive suits stepping out and trying their best to look busy for everyone to see. Nathan Gibraltar stepped out among them, a smile plastered on his face.

The stage manager approached, looking as if he'd been through a battle. "Lt. Governor. Thank you for taking time out of your schedule for our event."

"You are most graciously welcome," Nathan said, shaking the stage manager's hand.

"Please follow me to your spot on stage."

"It's not event time yet," Nathan said. "Wouldn't be proper if I went out before the ceremony got started."

"But…"

Nathan's chief of staff stepped in front of Nathan. "I'm Steven Falcone, Mr. Gibraltar's chief of staff. Mr. Gibraltar will be available when this event is ready to begin and only then. Which shouldn't be much longer if I'm not mistaken?"

The stage manager looked at his watch. "You're right. Took too long fighting with one of the men giving a speech today. If you'll excuse me…" He turned and headed for another part of the back stage area. Steven turned to Nathan.

"Are you sure you're ready? I can cancel and claim you were sick."

Nathan turned serious. "Maybe I was a little glib with the stage manager. I'm all right. I'm ready and able to do this speech."

Steven looked at him. "If I wasn't mistaken, I'd say you had something up your sleeve."

****

Robert looked out of his scope one last time, knowing that at any moment, Nathan Gibraltar would be in his sights. His time had come.

He wondered what the publicity would be. Would they give him a chance to explain himself or would they just seek to crucify him? It was worth the sacrifice. Come what may, a world without Nathan Gibraltar would be a better world indeed. He was well prepared for the sacrifices.

He looked at the stage and noticed that things were settling down, the participants all in their places. He checked his rifle one last time to make sure it wouldn't fail him. Things had to go right today. Something had to go his way. He looked through the scope.

3:00 PM-4:00 PM

The emcee stepped up to the podium. The audience gave polite applause. The emcee cleared his throat.

"Ladies and gentlemen, we at The Brisbane Foundation wish to thank you for attending the re-dedication ceremony of the statue of our town father, Otis Brisbane."

The audience applauded. "First today, let us welcome town historian Ferrell Denton who would like to say a few words about the esteemed Otis Brisbane."

More applause as Ferrell Denton took the stage. Ferrell soaked it all in, doing a smashing job at feigning ignorance to the fact that the applause was polite at best. He took out a stack of three by five cards and placed them on the lectern, each in their own place. The audience watched as a man with an obvious case of O.C.D. organized himself and began speaking.

"To begin at the beginning would not do justice to such an important figure in history."

The crowd could sense it. The man onstage would be talking for a long time.

****

Curtis got the last item into place and looked at the little creation he'd just built. His very own sniper rifle with designer stand. Curtis whistled.

"It's about time you finished," the woman said from the earpiece.

"You're lucky I did it in the first place," he snapped back. "I didn't know I'd have to put the damn thing together."

"If you continue with your rant, the other people listening in will get upset and demand I take you out."

Curtis kept silent. Only because he didn't want to prove this bitch's claim true.

"What are my instructions?" he asked finally.

"What do you do with a sniper rifle?"

Curtis rolled his eyes. "I don't know. Take it to a house by the lake?"

"No. You shoot things with it. When you hear a beep from your earpiece, I want you to shoot the gun out of the hands of the man on the roof of the middle building. Remember, do it only when you hear that beep and you won't die from bullets yourself. Until then…"

A loud, piercing sound erupted through the earpiece, ripping through his skull. He put his hand to his ear.

"I get the point. You don't have to be a…"

"Like I said, watch that potty mouth of yours."

Silence. Curtis took a breath to keep him from doing something he would regret. Then, out of curiosity, he looked through the scope of the rifle at the roof of the middle building. Curtis whistled.

"Damn."

A man lay on the roof with a sniper rifle aimed down at the stage. This could be fun, he thought.

****

"I'm looking for a Mr. Reardon," Phil said.

"That would be me. Come on in."

Phil walked into the man's office and closed the door. This was the fifth person he'd seen at the post office with it's never ending bureaucracy and he was hoping this man could yield something worthwhile. Phil grabbed a chair and put on his working smile.

"My name is Phil McKnight. I'm a private investigator. I'm looking for some information on the owner of a certain PO box."

"Any information in regards to owners of post office boxes I'm not at liberty to give out."

"I understand but this person is a suspect in the theft of a very expensive item."

"Again sir, that's information I can't give out."

Phil laughed. "Let's talk off the record, can we?"

Mr. Reardon gave a small smile. "We can."

"How much is it going to cost me?"

A pause. "Two thousand dollars would make me more open to rule breaking."

Phil cringed, taking the ever-decreasing wad of cash out of his pocket and counted out two thousand. Once it was all in his hand, Mr. Reardon put it in his pocket.

"The address please?"

Phil handed him the slip of paper with the post office box written on it. He waited while Mr. Reardon typed the appropriate information into his computer. Finding what he wanted, he picked up a pen and wrote a name.

"Here you go, Mr. McKnight."

Phil read the name and smiled. He hadn't expected this.

****

Nathan paced backstage, much to Steven's chagrin. After all the alcohol he'd consumed on the trip here Steven was nervous that it would coming back to haunt Nathan. He knew Nathan was a professional and did his job well but something about this speech seemed to be making Nathan squirrelly. Moreover, Nathan wasn't talking to anyone, much less him, so damned if he knew how to help. He walked up to

Nathan and put his hand on his shoulder.

"What's going on?"

"Nothing," Nathan barked.

"Then why are you pacing around like an expecting parent in a maternity ward?"

"Pre-speech jitters? Don't worry. I'm fine."

"You can't be. Something's on your mind and…"

Nathan smiled. "Nothing is on my mind. I'm a politician with a full workload to deal with and I'm just taking time to think. I don't mean to make you're scared."

Steven sighed. "I have a lot on my mind as well. I want things to go perfect today."

"I realize how important this is. Trust me. I can do this just fine."

What could he say? Steven resumed his place by the door of the limo, watching Nathan pace some more.

****

"You got that name?" Phil asked.

"I do," English Bob replied.

"What should be our next move?"

"We'll head over there and see if this person knows anything."

"That's a given. But what if this person doesn't know anything? What if they're just there to hand out cash and not ask any questions?"

"What, you think we're going to find some little old lady who invests her cash in criminal activities as a hobby? Whoever we're meeting at this place is knee deep in something and we're going to find out when exactly they're knee deep in."

Phil sighed. "I was hoping this would be easy, that's all."

"Dude, you of all people should know life ain't easy. I'll be heading over to the Spanish Moon to check out this name. Meet me there when you can."

Phil hung up the phone. "So what's going on?" Darrell asked.

"We get our butts to the store and buy some lunch. Then we head to the Spanish Moon to do a little old-fashioned person search. You up for it?"

"I could be in worse places."

Phil's phone rang. He stared at it a moment wondering who would be calling.

"Hello?"

"Am I speaking with Phil McKnight?"

"That would be me."

"I'm pleased to speak with you. My name is Ray. I'd like to talk."

"I'm a busy man. Can you tell me what this is about?"

"Richard Wilcox."

Phil paused. "Ok. You got my attention."

"I have something important to discuss with you. However I would feel better if we discussed it in person."

"I'm sorry. I don't think I want to discuss anything with a person with such terrible association in friends."

"I agree Richard wasn't the best which is why he's not around anymore, but I think you will feel our talk will be quite fruitful."

"That may be true but I don't think I want to meet you just yet. Richard Wilcox didn't exactly show good intentions when he hired me so I'd rather not walk into something I'm going to regret."

"I understand. But let me ask this. Do you know the whereabouts of the missing flash drive?"

"Why?"

"I want that flash drive back. I'll offer you five hundred thousand dollars in cash, no questions asked."

Phil paused, looking at Darrell. "What happens to the kid who took it?"

"What does it concern you?"

"It does. Call me crazy."

"Depending on what he knows, we can work something out."

"What do you mean by that?"

"If he knows something that could damage any interests of mine then I may be hesitant to let him go. With his record I don't think the authorities will be lenient with him."

"Call me back in an hour. I want a chance to think about this and I'll give you the answer then."

"Thank you. I agree to your terms."

"Good enough. Bye."

Phil shut off the phone. Darrell turned his head.

"Who was that?"

"A man named Ray."

"Ray?"

"Know him?"

"If he's here, I'm a dead man."

Phil paused. "You're going to have to tell me more about your employment with Mr. Wilcox. Anything you can tell me would greatly help."

Darrell slapped the steering wheel. "I sold computers. I worked on them. I bought them cheap at one store, brought it back to ours, and sold it for more. But," he sighed, embarrassed, "most of the time I delivered drugs across town."

"Just drugs?"

"Yeah, shit like that. Does this mean we can't date anymore?"

"Funny. Why'd you do it?"

"Money. I know more about computers than most people. But I didn't have enough dough to get to college. I had bills to pay like anyone else."

"Listen kid, I will do anything in my power to keep you safe and if we get through this, you'll go to college."

Darrell sat back and sighed. "You know, I trust you. You're kind of like my brother. He's the kind of person that can say the right thing at the right time. He's always been there for me."

"All right. Let's go. I'm hungry."

****

On and on he went, making every word he spoke feel like a monotone reading of The Lord of the Rings. This tubby pile of crap is making this day worse, Nathan thought.

He walked up to the stage manager standing by the stairs looking like he was nursing a belly full of ulcers. "What's your name?" Nathan asked.

"Antoine sir."

"Antoine, I'd like you to do something for me. I need that fat fuck off as soon as possible. What can you do to help me out?"

"I wish I could do something sir. I would personally love to get him off stage but I can't interrupt the show. I'd get into big doo-doo."

Nathan put his hand on the man's shoulder. "Do you know how I got to my position in life?"

"Hard work sir."

"That helps, sure, but the biggest reason I got to the top was by getting things done, no matter the cost. I need him off now. If you want to get somewhere, you'll get his ass off that stage."

Nathan pulled out some money and slapped it into the man's hands. The stage manager thought it over, the handful of paper with Benjamin Franklin's photo on them helping to convince him of what to do. He decided that anything that involved getting Ferrell Denton out of his life would be a great idea. He walked off.

Nathan smiled. It will be soon now. Thank God. Days like these can be rough on a man.

****

The stage manager walked up to Colin, the man working the soundboard for the event. The slug was still giving his speech, testing the patience of everyone in a thirty-mile radius. Colin looked up.

"Hey Antoine."

The stage manager smiled. "Colin, I need a favor."

"What do you need?"

"Get that parasite off the stage."

"Ain't that your job?"

"It's going to take more than me persuading him for him to leave. Cut his mic. He'll be so apoplectic that he'll damn near have a heart attack."

"I heard you and him argue earlier and all that but I can't be risking my job for…"

Antoine passed him some of the money Nathan gave him. "Is that good enough to change your mind?"

Colin thought it over. He held his hand out again, motioning for some more. Antoine obliged. Colin organized the money and put it in his pocket.

"This job sucked anyway," he said.

Xander's phone finally rang, whatever call he was taking before finally decided to end. Ray sat back in his chair and waited for him to answer.

"Hello?"

"Xander. It's Ray. I got a hold of Phil McKnight."

"You did? I'm impressed," Xander said.

"He sounded receptive to a meeting. Wilcox did a lot to make him nervous understandably but I tossed something in that'll make him see the light."

"I couldn't care less about him as long as he gives us what we need. We're only talking about some ignorant private eye here. I don't need any more headaches. Do what you have to do to get this over with."

"I got it covered."

Xander hung up the phone. Ray leaned back in his chair and sighed. His cell phone vibrated in his hands. He flipped it open.

"Hello?"

"Ray?" a woman's voice asked.

"Yeah."

"It's Leslie. Do you have a report?"

Ray smiled. "Yeah. How much time you got?"

Ferrell tapped the microphone harder, hoping desperately that the cord was loose thus preventing him to speak. It wasn't. He knew he was the victim of sabotage. Ripples of laughter erupted from the audience. He turned to his right and saw the emcee walking on stage with microphone in hand.

"What is going on here?" Ferrell demanded. "I must finish my speech."

"Thank you for that rousing and educational speech on the life and times of Otis Brisbane," the emcee announced. The crowd erupted into cheers.

"My speech is not done," Ferrell screamed, causing further ripples of laughter from the audience.

The emcee turned to face him. "We thank you for such a great speech and look forward to your involvement at the conference later today at the university."

"I am not leaving this stage," Ferrell announced, causing more laughter from the audience.

The emcee lowered his mic. "Listen tubby, you're gone. Either leave the stage like a good little penguin or I'll have no choice but to call security."

"You have no right to do this to me. I was contracted to give my speech in its entirety. I am not leaving this stage until I give my speech. As for your comments, you will be hearing from my lawyer. I will not be discriminated against because of my weight."

The emcee motioned to someone behind Ferrell. Ferrell turned and saw a six-man security team approaching him. Ferrell stood his ground.

"I have the right to finish my speech as contracted. I will not..."

The sharp sting of the taser hit him in the belly. Thousands of volts of electricity shot through his body, much to the audience's delight. They roared with laughter as the guards continued to taser him, then beat him with batons to get him under control. He was dragged off stage with an ovation from the audience.

When the stage was clear, the emcee walked up to the podium. The microphone on the podium suddenly worked again. "Now that we have that out of the way, let's continue with our ceremony. Here to officially re-dedicate the statue of our town father, please give a warm welcome to the Lt. Governor of the state of Michigan, Nathan Gibraltar."

****

Robert felt a tingle of excitement work its way through his body. His moment with destiny had arrived. He thought about everything one more time. The way he saw things, he was in the clear as long as he was precise as a clock.

He saw Nathan Gibraltar walk on stage, a plastic smile on his face, waving to the audience that probably would vote him in to be Governor in four years without realizing what sort of man he truly was.

Well, thanks to him, they wouldn't have to find out. Robert took a deep breath and relaxed.

****

"Do you copy Curtis?"

"I knew I'd be hearing from you."

"It's going to happen any second now. I want you prepared. This has to be done right."

"I know. I know. Take him out when I hear the beep," Curtis said.

"No. Just shoot the gun out of his hands. We want him alive."

"I misspoke. It's still stupid leaving him alive though."

"It's not your job to criticize the plan. Just have to execute your end of it."

"I will if you leave me alone."

Silence. Finally, he didn't have to hear from that silly broad. He could get down to work. He looked through the scope and got his sights on the man on the roof. This was definitely a weird job. He figured it odd that if they were trying to protect the guy on the stage, why would they wait until the very last second to save him. That was thinking bass ackwards as they say.

He cleared his mind, focusing on the job. He figured it wouldn't do any good to be thinking about other things when...

BEEP

He aimed and fired the gun. The man's gun went sideways then fell from his hands to the ground below. The man stood up and ran to the back of the roof out of sight. Curtis stood up.

"There you go," he said. "A job well done."

"You fired a second too late."

"Huh? I did everything you asked."

"I told you to shoot when you heard the beep, not one second later. For that, you're going to have to pay the price."

"What's that? A cut in pay? I know you won't gun me down because we have a deal."

"You're right; I'm not going to gun you down."

Curtis smiled. Then he felt the earpiece get hot. He grabbed at it. Before he could do anything, it exploded.

****

Nathan was shoved into the back seat of his limo. His breathing came in hard gasps, hard grateful gasps. Steven sat next to him.

"I can't believe this," Steven said. "They told me security would be tight at the event."

"It's all right," Nathan replied calmly. "Accidents happen."

"What? You could have been shot. Wait a second. Is that blood on your ear?"

Nathan felt his left ear and cringed. "Well I'll be. The bastard got me."

"Everyone's out there looking for this person, I assure you that. We'll get this son of a bitch before he realizes what's going on."

****

The cell phone rang, making Xander jump in surprise. Xander picked it up.

"Hello?" he asked.

"The job is finished," Annie said.

"And?"

"Your boy fired a second later than I would have liked but other than that things went fine."

"Good to hear. I need you on standby until tomorrow. Who knows what messes will need cleaning up after this. After that, I'm throwing some money your way and I want you to go wherever your pretty heart desires."

"Thanks."

"Keep that phone with you."

Xander hung up. He pulled a piece of paper out of his pocket and looked at the number listed on it, punching it into his cell phone.

The phone rang. The other party answered.

"Hello?"

"Yes," Xander said, "may I speak to Onyx?"

"Yeah. Just a minute," the person on the phone replied.

Xander leaned back in his chair. "Yes?" Onyx said, coming on the phone.

"How are you my friend?"

"I'm fine. But let's dispense with the pleasantries. We both know this isn't a social call."

"All right. I'm calling in a favor."

"What is it?"

"This may seem odd but I have a method to my madness. I need you to remove Governor Davis Creston from office by ten o'clock tonight."

"Why?"

"I have my reasons. Can you do this?"

"Of course I can. I would like to know what I'm getting in return."

"You will find out at seven tonight. I'm sending someone over there with a gift."

"While I appreciate the gift, this favor you ask of me to do doesn't make me happy. I have an idea, no matter how dim, who this whole plan of yours is for and I don't like it. I may not be the most reputable person alive but I know good people when I see them and Davis Creston is a good man. After I do this, we're done."

"So be it. It's been nice dealing with you."

Xander hung up the phone. This news hurt but wasn't unexpected.

****

Robert walked down the sidewalk, oblivious to the people around him. How could this have happen? How could he have failed at the last possible second?

Someone knew he'd be up there. There was no other way to explain it. He'd made sure everything was full proof. No one could have possibly known he would be on that roof. So how did that explain his gun getting shot from his hands?

His cell phone rang, breaking his concentration. He took it out of his pocket and turned it on.

"Yeah?"

"Why did you fail?"

Robert sighed. "Hello Leslie. Someone knew I was up there. They shot the gun from my hands."

"They must have been staring at you an awfully long time before they took a shot. You mean to tell me that you never saw anyone staring back at you?"

"I had my attention on the target, not on anything else. That's what you paid me for."

"We paid you to get the job done. What are your plans now?"

"We find out where he's at next on his itinerary and go from there."

"Hopefully his itinerary hasn't changed. Can we trust you to get the job done?"

"Why else did you hire me?"

Robert hung up the phone. Damn he hated that woman. He hated having to deal with people like that but it was a means to an end. He had to get off the streets quick. Not that he thought he was spotted or anything but under the circumstances it would be best to keep a low cover. But how best to do it? It would be great if he had a ride. What if…? He smiled. It just might be crazy enough to work. He took out his phone and dialed Lydia.

****

Leslie knocked on the door, waiting for a reply. Her boss could be quite irritable at times and she didn't want him upset now. The red light above the door turned off and she opened the door.

The room was dark, illuminated as though by a candle. She headed over to her boss' desk.

"I have some news," she said.

"Give it to me."

"Robert failed. He wasn't able to kill Nathan Gibraltar. He said someone shot the gun out of his hands."

Her boss drummed his fingers on the desk. "All right. Is he making preparations for his next opportunity?"

Leslie paused, not sure of what to say. "He, uh, told me he was making the appropriate preparations."

"Good. Things are going along nicely."

"How can that be? If I may be frank sir, we hired Robert Sampson to assassinate Nathan Gibraltar and he failed. Do we want to trust him by taking another chance at this?"

Her boss turned around in the chair, looking at her. "Robert is doing just fine. You'll see when this is over. You may leave now."

Leslie couldn't respond. She stood staring at him. What was he planning? She'd underestimated him before however she couldn't contemplate how things could turn to his favor as is. Leslie turned and left the room.

****

"Why couldn't we have just gone to a deli or something?"

"In this cheap ass town, this is a deli," Phil said, putting the last bit of mayo on his sandwich. He put the bottle back in the bag and slapped the piece of bread on his food.

"Thanks," Darrell said.

"You start the day thinkin you'd be getting shot in the head, now yer in a stranger's car eatin bologna sandwiches."

"Why couldn't we go to a restaurant?"

"Think about it. You pay about five or six dollars for a sandwich like this at a restaurant. For that amount, you're able to buy the bread, meat, and condiments and have it last you for more than a week. It's perfect."

Phil's cell phone rang. Phil cursed and put down his sandwich, smudging some mustard on his tie in the process.

"Hello?"

"Phil McKnight?"

"That's me."

"My name is Robert Sampson. We have to talk."

Phil turned to Darrell. "I'm all ears."

"I have a favor to ask. I need a ride to my place in town here and I have no one to turn to. I know you worked with my brother today so I was hoping you might help me out. I'd be more than happy to compensate you for your time."

"I usually don't offer cab service but I can make an exception in your case. Where can I pick you up?"

"Downtown. By the Calder. How soon can you get here?"

"Five, maybe ten minutes. Will you know…?"

"I know what your car looks like, yes. I'll see you soon. And I'd also like to thank you for what you've done for my brother."

Robert hung up the phone. Phil folded his phone up and put it back in his pocket.

"Who was that?" Darrell asked.

"Your brother."

"What?"

"You heard me."

"How the hell did he know to find me here?"

"He wasn't looking for you actually. He asked me to give him a ride somewhere."

"I wonder why he did that. That's strange."

"You're tellin me."

"Don't we have to go find English Bob?"

"He's got my number. Bitch can call me. Let's head downtown to the Calder. I'm curious to see why you're brother called me out of the blue and why he knows what kind of car I drive."

****

He knew there would be trouble when he saw the building. English Bob pulled up to the parking meter and shut off the engine. He took a more detailed look at the building housing the old karate studio.

Below it, a mom and pop Italian restaurant that he'd visited before was taking care of its lunchtime crowd. The door of the studio was just off to the side. He hoped that he'd find the place empty. The thought of being in a place where everyone could beat you with their feet made his bones shiver.

He found this location from an old buddy of his at the Spanish Moon, an old man from Brooklyn, New York back when the Korean War was more than a TV sitcom. It had cost him a pretty penny but English Bob knew that this old man was one thing. Honest.

He got out of the car and crossed the street. He opened the karate studio door and went up the stairs. Pictures of various people in various poses lined the stairway. Seeing these pictures filled him with more dread than he cared to admit having. Something in his head was screaming at him to run from danger. Something was about to happen and he realized he wouldn't be the victor. Maybe in traction but he wouldn't be winning anything. He got to the top of the stairs and opened the door.

The studio filled his vision like a close up in an Imax movie. The room was empty apart from metal beams spread throughout the room. The entire floor was covered with those mats you find in most high school gyms. An office was at the far end of the room. English Bob saw someone inside talking on the phone. He hoped it was the man he was looking for and that he'd be out of here soon so he could get some lunch at the restaurant downstairs. He walked over to the office door and knocked out of courtesy.

The man waved at him. Once he finished his phone conversation he rose and opened the office door. "May I help you?"

"Yes. Is your name Wallace Nelson?"

"That would be me."

"My name is Bob Terwilliger. I'm a private detective. May I ask you a couple questions?"

"Sure. Give me a moment and I'll be right with you."

Wallace walked back into his office and began putting away some paperwork. English Bob turned and paced, wishing each step would take more time off the clock than it did. Sooner than he would have liked, he heard the office door close and Wallace approach.

"How may I help you?"

English Bob took the printout from his pocket and opened it up. "I would like to ask you about an account in the Cayman Islands made out in your name."

"Like why do I have it and what not?"

"So it's safe to assume you have an account there and the information on this paper is correct?"

Wallace laughed. "Hmm. I don't want to share that information with you."

"I assure you sir that I'm only asking in order to get a stolen item returned for an important client of mine."

"Cut the crap junior. You don't ask someone about an off shore bank account when someone steals a car. You're looking for something that you shouldn't be messing with Bobby."

English Bob backed up, eager to split as soon as he could. "I'm sorry to use your time like this. I'll be on my way."

The kick swept him off his feet. He crashed to the floor, feeling the hard concrete through the mat. Wallace slammed his foot on the back of his head before the thought of retaliation entered his mind. Wavering bolts of pain and anger surged through him. He tried to stand but was met with another kick to the head.

"Why did you have to come snooping around looking for something you know nothing about? Why couldn't you just leave well enough alone?"

A flurry of kicks pummeled his body. English Bob tried in vain to get up but was knocked down with each attempt. The only thing he could hope for was Wallace making a mistake. Hopefully he would have energy to attack him if he did.

He almost missed the moment when it came. The kicks came down like rain from the clouds until they stopped for a moment. Wallace stopped to hear something. Just as he turned his attention back to English Bob, he felt Bob's fist crashing into his groin. He slunk to the floor in pain. English Bob got to his feet.

"Ahh, you love to give out pain but you sure don't seem to like taking it."

English Bob gave Wallace some good old-fashioned American kicks to the kidneys. "Now my friend, you're going to tell me what's going on here?"

English Bob got to the ground and pinned Wallace with his knee. He gripped his wrists and held them. Wallace grunted.

"I work for someone. You happy now?" Wallace said.

"I would be if I was five. Who do you work for and why did they give you money in an off shore bank account?"

"If you come to my office I'll show you."

"The moment I let you up, you're going to try and come at me again."

"No I won't. I promise."

English Bob thought for a moment. "I have a better idea."

He slammed his fist into Wallace's head until he was sure Wallace was knocked out. He rose from the limp body of the karate instructor. He dragged Wallace to a metal beam, securing him with his black belt. Once he felt confident Wallace couldn't escape, he headed for the office.

The office was tiny and smelled of gym sweat. English Bob inspected it, looking for anything out of the ordinary. He stepped over to the desk and searched the papers.

The papers had info relating to the karate school. Bob dismissed these as quickly as he could. Then he started seeing something interesting. Financial papers. A bunch were spread out on the desk. He sifted through the papers to see if he could find anything.

He saw Wallace's name listed as a C.P.A. on some of the papers. That's not what shocked him. What did shock him was the name of the other person on the forms.

Lt. Governor Nathan Gibraltar.

4:00 PM-5:00 PM

Phil's car came to a stop in front of a parking meter. Phil and Darrell stepped out and looked around. Foot traffic was picking up Downtown, especially at the courthouse across the street. Phil stepped onto the sidewalk, Darrell joining him at his side.

"Why did you drive past the Calder?" Darrell asked.

"You never just walk into a situation without giving it even the slightest inspection. Haven't you read any novels?"

"I don't read that much."

"No wonder you're a criminal."

They walked to the Calder stabile in silence, passing the miniature Calder created for the blind before reaching Calder Plaza. Phil stopped, holding Darrell back with his hand.

"This is called surveillance son. Leave it to the professionals."

Phil looked over the plaza for anything or anyone that seemed like they shouldn't be there. Things seemed normal, nothing out of the ordinary. Phil turned to Darrell.

"Do you see your brother?"

Darrell gazed over the crowd assembled at the plaza. "He ain't here."

"We're leaving," said Phil.

"Why?"

"It was something he said on the phone. He said he wanted to thank me for helping you today. The more I think of it, the more I think he thought you were dead."

"What? Why would he think that?"

"Remember the dart? Me thinks he has an accomplice who saw you get shot."

****

Robert watched Phil and Darrell head back to Phil's car from inside the bank across the street from Calder Plaza. He took his hand off the gun in his jacket. The son of a bitch McKnight guessed his plan. He walked out of the bank and headed to the sidewalk.

Darrell was alive. That he could be happy about. However, his apparent survival opened up a Pandora's box of its own. Why would Lydia lie to him?

She couldn't have lied, he reasoned. She probably saw him get shot and didn't bother to stay around to see if he was all right. That had to be it.

Robert took out his cell phone and dialed Lydia. Each ring felt like a part of him was being ripped off his body. Finally, she answered.

"Hello?"

"Darrell is alive."

A pause. "What? How can that be? I saw him get shot."

Robert sighed, relieved with Lydia's explanation. "You didn't stick around long enough to see what happened to him. Where you at now?"

"That old abandoned store up north from you."

"I'll be there as soon as I can."

He hung up. He searched his pockets for bus fare and headed for the bus stop.

****

The man whispered into Xander's ear. He winced when he heard the news. This wasn't what he wanted to hear.

He took out his cell phone and dialed the number of his favorite femme fatale. He needed a quick resolution to this problem and if Annie Walker couldn't get it done, he couldn't think of anyone else that could.

"Hello?" she replied.

"Annie, my darling. How goes it?"

"I've had a chance to meditate and have some tea. And you?"

"I'm doing fine, thanks for asking. I have some work which needs to be done. I need you to find a man who's been causing our organization some problems."

"I see. Where may I find this gentleman?"

"You'll find him at a chiropractor on 44th street. A car will be waiting for you in the parking lot of a gas station a block away. Instructions will be inside. I've arranged for a warehouse to be open for you. I believe you've worked there before."

"I'm on my way."

Xander shut off the phone. He sighed, relieved this problem would be disappearing soon.

****

Nathan found the mini bar and took out the vodka. He grabbed the first glass he could find. The vodka splashed into the cup, filling quickly.

"Are you sure you should be drinking that?" Steven asked.

"Were you just shot at?"

A room at the Brisbane Grand Hotel became available when the news reports hit. They drove into the service entrance and were escorted to a suite on the top floor.

Nathan had not been able to relax since he'd arrived. He felt almost electric, his body humming with an extra serving of adrenaline. He'd paced while watching the news of his attempted assassination. He had fun mocking the reporters and their faux serious delivery.

It wasn't that which bothered Steven. It was more the fact that he seemed like this wasn't something worth getting upset over. Why was he doing this? He hadn't once thought of calling his wife and children. It also didn't seem right that they hadn't contacted him but if those rumors he'd heard were true, he was sure they wouldn't be too upset at this news.

"Are you going to call your family?" Steven asked.

"I should. Quick question. Wasn't Davis' wife in town?"

"I believe so. If I'm not mistaken, she should be staying in this same hotel for the night."

Nathan smiled. He went over to the phone.

****

Audrey Creston stepped out of the shower and grabbed her bathrobe. It had been a long day at the charity event for the schools, having to be a server to all those sniveling brats in order to raise money for the school district that would only prepare those children for a life in fast food. However, it had to be done for the sake of the cameras because at the end of the day, it wasn't what you said that mattered, it was how you looked while saying it.

She picked up a towel and wrapped it around her hair. The phone interrupted her. She finished wrapping the towel on her head, walked over, and picked it the phone.

"Hello?"

"Hmm, that voice."

Audrey smiled. "Nathan Gibraltar. I heard you were in town."

"Yeah, I sure leave them with a bang as they say. How are you doing?"

"I'm fine now. Thankful I don't have to be around those ungrateful brats anymore. What brings you to the Brisbane Grand?"

"I'm here until they declare things safe. Had a whack job take a shot at me today while I gave my speech. When they brought me here I heard you were in the building and I just had to give you a ring."

"Oh my God. You were shot at? Are you ok?"

"I'm fine. Had my ear slightly grazed by a bullet but I survived."

"That is good to hear. Do you have some time on your hands?"

"I believe I do," Nathan smiled.

"Come to my suite. It's number 1346."

"Ahh, downstairs. I can be there soon."

"Knock before you come in."

Audrey hung up the phone. She smiled. She had to get prepared.

****

"I've got some news for you," English Bob said.

"What you got for me Bobby?"

"I found the man we've been looking for and he's a CPA."

"Huh?"

"A CPA who's also a karate instructor. Imagine that."

"I've heard of stranger. What else you got?"

"He works for the Lt. Governor."

Phil paused. "The Lt. Governor? Since when has he done anything illegal?"

"That's just it. A CPA setting up an offshore bank account for the Lt. Governor is not entirely inconceivable but it still doesn't make much sense under the circumstances."

"I agree. Why would all this crap be happening if this were all a legit enterprise? We just have to find what we're missing. I know it's staring me right in the face yet I can't see it."

"Well spoken Confucius. Do you want to get your ass over here to help out at this place?"

"Yeah. I'll be there soon."

"All right. See you soon."

English Bob hung up the phone. He peered over to Wallace. Still out cold. Let that lumbering fool stay quiet for a while. He went back to looking through the papers.

****

Robert opened the garage door and shut it behind him. He went to the stairs leading to the attic.

The woman in the rocking chair faced the wall, slowly rocking back and forth in rhythm to the creaking floor. Robert ambled up to her.

"Quaint little place," said Robert.

"I thought you would like it," Lydia said. She stood and turned to face him.

"Why did you tell me my brother was dead?"

"I thought he was. I'm glad he's alive."

"He was with Phil McKnight. I almost killed Phil for letting him die. You should have told me."

"I swear I didn't know. I would have told you if I knew."

Robert stared at her for an uncomfortable minute. Then he smiled, pulling her to him in an embrace.

"I love you," he said. "I just care about my brother, that's all."

"Who wouldn't? If you can't trust me, who can you trust?"

She stared into his face and smiled. He tried to return her smile but it just wasn't in him. He turned his head.

"What is it?" she asked.

"I…, forget it. It's nothing."

Robert turned and walked to a window. Lydia stared, not sure how to react or what to do.

"Maybe Leslie was right. You're not able to do this."

"Kill Nathan Gibraltar? I can do that no matter how I'm feeling."

"That's it though. You shouldn't be feeling anything."

"I feel anger. Isn't that an emotion?"

"No. Anger is a reaction to an emotion. You have to be able to do this as though you were going to buy some milk."

"I don't need another lecture."

"This is not a lecture," she said, brushing her hand across his cheek. "This is reality. You can't be having an emotional moment when you're holding the gun."

Robert turned and started to pace. "I just don't need to hear it. I'm beyond that. I thought you would have seen that already."

"All I'm seeing is someone who needs some tissues for a good cry."

Silence. Robert stared out the window and at the traffic.

****

The magical hands of the miracle worker kneaded the flesh of Maury Finkelstein. He moaned in ecstatic delight. This was the best.

Anything that diverted his mind from business was a pleasure. Diverted. Ha. That seemed to be his business these days. Diverting the cash from accounts made from dishonest gain. What were these criminals going to do, call the police? Maury turned his head toward the masseuse.

"You are doing one hell of a job honey."

"Call me that again and I'll call security. We're not a massage parlor."

Maury laughed. Skank. If she only knew how much money he had, she'd be on her knees begging him to rub his real muscle. He used hundred dollar bills for tissues. He wasn't one of these over worked housewives' that came in here with their husband's money to get touched more than they would at home.

Oh well. Can't have everything go your way. He laid his head back down on the table.

The door to the room opened. Someone walked in and whispered something into the masseuse's ear. He heard footsteps again as someone left. Maury's mind drifted off to his date tonight. A sloppy smile spread across his pudgy face.

The masseuse's hands started going down his back until they reached his ample posterior. Before he realized it, his rump was being kneaded like dough. Whatever was just said, he was happy to be on the receiving end of this massage.

"What changed your mind honey?"

"I don't know. Maybe I'm attracted to balding fat pigs," a new female voice said. Maury turned his head.

He saw a tall, sexy vixen standing over him. In her hand was a syringe. Before he even thought of this not being kosher, she injected him with a sedative. He tried to curse her out but his response came out as a wobbly grunt before his head hit the table in unconsciousness.

****

Phil and Darrell walked up the stairs to the karate studio, not knowing what to expect. They got to the top and entered the cavernous studio. Phil spotted Wallace tied up to the pole, his hands and feet bound with some black belts. Phil spotted English Bob in the office and headed over there.

"Took a lickin huh?" Phil asked.

English Bob snorted. "You can say that. I don't mind the beating but come on, let a guy get a punch or two in."

"Find anything else out?"

"No. He's still out. I was a little over zealous putting him in his current condition."

"We'll let the kid wake him up while you show me the papers."

Phil's phone rang, catching him off guard. He took it out of his pocket and motioned for Bob and Darrell to be quiet.

"Hello?"

"Mr. McKnight. It's Ray."

"Ahh, yes. I was expecting your call."

"Are you up for a meeting?"

Phil paused. "I will only agree to a meeting if it's in a public place. I'm not looking for any trouble."

"Understandable. I assume you'll be bringing the flash drive?"

Another pause. "We'll talk. Like I said I'm not looking for trouble but I do want to hear you out first."

"All right. Sounds reasonable. Let's meet in the lobby of the movie theater on Knapp. That should be public enough for you. Meet me there at 4:45."

"Got it."

Phil hung up the phone. "That was Ray."

"Who the hell's that?" English Bob asked.

"He's just this guy who wants the flash drive back."

"You're not going to give it to him are you?" Darrell asked.

"I'm not going to show up there with it or anything like that. I wanna bargain with him first to see if I can get anything then he can have it. Don't you have the contents of it on your laptop?"

"I, uh, yeah. But we haven't got that secured part opened yet."

"I understand. I just want to see what this guy's so eager about."

"What if he thinks you saw what was on it?" English Bob asked.

"He probably thinks I'm some dumb PI brought into this by one of his former employees. He wants his flash drive then he'll be gone."

"What about me?" Darrell asked.

"I'm going to hear what he has to say before I do anything. I like you kid but you're new to all this. I won't put you in a situation where you'll get hurt."

"You don't know me," Darrell said. "I know how to handle myself."

Phil sighed and walked up to Darrell. "That's what I'm afraid of."

Darrell turned his head and sighed. "Thought so," Phil said.

"Why are you doing this?"

"Because I can. Are you taking my offer or what?"

"I guess. I wanna talk to my brother first."

"Not a problem. I got caller ID. Now wake that silly bastard up for us while I talk with English Bob."

Darrell walked over to the unconscious Wallace. English Bob turned to Phil.

"Nice speech man. Almost made me cry."

"Ahh, shut up. Show me the papers."

****

Eva Gibraltar sat next to the toilet recovering from her latest bout of vomiting. She had told herself in the past that Nathan wasn't that bad. She told herself that the bruises he left on her body were not intentional. That he really loved her but couldn't communicate his anger properly. Everyone has his or her limits though. How many times could she cover up his anger with makeup before she realized he wouldn't stop?

What am I going to do? Where can I go? Who would want to help me? Nathan had control over her entire life. The only way she could escape would be to destroy him. But how? What could a lonely scared woman do to a man like him?

A sentence popped in her head that never occurred to her before. The pen is mightier than the sword. What if I call a reporter and dish some dirt on him? Then he couldn't do anything to me. One little comment to the right person and he could be ruined.

Whom could she call? She didn't get a chance to watch much television so the names of the reporters generally escaped her. Who was that reporter that covered Nathan's promotion to Lt. Governor? The one Nathan seemed to loathe the most. Yes, Clarissa Day. Eva rose, heading to her phone in the bedroom.

****

Nathan uncorked the wine and poured out the expensive alcohol into two glasses. When done, he took a whiff of the sweet fragrance emanating from the bottle. He smiled, placing down the bottle and picking up the two glasses. He joined Audrey on the couch.

"I'm glad you could take time out of your schedule for me," Audrey said.

"Miss the chance to spend time with you? I would be a fool to miss it. So my dear, how's life in the Governor's mansion?"

Audrey Creston smiled. "Without you quite boring."

Nathan smirked and pulled her close to him. He set his wine glass on the side table.

"Aren't you going to drink your wine?" she asked.

Nathan smiled. "I'm not thirsty for wine."

****

Clarissa slammed her front door and stormed into the kitchen. She'd had another yelling match with her editor and her nerves were frayed. At the moment, she needed something to drink to calm her nerves. Some Earl Grey tea sounded good about now.

Her phone rang breaking her concentration. She cursed it for the interruption. She took out her cell phone and answered.

"Hello?"

"Is this Clarissa Day?" a weak voice replied.

"Yes. Who is this?"

"Eva Gibraltar. You're office said you'd be at this number."

Clarissa almost dropped her phone in surprise. "Why hello," she said, turning on the charm. "How are you?"

Eva coughed. "I want to talk to you about a hobby my husband has. He beat me today."

Terrible news, she thought, but at least the news came to her first. "Have you called the police?"

"Of course not. If I call, they would just report it back to him. Besides, this would hurt Davis Creston as well and I don't want to do that. Then Nathan would really hurt me."

"Where are you now?"

"In my bedroom."

Clarissa rose from her chair. "I know where you live. I'll be there as soon as I can. I need to get you out of there."

"I don't want to leave. He's going to hurt me."

"Mrs. Gibraltar, listen to me. Men who hit women need to be punished. You don't need to be the woman who dies because she wanted to give her man a second chance."

A pause from Eva. "I'll be waiting for you at the front entrance."

Clarissa hung up her phone, did the happy dance inside her head, and ran out of her house. It would take a while to get to Lansing but damn if she wasn't going to ride the highway like a speed demon.

****

Phil walked up to Wallace. "How's it going?"

"Who the hell are you?"

"Phil McKnight. Private Investigator. I got a couple questions I need answered. You gonna be good and answer them?"

Wallace spit on Phil's shoe. Phil kicked him in the stomach. "Do that again you get worse," Phil said. "You gonna answer my questions?"

"I'll answer your questions. Then when you set me free, I'm going to kill you."

"Gotcha tough guy," Phil said. "You're Nathan Gibraltar's accountant?"

"You saw the papers. I don't have to tell you more."

"Who do you work for?"

"Well obviously Nathan Gibraltar jackass."

Phil kicked the man in the groin. He screamed in pain. Phil grabbed Wallace by the chin and pinned his head against the beam.

"Who do you really work for?"

Wallace tried to fight through the pain but his will power left him. "Leslie. A woman named Leslie."

Phil paused and stepped back. "If Leslie is your boss then what work do you do for the Lt. Governor?"

"We're trying to get him into office."

"Isn't he already in office?"

"No, not the Lt. Governor office. We want him to be Governor."

"And who would those people you call we be?"

"I don't know."

"What do you mean you don't know?"

"Think about it. I'm told what I need to know and that's it."

Phil nodded. "All right. I can accept that. How can I get in contact with this Leslie?"

"There's a directory by the phone on my desk. It's in there."

Phil pointed at Darrell and motioned for him to get it. Phil turned to English Bob. The two took a couple steps away from Wallace.

"What do you think?" he whispered.

"I think he's telling the truth. Somewhat."

"How do you want to handle this?"

"We should get some feelers out for this Leslie before we go calling her. Then we dive in and hope we don't get shot."

"Knowing us, we better get a bed ready at the hospital. I gotta get going now." Phil took some cash out of his pocket. "Send the boy on a Greyhound to anywhere far away that you can get him. Give him some of your own cash if you have to and I'll pay you back."

"Gotcha. Makin your tab bigger huh?"

"That's how I roll. I'll call you when I'm done. Oh shoot, got a pen?"

"Yeah."

"Take down this number." Phil took out his phone and checked the numbers on his caller ID. "555-8394. That's his brother's number."

"All right. See ya."

****

Annie wheeled the gurney into the heart of the empty warehouse. Her equipment lay spread out on a table, waiting for the expert to work the tools like a piano. She brought Maury next to the table and locked the gurney in place. She took the sheet off him, turning his obese over. She turned to her table and grabbed two leather

112

straps underneath. She strapped one across his chest, pinning his arms and the other across his legs.

She turned to the various medications on the table. She inspected them and grabbed the right one to get this started. Inside was a medication called Dazalone that would turn off all muscle movement yet keep him conscious for her questioning. She grabbed a syringe and filled it. She turned to Maury, searched for a vein in his arm, and injected him. It would take a minute for it to work.

She arranged her tray to best suit her during the procedure. Scalpels, hooks, lighter fluid, all a quick grab away.

Her patient moaned. She put her hand on his chest and smiled into his opening eyes.

"Morning," she said, giving him a bright smile.

"Wha…dis," he slurred.

"You are in an empty warehouse. You screwed up Mr. Finkelstein. I am employed by a man whom you've stolen a lot of money from and he would like to know why. I'm a kind person. I will give you one chance and only one to tell me why you stole my employer's money. And believe me, if you don't take this chance, you will regret it."

Maury looked scared and confused. She could tell that she'd get no response. She picked up a scalpel and a lighter. She snapped the lighter on and held the scalpel blade over the flame. She held it in front of Maury's face, his portly flesh wiggling in terror as the blade grew red with heat. He started to moan.

"Pleez don…," he moaned.

She turned off the lighter. Annie smiled.

"I'm going to get right to the point."

She lowered the blade.

****

Darrell took the piece of paper from English Bob and went back to the office. Just the thought of hearing his brother's voice was calming his tension. And if he could help him get out of all this, that would be da bomb as they say.

He walked in and went to the phone. He picked it up and dialed his brother's number. He sat in the chair and relaxed the phone on his shoulder.

"Hello?" Robert asked.

"It's been too long."

A long pause. "I can't believe you're alive."

"Why would you say that?"

"I heard about you getting shot today. I was told that you were killed in the melee."

"Oh my God."

"Yeah. You're all right."

"We have to get together."

"Are you still with McKnight?"

"No. He went to have a meeting with someone. He's coming back later."

"Who's he meeting with?"

"Someone. What's it to you bro?"

"Just curious. Appease my curiosity. Who's he meeting?"

"A guy named Ray."

Another pause. "Why would he be dumb enough to meet with him?"

"You know about Ray?"

"I should be asking you that. Why did he go see him?"

"I told him it wasn't a good idea. He said nothing would come back on me."

"Why would anything come back on you?"

"I haven't had the chance to tell you about the flash drive."

"Wait, wait. Start from the beginning."

"I had been working with a guy named Richard Wilcox for a while delivering some stuff for him."

"You mean drugs," said Robert, disgust evident in his voice.

"You could say that. Anyway, one day I see this flash drive at his shop that I thought was just left there so I took it home. When I checked it out, I found out that it held some banking information for someone with an account in the Cayman Islands."

"What?"

"Yeah. Phil helped track down the guy who the money was going to and found out that he was an accountant for the Lt. Governor."

"Nathan Gibraltar eh? Interesting. Did he find out who this accountant works for?"

"Someone named Leslie."

Darrell sat through the silence. Just when he was going to ask Robert if he was there, his brother began to speak.

"You need to get out of there now. Can you do that?"

"Yeah. I'll just tell…"

"You're with other people?"

"Yeah. I'm at the place where we found the guy who created the account. A guy named English Bob is here. I don't know what else to tell you."

"Kill the accountant."

Darrell looked at the phone as if it had a strange growth on it. "Excuse me?"

"Kill that man. He is dangerous and if he's allowed to live then you could be in danger."

"What the hell have you been smoking since we've met last?"

"When have I let you down Darrell?"

Darrell didn't answer. "Listen to me. I wouldn't tell you this if I wasn't absolutely sure I was right. Please follow my instructions."

Darrell hung his head. Why would his brother want him to kill the accountant? He wasn't one to be horrified at the suggestion goodness knows but there was a difference between a survival kill and a bad action movie type of kill. Why would Robert tell him something like this if it wasn't important though? His brother would not put him in this position if it wasn't worth doing.

"All right. I, I'll do it I guess."

"Good. Where are you at?"

"Do you know Mancino's restaurant?"

Robert chuckled. "I know it. Be outside in ten minutes."

Darrell hung up the phone. He felt numb. After all this time, his brother actually expected him to just go off and kill someone. Oh the tangled webs we weave.

He walked out of the office and stared over at English Bob. Life dealt you weird hands at times. Spending these last few hours with Phil and Bob were by far the best he'd had in a while. Better than that entire nail biting crap he'd had with all those drugs. But his brother. His brother always looked out for him no matter what he did to mess up his life. Why should he take this moment to doubt that he didn't have the best in mind for him now?

Darrell stepped forward, each footstep feeling like a ton of concrete slowing him up. He went to his backpack by the wall and pulled out his gun, putting it in his waist pocket. He had to take out English Bob without hurting him too bad. He looked over, saw a metal folding chair, and could feel the light bulb turning on over his head. He walked over and picked it up, making sure he was still undetected. He headed toward English Bob.

Bob turned just as the chair crashed down on his head. He took a weak swing at Darrell before slumping to the ground, sleeping for who knows how long. He put the chair down. Wallace started laughing.

"Good boy. Now someone is doing something productive around here."

"I've never been one for productivity."

Darrell pulled out his gun and fired, putting two holes into Wallace's chest. He ran over to his backpack, sticking the gun and flash drive inside. He headed for the exit.

****

Phil took a bite from the bucket of popcorn he'd bought from the concession stand. He looked around the busy movie theater lobby from the stool by the arcade entrance. Business was brisk now, causing the lobby to be congested. This could be a good or bad thing for him. He didn't know which yet.

He scoped the place out in the off chance that he was being set up. He figured that he was too minor a person at this point for them to want to waste any muscle on. But assuming things would be safe was a good way to find some metal in your head.

So intent was he on checking out the crowd that he didn't spot the man sitting next to him. He jumped in surprise. The man smiled and took some popcorn from Phil's bucket.

"How ya doing McKnight?"

Phil smiled. "Ray I presume?"

"You presume correct. This is good popcorn."

"It tastes better when it's fresh."

"Needs more salt. So how come you didn't want to bring the flash drive?"

"I wanted a chance to talk about the kid who took it mostly."

"What about him?"

"He's a good kid, just not that bright. Doesn't know what kind of people he's messing with. He's not really someone to waste any energy on."

Ray smiled. "Love the sentiment but leave the business matters to me. As it is, I'm not too worried about what he saw because as you say, he is a dumb kid no matter how good he is with computers. My question is have you seen anything?"

"I have. Just a bunch of numbers."

Ray laughed. "I love yer spunk. You gotta appreciate someone who has balls. I'm not going to lie to you. That flash drive is important to me. I would like my property back and am willing to pay you more than you deserve for it. And I know how much you need the money. I read about what you did last week in the paper."

Phil smiled. "Yeah, The Mayor of Grand Rapids didn't appreciate my shooting out the windows on the walkway over Fulton Street."

"So when can I make that problem go away with more money than you can hold?"

Phil laughed. "When did you want it?"

"We can meet back here in an hour. I'll have your money, you bring the equipment, and maybe we can watch a movie. Who knows?" Ray took some more popcorn. "I was right. More salt."

"Where are your bodyguards?" asked Phil.

"My guys? All over the place. Why?"

"I staked the place out before you got here and couldn't figure out why you'd show up here alone."

"I would never do that. Besides, I own the place."

Ray stood and walked off. Phil watched him off, finishing his popcorn before he left.

****

The man looked over the business report wincing at the stocks that were costing him money. Not that his lifestyle was in any danger of changing but losing money was losing money. He hated the loss of control. Whether it is losing money, bad business decisions, or other people's opinions, the idea that he couldn't control all aspects of his life was frustrating. Most people had the misfortune of having to deal with these events in life without any chance of changing anything about it.

Not him. Money gave you the opportunity to control the forces in life that many people didn't know controlled them. Power. In the palm of his hand. Yeah it was cliché, but when something fit's, use it.

His hand held PC beeped. He put the paper down and picked it up, turning it on. The screen lit up, showing the library of his house. He hooked up his earpiece and listened. Two people had entered the room. His children. His two ungrateful children.

"I can't believe Dad took away my car," his daughter said.

"Why did he do that?" asked his son.

"He caught me with Stan."

His son laughed. "I hate to ask, but he caught you doing what?"

"You know."

"No. I don't know."

"He didn't catch us studying."

That's for damn sure, the man thought.

"Why were you dumb enough to get caught? I've done worse in this place and he hasn't caught me."

Like hell I haven't. You don't realize what I have on tape, he thought.

"Do you think I was cavorting in the living room with the guy? I was back in the utility shed by the pool. Why the hell would anyone know I was back there?"

"If you were wailing like an alarm…"

"I am not a fool. Dad is insane. I mean, we knew he was paranoid growing up and all that but he's gone nuts."

"You need to calm down. So what he caught you. Sure, I'd be pissed and a little weirded out but accidents like that happen. They wouldn't have sitcoms or therapists if they didn't."

"It's not only that. I found this."

His daughter took a small object connected to wires out of her purse and showed it to her brother. He took it from her and inspected it. The man leaned forward, slightly concerned.

"It's a camera. I went to the college computer lab and had them check it out for me. He's spying on us."

His son handed back the camera to his sister. "Why does it have to be all Big Brother like? Can't it just be the bloody obvious? We're a rich family and have state of the art security equipment at our home in order to protect our belongings."

"I didn't tell you where I found it. It was in my room. Above my bed."

Silence. The man sat back, angered that the little bitch found the camera. It wasn't that a man of his stature got any excitement from watching his daughter cavorting with people on her bed. That was not it at all. He just had to know what his family was doing. He had to know everything. For their own good. For his own good.

He'd had enough. He turned off his hand held, sick of the squabbling of two spoiled brats who earned none of their gain in life.

A knock came from his office door. "Come in," he said.

Leslie walked in. "Sir, we have a problem."

****

Nathan adjusted his tie in the mirror. Damn I look good, he thought. Satisfied, he turned and gazed at Audrey Creston's nude body on the bed.

"So what do you think?" he asked.

"I could just rip your clothes off and ride you like a pony all night."

Nathan smiled, walking toward the bed. He sat down and ran his hands over her body. Audrey ran her fingers over his thigh.

"What about us?" she asked.

"What about us?"

"Is there a future for us?"

Nathan laughed, rising. "Future? I'm a married man and a politician. I have an image to keep."

"I just thought that with the moments we've shared..."

"What moments? All we do is mimic animals in heat. That's not a moment. That's an exchange of fluids."

Audrey sat up. "Why are you saying that? You tell me such beautiful things when we make love. Don't tell me you didn't mean any of it."

Nathan knelt down and kissed her. "Audrey, never take a man seriously who has a speechwriter."

Audrey stared at him, the life draining from her face. "So I've been your whore this whole time?"

"I wouldn't say that. Let's just say you've saved my wrist a workout."

"How dare you. I'm going to tell everyone about you."

Nathan smiled. "Save it. Most journalists in this state know about your daily meetings with everyone from the pool boy to your neighbor's sixteen-year-old son. All it would take from me is a phone call and that information will be on the front page of every newspaper across the state. Understood?"

Stunned, she lay back on the bed. Nathan walked to the dresser and picked up his suit coat. Before he left the room, his cell phone rang. He took it out from his suit pocket and turned it on.

"Hello?"

"Dad? It's Alex. Mom just called a reporter. I heard her tell the maid she was expecting her a little later tonight."

Nathan clutched the cell phone. "Thanks."

He ended the call and left the room. Audrey's sobs followed him out. He dialed a number and called Steven.

"Hello?"

"We have to get back to the mansion. How soon can you get a car?"

"Why the hurry?"

"Alert my limo driver to prepare for my arrival."

"Hold on. We can't just leave. We can't go anywhere until we're cleared by security."

"When is the soonest we can leave?"

"Seven thirty, eight o'clock tops."

Nathan hung up the phone. He paused then hit his hand on the wall in frustration.

5:00 PM-6:00 PM

The human body has a limit as to how much pain it can take. That Maury was still alive despite the torture he'd endured annoyed Annie. Despite her best work, he'd still not given her the information she wanted. As long as he's breathing there's still time, she told herself. Stay patient.

"You can end this by telling me why you stole the money," she said.

Maury whimpered, not having the strength to respond. Annie sighed. Back to work.

Annie picked up the lighter and scalpel again. She sparked a flame from the lighter and held the scalpel over the flame so Maury could watch. The scalpel soaked in the fire, the tip turning a bright orange. Annie turned off the lighter and placed the scalpel over Maury's stomach. He cringed, anticipating the pain. Annie plunged the scalpel into the skin, blood bubbling up from the fresh puncture wound. She pulled the scalpel towards her, opening a huge gash into the physically drained man. Maury gave a guttural, primal scream that sent shiver's of delight into her. She slipped her index finger into the hole and moved it around clockwise.

"You're going to irritate me if you don't tell me what I want to know," she said.

"I can't," Maury cried.

"Why not?"

"They'll kill me if I tell."

"And you'd rather endure more of this?"

Annie leaned down to Maury's face. She stroked her hand across his cheek and smiled in a motherly way.

"I don't want to hurt you. Tell me what I want to know and this will all be over with," she whispered.

Maury started shaking, trying in vain to fight back tears. Stubborn fellow, she thought. She walked out of his sight a moment and headed toward a cupboard. She opened it up, taking out a box. She turned back to Maury. Scratching noises from inside the box made his eyes bulge.

"Have you ever taken the time to enjoy God's creatures? Taken the time to enjoy the beauty of creation? Not the technical stuff that we live off of or can't live without. Our society, we can't live without technology but the beauty in the simplest things we take for granted. Take animals for instance. They live, they feed their young, and they survive through anything. They can eat anything, digest anything, adapt to any environment. And given the right circumstances they can tear into human flesh so slowly that it would take days for a person to die. Now lots of animals are capable of that but," Annie paused, "my favorite would have to be a nice fat, hungry rat. That's right. Do you like rats? Did you know that a hungry rat would respond to the smell of blood? They're quite beautiful creatures. You've got one more chance to tell me who your boss is before these rats make a buffet of your intestines."

Maury stared at the box, unwilling to accept the reality of what was inside. Annie opened it and the rats poured out, drawn to the fresh meat that lay before them. Maury felt bits of flesh rip from his body by the killing rodents. He used the last of his strength to whisper the answer.

"Repeat that," Annie said, leaning down.

Maury did. Annie heard his answer and smiled.

"Good. Now relax and this will soon be over with."

She grabbed a needle from the table and injected him with it, immobilizing him, making him immune to the pain but conscious enough to witness his own demise. She left the room. She had calls to make.

****

"How's my little man doing?" Laura asked.

"I love you Mommy."

"I love you too Ty. Do you like it at Cora's?"

"I do. She made me some cookies."

Laura smiled. "She is nice. I should be out of work soon all right."

"Ok. Can I have some more cookies?"

"I'm sure she wouldn't mind. I'll see you soon baby."

"I'm no baby Mama. I'm a big boy."

"I know. You're my little man. See you later."

Laura hung up her cell phone and put it back in her purse. She leaned back in the chair and yawned. It had been quite an interesting day at the Senator's mansion inspecting his security systems. For the most part, she saw the mansion was as protected as Fort Knox. She hadn't seen a home with as many security cameras or other type of security equipment than this place. It made her wonder what this guy had to be scared of.

The door to the room opened and she turned. It was the Senator's maid, Emerald. She'd met her earlier in the day and had enjoyed the few minutes she had to spend with her. Emerald went to the coffee machine and poured herself a cup. She joined Laura at the table.

"So how do you like it here?" Emerald asked.

"It's nice, quiet work. Better than a working mother could ask for."

"How many kids you got?"

"One. My son Ty."

"That's a nice name."

"Wish I could take credit for it. My husband came up with it just before I went into labor."

"I only wish my husband were that involved with my kids. I got three boys and two girls."

Laura winced. "You have a busy house."

"That's an understatement. If I didn't know any better, I'd think they were monkeys,"

They laughed. "I sometimes think my husband Phil is the head monkey in my house," Laura said.

"That bad huh?"

"He's not a bad guy, just not always prepared for being a husband or father. If he just got smacked in the head more often, he'd be a good guy."

"Wish I could say that. Bastard wants to leave me with those kids that he said he wanted for some little blond bitch. If I see him, I'm gonna cut him."

Laura laughed. "Sounds like you could be on a talk show."

Emerald smiled. "Or maybe Cops."

"How long have you worked here?"

"Oh, about five years. Mr. Wilson is a good man. He pays good money."

"I agree with that."

"One thing though. Whatever you do, keep to yourself. Any sort of problems happen here at all he fires you no questions asked. Get what I'm saying?"

"What do you mean?"

"The Senator knows everything that goes on around here. It's as if he has eyes and ears everywhere. I can't explain but it's just weird you know?"

"The security here is pretty considerable I know but I don't see why he would spend any significant time inspecting his employees."

Emerald glared at her. "This is your first day. You'll see what I mean if you spend any time here."

Laura took a sip of coffee, not sure how to respond to a woman who'd have no problem cutting someone at a moment's notice. This job just got a little weird, she thought.

****

Phil splashed a cup of water onto English Bob's face. Bob grunted, shaking off the grogginess. He sat up.

"I'm gonna kill that little son of a bitch," he said.

"What happened?"

"Bastard hit me in the head with a chair. I don't know what for but if I ever see him again…"

"Consider yourself lucky. Wallace got worse."

English Bob turned and gasped. He stood up and rubbed his throbbing head.

"This doesn't make sense," said English Bob.

"Something must have happened. What was he doing before he hit you?"

"He was on the phone with his brother."

"The dark clouds may have cleared a bit for us. Where's the flash drive?"

"Probably with that little bitch."

"Shit. You transferred that data to your computer so we don't have much to worry about when it comes to that but I did promise Ray I'd give it back."

"Now why would you do something as stupid as that?"

"Seemed like a good idea at the time. You think we can come up with a suitable replacement that will get me through my next meeting with him?"

"I should have something back at the Moon but that won't guarantee you'll get through the day alive."

"I'll deal with that problem when it comes. We gotta find out how Darrell's brother fit's in all this, since he was the last one Darrell spoke to."

"You think it might have to do with that Leslie chick?"

The silence answered his question. "All right," English Bob said. "We should head back to the Spanish Moon so I can grab an aspirin. We'll also check out the files again on my computer to see if there's a thread we're not seeing that we can follow. If all else fails, I'll threaten one of my scumbag regulars with paying their tab if they don't give me some information. That kind of thing always works."

"I gotta call Campbell first, give him a heads up about this. Then we hit the road."

****

"Xander, its Annie."

Xander smiled. "What's the word?"

"It took a little longer than I would have liked but he cracked."

"What did he have to say?"

Annie told him. Xander's jaw dropped.

"How sure are you of this?"

"I had him begging to tell me the truth."

Xander smiled. "I'm glad you're on my side."

"On that note, have something else for me?"

"Not at the moment, but you know how these things go. Keep your phone on."

"All right. See ya."

Xander turned off his phone and put it back in his pocket. This wasn't good. He walked over to one of his assistants.

"Who do we have that's pretty new but is trustworthy enough to do some spy work for us?"

"I told you about my son right?"

"Donnie?"

"Yeah. He's available."

"I thought you said he didn't want any part of the business."

"You know kids. He found out saving the world don't pay much."

"Kid needs some cash?"

"Exactly."

"Give him a call. Tell him this isn't illegal and that he'll be paid nicely for his work."

"Will do. Thank you sir."

****

Lydia looked over at the young man who slightly resembled her boyfriend. Why did he have to be here? She couldn't think of any logical explanation for it other than Robert's silly emotional ties. When was he going to learn that emotions like these that would end up destroying him?

She turned and walked over to Robert who stood by the window seemingly enjoying the view of the cars that drove by. She put her arm around him.

"I know what you're thinking," Robert said, not turning his head.

"What's that?"

He faced her. "You don't want my brother here."

"What makes you say that?"

"You're not as mysterious as you'd like to think. You've been giving him dirty looks since he got here."

"You never really told me why you had to bring him here in the first place."

"He's my brother. He needed help. You do that for family."

"Why do you need to help him? He's old enough to take care of himself."

"I feel responsible for him. He was only fourteen when my parents passed away. I've been looking after him ever since."

"That's sweet dear. But today is not the day to be distracted with silly family ties."

"He's my brother. He can handle himself and be a big help to us. Trust me."

"I don't know if there's time to do that. We have an important job to do and we don't need anything stopping us. If he helps us, great. If he doesn't, then I'll kill him."

Robert looked at her, his face turning cold. "Don't even joke about that."

"It's not a joke. I'm not saying I will but if he prevents us from getting Gibraltar…"

"If he does that, I'll take care of him myself. He's family. I deal with family, you got that?"

Lydia stood, silent. She wished he would have some of that fire when it came to Nathan Gibraltar. He used to have it but like a flashflood on a campfire, it went out a while ago. She stepped up to Robert and kissed him.

"I'm on your side you know."

Robert smiled. "I know. I'm sorry for blowing up."

"We should be hearing from Leslie soon."

"Good. I want to get Nathan out of my life forever."

"I want you in my life forever."

Robert pulled her to him and kissed her again. "I hope so," he said.

****

Somewhere in Southern Kentucky

Zeke poked his head out of the door, getting a visual on the perimeter. Everything clear. He motioned to the men behind him to follow.

They burst through the door, Zeke in the lead. He held his machine gun close, prepared to use it if need be. Two men followed behind him holding a metal chest. The men ran toward a jeep about a hundred yards in front of them.

The two men holding the box loaded it onto the jeep and ran back for the bunker. Zeke ran to the driver's seat of the jeep, started it up, and sped off.

He didn't know what was in the box. None of them did. However, being how the economy was what it was, the money they were paid to do this little task made it worth the effort. Damn government wasn't so giving to their ex-soldiers anymore like they used to when his Daddy was in the Marines. You give your all for the US of A, risking your life for all the little brown people you're told to kill and what do you get? A case of malaria and a boot in the ass.

A hill was up ahead. He hit the gas, wanting to see if he could get a good jump off it. He loved the thrill of being airborne, nothing between you but a hope and a dream. That was a damn good feeling. He hit the hill and shot up, the wind whipping back his hair. He shot over the top of the hill.

The men with guns waited for him.

Gunshots spit out from their guns, poking holes into the jeep like a gopher chewing up a golf course. Zeke took a gun from a shoulder holster and fired back at the men, hoping beyond hell that he'd get lucky.

The jeep landed. He braked, grabbed his gun, and dived out the side. He turned, getting some shots off. The opposing fire was relentless. The men approached the jeep, getting into position to take out Zeke quickly.

His ammo wasted, Zeke threw his gun to the ground. He had to do the only thing he could do. He rose, putting his hands in the air.

"I give up. Ya got me."

The four men paused, looked at each other, and shot down Zeke. Two of the men went to the back of the jeep and grabbed the box. The leader of the group got on his cell phone and dialed a number.

"Hello?"

"Sir, we've retrieved the package," the lead man said.

"Very good. Proceed to the rendezvous."

****

Phil got out of the car and shut the door, English Bob following behind. They walked into the Spanish Moon. The crowd was the same as before, at least they looked like the same people. Phil guessed that was the case with most bars, pubs, and taverns around the world. English Bob was greeted with an assortment of greetings and yells of anger at the price of booze. English Bob returned the greetings when appropriate and gave the finger to the rest of the complainers.

"Now, which one of these douche bags has some information for us?" English Bob mused.

The two walked to the end of the bar and approached a man who seemed to enjoy his privacy. The stools around him were clear by five stools on either side of him. English Bob put his hand on the man's shoulder.

"Howdy Nick."

The man looked up, his face being the definition of sad sack. "Bobby."

"I was wondering if we could talk."

"We're doing that now I guess you can say."

"I guess you can. Have you met my friend Phil McKnight?"

"No I haven't."

Phil sat on a stool offering his hand. Nick didn't care to shake it.

"So," English Bob said, "how's life been treating you?"

"The more you talk the less beer I can drink," Nick said. "Get to your point."

"I'm looking for an identity to a name. I was thinking you might be able to help me out."

"Tell me everything."

"We got the name of a woman named Leslie from a man named Wallace Nelson. I need to know who that woman is and where I can find her."

Nick thought for a moment taking a sip from his beer. Just as it looked like he was about to respond, he raised his hand to get another beer from the bartender. Phil tapped the bar in frustration.

"Have you got anything for me?" English Bob asked.

"Less talk, more beer."

The bartender came back with a fresh glass. Nick took a long swallow, sighing in relief.

"I've worked for Leslie before," said Nick.

Phil looked at English Bob, excited. "Can you tell me about her?" Phil asked.

"Well, she's a woman. Does that help?"

"I got this Phil," English Bob replied. "Give me all you got and you get free beer for a month."

Nick smiled. "How sweet. Leslie Dubois is the chief of staff for the good state Senator from Grand Rapids, Senator Joe Wilson."

Phil and English Bob looked at each other. Phil motioned English Bob off to a quiet corner.

"We got a problem."

"What's that?" Bob asked.

"Laura started working for the Senator today."

"What do you want to do? I mean, if you want to stop…"

Phil held up his hand. "I'm just stating a fact. Until things look like they might get bad, I still want to do this. I ain't looking to get Laura pissed off at me or anything."

"All right. Let's see if he knows how to contact this broad."

They walked back over to Nick. "So how do you know the connection between Leslie and Wallace?" Bob asked.

"I'm the sum bitch who introduced them. Dim boy if you ask me but he got the job done."

"What kind of work did he do?"

Nick looked at Bob. "I don't think I have to tell you. Somethin tells me ya already know. Now, how's about da free beer?"

English Bob motioned for the bartender. The bartender walked over to them.

"Put Nick on my list for a month."

"All right," the bartender replied.

English Bob motioned to Phil and the two went to go to Bob's hidden office. The women inside the restroom screamed as the two men entered. Fear turned into confusion as they entered the stall marked out of order and disappeared.

"So what do you think?" English Bob asked when they were inside.

"You got that replacement flash drive?"

"I got one that looks like it sure but I don't know how long it will pass. What should we do to get you out of that meeting?"

"I'll worry about that," Phil said.

"No you don't cowboy. We're in this mess together. You get that meeting finished and head right back here."

"Just as long as we don't have to bother Stone again."

"Oh, that guy can go kiss my…"

"Dude."

"He just wants to scare you. He's full of it. It's like he sweats bullshit, know what I mean?"

"Look, I gotta be back at the movie theatre by five forty-five."

"Let me get that flash drive. Why the hell did you offer to give it back anyway?"

"I ain't looking for trouble from this Ray guy. Shit, I got bills to pay ya know."

"Listen to you."

Phil laughed. "Get that shit together scumbag."

****

They descended the stairs into the garage. Robert led the way, followed by Darrell and Lydia. Robert took the cell phone from his pocket and dialed Leslie.

"Hello?"

"It's Robert. Where do you want me?"

"As far underground as you can go."

"Not the right answer. I want some action and I want it now. If I can't have Gibraltar, I want to destroy his means of living. Got me?"

Silence. "Thought so," Robert said. "Where are you sending me?"

"There's a warehouse in Walker I need you to check out. We've suspected that Nathan's used it to ship some things that have made him a lot of money."

"Shipped what exactly?"

"That's where you come in. You want something to do, you got it pal. I'll text the address to your cell phone. You're doing this on your own time."

"I understand."

Robert hung up the phone and slipped it back in his pocket. He opened the driver's side door and got in. Lydia and Darrell followed suit.

"So what's the plan?" Lydia asked.

"We're heading to Walker to check out a warehouse. Leslie seems to think Nathan has some stuff stored there."

"This is not a good idea at all," Lydia said.

"I know. I agree. I just want out of the house if you know what I mean."

"You're risking a lot. What if some of Gibraltar's men find out where we're at?"

"Then I get some target practice right?"

"I agree with Lydia," Darrell said. "It's too damn risky going out."

Robert turned and faced his brother. "You don't have the authority to give anyone advice much less me got it?"

Darrell looked at his brother, his humiliation preventing him from replying. A beep came from Robert's cell phone and he took it back out. The text message came. He opened it up and got the address.

Satisfied, Robert hit the button for the garage door opener. Once it was raised, he started the car and drove out.

****

The truck drove across the blacktop on the highway, speeding toward its destination. The driver, Thomas, sat behind the wheel, blissfully unaware of the traffic around him. Derrick sat in the passenger seat, gripping the armrest with a choking grip.

"Do you have to drive this fast?" asked Derrick.

"Calm down man. I drive just fine."

"I wanna get there just like you but I don't want to get there sailing through the windshield."

Thomas laughed. Before he had a chance to reply, the truck lurched forward. The two men looked behind them, Derrick taking out his gun out. A larger truck rode behind them smashing the back end again.

"What the hell's going on?" yelled Derrick.

"What a dumb ass question? If you think I knew, wouldn't you think I'd try to stop it? Fire that damn gun."

Derrick leaned out the window and fired a couple shots. Someone from the bigger truck fired back, forcing him back in. The gunshots from the truck took out one of their tires causing the truck to lose control. Thomas tried with all his might to straighten it out but lost out when the truck spun out of control and tipped over, sliding onto the shoulder of the highway.

The big truck pulled up behind Thomas and Derrick. The driver got out and walked over to their truck. He aimed his gun at Thomas's head through the windshield and fired. Derrick lay bloodied, every ounce of energy he had being used to try and breath. The driver walked up to him. Derrick raised his gun in a shaky hand.

"I'm going to kill you," Derrick said.

The driver smiled. "Maybe. First, we must talk. Do you know what you were going to pick up today?"

"No. I wasn't told a damn thing."

"Good. Ignorance is always best in our business. I'm going to tell you something now that may shock you a bit."

Derrick didn't respond. He raised the gun, firing off a couple shots everywhere but his intended target. The driver laughed, not even flinching.

"Nice shot. I'm surprised you never found out about our little operation. We've been monitoring you guys for a long time now. We know all about what you got planned and what you were picking up today. Just the thought that you guys thought you'd get away with anything is laughable. As we speak, what you were supposed to pick up is in our hands."

"Save me the monologue," Derrick wheezed.

"Ok."

The driver raised his gun and fired a shot into Derrick's head.

****

Xander heard the phone ring and picked up the phone from its cradle. "Yeah?"

"Sir. We have a problem."

"What is it?"

"We got a call from our people in Kentucky. Our man was ambushed before he could get to the checkpoint. Someone took him out and confiscated the box."

Xander almost dropped the phone. Of all the things that didn't need to happen, it was this. Fate was slapping him around like a kid being punished for breaking a window.

"Any leads?" Xander asked.

"We're checking with people in the area who may have seen it. I don't know how successful that will be under the circumstances but…"

"Listen to me. Use any methods necessary to find out who took that box. Make it known that the man that finds it will be rewarded. Understood?"

"Gotcha."

"Get to work."

Xander hung up the phone. He closed his eyes, rubbing his hands across his face.

What was going on here? Stupid, stupid people. Someone was messing with things. Someone with knowledge of his plans was doing their best to sabotage everything that he'd been planning for months now.

Xander grabbed a bottle of booze from the mini-bar. He poured himself a liberal shot that he downed in one gulp. He had to get out of here and head to a place with some class. Some place he could think.

"Where's a decent place to eat in this town?" he asked his assistant.

"The 1917 room is a wonderful place to eat."

"Stop right there. Get me a table."

"Yes sir."

He needed to take a break. When he had a couple drinks in his system then he'd make his calls.

****

Phil got out of the car and walked to his trunk. He put in the key and opened it up. The tricks of his trade were scattered inside. Books, his briefcase, a spare holster. What a life.

He rummaged through his belongings and found the flash drive. He closed the trunk and headed into the movie theater, putting the flash drive into his pocket. He opened the doors of the theater and felt a little relief from the humidity outside. He looked around, spotted the concession stand, and headed to it. He got in line with the other customers and waited until it was his turn.

"Can I help you sir?" the attendant asked.

"Give me a large pop, doesn't matter what kind ya got."

The attendant gave him a cup. "The soda fountain is over there. You can get it yourself. Four fifty."

Phil paid her, grabbed the cup, and headed for the fountain. He poured his favorite soda into his glass until it couldn't hold anymore, took a sip, and filled it up some more. He found the lid to put on the cup, grabbed a straw, and found a bench to wait for Ray.

He thought about the price he had to pay for the drink and cringed. He wasn't that old be he did remember the day when you didn't have to take out a mortgage to buy some refreshments at the movie theater. He felt sick thinking that the price he paid for the pop in his hands he could have went to the store across the street and bought four two liters of the same pop and have it last him a whole week. Greedy bastards.

"I wouldn't drink the soda here. They water it down."

Phil turned. Ray stood above him, a smile on his face.

"Nice to see you," Phil said. "You have the money?"

Ray smiled, taking a think envelope out of his suit jacket. Phil took out the flash drive and the two men made the switch.

Ray sat next to Phil examining the flash drive. "So this is what all this fuss has been over?"

"That it is. How's it going?"

"Things are great. Got to ask you a couple questions my friend."

"Shoot."

"What happened to the kid?"

Phil shook his head. "Once he heard I'd been in contact with you he attacked a friend of mine and escaped. I would have brought him here if I had him."

"Fair enough. Why are you an investigator?"

"Pays the bills."

"I've checked. It doesn't. Why haven't you done something with your life other than this? I mean, the life expectancy of a gas station clerk is a lot higher that a private eye."

"Gas station clerks don't go home at the end of the day knowing they've helped someone. I do. Despite the lack of work that is."

Ray smiled. "Phil, I like you. I would even hire you but I know you have this bizarre notion of good and evil so your conscience wouldn't allow you to work for me. All I have to tell you is this. I don't want our paths to cross while you're on a job. I'm a powerful man. I can smash you like a bug."

Phil laughed. "It usually takes someone a few weeks to say something like that to me, Ray. Guess I should be honored."

"You're not lying to me when all you said you seen on here were some numbers?"

Phil stood up. "If I'm lyin I'm dyin."

Ray shook Phil's hand. "Hope you're not fucking with me Phil. I really hope you're not fucking with me."

****

Governor Creston sat in his office reading the final copy of a speech he had to make tomorrow. His mind was distracted though with the attempt on Nathan's life. He couldn't believe the insanity of the assassination attempt. Why would somebody want to kill Nathan Gibraltar? What could he have possibly done that would make someone want to do that? Moreover, why was this line of thought his first reaction to the news?

The phone broke the silence. Davis picked it up. "Hello?"

"Davis. I just thought you'd like to know I was o.k."

"Nathan, I was just about to call you," Davis lied.

"I'm sure you were. I was wondering how your day was going?"

"Let's not talk about me. How's your wife?"

"She's fine. She's at home now with Alex."

"When are you going to bring that family of yours over for a visit?"

"Call my secretary and set up a date. I have to go. Just wanted to check in."

Davis hung up the phone. What turned him into Mr. Happy? he asked himself.

Davis rose from his desk and stretched. He'd spent enough time in here and was beginning to feel cramped. He left his office, walking past his secretary, ignoring her pleas to know where he was going. He walked down the hallway until he arrived at the head of security's office, a man named Rufus Jones.

Rufus turned when the door opened and smiled at the Governor. "Sir, I thought you'd forgotten me."

"I got a little claustrophobic in my office so I thought I'd come and see if I can leave."

"Do you have to leave now? I'd like to keep you here a little longer until we can be sure you're safe."

"It's not a question of have to go. I want to leave. If I stay here any longer, I'll explode. Besides, the attempt was made against Nathan in Grand Rapids, not me in Lansing."

"I'm not comfortable with you leaving sir but I guess this isn't a prison."

"Depends on the day. Am I free to go?"

Rufus smiled. "If you go, then I'm escorting you to your car. There's no arguing that."

"Then let's go," Davis said.

Rufus turned and escorted Davis down the hallway to the rotunda. They took a right and reached the elevator banks. Davis pressed the button heading down to the parking garage. They waited a moment until the elevator door slid open. Both men walked in. Rufus pressed the button heading down and the elevator began to descend.

"I can't believe the world we live in," Rufus said, breaking the silence. "Nathan's not the greatest guy in the world but I sure wouldn't put a bullet in him. It would be a waste of metal."

"No one deserves to die even if they aren't the greatest human alive. I just wish it were happening at a different time. I've got too much to deal with."

"I don't see what you got to worry about. Think about it like this. You bring in some news cameras, have Nathan give a sob story that will attract the female vote, and watch the estrogen tidal wave hit on Election Day."

"Believe it or not, there are still politicians who use their campaigns to focus on the issues and not on turning it into a beauty contest."

"I don't see how you do it. I thought your kind got killed off with the dinosaurs."

The elevator doors opened. "Well, if the people want this fossil to continue working for them, they'll vote for me on election day."

The two men walked out of the elevator and into the parking garage. Rufus lead the way to the Governor's car. Davis followed along, lost in thought. That's why he didn't notice the footsteps behind him.

A man crept up from behind with a rag in his hand. The rag dripped with chloroform. Systematically he walked, until he was behind the Governor. Before Davis realized it, the man punched him in the kidney. Davis fell on his knees clutching his back in pain. The man forced the rag on the Governor's face, keeping it in place while Davis struggled. The chloroform did its job and Davis sunk to the ground. The rest was foggy. He heard the man whistle.

"Hey Jonesy, he's down."

The two men picked him up and placed him in the back of an open car trunk. Maybe it was the chloroform but Davis swore Rufus was one of the men.

"Do you know what Onyx has planned for him?" Rufus asked.

"No. I like things that way. Just remember, clean out your office, and leave within the hour. We don't need people asking questions now do we?"

Rufus closed the trunk.

6:00 PM-7:00 PM

The man looked at the monitor. The time had come for the package to be opened and he wanted to be the first to see what was inside. His men put the package in sight of the camera.

"Are you ready sir?" the team leader asked.

"Open it."

The team leader snapped off the lock and pulled off the top of the package. The camera showed what lay inside, bringing a smile to the man's face.

"Is that good sir?"

Senator Joe Wilson smiled. "Very. Ship the package to my estate."

Senator Wilson cut the image from the screen. He smiled. Before he had the chance to reflect, his phone rang. He picked it up.

"Hello?"

"Greetings Senator."

"Xander, what brings this pleasant surprise?"

"Our deal. I feel it's time to renegotiate."

"What do you mean?"

"I want a meeting. Can we meet in a half hour?"

"That sounds reasonable. I've heard you're in town today. Where are you staying?"

"I'm at the Brisbane Grand. Is dinner at the 1917 Room all right?"

"If you're paying."

"I'll see you then."

Joe hung up the phone. With a half hour to the meeting, he had no time to waste. He couldn't wait to see Xander's reaction when he told him he had the package. Then the real negotiations could take place.

****

"So where do we go from here?" Phil asked.

English Bob looked down at his margarita. "I got some more out of Nick bout that Leslie chick. She's the personal aide to Senator Joe Wilson. I did some looking on the computer and found out that she has a place in East Grand Rapids."

"Maybe we should head over there and do some of our creative questioning if you know what I mean. What will this woman have to offer us?"

"Simple. The reason for the off shore funds. What it's for and why it's there."

"Think we can get close enough to her to ask these questions?"

English Bob smirked. "If we can't then we'll have a good time trying."

"What do you think the money's for?" asked Phil.

"Somethin big and bad that's for sure. Let's pack up and move out to this woman's place."

"Good idea."

Both men rose and headed out of the office. They headed through the bathroom and onto the main floor of the Spanish Moon. As they headed for the exit, the bartender stopped English Bob.

"Bobby!"

"Yeah."

"Call."

English Bob turned to Phil. "Hold on a sec."

He took the phone and answered it. He turned back to Phil.

"I gotta take this. I'll meet you in the car in a sec."

"All right," said Phil. He turned and left.

He opened the car door and slid behind the wheel. He stretched, letting some of the tension of the day escape from his aching muscles. Why was he still doing this? Laura would call him bullheaded or any variation thereof. But why did he still have the drive to pursue this case to the end? Why couldn't he just tell himself this was all a waste of time and leave something like this to the professionals?

The explosion rocked his car. Debris smashed onto his hood. Phil dove to the floor of the car, avoiding the shattered glass from his windshield. When the debris died down, he opened the door, looking around.

The Spanish Moon was gone. Everyone inside, dead. What the hell is going on?

****

Trying to regain his consciousness was like trying to swim through a thick vat of clear gel filled with sharp razors. Davis moved his arm as fast as his body allowed and rubbed his head. Where am I? he thought. He felt the car rumble beneath him and remembered what happened in the parking garage.

He'd been kidnapped. The thoughts, the possibilities of what could be happening ran through his mind. What's going on? What do I do?

He cursed himself the moment he looked at his wrist and noticed his watch gone. He had taken it off earlier when it caused his wrist to flake and itch. Of course, he hadn't anticipated on being kidnapped so he guessed he shouldn't blame himself too much but the fact that he didn't know how long he'd been here really gnawed at his him.

Davis had no idea where he was going. He couldn't think of any possible outcome to his predicament that ended well. Why couldn't they have been polite, pointed a gun at him, and told him to get in the trunk? He would have complied. He made it a point not to be disagreeable with people with guns. However, you had to go with the cards you were given in life. If one was being knocked unconscious and stuffed in a trunk then he would have to thank the maker for ibuprofen.

He had to rest his mind for the moment. He didn't know when but he'd soon be confronted by his kidnappers and he wanted to be as mentally alert as possible. If that was possible, that is.

****

"Stone, it's Phil. I have an emergency."

"What now?"

"The Spanish Moon exploded. English Bob is dead."

"What are you talking about?"

"Get your ass to the Spanish Moon. There's been an explosion. I don't know how many people died in this thing but it's bad."

"I'm on my way."

Phil hung up the phone. He stared into the burning rubble of his former friend's bar. Why the hell would someone want to blow up this dump and kill all those people?

Phil turned his head, scanning the area. Something, that is someone, grabbed his eye. A man across the street sat on the hood of a car watching the building burn with no emotion. After the day Phil had been having, he sure could use a confrontation now. He walked across the street.

The man's attention was on the fire. He didn't turn his head until Phil was within arm's reach. When he turned, his face went white at Phil's appearance. The man bolted down the sidewalk. Phil ran after him.

He rounded a corner, Phil on his tail. He ran until he came to a chain link fence. He hopped over the fence into a preschool playground. Phil followed him and pulled out his gun. He fired a shot at the man to get his attention. The man turned course and headed for the swing set. Phil cornered him. The man stopped and raised his hands.

"Who the hell are you?" Phil asked.

The man smiled. "A man enjoying the view."

"The view of a building that just blew up? I'm thinkin you had something to do with it."

"What makes you say that?"

"I don't know. Maybe that dopey ass look on your face."

A pause. "I wouldn't be telling you this if you didn't have the gun. The answer is no, I didn't set that bomb. I was here to make sure you and your friend were in the building when the bomb went off."

"Well you got one of us. Who ordered the place to be bombed?"

"Aww, who likes a snitch?"

Phil made as if to hit the guy. The man flinched.

"What are ya, some kind of pussy?" Phil mocked.

"I have an aversion to pain."

"I have an aversion to bad TV shows myself but that's just me."

"I'll tell you who put that bomb there, just promise you'll let me go when you're done."

"Depends on how juicy the info is."

"Oh, you'll let me go all right. The people who put the bomb in the Spanish Moon have your family."

Phil looked at the man, his body going cold. "What are you talking about?"

"You remember Nick? Man couldn't shut his mouth. He just went on and on and before you know it, the crap he told you today reached the wrong ears. You found something big McKnight. You're just too weak and poor to do anything about it. If you want your family to live, go back to that nickel and dime business of yours and forget all about this."

Phil leveled the gun at the man. "I love my wife and son. But ain't no two bit punk like yourself going to threaten me like that and think he'll just walk away."

Phil pulled the trigger, shooting the man in the shoulder. The man fell to the ground and screamed. Phil walked over, kicking him onto the ground and putting his foot on the wound.

"Now," Phil said, "who bombed the Spanish Moon?"

"Leslie Dubois ordered it. If you know what's good for you, you'll leave her alone."

"Where can I find her?"

"I'm not telling you…"

Phil pressed his foot harder on the wound. The man screamed, his body writhing like a Pentecostal getting the Holy Ghost.

"Where the hell can I find her?" Phil yelled.

"At her mansion in East Grand Rapids."

"Thank you."

Phil picked the man up and began dragging him back to the Spanish Moon. "Where are we going?" the man asked.

"I'm up for a little stroll. Besides, maybe you'll tell a little more when the police arrive."

"Then I'll tell them you shot me."

"You go right ahead and do that."

****

Laura replaced the book on the bookshelf and marked it on her list. Her time in this room was complete. Senator Wilson had one dominant trait, she observed. Paranoia. This made her job easy.

She picked up her equipment and was prepared to leave when Leslie Dubois came into the room. It was a surprise but one she hoped would be good.

"Hello Ms. Dubois," Laura said.

"Hello. I just came by to tell you what a fine job you're doing."

"Thank you. That means a lot being my first day and all."

"The Senator is pleased with your work too. In fact, he'd like to see you right now."

"I still have some things to finish…"

"It can wait," Leslie said. "Follow me."

Leslie led Laura down the hallway to the stairs. Once they reached the top, they took a left and headed to the room at the end of the hall. Laura saw the red light over the door and wondered why it was there. She never recalled any of the Senator's family being involved in music. Maybe he had a studio to practice his speeches. Who knows? She didn't have time to worry about the eccentricities of the rich.

They stopped at the door. Leslie pulled something out of her pocket and pressed a button. The red light above the door went off and Leslie opened the door. She motioned Laura inside.

"I'll see you later," Leslie said, turning to leave. The door shut behind her with a thud, leaving Laura in a soundproof room.

"Hello Mrs. McKnight."

Laura turned, startled by the speaker where the greeting came from.

"Nice to meet you," Laura said.

"I have been quite impressed with your work today and just wanted to give you a word of commendation."

Laura smiled, not wanting to show her uneasiness. "Thanks."

"I would like to discuss something with you."

"Yes?"

"Your husband, Phil McKnight."

Laura looked confused. "What about him?"

"When is the last time you spoke with him?"

"What does that have to do with anything?"

"It has more to do with it than you may think. I'm a man of means as you can see by my estate. To come to the amount of wealth that I have I had to diversify my interests in many different areas. Your husband has chosen to involve himself in my affairs to the point that I am losing money. I don't like losing money. In fact, I make sure the people who try and lose me money are stopped with any means necessary."

"What are you talking about?"

"You will not be leaving that room until Phil has stopped putting his nose in my business. If he continues with his snooping I'll have to resort to other means to get him to comply."

"What do you mean by that?"

Silence. The weight of the silence felt crushing. Laura collapsed to the ground. Phil would never do anything that would put her in any harm but he did have the tendency to get into situations that he couldn't resolve on his own. Same old Phil, she thought. I'm going to kill him.

****

The limo pulled to a stop. The Senator got out and walked into the Brisbane Grand Hotel making his way through the crowd to the elevator. The restaurant was on the top floor of the hotel and was the best in the state. He got to the doors, pressed the button, and waited until they opened. Once they did, he got on and pressed the button for the top floor.

Arriving at the top floor, the doors opened and Joe stepped out. He met the maitre de who led him to his table in a secluded part of the restaurant. Xander wasn't here yet. Always best to start meetings like this with an appetizer. A waiter approached the table and he ordered a drink.

After a few minutes, Xander walked up to the table and sat across from him. The Senator didn't look up.

"Hello Xander."

"Thanks for coming."

"My pleasure. You can thank the wonderful taxpayers of this great state for our drinks."

Xander laughed. "If your constituents could hear you now."

"I'd be hung from a tree."

"Let's get down to business. The package is missing."

The Senator smiled. "I have an idea where it's at."

Joe pulled out his hand held PC and showed Xander a picture of the shipment. Xander leaned back in his chair and sighed.

"I was wondering how someone knew where to find it."

"It's in a secure place."

"Why did you take it?"

"You know me. I like to stay one step ahead."

"You're breaking our deal."

Joe took a sip from his drink. "You broke that deal when you sent that son of your limo driver to spy on my children. You can tell your driver to order up a casket for his boy. Besides, deals are meant to be changed."

"Why you doing this?"

"Nothing personal. It's just business."

Xander drummed his fingers on the table and looked around the room. "Joe, I've known you for a long time. I've even helped you in a couple situations that don't need to be brought up. This just puzzles me why you'd try and screw us over."

"No one's screwing anyone. Now if we can get down to business before the food arrives I'll be a happy man."

****

Clarissa pulled into the parking lot of the Gibraltar mansion. The light was on by the front door. She only hoped that Eva hadn't changed her mind and sent some unruly security guards to remove her from the property.

She turned off her car. She grabbed her purse and opened up the glove compartment, reaching for her notebook and tape recorder. She could usually trust her memory with things like this but damn if she wasn't going to use every tool at her disposal to record this event.

She opened the car door and walked to the front entrance. She rang the doorbell. She waited. She rang it again. Finally, a man answered.

"Yes?"

"I'm here to speak with Eva Gibraltar. My name is Clarissa Day."

"She's expecting you. Come with me."

The butler led her inside. She followed him down the hallway to an open dining room area. Clarissa saw Eva inside waiting at the end of a long table. Clarissa walked up to her and sat down.

"Thank you for calling me Mrs. Gibraltar."

"I wish I didn't have to. Would you like something to drink? Something to eat?"

"No I'm fine. How are you doing?"

Eva hung her hand. "My body is feeling better but nothing can make the pain in my head go away."

Clarissa sighed, unable to go on for the moment. She'd been around women who've had to go through this before. Her sister had been a victim of abuse from her husband so seeing this brought a pain and rage inside her that she didn't know how to react to. The only thing she could do was listen to her and pray to God she could help.

"Mrs. Gibraltar, I'm starting this off informally. I realize this is a terrible situation for you and I want to make sure I do everything in my power to protect you."

"Thank you. I want to get this over with so if we can begin?"

Clarissa put her tape recorder on the table and turned it on. "When did Nathan start abusing you?"

****

The car pulled to a stop. Davis figured it best not to let them know he was awake. As the occupants exited the car, he closed his eyes.

Someone opened the trunk. Davis was dragged out by two men. They dragged him into a building that by the sounds of the echoes he guessed to be a warehouse. After walking deep into the heart of the building, he was placed into a chair and tied up. He heard some voices talking in a low murmur behind him. Someone slapped him on the cheek. Davis took a moment to open his eyes.

"Where am I?" he asked.

"That's not important. Someone wants to talk to you."

"They couldn't just call me?"

The Governor received a slug in the belly for a reply. Davis wheezed as the air left his body.

"Leave the Governor alone."

Davis turned his head in shock. Tony Palermo, his friend and restaurant owner, stood behind him. Tony put his hand on Davis's shoulder.

"Don't speak. You've had a rough time. Besides, nothing you could say right now could be of any help to you. Just let me do the talking."

One of the men walked up and offered Tony a chair. Tony took a seat in front of Davis.

"The world as you know it has ceased to exist. You've known me most of your life as the man who ran a nice little trendy restaurant in the heart of Lansing. In truth, that's only my hobby. In reality, I run an outfit that makes its gains from criminal activity. You may have heard my name tossed about in the newspapers. They call me Onyx."

Davis couldn't believe what he just heard. Could this man he'd known as a simple businessman be the monster known as Onyx? He had read enough to know his reputation.

"Now let me get down to business," Onyx resumed. "I need you to do your old friend a favor. I want you to resign as Governor of this fine state tonight. Hand the office over to Nathan Gibraltar and take a plane trip to Bermuda. I'll finance it if you're agreeable."

"And if I'm not?"

Onyx leaned forward. "Don't make me answer that."

"Why are you helping Nathan Gibraltar?" Davis asked.

Onyx leaned back in his chair. "Call it family business. Something a guy like me can't refuse."

"Politicians working with gangsters. The stereotypes are true then," Davis said with disgust.

Onyx looked at Davis a moment. "I'm not your enemy here. I hate doing this to you but its just business."

"Business huh? You're one of the biggest criminals in the country. Your business affairs have led to the deaths of countless thousands of people. Don't you have a conscious?"

"I do. I hate this stuff as much as you do. In fact, I'll contribute ten dollars to your campaign to clean up crime. However, I run a business. A business that exploit's the weaknesses of others. What people do after they go their way is none of my concern."

"I can't believe this. Someone better pop out now and tell me this is all a joke."

"I'm afraid it isn't."

"What about my wife?"

"I wouldn't worry too much about that woman. She isn't your type."

"What the hell are you talking about?"

Onyx pulled a set of pictures from his pocket and showed them to Davis. As each picture flashed in front of him, Davis's body began buzzing in shock. The pictures were of his wife, in various positions, with various men.

"I've known this for a while but couldn't think of a way to get it to you."

Davis tried in vain to escape from the chair. The knots were tied in such a way that the more he struggled, the tighter they got. After a few moments, he gave up, tears flowing from his eyes. Onyx rose from his chair and put his hand on Davis's shoulder.

"Take my advice and leave. I don't want to be your enemy but if you push me I can be."

Onyx walked off. Before he got out of earshot, he turned. "I'll give you some time to think this over. I'll be back later with your decision."

Onyx turned and walked away. Davis sat staring at the man he thought was his friend, the rage inside him filling up like water in a bucket.

****

Xander looked across the table at the Senator and couldn't find a word to say in response. This was not good. Joe Wilson had control of the package and demanded a bigger cut that he wasn't sure he could guarantee. He took a bite from his salad.

"Bold move Senator. After all we've been through together, why did you decide to do this now?"

"I'm not stupid Xander. I have my reasons and I refuse to tell you even one of them. This is not a request. This deal will go down my way or it won't go down at all. For you that is."

Xander took a sip from his drink. "Let me make a call. I have to talk to others about this."

"You go right ahead."

Xander rose from the table and headed for the restrooms. He took his cell phone from his pocket and dialed a number. As the phone rang, he entered the men's room and walked into a stall.

"Hello?"

"It's Xander. We have a problem."

"What's that?"

"Wilson got the package. I don't know how but that shifty little bastard is running things now."

A pause. "I told you not to trust him. I don't know why he had to be brought in."

"We need him down the road but using him this early was a risk we shouldn't have taken. That's what I get for taking your advice. It's the same old problem. The more parts there are in a machine, the better chance it has of failing. I'll contact you later."

Xander hung up the phone and stepped out of the stall. He went to the sink and washed his hands, examining his face in the mirror. He hated being one upped on anything. Oh well, he thought. The day's not over.

****

"We have to talk Phil. What the hell have you gotten yourself into?"

Phil rubbed the back of his neck. "I ain't quite sure man. It started out as a simple job and turned into this, this thing that's made me question which way is up."

"Start from the top."

"I was hired to find a stolen flash drive. Wasn't told what was on it, just told to find it. Also, they wanted the kid who stole the thing as well."

"That Darrell kid?"

"Yeah. I end up finding him and the flash drive rather quickly. He tells me there was some information on there that was big. I had him show me and it led me to an off shore bank account held by Wallace Nelson."

"That CPA karate instructor you found dead?"

"Uh, yeah. He did work for Lt. Governor Nathan Gibraltar. His main employer was a woman named Leslie Dubois. She's and aide for Senator Joe Wilson."

"What's the connection?"

"I'm not quite sure."

The two men stood silent for a moment, watching the fire fighters kill the last fleeting flames. "I know how your mind works Phil. I've seen you pull cases together in a matter of days that would take any other man at least a month. You know I've covered for you on things others wouldn't. What are you getting into here?"

Phil looked at the rubble. "I've got a thread. It's thin but I think I can string it together. I got myself into this, I'll get myself out."

"You won't be able to do this alone."

"The only help I had is roasting in that building now."

"Not anymore. I'm working this with you as an official criminal investigation."

"Oh come on…"

"It's that or I arrest you for shooting that guy."

Phil snorted. "Great compromise."

"You have my number. I want constant updates on your progress. I want to make sure that your ass is covered when you need it if this is what you think it is."

"What can I say?"

"I don't think you have much to say. I'll do what I can to find your family and keep them safe. The rest is on your shoulders."

Phil smiled. "Great."

"Just don't treat me like one of those old broads whose foolish enough to hire you. I know when you're bullshitting me."

"Me? Bullshit? You must have me mistaken."

****

"He got our man," Leslie said.

"Either he's smart or our man was dumb," Joe said.

"Little of both I believe. I think we need to bring in his son and the nanny."

"Are you sure that's wise?"

"He'll fight to save them. We don't need any more snooping around by this guy. Sooner or later he may fall into some real information he can use against us."

"How would he know how to use it?"

"Never underestimate an idiot."

Silence. Leslie thought of checking to see if he hung up before he spoke. "Grab the boy. Kill the nanny."

****

Darrell opened the box and dumped the contents onto the floor. More of nothing. Children's schoolbooks littered the warehouse floor around him.

What am I doing here? he thought. His brother spent more time ripping open any box he could grab than he did catching up on old times with him. He seemed different. And his new girlfriend the ice queen. He suspected that this change in his brother had a lot to do with her but when was he going to begin sorting all this out?

He was stuck. Chained. Super glued to this silly ass situation. This was just another instance of these non-decisions that were ruining his life.

He heard a crash a few aisles down. He walked over to the noise, feeling guilty that his first thought wasn't about his brother's safety. Lydia stood at the entrance staring at the top of the shelf. Robert stood on top looking at the skid of boxes he'd pushed to the ground.

"Darrell my boy. I think I found something. Find that black box in the middle there and toss it up."

He sifted through the rubble and found what his brother wanted. He tossed it to him. Robert caught it, tearing it open. He looked inside and smiled. He made his way down the shelf.

"What is it?" Lydia asked, coming up from behind Darrell.

Robert took out the contents of the box and showed it to them. "Here's something that shouldn't be in a children's schoolbook warehouse. It's a timing device for explosives."

"For what?" replied Darrell.

"It's not for making cookies that's for sure," Robert said.

"Are you sure this is what we're looking for?" Lydia asked.

"I highly doubt that a timing device for an explosive will be a part of a package teaching children about the military. There's something in this building that someone has done a half-assed job of hiding. Looks like we have to find out what that something is."

"Where's all the adventure and excitement?" Darrell asked.

"Adventure. Excitement. Real men don't crave those things. Lydia, toss me the phone."

Lydia grabbed her phone and tossed it to Robert. He walked off and dialed someone. Darrell knelt down and inspected the package more closely.

"What's going on with all this?" Darrell asked Lydia.

She looked at him, trying to hold back a sneer. "It's none of your concern."

Darrell paused. "What's your problem with me?"

Lydia turned her full attention on him. "This is an important day for Robert. He doesn't need some domestic bullshit distracting him."

"You are one crazy bitch you know that? I don't know what the hell he's got planned but I'm not exactly a pipsqueak who's barely out of his diapers?"

"Oh. You learn how to use a gun from playing some video games and now you're a gangster?"

"What the…"

"No pal, pay attention. I don't trust you. I don't like you. And one wrong move on your part, I'll cut you off at the knees."

Before Darrell had a chance to respond, Robert joined them, handing Lydia back the phone. "What's going on?"

"Nothing I can't handle," Lydia said, not taking her eyes off Darrell.

Robert looked at his girlfriend and brother. "I've been told there's more to find here. Unfortunately, we have as much to work with as we had before."

"Why are we doing this crap? Darrell moaned.

"Because we're going to. This may seem like crap work but every little bit we discover helps bring a bad man down, understand?"

"I don't like working on something I know nothing about."

"Listen bro, you're in no position to know anything. Just do what I say. Darrell, I need you today. I know you need me too otherwise you wouldn't have called. I know you're predicament because I've been in your shoes plenty of times. You feel trapped, as if life is squeezing you until you suffocate. Guess what? You're going to have to suck it up for a while longer and do what I tell you. You know I won't hurt you. I only want to help."

"But…"

Robert raised a finger. "This is not the day to be stubborn. If you act ignorant, you may choose to make me forget our family bonds. Understood?"

Darrell looked at his brother. "What's gotten into you?"

Robert turned away. "Nothing. I'm a perfectly well adjusted human being. Everyone else is crazy."

"Does this have anything to do with Monica?"

Robert turned and faced his brother. "Shut yer mouth."

Darrell frowned. "It is."

Robert grabbed his brother by the throat and rammed him against the wall. "You don't know what loss is boy. Until you do, keep that little mouth of yours shut and follow my lead." He paused, releasing his grip on Darrell's throat. He took a breath. "Please."

"What are you involved in?" Darrell asked.

"I'm not telling you."

"Why?"

"I suggest you trust me," Robert said. "That's all I need from you."

"You were always the good guy in the family. Why are you getting involved in silly shit like this? You were always the one to give me a lecture every time I screwed up. Said I was a fool to try to mess around with the law and everything. And now you do this? What's wrong with you?"

Robert looked at his brother, trying to plead with him without knowing what exactly he could say to make him see his point. He shivered, using every ounce of will power to keep his emotions from boiling over. Lydia came up behind him and put her hand on his shoulder.

"Don't we have work to do?" she asked.

He sighed. "Yeah. Darrell, follow me."

Robert turned and headed back to the shelves. Darrell stood, watching him, seeing how much pain his brother was in. Lydia walked up to him.

"Your brother may want to look out for your well being but I don't. If there are anymore disturbances like this, I will kill you, got it?"

Lydia whipped out a knife and sliced Darrell's arm. He pulled his arm back in pain, feeling the warm gelatinous blood flow from the wound. Lydia pulled his ear to her mouth and spoke.

"That's you're final warning. Don't fuck this up for your brother."

She turned, heading in Robert's direction. Darrell watched her walk off. What had his brother gotten him into?

****

Cora peeked out the curtain again, instinct telling her that something, heck, everything was wrong. Laura hadn't called yet to check on Ty, which wasn't like her. All these years of being a mother sure brought more stress than she deserved.

She turned and looked at the boy she considered her grandson. He sat in the living room playing with a group of ragtag teddy bears that had been in her family for a few generations. Her thoughts drifted back to his father playing with the same teddy bears. She shook her head. Time to take her mind off this stress. She headed for the kitchen.

She opened the door of the refrigerator and grabbed the milk. She set it on the counter and headed for the cupboard.

"Do you want some chocolate milk Ty?" she asked.

"Yeah."

"And do you want some cookies?"

"Yes, yes, yes!"

She smiled, opening the cupboard. She took out the package of cookies and the powdered chocolate, setting it on the counter. She grabbed a couple plates and glasses, setting them next to the cookies.

The sound of broken glass snapped her to attention. She stepped into the living room. Nothing out of the ordinary as far as she could see. She went back into the kitchen and headed for the broom closet. She opened the door and reached for a lever in the back. She turned it and a secret door opened up. She reached inside and grabbed what she wanted. Her gun. She stepped out, expecting the worst.

More noise, this time coming from upstairs. She took off her shoes and crept back into the living room. She stepped over to Ty and knelt next to him.

"Ty, we got some trouble. Can you be real, real quiet?"

Ty held his finger up, shushed her, and smiled. She took his hand and walked toward the front door.

Her favorite vase flew past her head smashing against the wall. She ducked, sheltering Ty. She picked him up and ran for the door, firing a couple blind shots behind her. Just as she reached the door, it burst open, forcing her and Ty to the ground. Armed men stormed into the house, converging on the woman and the child.

"What you all want?" Cora yelled.

The men didn't speak. They picked up Cora and threw her against the wall. They ripped Ty from her arms. Ty screamed, reaching for Cora like a drowning person reaching for a life preserver. Cora pulled the gun up, ready to fire at the first person who got close to her. One of the men approached.

"I suggest you put that away ma'am."

"Who the hell are you?" she yelled.

"The only thing you need to think of is the safety of this kid. If you don't want me to hurt him, then you need to hand me your gun."

"Ain't no bastard like you gonna make me give up this gun."

The man nodded to one of the men holding Ty. He pulled out a razor and inched it toward the boy's throat. Cora tried to run toward the man but was held back.

"I know I'm going to hell already," the man said. "Please don't make my stay there worse."

She started shaking, her options taken away from her. Cora closed her eyes and held out the gun.

Gunshots rang out. The men holding Ty clutched their chests, blood bursting out from the freshly made gunshot wounds. Cora looked around. Her neighbor Stan stood in the doorway firing at the men before they had a chance to take him down. Cora raised the butt of the gun and hit the man holding her in the head. He fell to the ground. She knelt next to him.

"Didn't yer Momma ever tell you not to make a black woman mad?"

She rammed the butt of the gun into his head, knocking him unconscious. She looked up at Stan.

"Thank you."

"What the hell's going on?"

"I'll tell you in the car. Let's go."

She ran and clutched Ty. The boy buried his face in her shoulder, crying tears of relief. Cora ran out the door and headed for her car with Stan on her tail.

****

The EMT's sifted through the rubble of the Spanish Moon's basement. Most of the main floor upstairs had caved in causing most of the rubble to land down among the empty beer cans and used kegs.

According to reports, there were about fifteen to twenty people inside the bar when it blew up. Their jobs now was clean up, getting the bodies out of the building as soon as possible so the police could come in and begin their investigation. Nothing worth making a movie about but it paid the bills.

The woman in charge, Jaime Cortez, lifted some broken wood from the ground and dug through the pile. She spotted something, hoping it wasn't an illusion. She smiled.

"Mark, get your skinny butt over here. I got something."

Mark looked up and headed toward Jaime. He helped her remove the last remaining bits of debris. Revealing a body. The body moved.

"We got a live one!" Jaime yelled.

7:00 PM-8:00 PM

The nurses wheeled the patient into the room, her battered body bandaged up after a particularly nasty surgery. They put the bed in place, hooking her up to the various machines that would monitor her through the night. As they finished, a young woman entered the room, her eyes reddened from a long day of tears.

"Is she going to be ok?"

"Miss Hunter was assaulted pretty badly but I think she's going to pull through," the head nurse replied.

The woman smiled, her relief blossoming on her face. "Is she able to talk?"

"She's asleep but she may wake up at anytime."

The nurses finished up and left the room. The woman walked over to the patient on the bed. Fresh tears flowed down her cheek.

"Oh my God. How could he do this to you Melissa?"

She stroked Melissa's cheek, avoiding any of the bruises on her cheeks. Melissa's eyes fluttered and then opened. When she saw her friend, she smiled.

"Roni. Thank you," Melissa whispered.

"Who could have done this to you?" Roni asked, choking back tears.

A pained look came across Melissa's face. Roni surmised that it wasn't due to physical pain.

"You know who did this to you, don't you."

Melissa turned away. "He did it."

A flame of anger flared through Roni. She stroked Melissa's hair.

"I'm so sorry. He's going to pay, girl. I'm going to make that bastard pay."

A tear dripped down Melissa's face. Roni wiped it away. She would make good on her promise. And she knew just the person that would help.

****

He moaned, or tried to, before he realized that the searing pain he felt was coming from his head. Curtis sat up. The agony he felt almost made him pass out. He lifted up his hand to feel his face. He stopped when he saw that his hand was missing a couple fingers.

That crazy broad tried to kill me, he thought. He brought his healthy hand to his head and felt around.

The touch to his jaw paralyzed him. He'd never felt pain like that before. It was like a nerve ending in your tooth being hit only a million times worse. He pulled himself up to his knees and crawled over to the window. In the dimming light, he was able to see his reflection on the windowpane.

The sight made him want to vomit. Half of his face appeared to be burned or charred off. The red, melting flesh that hadn't burned off appeared to be hanging on for dear life. He turned away.

He had to get out of here. They obviously left him for dead so it wasn't as if he had to worry about people looking out for him. He'd be damned if he was going to let that bitch get away with this.

He rose cautiously, not wanting the nausea to overwhelm him. Once he was confident he could walk without falling or vomiting, he left the office and walked downstairs.

He spotted a closet on the ground floor. He opened it up, looking inside for anything he could wear that would make him inconspicuous. He found a gray hooded jacket that looked big enough to hide his face. He took it out and put it on. He spotted a mirror and checked out his reflection. Nice, he thought. I look like the Unabomber's bastard son.

He looked around the office for anything else he could use. He spotted something on the floor and walked over to check it out. I'll be damned, he thought. Another dead body. What kind of shit went down before he woke up?

He checked out the body and found a wallet. He looked inside and grabbed the money, about a couple hundred in twenties. He put the cash in his pocket and tossed the wallet aside. He searched in the other pockets and found some car keys. They were connected to a remote car starter. Hopefully this prick parked somewhere near here so he could get back to his place without being noticed. He rose and left.

****

Phil pulled up to the ratty old house and shut off his car. He closed his eyes and sighed. Damn, he thought. What started out as a simple case had turned into a nightmare possibly involving his family. In addition, one of his best friends lay dead in the burned out rubble of the Spanish Moon. This never happened to the people in the movies.

Phil got out of the car and headed to the house. It had been awhile since he'd visited his friend The Ganj. He was your everyday, average American drug dealer, specializing mainly in marijuana but sometimes able to get some shrooms or acid if the customer had enough cash. Their friendship used to bother him thanks to The Ganj's profession but as time went on, Phil discovered one thing. Many people, including people he needed dirt on, occasionally hit the bong in times of trouble. So he figured it was a trade off. Besides, the guy just oozed charisma.

Phil stepped onto the rickety porch and knocked on the door. He turned and gazed over the neighborhood. There were some houses struggling to maintain a respectable appearance but were losing the battle to not become part of the bad side of town. Phil turned and knocked again.

The locks were fumbled with and the door finally opened. The Ganj appeared through a thick cloud of smoke that instantly gave Phil a contact buzz. He smiled.

"Damn boy. You been hitting it all day?"

The Ganj smiled. "Well I'll be. What happened? English Bob cut you off or something?"

"English Bob is dead. That's why I'm here."

The smile on The Ganj's face disappeared. He pulled Phil into the house and led him to what he referred to as his chambers upstairs. As they reached the top of the stairs, a plain looking, plump woman waited for them.

"I need some smokes Joseph."

"I told you not to call me that Princess."

"I need some smokes now. Where are they?"

"Why the hell should I get them for you? I mean, you don't exactly work for them you know."

The two stood staring at each other for a moment. Finally, The Ganj lowered his head.

"Check in my pillow."

Princess bounded down the steps, allowing Phil and The Ganj to pass and head for the chambers. They entered. The Ganj shut the door, locking it behind him. He stepped over to his stereo and turned it on, a rather untalented hip-hop act erupting from the speakers. The Ganj sat next to Phil.

"What the hell is going on?" The Ganj asked.

"I've started a case today that's just turned crazy. Someone trying to get me got English Bob instead."

"Fill in the detail's man. Then we'll see how I can help."

****

Nathan burst through the doors of the hotel and headed straight for his chief of staff. "Get a god damned jet ready. I have to get back home."

"But Nathan…"

Nathan raised a hand. "Enough. You know how much I hate this crap to begin with. I have an urgent matter I need to resolve now. Get me back to the mansion."

"Yes sir."

Steven walked out of the room. Nathan walked over to the window and pulled out his cell phone. He dialed home, calling Alex's cell.

"Hello?" his son replied.

"Is that reporter still there?"

"Yes."

"I need you to do something for me. Try your best to keep that reporter there for as long as you can. I'll be home within the hour."

Nathan hung up the phone. *Eva my dear, what do you think you're doing?* The beginnings of a plan formed in his mind. *Hmm an hour. That would give me just enough time.*

****

Senator Wilson sat in front of his computer typing up his proposal for a new spending bill that he was sure would get voted down. Though he hated losing, by creating this bill he would be able to get some advantage for a road project that would come Grand Rapids' way, or more precisely, would come his company's way. Compromise was sometimes worth the loss.

His cell phone rang. Joe stopped typing and picked it up.

"Hello?"

"It's Xander. We'll up the percentages. Seventy, thirty in favor of you."

The Senator smiled. "Now that sounds like a deal. I'll notify you when the package arrives."

He hung up the phone. One problem solved. Time to inquire about his other problem. He dialed Leslie.

"Hello?"

"Give me a progress report on the McKnight problem."

A pause. "He disappeared after the explosion at the bar."

Joe closed his eyes. "Then we have to assume he can't take a hint. Expect him to be visiting tonight."

"Why do you think that?"

"It's what I would do. Keep me updated."

Joe hung up the phone. This wasn't the best of news but at least the situation was manageable. He turned his attention back to the computer.

****

"I see you're at it again Phil."

"What's that?"

"Fucking up your life as usual."

"Hey. This time it ain't my fault."

The Ganj laughed. "So let me guess what you want to do. You want to search out this Leslie and see what the hell she knows, am I correct?"

"There must be some imported hashish that makes you read minds."

The Ganj smiled. "I can help you. But I only ask for one thing."

"What's that?"

The Ganj went down on his knees. "Please take me with you. I can't stand being in the same room with Princess, much less the same planet."

"I could use a partner. If we're going to do something we gotta do it now while the getting's good."

"All right. I'll meet you outside. Follow the Ganjmobile to a customer of mine in East Grand Rapids who I think can help us out. Before that, I'll smoke one last bowl and we should be set."

Phil smiled. He stood and headed for the door. The Ganj unlocked it for him, allowing him to go downstairs and head outside to get some fresh air.

****

Davis heard the footsteps behind him but didn't raise his head. Onyx sat in the chair in front of him.

"Have you made your decision?"

Davis sat for a moment then looked into the face he'd trusted for so many years. "I'll arrange a press conference for nine tonight. I'll announce my resignation then."

Onyx smiled. "Good. I'm sorry I had to do this."

"I'm sorry too."

"I like you Davis. I've done everything I could to prevent this but I had no choice. I hope you understand."

Davis looked Onyx in the face and spit on him. A guard approached Davis ready to punch him but Onyx held him back.

"Don't. He doesn't need any bruises for his press conference." Onyx walked away, wiping Davis's spit from his face.

****

Alex crept up to the door and observed his Mother with the reporter. Who does she think she is? His Father had done so much for her only to have her disrespect him like this. Well, he had to do something to teach his Mother a lesson.

He pounded on the wall. The conversation stopped. He heard footstep's approach and the door swung open. His Mother looked at him.

"What do you need Alex?"

"What is there to eat?"

"Well, if you ask Esmeralda…"

"I'm not asking that filthy spic, I'm asking you."

Eva slapped him. "You never say that. How dare you."

Alex slapped his Mother back. "I only asked you a damn question. I hate you."

Alex turned and ran away, leaving his Mother standing there, tears in her eyes. The sound of her crying somehow made him feel good. And he wanted more of that feeling.

****

Curtis entered the basement of his house and turned on the light. His dog, lying next to the water heater, turned its head up and rose, approaching him. Curtis ignored the dog and headed for the basement bathroom.

He kicked open the door and went inside. The bathroom had a motion controlled light that turned on when he stepped in. He looked at himself in the mirror.

He quickly turned away. He couldn't understand how anyone outside was able to look at him and not run away screaming or call the damn police. He turned back. Dried up blood covered almost half his face. Parts of his face were either scorched or blown away. One positive thing was that despite the mess, with enough energy he'd be able to hide it.

He had to get someone to help him. Whoever did this was going to pay a hard price for screwing with him. He was an easy enough guy. If someone had trouble with him, they could talk to him about it and he would change whatever needed to be changed. They didn't have to stab him in the back like this.

His dog nudged his leg, not sure yet how to react to his master's appearance. Curtis opened his mouth to talk…and realized he couldn't. He cleared his throat and still found himself unable to speak.

Great. What could he do to fix this? He looked around the basement and spotted his laptop. There was a program on it that did the job of those old See and Say toys. You typed in a sentence; it spoke it back for you. He grabbed the laptop and brought it over to the phone. He turned it on the computer and found the program he was looking for. Curtis typed in the starting message he wanted the caller to hear. He dialed the number.

"Hello?"

Curtis pressed the button on the computer. **"PETE, THIS IS CURTIS. I'VE BEEN HURT. COME OVER TO MY PLACE RIGHT AWAY."**

Pete laughed. "What the fuck is this?"

Curtis typed in another message. **"JUST GET YOUR ASS OVER TO MY HOUSE NOW OR I WILL FIND YOU AND SLICE YOUR FUCKING THROAT."**

A pause. "All right. You better not be fucking with me man."

Curtis hung up the phone. He walked over to his chair and sat down. Someone will pay. I'm going to find the bitch that did this and bam…he thought. A throb in his head forced him back to the bathroom for some kind of medication.

****

The security guard opened the door to the warehouse to do his nightly inspection. What a job to have, walking around these damn warehouses, making sure no one is robbing any machine parts from these tool and die companies. Like that would ever happen.

He'd been working for the security company for five months now. It was a better job to have compared to a gas station clerk and if he ever was attacked, he could at least defend himself here.

He turned on his flashlight and made his way around the building. He'd have to do a visual inspection of the place before he went back into the office to check the new digital security camera system that had just been installed two weeks previous. The owners of this particular warehouse had complained that people were entering when no one was around. He thought they were full of crap but hey, their paranoia paid his bills.

Same old greasy metal products, he observed. It would be great if he could have one of those security jobs people had where he could kick back and read all night. Inspecting the same old things like this each night seemed tedious and unnecessary.

He made his way back to the office and unlocked it with his master key. He turned on the light and headed to the back to watch the tape. Before he got to the room, he got the scare of his life.

A giant rat was sitting on a desk looking at him. He screamed in shock. The rat hissed at him and walked away. I thought this place was regularly fumigated, he thought. He made his way into the room, keeping an eye out for the rat or any friends he may have.

He turned on the computer and accessed the security camera files. He started from the beginning and turned the fast forward on. There was no need to exam nothing happening at regular speed.

He examined the tape until he saw something strange. He pressed the button to play back at regular speed. Once he realized what he was seeing, he almost vomited. He took the walkie-talkie from his belt.

"Call the police. We have an emergency at the Macgruder warehouse."

****

Phil and The Ganj walked up the door of a pretty decent looking house in the poor side of East Grand Rapids. The poor side of East Grand Rapids consisted of lawyers starting their practices, managers of major grocery stores, and others of their financial caliber. The Ganj knocked. After a few moments, the door was answered.

The man who opened the door tried to shut it after he saw who was on the porch but The Ganj put his foot in the door. "Happy to see me?" The Ganj asked.

"I told you I don't do drugs anymore."

"I'm not a drug dealer. I just sell weed. And all I want to do is talk."

"We have nothing to talk about."

"Alright. But do you think your lovely wife Esther wants to know about your little tryst with my sister Frederica?"

The man looked at him. "She wouldn't believe you, you ignorant bastard."

Phil kicked the door in forcing the man back. Just as The Ganj walked through the door, he spotted an old couple on the sidewalk staring at them. He smiled.

"It's ok. We're Jehovah's Witnesses."

The Ganj went into the house. Phil had the man pinned against the wall. The Ganj approached.

"Dirk, I'm not looking to cause you any problems. I never have done that and I never will. All's I need is some information."

"What kind of information can I give you?" Dirk spat back.

"Leslie Dubois," Phil said. "I need to see her tonight. How can I do that?"

"Do you think I'm stupid giving information like that to some crack head and a..."

Phil got in Dirk's face. "You wanna finish that sentence? I didn't think so. Give me the info I need or you'll see what it's like when a cheap ass Dutch man gets pissed."

Dirk stared a Phil. "I'm sorry."

"All I want is to meet Leslie tonight then you'll never see me again."

"All right. I'll tell you."

Phil let go of Dirk. Dirk motioned for the men to follow him. They did so, heading to Dirk's office. He rummaged through the papers on his desk until he found what he was looking for.

"This is her address and phone number." He held the paper out.

The Ganj laughed. "Sorry my friend. You're bringing us there."

"No I'm not. I've had enough of her."

"But," Phil said, "I'm sure her place is quite secure so we're going to need any help we can to get in there. Understand?"

"Look. I can't and won't do it. But I know someone that can help you."

Phil looked at The Ganj. "Why should we believe you?" The Ganj asked Dirk.

"Look, consider this a trade off. I'll help you out, you forget about me, all right?"

The Ganj stared at him for a moment. "I'm willing to take you up on that as long as your help is legitimate. One wrong move and I'll start a web page with the videotape my sister has."

Dirk's face went pale. Phil smiled. The ignorant bastard got the point.

****

Cora looked out the curtains to the road outside. The black car was still there. How could they have been followed? She closed the curtain and headed back to Stan and Ty.

"What do you think?" Stan asked.

"I think we're in trouble."

"What are we going to do?"

"We're not going to startle Ty that's for sure. Give me your phone."

Cora took the phone and dialed. "Hello?" Phil replied.

"It's Cora. There's a problem."

"What's going on?"

"Well, someone tried to kidnap your son and kill me. And they may still be outside the house I'm at now."

"What the…"

"Now don't be cursing on me. I need you to get me out of this mess."

"Where you at?"

"You remember Stan?"

"Your boyfriend?"

"He's not my boyfriend. Now ain't the time to be joking around son."

"I wasn't joking around."

"Just get yourself to Stan's house. Come in the back way."

****

Phil turned to The Ganj. "Dude…"

"What's going on?"

"Some people are after my nanny and son. They tried to kill them."

"All right. I'll go to Leslie's and see what I can find."

"Cool. My cell is on so keep in touch."

Phil walked outside and ran to his car. He got behind the wheel and put the key in the ignition. He closed his eyes a moment. It's true. They're making this personal, he thought. He started the engine.

****

The phone rang. Xander, annoyed at the interruption, picked it up and answered.

"Yes?"

"There's a problem sir."

"What's that?"

"There was a tape found of the liquidation of Maury Finkelstein."

Xander sucked in a breath in shock. "What?"

"The company had installed a new security system that I guess we weren't aware of."

"I guess we weren't."

"I called sir because of the problem this raises. The police are already on the scene. What are we going to do?"

Xander paused, looking out the window. "Put the word out. Eliminate Annie Walker."

Xander hung up the phone. He shook his head. Of all the problems he faced today, this would be the worst of all. Hell hath no fury, he mused.

****

Lydia searched through the boxes for whatever Robert thought he would find. Robert and his silly brother were off in a different part of the warehouse searching through boxes. She hated doing this but it was for a reason.

Her cell phone rang, giving off a VIP ring. She looked around to see that no one was watching and answered the phone.

"Hello?"

"Lydia. Are you free?"

"Yes Xander but I told you not to call on this phone."

"There's a problem."

"What's that?"

"I need to have Annie Walker taken care of. You free?"

"What did she do?"

"She wasn't careful. Is this a problem?"

Lydia took a moment to think about it. "Uh, yeah. How do I explain it to…?"

"Try lying."

Lydia heard the line click and folded up her phone, putting it back in her pocket. She had to get out of here. This whole charade of letting Robert believe certain things to accomplish her goal made her nerves frazzled at times. She liked the guy, she really did. However, he was just a little on the intense side for her to actually get feelings for.

She left what she was doing and went to find Robert. She found him on the other end of the building on top of a shelf.

"Robert, we need to talk."

Robert climbed down and walked over to her. He pulled her close and kissed her.

"What's going on?"

"I got a call from Leslie. I have someone to find someone."

"Who?"

"Her name is Annie Walker. Leslie told me to find her and kill her."

"Why's that? I need you here."

"She's an assistant on Nathan's staff. Leslie found out is responsible for covering up Nathan's messes, like the death of your wife."

Robert looked at her. "Then let me be the one to kill her."

"I can't. Those were the orders. You stay here. I'll be back before you know it."

She turned and walked away before he could respond. Annie was a tough customer. If anyone on the planet knew that, it was her. But duty called, and she would make sure she fulfilled her duty.

****

Annie sipped her tea, eyeing the cop car coasting by the coffee shop. It had circled around for a third time, which piqued her curiosity. There was nothing she could think of that would give them a reason to look for her, but in this business, you just never knew.

She put her cup down. She couldn't be trapped in a place like this if something went down. Annie liked the place too much to allow it to be the scene of a bloodbath. She went to the counter and put a large tip in the jar for the cashier. Annie walked out the door and took an immediate left.

Each step brought her closer to her car. She had to get there. Her equipment, as well as the half-eaten body of Maury Finkelstein, was in the trunk. She picked up her pace and ran for the car.

She reached for the door and opened it. She sat down in the seat and took out her keys from her purse. Just as she put the keys in the ignition, there was a knock on the driver's side window. Annie looked up and stared at the police officer outside.

"I'll have to ask you to step out of the car ma'am," the officer demanded.

Annie looked at the steering wheel. She pulled the keys out of the ignition and followed the officer's order.

"How can I help you officer?" she asked, stepping out of the car.

"I have a couple questions for you. We're looking for a woman that fits your description. Where have you been tonight and can someone verify your whereabouts?"

She moved her fingers over the unlock button on her remote car starter. It wasn't just a remote car starter it was also a taser. "Well, I don't see how that's any of your business officer. You haven't arrested me for anything so I'd like to know why you're asking me this."

As the officer was about to answer, she rammed the remote car starter into the officer's neck and pushed the button. Thousands of volts of electricity pulsed through his body, paralyzing him. He slumped to the ground, unconscious.

Annie knelt down and took out the officer's gun. She unlocked the safety and pressed the gun against the officer's head.

"You made a big mistake pal. And you seemed like you knew what you were doing."

She pulled the trigger. The barrel of the gun sunk in the new hole she created in his head. She looked around. Another officer was running toward her, gun drawn. She raised the gun and delivered a bullet into his skull. She heard screams. Annie stepped into her car and started it up. Sirens seeped through the windows of her car. She hit the gas and the car shot forward. Darting through the stunned bystanders, Annie directed the car towards an unknown destination. She had no idea where to go now. Something was terribly wrong and she needed to be out of site. Could it be that someone, maybe Xander, had turned on her?

A line of police cars barricaded the road a few blocks ahead. Whatever was going on, it was big. She reached over and opened up her glove compartment. She took out a metal tube designed with purple flowers that had a button on the side. Annie rolled down the window and aimed the tube directly at the police cars up ahead. With a press of a button, the tube shot out a small rocket that exploded upon impact with the police cars. The officers dove for safety, some successful, some not.

Annie's car broke through two of the destroyed vehicles. Some of the remaining officers shot after her, their shots nowhere near their marks. Her car disappeared in the distance. This car would have to disappear fast. She would have to disappear faster. Then she could find out what the hell was going on.

****

Phil pulled his car to a stop and shut off the engine. He dialed Cora on his cell phone.

"That better be you Philip."

"It is. Any change?"

"No."

"I'm a block away from you now. Tell me what I'm looking for."

"A big black car that sticks out like brown on pink. Need anything more?"

"No. I'll be there before you know it."

Phil hung up. He stepped out of the car and surveyed the neighborhood. A liquor store sat on the corner, open at all hours for business. Phil crossed the street and headed inside.

He headed down an aisle. Gazing over the various brands available, he found the cheapest brand of whiskey and picked it off the shelf. He headed up to the cashier.

"Starting early?" the cashier asked.

"Why do I have to be hitting the bottle just because I'm buying it now?"

"Sorry."

"Comments like that get yer ass shot." Phil handed the cashier the money and left.

He walked down the block and spotted the car Cora was talking about. He opened the bottle of whiskey and poured some on himself. When enough was on him to make the stench of whiskey evident to people a mile away, he started staggering toward the car.

When he was close enough, he stumbled onto the hood. The two men inside looked at each other and got out.

"Listen bum," the driver said, "this car costs more than you. Get your ass off it."

He pulled Phil off his car. "Hey man. I'm jus a cizin of Merica dat loves him some whiskey. Gimme a dolla."

The passenger pulled him up to his face. "I hate people like you."

Phil smiled. "Why's that?" he asked in a clear voice.

The passenger gaped at him, not comprehending. While he was figuring this out Phil's ruse, Phil punched the man in the gut. The driver approached Phil, pulling his gun out. Phil took out his gun and leveled it at the driver's head.

"Who sent you to hurt my boy?"

The driver realized whom he was talking too. "You're Phil McKnight?"

"Correctamundo! Who sent you?"

"I'm not telling."

"Then I'll send you to intensive care."

Phil shot the driver in the shoulder. He fell to the ground screaming. The passenger made a play to do something but Phil put the gun on the man's head.

"If I'm silly enough to do that, you think I won't do it again?"

The passenger raised his hands in the air. Phil bashed the handle of the gun on his head. The man slumped to the ground. Phil walked across the street to Stan's house. He knocked on the door.

"Cora, it's me."

He heard a noise. He kicked the door in and ran into the living room.

He stopped. Cora and Stan lay on the floor dead. Ty sat on the couch, two men stood over them with guns pointed at his head. Sitting in a chair on the side was Ray, a smile on his face.

"We meet again."

8:00 PM-9:00 PM

The Ganj walked up to the side door of the duplex and tapped lightly on the door. He waited a few moments, looked around to see if anyone was looking, and turned the knob. The door was unlocked. He smiled, walking inside. Dirk gave him information that the woman who lived here was Leslie Dubois's maid. If anyone would be able to get him into Leslie's home if would be Isabel Sanchez. With some of the information Dirk told him about Isabel's activities with Leslie, he was confident he'd be able to get some information from her.

He heard noise coming from the kitchen so he headed there, careful to keep his footsteps quiet. As he got closer, he smelled dinner being made for the night. The Ganj stepped into the kitchen.

A woman was busy preparing food at her stove. The Ganj cleared his throat. The woman turned, not reacting to the strange man that appeared in her kitchen.

"Who are you?"

"They call me The Ganj. I'd like to ask you some questions."

"Tell me why I shouldn't call the police?"

"You can do that. Then I can call immigration and tell them about that kilo of heroin you helped bring across the border when you illegally entered the country. I'm not here to cause you any harm. I just have some questions. I won't even leave this spot if that makes you feel better."

The woman looked at him. "I've made enough for two. An old habit of mine. I always prepare for two since my husband died. Please join me at the table."

The Ganj thanked her, heading for the table, taking a seat. The woman prepared a plate and placed it in front of him. She sat across from him.

"What's your name?" The Ganj asked.

"Isabel."

"How long have you worked for Leslie Dubois?"

"Too long to remember."

"Tell me what she's like."

Isabel looked at him. "You don't want to know."

The Ganj smiled. "I know people like that. How many times has she sent you on drug runs?"

Isabel played with her food. "The time you mentioned earlier wasn't the first time."

"When was the first time?"

"Maybe nine, ten years ago."

"Interesting." The Ganj took a bite of the food. "This is great cooking by the way."

"Thank you."

"Can you tell me about a man named Wallace Nelson?"

"He's Leslie's assistant. Does all the dirty work for her."

"I heard he was a CPA."

"He probably is but I never spent too much time worrying about stuff that didn't concern me."

"Do you have any idea what they've been planning lately?"

"They don't tell me. I just do what I'm told."

"Do you like what you do?" The Ganj asked.

"Getting chased by dogs in the desert and having to look over my back every day just to earn a living for my family? What do you think?"

"Then I have a proposal to make."

Isabel took a bite of food. "Go ahead."

"Give me what I need to get into Leslie Dubois's house. I need in there tonight."

"You looking to die?"

The Ganj smiled. "Not really, but others think so."

"I think we can work something out. First, we eat."

****

Phil looked up at Ray from the floor. The two guards that had been holding guns to his son's head had gone on to give him a good thrashing.

"You gonna tell me the truth about that flash drive now?"

"I already did. That little punk took it."

"Then tell me why you lied to me at the movie theater?"

"Because when I gave it to you I thought I had the original. What reason would I have in lying?"

Ray smiled. "That's right. If yer lyin yer dyin right?"

"Honestly, I have some questions to ask that little bastard Darrell myself."

"Get up," Ray said.

Phil stood up, rubbing his sore limbs. Ray directed him to the couch next to Ty. Ty jumped up and clung to his father like a life preserver. Ray took a seat in his chair.

"What if I tell you I believe you?" Ray said.

"I'd tell you that was a good choice."

"I'm willing to give you until midnight to get me the original flash drive along with the kid who took it. If successful, we both walk away happy. If not, I'm going to be forced to do something I don't like."

"And what's that?"

"Let's not get into that. I am a positive man you know."

"I'm taking my son with me."

"No."

"If you hurt my son..."

Ray held up his hand. "Please. That's cliché. I expect more from you. Your son will not be harmed as long as I get that flash drive along with the punk who stole it by midnight. I'm a man of my word. As long as you keep yours."

Phil clutched Ty to his chest. He looked into his little eyes.

"You deserve better little man. I love you so much."

His son, trying to be brave, smiled. "I love you too Daddy."

Phil turned back to Ray. "If I refuse?"

"Then my men have two bullets with your names on it. There's no compromise with this. You either do what I want or die. I think the answer's quite simple if you ask me."

"Then I guess I have to agree."

"Good. Find that flash drive. Be back here by midnight. If you try and call the police, the first one to die is your son."

One of the men came and ripped Ty from Phil's arms. The boy burst into tears, not wanting to be away from his father. Phil didn't take his eyes off him until the man left the room.

"Don't worry," Ray said. "He's being put to bed."

Phil glared at Ray. That certain intangible feeling he had about the man earlier came into focus. Ray was dangerous. Dangerous because he was smart. Phil pointed a finger at him and left the room without saying a word.

****

The jet taxied onto the runway and headed toward the hanger. It slowed until it finally came to a stop. The technicians came out and did their duty of refueling the plane. A limo waited for them about a hundred yards away. Two of the passengers stepped off, walked down the stairs to the tarmac, and approached the limo, getting in. The limo took off.

Nathan Gibraltar sat back in his seat and closed his eyes. Steven looked at him.

"You've been awfully secretive since we got on the plane," Steven said.

"Not more than usual."

"Something on your mind you want to talk about?"

"Not particularly."

"You would tell me if there were problems at home would you?"

Nathan turned to face his chief of staff. "My family business is none of your concern. I would like the driver to drop you off at your place first if you don't mind. I want to relax when I get home."

"It has been a long day. I'm ready for a shower and bourbon myself."

Nathan signaled the driver. "How long do you think that should be?"

"It should take about fifteen, twenty minutes' sir."

Nathan leaned back and smiled.

****

Phil held his cell phone in his hand as if he wanted to throw it at something. The battery was dead. He'd been working all day and neglected to look at the power bar.

His hands shook. He leaned over to the glove compartment and took out the car charger for the phone. He plugged it in, turned it on, and dialed The Ganj.

"Hello?"

"It's Phil. What have you got for me?"

"I learned a little about your friend Wallace Nelson. Turns out he's Leslie's number one man and that he coordinates drug runs in Mexico."

"Drug runs?"

"Yeah. Kind of funny that the Lt. Governor's tax man is also the point man for heroin in Michigan."

"Anything else?"

"Yeah. Leslie hires the best damn cooks. You gotta try some of this food Isabel made. When you coming back?"

Phil sighed. "That's the thing. Something's happened?"

"What?"

"Remember Ray? He has my son. He's given me until midnight to find the flash drive and the little douche who took it."

The Ganj whistled. "Damn. I got things covered on this end man. You get that flash drive back and get your son. And remember Phil…"

"What?"

"Jesus don't like it when you lie."

Phil hung up the phone. Wallace Nelson is Leslie's number one man and a drug runner. Now how does Ray fit in all this?

****

"Doctor, I think John Doe is regaining consciousness," the nurse yelled.

Activity filled the hospital room and the doctor and other nurses filled in to work on the patient. The man on the bed moved his head back and forth and opened his eyes with a struggle.

"What's going on?" the man asked.

The doctor stepped forward. "You're at the hospital son. You're lucky to be alive."

The man chuckled. "Hooray for me."

"What's your name?"

"Bob Terwilliger. How's my bar?"

"It's gone. Went up with the explosion."

Recognition spread across English Bob's face like acne on a teenager. He sat up in bed, the pain making him swoon.

"I gotta get out of here," English Bob said. "I gotta call Phil McKnight."

"I don't know who that is but you'll do no such thing. You're very lucky to be alive. You were standing on a part of the floor that had been attacked by termites for years so when the explosion hit, it collapsed and you fell into a room filled with empty beer cans."

English Bob smiled. "Lucky I didn't fumigate the place."

"You only came out with a concussion. I'd like to keep you overnight for observation."

"Just give me a couple Vicodin and let me go."

The doctor looked at the nurses and they left. He put his hand on English Bob's shoulders and eased him back on the bed.

"Look, you just woke up from a terrible ordeal. Give yourself a couple hours. If you still want to leave then I won't stop you. Your injuries aren't too severe. But for now you need rest."

With each syllable of the doctor's speech, English Bob's head throbbed more. He decided that taking him up on his plan wasn't that bad an idea. For now at least. He closed his eyes.

"I'll need a phone in here. I gotta call some people."

"Consider it done," the doctor said. "Just get some rest."

****

Annie saw the coast was clear and took off the manhole cover. She stepped inside and, just as she was consumed by the hole, moved the manhole cover back. She descended the ladder into the sewer.

She put her feet on the concrete walkway and stopped. Her nerves had been rattled from escaping the police. She'd been able to dump the car. Now she headed to her secret hideaway, made for an event such as this. She followed the walkway toward her hideaway.

She stepped inside the abandoned control room and turned on the light. Annie had redecorated the room herself. She thought of it as her version of a bomb shelter. She had everything she needed to keep her safe for months. She also had everything she needed to wage a little war, which she planned to do now. She went over to a digital punch pad on the wall and typed in a code. The wall opened up, revealing various weapons, a computer, and a satellite phone. She grabbed the phone and dialed a number. She had to confront the man who put her in this position before she killed him.

"Hello?"

"Ahh Xander. You're home."

A pause. "Annie. I see you're alive."

"You've made me angry Xander. I want to know why you've done this. I've been nothing but loyal to you."

"That you have. But that job I sent you on today, taking care of Finkelstein, that warehouse had installed a new digital video system that recorded your little adventure."

"You sent me there."

"You know how this business is Annie. You take responsibility for your mistakes whether you were aware they could happen or not. I run a business and I have to eliminate any threat to my business that could destroy it."

Annie smiled. "Then rest assured, you're going to regret your decision. No one crosses me and lives."

She hung up the phone. There was no need to hear his response. She knew he'd give the usual male bravado retort. Nevertheless, she also knew he had secrets that could make him reconsider any action against her. Secrets that could destroy him.

Secrets like his plan for tomorrow. She smiled. He had a big shindig planned and she was going to crash it. Then he'd learn it wasn't wise to make a woman angry.

****

The Ganj walked across the lawn and headed for the side door. He pulled out the key Isabel had given him and put it in the door. He turned it slow, trying not to alert anyone inside. It unlocked and he stepped inside. Damn, he thought. You'd think I'd done this before.

For a mansion, the place was as empty as a mausoleum. He closed the door and locked it. Following Isabel's instructions, he crept to the hallway and climbed the stairs.

Leslie's office was at the end of the hall. His actions were risky to say the least. Isabel told him the office contained the answers to any questions he might have. He wasn't sure he could believe the woman but doing this was more fun than sitting at home listening to Princess bitch. He reached the door to the office and turned the knob.

Locked. He cursed. What could he do? He remembered an old trick he discovered in grade school. He pulled out a credit card and slipped it in the crack, jimmying the knob until it finally opened. The Ganj stepped inside.

Simply furnished, it contained a desk with a computer and bookshelves on either side that contained lengthy tomes on subjects that didn't really matter. On his left was a coat closet. He headed for the desk and began searching.

The papers didn't say much. Just the usual business as it pertained to Leslie's day job. He set them down and opened up the drawers. Yet more useless papers. Just as he was about to close the bottom drawer, he noticed something. He opened the drawer again and reached inside, pulling out a small metal lock box. He put it on the desk.

Now we're in business, he thought. He opened it up and took out the papers inside. The Ganj started reading. His jaw dropped.

Footsteps on the stairs startled him. He grabbed the lock box and ran into the closet.

The Ganj hid in the closet, sure that every breath he took would be heard by the two people that walked in the office. Of all things he'd ever been trapped doing, he sure as hell didn't want to be caught here. After reading what little he did from those papers, he knew his life was on the line.

He shivered in fear. The papers told of an evil plan that, while bold, shook him to the core. A large shipment of pure Colombian cocaine was on its way to Grand Rapids. The people who stood to make money off this plan were the same people in the state who were supposed to fight against drug deals like this. No wonder Phil is going through the crap he is. If I were one of the people involved, I'd be willing to kill some people too.

The Ganj leaned further back in the closet. He closed his eyes, focusing on the conversation in the office.

"How soon do you expect the shipment in?" Leslie asked.

"Should be here around three in the morning."

"Good. You've stepped up security like I asked?"

"Yes ma'am. I took care of it."

"Excellent. The Senator thinks I'll be expecting a visitor here later and I want to be prepared if they arrive. Make sure that doesn't happen."

The man left the room leaving Leslie alone. The Ganj heard Leslie sit at her desk and pick up the phone. Who's that bitch going to call now?

"Senator? The room is clear. Can I put you on speaker?" She waited a moment before flicking a switch. This is getting good, The Ganj thought.

"I'm getting things ready for the shipment tonight. I wanted to know your plans for tomorrow?"

"I plan on being at the book warehouse tomorrow for the Governor's speech. From there I can monitor the execution of our plan. As long as Xander doesn't play any games."

"Should I have any contingency plans covered?"

"But of course. Have you heard from Nathan?"

Nathan? The Ganj wondered. Nathan who?

"He hasn't contacted me today what with his troubles and all."

"Send a call to his residence. I need to speak with him tonight. If you can't reach him there then that chief of staff of his will be sure to know where he is."

"Yes sir. Is there anything else?"

"I'll contact you if I need anything."

Leslie switched off the phone. The Ganj tried to control his breathing. Something had just been said that meant something. The dots were not all connected yet but he knew something was there. Until he could get out of here and get to Phil, he'd have to sit tight and hope he wasn't caught.

****

Clarissa looked at the sad face of Eva Gibraltar. This woman has been through hell, she kept telling herself. What little she had thought of Nathan Gibraltar before was nothing to what she thought of him now.

"Is there anything else you want to tell me?"

Eva shook her head. "I could tell you more but the rest is conjecture."

"I'm just wondering why you haven't done this sooner."

Eva looked down for a moment before answering. "Sometimes a person needs to prove themselves wrong. I saw what he was doing but for some reason I thought there was something in him, something good, something to keep us together. I was wrong. I've paid so much in order to have this hunch of mine proven wrong."

"Mrs. Gibraltar, everything is going to be alright. I have one more question. Can anyone corroborate your statements about his chief of staff?"

"Yes. Steven Alexander Falcone is not as bright as he thinks he is. I have someone who is able to corroborate my statements, though they won't do so in front of a grand jury."

"As long as they speak to me, I could care less who else they talk to. I'm not a cop."

"Is there anything else I can do for you?"

"I should ask you that question Mrs. Gibraltar."

"You've done enough. You've seen what's been done to my family. All I want is to pay him back."

"Then I should be all set."

Clarissa rose from the table. "Do you mind if I use your restroom?" she asked.

Eva nodded. "Out the door at the end of the hall. When you're done I'll escort you to your car."

Clarissa left the room and headed for the bathroom. She walked in and closed the door, locking it. She took her cell phone out and, just as she was about to make a call, noticed she had a voice mail. She connected to her voice mail and listened to her message.

"Hey sis. It's me Roni. Please call me when you can. I need some help. Talk to you soon."

What is that about? she thought. She'd have to call her when she got to the car. She shut down the voice mail and made her call. She cursed when Stu's voicemail answered.

"Stu, I'm on my way back to Grand Rapids. I'm heading straight for the station. I got a big one here."

She hung up the phone and put it back in her purse. She straightened her hair then left.

Eva waited for her by the front door. The two women headed to Clarissa's car.

"Are you going to be safe tonight?" Clarissa asked.

"As safe as I've ever been."

"Are you sure you shouldn't be somewhere else tonight?"

"I'll be fine. After this gets out he won't think of touching me."

"I don't know how you do it."

"I don't know either."

Before Clarissa could reply, the front door of the mansion flew open and Eva's son Alex stood in the doorway. He held a cell phone in his hand. A smug, evil little grin shone on his face.

"I just wanted to tell you that Daddy's home."

Clarissa stood there confused. The blood in Eva's face drained. She ran to her son.

"What have you done Alex? What have you done?"

"I told him everything you told that reporter."

She grabbed her son by the shoulders and shook him. "How could you? You don't realize what kind of monster he is."

As the words came out of her mouth, a limo pulled up to the mansion. Nathan Gibraltar got out, closing the door. The limo drove off.

"Now what do we have here?" Nathan said with a smile as genuine as cancer.

Nathan walked up to the porch. His wife stared at him, hypnotized. Clarissa took a couple steps away from her car, not wanting to leave a situation this dangerous. Nathan stepped up to his wife.

"Alex, step onto the lawn please," he said, not taking his eyes from Eva.

His son obeyed. Clarissa put one hand on her cell phone, feeling it may be needed.

"So I hear you were talking to a reporter."

"Yes I was," Eva said, showing more courage than she felt.

"May I ask what you were talking about?"

"You know what I talked about."

Nathan smiled. "You were talking about business dear? My business?"

"And what if I did?"

"What exactly did you tell her?"

"I won't say."

"You won't say. Like you have any right to say that to me. What did you tell that reporter?"

"Mr. Gibraltar, I'm Clarissa Day. Anything you say will get to the public, I assure you."

"That's the problem with people like you," Nathan said, turning to Clarissa. "You throw out any bit of information you get your filthy little hands on and give it to the uneducated masses. Yet when problems arise, you blame the people who held the secret in the first place for the mess you created."

"The information your wife gave me is something the public has a right to know. I don't think they'd like to hear that an elected official was using their tax dollars for illegal purposes. And rest assured, if you try anything, my boss has everything Eva told me at my station in Grand Rapids ready to hit the airwaves."

"Good luck trying to prove it."

"One thing I can prove is that you beat your wife. Eva, I don't think you're going to be safe here. Come with me and I'll bring you to my place."

"She will do no such thing. My wife will stay here, in my home. And when you leave I will be calling your boss about your behavior."

"Nathan, I'm leaving," Eva said, her voice small.

Nathan turned to his wife and glared at her, laughing. "Excuse me?"

"This is a free country Mr. Gibraltar. She said she wanted to leave with me so she can leave. Let's go Eva."

Eva stepped away from her husband and headed towards Clarissa. Nathan stared at her in disbelief.

"Come back here Eva," he said in a calm voice.

She kept walking. Clarissa held out her hand.

"You don't do this to me. Who do you think you are?"

She kept on walking. Nathan put his hand inside his suit coat.

"Eva, I love you," he said.

Eva stopped. She paused, and turned. Her body language told the whole story. She wanted it to be true. However, her hope vanished when Nathan pulled out a gun. He fired. She fell to the ground. Clarissa stared at Eva's limp body and screamed.

9:00 PM-10:00 PM

"We interrupt this broadcast to bring you this special report. An emergency press conference has been scheduled at our state capitol by Governor Davis Creston. We bring you there live with our capitol reporter William Rodriguez."

"Thanks Bob. Speculation has run high about why this press conference has been called. It's anyone's guess at this point what the Governor could want to discuss. But I see the Governor approaching the stage now so let's head up to him."

Governor Creston emerged from the back and walked to the podium. He rubbed the back of his head and sighed.

"I'll make my statement short and sweet so please, no questions." Davis picked up a glass of water on the podium and took a sip before resuming. "I'm here to announce my resignation from the campaign and from the Governorship effective immediately. Some problems have arisen in my personal life that I must attend to before I can put my attention to other matters. I believe in the old bit of wisdom my grandmother taught me. A man who can't solve his own problems is not a man who can solve the problems of other people. I hope the citizens of the state can understand and respect my decision. Thank you."

Davis walked offstage, leaving the reporters in rare silence. William Rodriguez stepped in front of the camera.

"Shocking news from our now Ex-Governor, Davis Creston. He has resigned his position, thus giving the reigns of the state over to Nathan Gibraltar. Why has Davis Creston resigned? What does this mean for our state? Back to you in the studio."

"Thank you William for that stunning announcement."

****

"Toss me your phone Alex."

The boy did as his father wished, his body in shock over what he witnessed. Nathan caught the phone and dialed his chief of staff, Steven Alexander Falcone. Xander.

"Hello?"

"Xander!"

"What is it?"

"I need the cleanup crew at the mansion."

"Why?"

"I have a mess I need cleaned up."

"What is going on?"

"Eva called Clarissa Day to try and spill the beans on me. She tried to leave. I tried to stop her. One thing led to another so I shot her."

"You shot your wife. How dumb can you be?"

"I am your boss. You do not talk to me like that. Tell me when you'll fix this."

"You know I'll fix it. But I've got damage control to think of."

"I can handle that part. Just get the mess cleaned up."

"How do I know you can handle things? You know the press has been sitting on the fact you've smacked her around. Hell, I've been pussy footing around asking about this myself cause I didn't think you'd be stupid enough to do take this too far. What are they going to do when they find out that a bullet from a gun you own killed your wife?"

"Don't give me your crap. We are hours away from the implementation of our plan. I never make a decision, personal or otherwise, out of emotion. Get the crew over here, get this mess cleaned up, then we'll find a way to sell our version of the story to the press. You got me?"

Xander paused. "Did anyone see you do it?"

"Alex and Clarissa Day, the reporter. I had to take her hostage."

"Of all the people you could have taken hostage..."

"She was trying to take my wife."

"I don't care if she was there trying to sell you some makeup. You kidnapped a reporter. We won't be able to let her go. When she disappears, that in itself will be big when her network runs a story on her disappearance and eventual murder investigation. Oh, I don't even know why I discuss some of this stuff with you. You've got the brain capacity of a watermelon."

"If you weren't my chief of staff..."

"Then I'd be working on getting your ass to prison, not saving you from it. You got me? I'm the reason you're the Lt. Governor. If you don't want to become a resident of the Gray Bar Hotel you'll start listening to what I say."

Nathan paused and took a breath. "Just get the cleaning crew over here."

"Don't touch the reporter. Leave her to me."

Nathan hung up the phone. He walked over and knelt next to Clarissa.

"Get in the house."

"You killed her," Clarissa muttered.

Nathan pointed his gun at her face. "I suggest you follow my orders."

"You won't kill me."

"Maybe, but I can scar that pretty little face of yours. I know what that would do to your precious little career. Now get up."

Clarissa rose and headed for the house. Nathan turned to his son.

"Go to the garage, get the tarp, and cover that up," he said, pointing to Eva's body. Nathan followed Clarissa inside.

****

The Ganj stepped out of the closet into the dark office. He clutched the lock box to his side, praying that the contents inside wouldn't rattle around. He crept to the door, opened it slowly, and stepped out.

The lights were out in the hallway. He headed down; each step took feeling as if it took an hour. He reached the stairs and glanced down. Lights were on in the hallway but it looked deserted.

He walked down the stairs and reached the bottom. The kitchen door was just ahead. He arrived at the kitchen entrance without notice. The kitchen was clear so he ran to the exit. I can't believe I'm doing this, The Ganj thought. He reached for the doorknob and turned.

The noise split his eardrums. He yanked open the door and ran out into the massive yard, the sound of the house alarm following behind him like the sea lapping up sand on a beach. He heard screaming behind him and the unmistakable sound of gunshots. He pushed himself to run harder.

The bullets whizzed by him. He started weaving, trying not to give the shooters a steady target. He neared the gate, getting confident that he would make it. He reached the fence and jumped over.

Two of Leslie's guards jumped out of nowhere and tackled him to the ground, forcing the lock box to go flying from his hands. The Ganj stood up and took out the first guard with a swift kick to the groin. He turned. The second guard punched him in the chest. The Ganj fell back, trying to get his breath back. He shot back with a kick to the guard's knee, causing him to fall. He looked around for the lock box, grabbed it, then ran for his car. He jammed his key in the ignition and started the engine. His humble little Ganjmobile shot forward, escaping any immediate danger. He took out his cell phone and dialed.

"Hello?" Phil replied.

"It's The Ganj. I got something here you need to see. I got a lockbox filled with some juicy information that I got from Leslie's office."

"What's in it?"

"You have to see it to believe it. Some shits about to go down and you won't believe what it is."

"Meet me at my office when you can."

"Will do."

The Ganj hung up the phone. Thank you Phil, he thought. This was turning out to be one hell of a night.

****

The cell phone rang. Nathan took it out of his pocket and answered.

"Gibraltar here."

"Congratulations. The office is yours."

Nathan smiled. "Davis Creston. How is your day going?"

"I may have not seen it coming but I know you're behind all this. Rest assured, this game is far from over."

"I would have thought you'd be beyond clichés Davis but you must really be one of those fat, ignorant, D.N.A. slop heaps that always came out voting for you in record numbers."

Nathan hung up the phone. The plan worked. He had the power in his hands to expand his empire to heights he only dreamed of. Nathan turned his head and spotted Clarissa staring at him.

"Why did the Governor call you?" she asked.

Nathan smiled. "It was a call of congratulations."

"For what?"

"Becoming the next Governor of this state."

Clarissa stared, dumbfounded. "What are you talking about?"

"I should have turned on the news for you. Davis Creston resigned as Governor."

"Why would he resign?"

"I've got people who can make really persuasive arguments to stubborn folk like him."

Nathan walked back into the study, leaving Clarissa handcuffed to the dining room table. He had a speech to write and it had damn well better be good.

****

They got the call from Xander and knew it wasn't good. They were the two-man team dubbed the Cleaning Crew. Xander had put them together due to their talent of taking any situation, such as the one they were about to descend upon, and making any illegal situation disappear. If there was no physical evidence, then how could it be proven that anything happened?

They pulled up to the mansion. The leader of the crew surveyed the situation from the driver's seat.

"Well, this looks like it'll be quick."

Mr. A stared at the mansion and shook his head. He sure hated the young punk Xander assigned him with. Xander thought it best to give them these names so they wouldn't be too attached to each other. Why he couldn't come up with something more imaginative than the letters of the alphabet was beyond him but he wasn't paid to come up with better names.

"Let's get to work," he said.

The two men got out of the van. Mr. A walked over to Mr. B.

"Get inside and get Mr. Gibraltar's gun."

"What're you gonna do?"

"I'll take care of the broad."

"Aww. Keeping the good jobs for yourself," Mr. B smirked, heading to the mansion.

Mr. A walked over to the body under the blue tarp. He uncovered it. The face. He recognized the face from the news. The bastard shot his wife, he thought. He knelt down and examined the body. No exit wound. Nice, he thought. No blood to clean up. He let the body fall back on the grass. A soft moan escaped from the woman's lips, almost sending Mr. A on his butt.

Please God, tell me I was just hearing things. Mr. A picked up Eva's wrist and felt for a pulse. A faint throbbing stimulated his fingers. He placed her wrist back on the ground. Eva Gibraltar was still alive. Mr. A looked around. No one in sight. He picked up Eva and walked to the van. He had to get her out of here. He knew he wasn't a saint but he couldn't let this woman die like this.

Mr. A pulled his keys from his pocket and pressed the automatic door opener. He placed Eva's body on the back seat. Closing the door, he sprinted to the driver's side door. A voice stopped him.

"Where you going?" Mr. B asked.

"Waste disposal."

"What? You gonna leave me here?"

"I've been doing this longer than you sonny which makes me twice as fast. I'll be back soon."

Mr. A got back into the van before Mr. B could respond. He put the keys into the ignition and started up the van. Mr. A backed out of the driveway.

****

"You're a mess Curtis. Why don't you go to the hospital?"

Curtis typed into his computer. "**I KNOW WHAT I LOOK LIKE. WE HAVE TO COME UP WITH A PLAN PETE.**"

"There is no plan. If you want to take on Xander and his men, what do you plan to do that could make a dent in this guy's organization?"

"I HAVE SOMETHING AGAINST THEM."

"What?"

"I KNOW ABOUT THEIR SHIPMENT TOMORROW."

"What shipment?"

"COCAINE. THE BEST SMACK MONEY COULD BUY."

"Oh God. Criminals dealing drugs? What is this world coming to?" Pete sarcastically replied.

"I'M NOT STUPID, PETE. WE'RE NOT TALKING ABOUT THE USUAL SUSPECTS HERE."

Pete sat for a moment. "Explain."

"WHAT WOULD YOU SAY IF I COULD PROVE THAT NATHAN GIBRALTAR IS INVOLVED IN THIS DEAL?"

"Then I'd say you'd better be damned sure you have some proof because if you're wrong, these people are taking you down."

"THE ONLY WAY I'M GOING DOWN IS IF I TAKE THOSE BASTARDS WITH ME."

"So you have this information. What do you plan on doing with it?"

Curtis smiled. I hope I don't get carpal tunnel typing this, he thought.

****

The Ganj closed the door to Phil's office. Phil sat at his desk, eager to get something done. He knew he was on the clock. If doing this brought him his son back then he wanted to dive into these papers as fast as he could. He kicked out a seat for The Ganj.

"What you got?" Phil asked.

The Ganj placed the lock box on the desk and opened it up. "Dive in and read. I think you'll like it."

Phil took some papers and read them. The more details of the plan that he read, the angrier he became. Everything he'd been through today, everything, had been all to support a drug deal. However, not all the answers were in these papers. Could they be in the flash drive Darrell had with him?

"This is pretty fucked up right here," Phil said. "I've been such a tool today. This even explains the involvement of Darrell's brother."

"How does this all fit in with that flash drive?"

"I'm not sure yet. Maybe there was something on there we didn't see."

"Any leads on where the flash drive's at?"

"No. I tried his brother's number but there was no answer. I don't know what to do."

The Ganj thought for a moment. "I think I know a guy who can help."

"You know a lot of guys that can help. I just want to know what the hell he can do."

"Well, if his phone is on, there's a good chance we can find its location via GPS. Once we get a signal, then we track them. Simple as that."

"You technological bastard. Who do you need to call?"

"Just gotta give him a call. I can get him here in like fifteen minutes."

Phil smiled. Finally, some action.

****

Mr. A sped through the dark streets wishing for no red lights or delays of any kind. He had to get to a doctor fast. And not any doctor. It would be somewhat awkward explaining to hospital security and the police why he walked in with the new Governor's wife nearly dead with a gunshot wound to the chest. He had to go to Dr. Fix It.

Dr. Fix It was a man dedicated to the medical profession until he became dedicated to drugs and alcohol. He lost his license performing a breast reduction surgery while drunk and doped up on pain pills. Since losing his license, for the right price he would perform any medical procedure you needed. Mr. A knew the man to be cautious. And since he owed him a favor, he hoped he'd do the job without telling anyone.

Mr. A found the right road and took a left. He pulled to the end of the block and pulled into Dr. Fix It's driveway. Mr. A got out of the van and ran to the front door, ringing the doorbell. After a moment, the door opened.

"What the fuck do you want?"

"I've got someone who needs your help."

Dr. Fix It walked past Mr. A to the van. He certainly wasn't dressed for a proper medical procedure. He was barefoot in boxer shorts with a bathrobe covering up what you didn't want to see. His face wore a thick layer of facial hair that wouldn't have known a razor if it saw one in a line up. Dr. Fix It opened the van door and looked inside.

"Where did you find her?"

"Nathan Gibraltar's front lawn."

Dr. Fix It looked at her more closely and backed away from the van. "You must be fucking insane if you think I'm touching her."

Mr. A got in Dr. Fix It's face. "You know me man. I can't let this woman die for no reason. If shit goes down I'll take responsibility for it, you have my word. Just do your job and save this woman."

Dr. Fix It paused. "All right, let's get her inside. Be careful not to make a scene. The neighbors love calling the police around here."

Mr. A picked up Eva and followed Dr. Fix It into the house. He brought Eva to the back bedroom. After laying her on the bed, he ran back to the front door. Satisfied no one saw what just went down, he shut the door and locked it.

****

Laura stood up when she heard the door open. She wanted to be as prepared as she could under the circumstances. A man with a gun waited for her.

"Follow me."

She stepped out of the room. The gunman motioned for her to walk ahead of him. They reached an elevator and went inside. The gunman pressed a button and the elevator car went down. It opened up in the garage. She was led to a black SUV. The gunman forced her in the back and cuffed her to the seat. Before the door closed, Senator Wilson appeared.

"Mrs. McKnight, pleasure to meet you in person."

"What do you want?"

Senator Wilson smiled. "I'm transferring you to another location. I think you'll be better off there."

"Where am I going?"

"I own some offices in the old gypsum mines on the south of town. I thought you may enjoy it better over there."

"Cut the crap. Something's going on and you want me hidden away. Phil must be getting close to busting your ass."

"Do you honestly think I'm concerned about that bumbling fool? I believe in contingency plans. This contingency plan involves you being stored away at a neutral location until this mess blows over."

Laura stared at him. "You want me dead."

"If I did we wouldn't be having this conversation. Enjoy the mines. I've been through them a few times myself. Fascinating place."

The Senator closed the door. Laura sat back. She had to figure a way out of here. If she didn't, she'd be dead by the end of the day.

****

Phil opened the door letting Pedro Santana into his office. The two men shook hands.

"I heard you needed a computer guy," Pedro said.

"You heard right."

The Ganj stood up. "His computer's over here. He'll give you the number he needs checked."

"Sounds good."

Pedro took his place in front of Phil's computer. Phil found Robert's number on his phone and showed it to Pedro. Pedro went to work.

"How soon do you think you'll find something?" Phil asked.

"It should pop up on screen here in a minute. I'll tell you when."

Phil stared at the screen. Suddenly a map popped up with a blinking red light on it. Phil looked closer.

"Is that it?" Phil asked.

"Correct."

"Well I'll be damned. What are they doing on 28th street?"

"Well," The Ganj replied, "it looks like they're watching a movie or something. It's near Twenty Eight Screens Theater."

"I doubt they'd do that. They're probably having dinner at one of the restaurants over there. Pedro, can you stick around the office here and keep me updated on their location from the phone?"

"I don't know man."

Phil pulled out a couple hundred-dollar bills and put them in Pedro's hand. Pedro smiled, putting the money in his pocket.

"Yeah, I can do it," he said.

"Good. If I get back here with that kid then maybe you can help me with the flash drive."

"Hey, whatever. I'm cool if there's money involved."

Phil and The Ganj got up and left.

****

Mr. A pulled into the Gibraltar Mansion at just the right time. Mr. B sat on the porch, his job apparently done. Mr. A pulled up next to him and shut off the van.

"Decide to come back when the work's done, huh?" Mr. B said.

"The dead body shop was closed so I had to look around for one that was open. Do you think it's easy to dump a body?"

"Where'd you dump it?" Mr. B asked.

"The only way you'd find out is if you joined her. Now let's get inside and see what Mr. Gibraltar wants done next."

The men walked into the house and headed into the study. Nathan was seated at his desk, writing. Nathan turned when they entered.

"Ah yes. I have to apologize for interrupting your night. I just need you to do two more things for me."

"What's that? Mr. A asked.

"Escort the woman in the dining room to a secure location. I don't care where but it must be secure. I also want you to take my gun."

Nathan grabbed the gun off his desk and handed it to Mr. A.

"Xander will speak to you later. Have a good night."

Mr. A headed into the dining room and aimed the gun at Clarissa. "You're coming with me."

She got up and followed the two men outside to Mr. A's van without objection. Mr. A opened the side door and gently helped her in. Mr. B got in on the passenger side. Mr. A got into the driver's seat and started up the van, taking off.

"So who are you?" Mr. A asked.

"Haven't you seen the news?" she replied with a hint of sarcasm.

"Contrary to what you think, I'm not a terrible guy. I'm a disposer, not a killer."

Mr. B started laughing. "You're Mr. Freaking Rogers's man."

Mr. A put his finger in Mr. B's face. "I'd shut that mouth of yours if I were you boy."

"What? You turn into an angel dumping that broad or something?"

Clarissa gasped. "He had her body dumped like garbage? That bastard."

There was a silence. Then before Mr. B could react, Mr. A grabbed Nathan Gibraltar's gun and shot his partner in the head. Clarissa screamed. Mr. A pulled the van to the side of the road and dumped Mr. B's body out.

"Why did you do that?" Clarissa asked.

"Listen to me. Eva Gibraltar is not dead. I took her to get some medical help. And now with this," he raised up Nathan's gun, "we burn him. A man who tries to kill his wife is scum. Like I said, I'm not a murderer. You with me?"

Clarissa smiled. "Deal. Let's see Eva."

10:00 PM-11:00 PM

Xander picked up the phone. "Hello?"

"Am I speaking with Xander?"

"You are. Whom may I ask is calling?"

"I'm calling on behalf of a former employee of yours. Curtis Banfield."

Xander closed his eyes and rubbed his temples. Not again, he thought.

"Ah, Curtis. How is he doing?"

"He survived. He can't talk but he's all right. He wants a sit down with you."

"Why's that?"

"He wants to be able to live the rest of his life in peace. In exchange for that, he wants some assurances. Consider it a goodwill offering for his safety."

"Why is he being so gracious?" Xander asked, trying to hide his sarcasm.

"Because he doesn't want to die. Once you see how fucked up he looks you'll understand."

Xander smiled. "All right. Let me call you back at eleven and I'll give you the details for our meeting."

Xander hung up the phone. This day wasn't going as planned. No time to think of that now, he thought. There were matters to attend to.

****

Clarissa burst through the door of the makeshift operating room at Dr. Fix It's house. Dr. Fix It looked up.

"What the hell is she doing in here?"

"Checking to see if Eva's alright," Clarissa said. "And who the hell are you?"

"Oh, you've forgotten? You're the one who lost me my job honey."

"Whatever. How's Eva?"

"She's going to be fine. The bullet didn't hit anything vital but then again my equipment here is pretty substandard compared to what I was used to working with. Again, thanks to you."

Clarissa stepped forward. "I don't care what kind of beef you have with me. You get her out of this."

"Then let me finish. And tell Mr. A not to allow anyone else in here."

Dr. Fix It got back to work. Clarissa turned and left the room. She met Mr. A in the kitchen.

"He's got a great bedside manner," she said.

"He gets the job done. That's all you can ask for these days."

"Why did you do this? Aren't you afraid Nathan will come after you?"

Mr. A grabbed himself a cup of coffee and took a sip. "I have not always made the right choices in life. I've seen that woman on TV though. She's done an awful lot of good and I just couldn't sit back and allow her to die because her husband was an ignorant bastard."

"What if he comes after you?"

Mr. A smiled, raising the cup in a toast. "You're already talking to a dead man."

Clarissa stood a moment, not quite sure how to respond. "What are they going to do with my car?"

"I have to head back now and get it. I don't know how I'll pull this off with Mr. B gone."

"What if I went with you?"

"No. Too risky."

"It's not like they'll be looking for me. Besides, that dead guy and I were about the same height anyway. As long as no one watches, I think we can pull it off. Especially if I stay in the van."

Mr. A thought about it a moment, taking another sip of coffee. "Oh hell. We got nothing to lose. Let's do it."

****

The streetlights illuminated off the puddles that remained from the rain earlier that day. Phil held his cell phone to his ear as he splashed through one, The Ganj a few steps behind.

"They still there?"

"Yeah. As far as I can tell they're about a block ahead of you," Pedro replied from the cell phone.

"Cool. I'll call you back."

Phil hung up. "They're probably at the diner just up the block. You ready?" he asked The Ganj.

The Ganj smiled. "As you know my boy, I'm up for anything."

Phil took out his phone and called Robert's number. The phone rang, indicating to Phil that he was being ignored. It went to voice mail. Phil hung up and called again. Finally, Robert answered his phone.

"Phil McKnight. What do you want?"

"We have to talk."

"Why's that?"

"I know all about why you want to kill Nathan Gibraltar."

A pause. "And why should I care?"

"There's a lot I've found out in the past couple hours. We're both being played by a group of people who have some nasty plans tomorrow. I would like to meet up with you to discuss what I've found out."

"What would you like to discuss?"

"I won't talk over the phone. I know you're at the diner just up the block. Let's meet. It'll be in public so you can be assured nothing will go down to endanger you."

"All right, I'll bite. But rest assured, you screw me over in any way, I will kill you."

"There'll be no need for that. I'll see you in a few minutes."

Phil hung up the phone. The Ganj looked at him.

"You sure this is a good idea?"

"No. Nevertheless, maybe we can figure some things out. They're a piece of this puzzle. I want to find out what they know."

****

Robert turned to his brother. "Give me your opinion of Phil McKnight."

"Nice guy. Why do you ask?"

"Just got off the phone with him. He wants to meet. Says he knows about my situation with Nathan Gibraltar."

"After what I did do you think it's a good idea we meet up with him? What if English Bob is with him?"

"I think we need to hear what he has to say. He won't pull anything as long as I'm here."

The doorbell chimed and Robert turned. Phil and another man walked in. Robert stood.

"That was quick," he said, welcoming the two to the table.

"We were just around the corner. We were able to track you through the GPS signal on your phone," Phil said.

"That's nice to know," Robert said, taking his cell phone out and turning it off. "So what would you like to discuss?"

"Ever since Darrell left I've had to deal with the people who wanted that flash drive. And let me tell you they can be quite difficult bastards. They've even kidnapped my son in the hopes that I would get the flash drive back."

"Will you?" Robert asked.

"I will do what it takes to get my son back but I will not be pushed around like someone's pawn. These people have something diabolical up their sleeves and I want to find out what it is."

"Again, how does that involve us?"

"My associate here came across some papers from one Leslie Dubois. Familiar with her?"

"We wouldn't be here if you didn't know that answer."

Phil smiled. "Stop being so tense man. Kills the mood."

A waitress came to take their orders. Phil and The Ganj ordered some coffee while Robert and Darrell asked for refills. When the waitress left, Phil continued.

"Those papers contained plans concerning a drug deal that's going down tomorrow. The players involved kind of complicate things. Leslie Dubois is involved as well as her boss, Senator Joe Wilson. Also Lt. Governor Nathan Gibraltar is knee deep in this along with his chief of staff Steven Alexander Falcone."

Robert's eyes told the story. This was something he hadn't expected to hear.

"That can't be."

"I'm afraid it is. And the reason I asked for this meeting is because you are also named in those papers."

Shock turned to confusion. "Wha…, why am I mentioned?"

"It talked about your hatred for Nathan Gibraltar. For some reason they're using that hatred to their advantage. The papers don't go into detail as to why or to what goal this will accomplish. I was wondering if you could fill me in?"

"My only goal is to see Nathan Gibraltar dead."

Robert took a sip of his coffee. "I'm not believing this," Robert said.

"How do you think Lydia is involved in all this?" Darrell asked his brother.

"Who's Lydia?" inquired Phil.

"My girlfriend. She introduced me to Leslie. Is her name in those papers?"

"I don't recall. You think she's involved?"

"It would explain a lot," Darrell said.

"No one asked you your opinion Darrell so I suggest you keep your mouth shut," Robert said.

"Listen," Phil said, "I don't care who this woman is. I think we have to agree that we're both being used here. I suggest we talk this out as much as we can so we can try to make some sense of it."

Robert sighed. "All right. But I want to look over those papers you found myself."

"Fair enough. Meet me back at my office. Darrell knows how to get there."

"Before you go McKnight, know this. You try to screw me I'll kill you. Got me?"

Phil stood up and nodded. "I heard you the first time you threatened me. See you at my office."

****

Annie looked at her reflection in the window and admired her newly styled hair. She had realized in the past that there might be times in her profession where she'd have to change her appearance at a moment's notice. She'd spent time with a theater group to learn some of the intricacies of makeup and hair styling for just a time like this. For what it mattered, the police were looking for a woman who looked nothing like the woman she saw in the reflection. She turned and entered the building.

A security guard sat at the reception desk watching a small television. He looked up at her and smiled.

"Well, well, for what do I owe this pleasure?"

Annie smiled. Men. "I have an appointment at Lowenstein and Brown. They're expecting me."

"Let me make a call upstairs to confirm it."

The security guard picked up a phone. Before he had a chance to dial, Annie pulled a small dart gun from her pocket and fired it into the guard's neck. He winced in pain before collapsing to the floor. Annie walked behind the desk. She knelt next to the fallen security guard.

"Didn't your mother ever tell you that women don't like being objectified?"

She pulled a taser from her purse and jammed it in the guard's neck. The guard writhed around like a fish out of water. Satisfied he wouldn't wake up anytime soon, she stopped, putting the taser back in her purse. She may have overdone it, but she had to be sure there would be no distractions. Annie ran to the elevators, stepped into an available car, and hit the button for the top floor.

The doors opened and Annie stepped out. She reloaded the dart gun and headed for the offices of Lowenstein and Brown. The only occupants on this floor would be behind those doors.

She reached the door and heard noises inside. Annie smirked. Based on the sounds some secretary was receiving an early bonus. Annie opened the door.

The head of the law firm, Arthur Brown, had his secretary bent over the desk. He was showing her how his clients ended up after he got through with them. Annie smiled, raising the dart gun and fired. The dart landed in the secretary's thigh, causing her to go limp. It took Arthur a few moments to realize his free legal lesson wouldn't reach a conclusion. He turned, spotting Annie. Annie put the dart gun in her purse while he pulled up his pants.

"Who the hell are you?"

Annie started to clap. "Bravo Mr. Brown. You sure know how to treat your employees."

Arthur went for the phone on his desk. "I'm going to call the police."

"You do that. Then I can tell them about some of your dealings with Xander Falcone and Nathan Gibraltar."

He held the receiver in his hands but couldn't raise it higher than chest level. He put it back in the cradle, taking a seat in his chair.

"What do you want?" he demanded.

"All of your files pertaining to Xander and Nathan."

"Why should I do that?"

Annie smiled. "Do you really want my answer?"

They stared at each other, two poker faces waiting for the other to budge. Finally, Arthur relented. He rose from the desk and walked toward the door. As he was about to leave, he turned suddenly and tried to attack Annie. She grabbed his arm and spun it, forcing him to the ground. She put her foot on his back and twisted the arm until she heard a crack. Arthur screamed.

"I have had a really bad day," Annie said. "What I need from you is obedience. Otherwise I can break the rest of the bones in your body as well."

"Yes, yes," he wailed.

Annie pulled Arthur to his feet. "Now, let's get those files, shall we?"

Arthur brought Annie to the records room. Annie opened the door for him, shoving him inside. He walked over to a filing cabinet.

"They're in here," he said. "Second one from the bottom."

Annie knelt down and opened it up. She browsed through some of the papers until she found what she the files.

****

Mr. A pulled the van into the Gibraltar Mansion driveway and coasted toward Clarissa's car. Clarissa sat in the passenger seat, her head held low so as not to be spotted.

"This ain't going to work," Clarissa said.

"You're the one who came up with the idea."

Clarissa took a glance out the window. Standing on the porch was Nathan's creepy son Alex. He stared at the van as it reached Clarissa's car. Mr. A put the van in park.

"If they spot us we'll need to get out of here as fast as we can. You ever drive a car fast before?"

"I got a speeding ticket once. Does that count?"

"It'll have to do. Here we go. I'll drive your car."

Mr. A got out of the van and went to Clarissa's car. Clarissa climbed over into the driver's side of the van. She waited until Mr. A had her car started and moving. She turned the van around. As they headed for the road, they passed by the porch. The kid had his eyes latched on them like magnets. Clarissa's eyes leveled onto the kid's. Alex's eyes widened when he recognized her.

Alex turned and ran into the house. Clarissa kept her attention forward. Why can't he drive faster? she thought. A limo pulled into the driveway, causing Mr. A to stop her car. She hit the brakes. She turned her head toward the front of the mansion. Just as she saw the door open again with Alex dragging the butler behind him, the limo drove past them, allowing the two vehicles to head back to Dr. Fix It's.

****

Phil opened the door to his office for Robert and Darrell. They walked in, finding places to sit. Phil went over to the coffee machine.

"Want some coffee?" he asked.

Everyone declined. Phil poured his coffee and took a seat at his desk. On the desk sat the lock box. Phil slid it across to Robert.

"The papers are in here," he said.

Robert took the box. He opened it up and gazed at the papers. Darrell fidgeted, nervous.

"So how you been doing Phil? Where's English Bob?" Darrell asked, trying to lighten the mood.

"English Bob is dead. I've had better days."

Darrell sat back, getting the hint that no one wanted to hear him speak. Robert glared at the papers, the anger becoming more evident in his face.

"I can't believe this," he said.

"Told you I wasn't making this up."

"So what did the kidnapper's demand in exchange for your son?" Robert asked.

"They wanted the flash drive and Darrell."

Robert stroked his chin in thought. "You have an idea?" Phil asked.

Robert smiled. "Yeah. I got something in mind."

****

Pete picked up the phone. "Hello?"

"It's Xander. Hope you don't mind an early response. Be at the Greyhound station on Grandville Avenue at eleven thirty. A man will be waiting for you at the entrance standing next to the elevator. He will have a laptop with a webcam that he will give you. Once you take it to your car we'll have a video conference."

"Sounds good. Talk to you then."

Pete hung up the phone. He turned to Curtis.

"We have a meet. You have any plans?"

"GET SOME OF YOUR BOYS TO STAKE OUT THE AREA SO WE DON'T HAVE ANY SURPRISES."

"Done. You think he'll try something?"

"WOULDN'T YOU?"

Pete nodded. "How good are his men?"

"IT'S MICHIGAN. HOW GOOD CAN THEY BE?"

****

Clarissa sat in the seat of her car in Dr. Fix It's driveway. Mr. A leaned in the open window.

"You promise to call me with news on Eva?" Clarissa asked.

"Yeah," Mr. A said. "You sure you know how to use that gun?"

She patted the purse with the gun he gave her. "Pull the trigger and shoot. Gotcha. Stay safe."

"You too."

Clarissa started up her car and left. She grabbed her cell phone and dialed her sister.

"Hello?"

"Roni. I'm returning your call."

"Thank God. Something terrible has happened. You remember my roommate Melissa?"

"Yeah."

"Nathan Gibraltar had her raped and beaten."

Clarissa gripped the steering wheel like a vice. "That son of a bitch."

"Please tell me you can do something about it."

"Roni, you might not believe me but I already am."

"What are you talking about?"

"I can't explain much now. What I do know is that you and Melissa need some protection. Is there anyone you know that can watch you two?"

"I..., I can't think of anybody. I'm at Butterworth Street hospital. I should be safe here."

Clarissa thought for a moment. "No, you won't be. Let me call you back."

Clarissa hung up the phone. She dialed another number.

"Hello?"

"Is this Phil McKnight?"

"Yeah. Who's this?"

"Clarissa Day. We spoke earlier today. I have a problem I was wondering if you could help me with?"

"I'll do what I can. What's up?"

"My sister's roommate was attacked and raped by some goons hired by Nathan Gibraltar."

A pause. "Did you just say Nathan Gibraltar?"

"Yeah. Why?"

"Nothing really. It's just a case I'm working on. What do you need?"

"My sister and her roommate need protection. They're at Butterworth Street Hospital downtown."

"Hmm. I can't do it personally but I can send someone over. Are you sure Nathan Gibraltar is involved in this?"

"I wouldn't be calling otherwise. My sister's name is Roni Day and her roommate is Melissa Hunter. I'll have Roni meet your man at the main entrance."

"All right. I'll get someone over there ASAP. What does your sister look like?"

"She's about 5'6" with brown hair. She wears black framed glasses. Thank you so much."

Clarissa hung up the phone. She dialed her sister back.

"Hello?"

"Wait by the front entrance. Someone will be meeting you there shortly. He'll protect you two."

"How will I know who it is?"

"I gave him your description. If you don't hear from him in a half hour then tell hospital security. But try and keep it as quiet as you can."

"Why? I want to bring this bastard down."

Clarissa smiled. "Trust me sis. He's goin down."

****

"That sounds like something Nathan would do," Robert said.

"Why would someone in his position do something so stupid?" Phil said.

"To paraphrase George Bush, because he can," The Ganj replied.

"But someone in his position is not going to do something like this unless he was certain he could get away with it. What's the end game here?"

"Well," Pedro said, speaking up, "he has a lot more at his disposal now that he's Governor."

"What are you talking about?" Robert asked.

"You didn't hear the news? Davis Creston resigned earlier. Nathan is going to be sworn in as Governor soon."

The men looked at each other. Another piece of the puzzle had revealed itself yet they didn't know how it fit. Phil turned to The Ganj.

"I want you to go to the hospital to guard those women. Find out anything you can while you're there. Robert, you sure you want to go through with this plan?"

"Yeah."

"Alright. Let's get going."

****

Lydia watched through her night vision goggles as the door to Phil McKnight's office opened and four men walked out. Robert was the last in line. She couldn't believe the dumb luck McKnight had in contacting them. All her months of planning were now ruined because of him. She took out her phone and called Xander.

"Hello?"

"It's Lydia."

"What are you calling for?"

"I've lost contact with Robert."

"How the hell is that possible?"

"Phil McKnight reached him with some information."

"That two bit PI Wilcox hired?"

"Yeah."

"What information does he have?"

"I wasn't able to make out everything over the listening device I installed in his cell phone but it sounds like they retrieved some papers from Senator Wilson's assistant Leslie."

Silence. "What do you suggest I do?" she asked.

"Pay Leslie a call. Find out what's going on."

"What if she doesn't cooperate?"

"Then you have carte blanche to use any means necessary to make her cooperate."

"What about the Senator?"

"He'll be in no position to do anything if she was dumb enough to lose important information."

"Gotcha. Do I put the search for Annie on hold?"

"You have to. This is more pressing."

Xander hung up the phone. Lydia put her phone in her pocket. At least she'd be able to take some of her frustration out on Leslie.

****

Annie ripped off the last bit of tape and attached it to Arthur Brown's head. She smiled.

"This looks good on you."

Strapped to his head were two small blocks of C4, a plastic explosive used by the military. They were connected to a trip wire that she was currently connecting to the door. Arthur stared at her in disbelief.

"Why are you doing this?"

"Because Nathan Gibraltar and his henchman Xander Falcone decided to screw me over. No one does that."

"Why do you want to kill me?"

"Because you're a lawyer and lawyers suck."

"What do you plan on doing with those files?"

"Knowledge is the greatest weapon a person can have. You just have to know how to use it properly."

She walked over to the filing cabinet and closed the briefcase she 'borrowed' from Arthur. Every file she needed was inside. She closed it and headed for the door.

"The explosives attached to your head are connected to the trip wire on the ground. Once I close this door, the bomb will be set. When the door is opened and the wire is freed, then you'll become a lot shorter."

"You think you can burn Nathan Gibraltar with them?"

"Honey, I know I can. Oh, before I forget."

Annie set the briefcase down and pulled out the tape. Annie tore off a piece and placed it over his mouth. She pulled off more strips until she was satisfied he wouldn't be able to get it off. She put the tape back in her pocket and stood up.

"I really wouldn't want another plan spoiled. Hope you don't mind."

She smiled, picked up the briefcase, and left, closing the door.

11:00 PM-12:00 AM

The news cameras were set in place for the perfect shot of the new Governor being sworn in at the capitol building. Nathan Gibraltar welcomed them with the appropriate, controlled smile. Just the right image the public wanted.

The state Attorney General entered the main room. Nathan walked over and shook his hand. Everything was set for his ascension to power.

"Are you ready?" the Attorney General asked.

"Impatiently so."

Nathan and the Attorney General approached the podium. The Attorney General adjusted the mike. "Under the circumstances, the usual ceremony associated with this event will have to be postponed for a later date. This state needs a new Governor so let's get to it."

He picked up a Bible from the podium and faced Nathan. The cameras faced them, catching every moment of the historic ceremony.

"Nathan Gibraltar, place your left hand on the Bible, raise your right hand, and repeat after me. I, Nathan Gibraltar."

"I, Nathan Gibraltar."

"Do solemnly swear."

"Do solemnly swear."

"That I will support the Constitution of the United States and the Constitution of this state."

"That I will support the Constitution of the United States and the Constitution of this state."

"And that I will faithfully discharge."

"And that I will faithfully discharge."

"The duties of my position according to the best of my ability."

"The duties of my position according to the best of my ability."

"Nathan Gibraltar, I am proud to announce you as the new Governor of the state of Michigan."

The reporters applauded. Nathan and the Attorney General shook hands. Nathan approached the podium to address the state for the first time as Governor. The

Attorney General took a seat.

"My fellow citizens. I take the office of Governor with great trepidation. Davis Creston was a good man who deserved to keep the Governorship as long as the good people of this state wanted him there. However, with his issues at home, he felt he needed to pay more attention to his family. And while it saddens me and many more across the state that he chose this particular time to do so, the man made a decision you have to respect."

The reporters applauded. Nathan took a sip of water waiting for the applause to subside before he continued.

"Our state faces a challenge not often faced in America today. Replacing a Governor as powerful and influential as Davis Creston on a days notice is not an easy task. However, with the cooperation of the state House and Senate this event will not affect the people of this state.

"My first pledge to you, my fellow citizens, is an increase in funding for law enforcement. As most of you know, I was the victim of an attack today. To think that what happened to me today happens on a regular basis to the citizens of this state shocks and appalls me. Therefore, my first act as Governor will be to issue an executive order calling for a major increase in the number of police on the streets effective immediately. With more policemen on the streets, the man who tried to shoot me and any other criminal in this state will see justice. I guarantee it.

"Another goal I want to focus on is something that's been plaguing our state for some time. That is drugs. Drugs have been poisoning our state for far too long. We have to do what it takes to get rid of these awful substances before they ruin our children and our future.

"The citizens of this great state deserve the best. They deserve a leader who will take this state to realms it never dreamed possible. They deserve the undivided attention of Nathan Gibraltar. Thank you."

Nathan left the podium. The reporters approached, trying to get him to answer their questions. Nathan walked out of the main hall into his new office. He walked over to his desk and picked up the phone. It was time to call Xander.

****

The Ganj walked up to the window of Butterworth Street Hospital and saw a woman that fit the description of Clarissa Day's sister that Phil gave him. He knocked on the window to get her attention. The girl approached and opened the door.

"Are you Roni Day?"

"Yes. Thanks for coming."

"No problem," The Ganj said. "Where's your friend at?"

"She's upstairs. Follow me."

They headed for the elevators. "So how bad was your friend hurt?"

"She was messed up pretty bad. It's sickening how someone could do that to another human being."

"How is Nathan Gibraltar involved?" The Ganj asked as they stepped onto the elevator.

"One of Melissa's faults is that she likes men. A lot. If she became enamored with a man, she didn't care what kind of jerk he was, she went and got them. She met Nathan about a year ago when she interned in his office. They became lovers. But he became too obsessive. She decided to break it off. When you see her you'll see his response."

The elevator stopped and the two got off. Roni led him down the hall. Once they reached the end, they took a right. Melissa's room was at the end.

The room was dark, illuminated only by the hospital equipment Melissa was hooked up to. The Ganj walked over to her. He winced. The sight made him disgusted. He turned to Roni.

"He will pay. I guarantee it."

****

Lydia approached the gate, examining the area for any guards. The gate was unlocked. No one was around. She walked across the lawn and reached the door. She knocked. A guard came and answered.

"Yes?"

"Tell Leslie Lydia is here to speak with her."

"Come on in. She's upstairs."

Lydia walked inside. They went upstairs to Leslie's office. The guard knocked.

"Yes?" Leslie replied.

"Lydia's here to speak with you."

There was a pause. Then the door opened. Leslie looked frazzled.

"Thank you. Leave us."

Leslie pulled Lydia into her office and closed the door. "What are you doing here?"

"We have to talk. Robert discovered something."

"What?"

"By your appearance I think you know."

The two women stared each other down. Finally, Leslie sat down at her desk.

"How could this have happened?"

"You underestimated Phil McKnight."

"What is his problem anyway? You think that with his wife and son close to being killed he would let up on his curiosity."

"Wait a minute. What's going on?"

"We kidnapped his wife and son with the hopes that it would encourage Phil to get the flash drive back along with that punk who stole it."

"Interesting. Who's running the operation?"

"An old flame of mine named Ray is dealing with Phil's son. Senator Wilson is dealing directly with Phil's wife. He'd hired her last week to work on the security system at his home and when this situation with her husband came up, he took it upon himself to keep her detained."

Lydia smiled. "So what were in the papers that were stolen?"

"My notes on everything that's gone down the past couple months."

Lydia turned her back on Leslie and looked out the window. She pulled out her blowgun discreetly.

"Why would you go and do that?" Lydia asked.

"Better to have it written down so I can cover my ass, know what I mean?"

Lydia turned and blew a dart onto Leslie's chest. Leslie tried pulling the dart out before the poison could enter her system but the effects of the cyanide quickly took effect.

"That's why you don't write shit down, Leslie."

Foam started gushing from Leslie's mouth. Her writhing body slowed until she finally stopped, dead. Lydia walked over to the door, shut off the light, and left the office. She loaded another dart into her blowgun.

The guard who brought her upstairs ran up to the door. "I heard a noise."

"Yeah. I killed her," Lydia said, blowing a dart into the guard's chest.

****

"I don't like this Phil," Darrell said.

Phil held him by the neck with his right hand. He held Darrell's backpack in his left hand. They headed to the house.

"If you want to be on my good side again than you're going to do what it takes to help get my son back."

Darrell remained silent. They approached the front door. Phil knocked. After a moment, the door opened.

"I got what Ray needs," Phil told the guard.

The guard let him in the house. He grabbed the bag from Phil. They walked into the living room. Phil took a seat at the couch, shoving Darrell to the floor. Ray joined them.

"Well, well. You came earlier than expected."

"You gave me ample reason to."

"True. Your son will join us shortly. And you must be the little troublemaker that caused all this mess," Ray said, turning to Darrell.

Darrell nodded. Another guard escorted Ty into the room. Ty ran to his father and gave him a hug. The first guard brought in a computer and set it up. The guard took the flash drive out of the backpack and put it into the USB port.

"I hope you don't mind but I'll check this out while we're all here to prevent any more problems."

"No problem at all," Phil said, smiling.

The guard opened the files on the flash drive and turned to Ray, giving him a thumbs up. Ray smiled.

"Thank you Phil for keeping your word."

Phil rose from the couch. Ray's guards went for their guns. Phil raised his hands in the air.

"What? I got something to say."

Ray motioned for his guards to lower their guns. "It's all right."

The guards complied. Ray glared at Phil.

"Now what have you got to say?"

"I just wanted to know if you can see in the dark."

Ray looked at him puzzled. Before he could react, the power went out in the house.

Phil shoved his son to the ground and covered him. Gunshots. Bullets flew everywhere. If Darrell had paid attention to the plan and stayed where he was, then he should be all right. Phil's vision adjusted to the dark. He spotted the guard's protecting Ray by the door. Phil got up and punched the guard in the chest. He stumbled, dropping his gun. Phil slammed his head against the wall. He picked up the guard's gun and shot the other guard in the shoulder. Phil ran over to the second guard and kicked his weapon away from him, making sure he wasn't in any condition to retrieve it. He turned to Ray and put the gun on his head. He pulled his cell phone from his pocket with his free hand. The phone was on speaker, connected to Robert's cell phone outside.

"Turn the power back on. Everything's under control."

The lights turned back on. Robert ran through the front door. He walked over to Phil and Ray.

"Howdy," Robert said.

"Well Ray, looks like we're going to have some time to chat," Phil said. "My friend and I have some things we want to ask you. And we're hoping you'll have some answers for us."

****

Pete walked back to the car with the laptop. He got into the passenger seat and set it up for the meeting. Curtis leaned back, sweat rolling off his face. The painkillers he'd taken were wearing off and the pain was becoming unbearable.

"Finished," Pete said.

He turned the computer on. Once the start screen appeared, he pressed the appropriate buttons to start the video conference. A waiting signal appeared on the screen. Finally, Xander appeared.

"Welcome gentlemen. We'll cut the bullshit and get down to business. What made you want to call this meeting?"

"Curtis wants a guarantee that he will be left alone in exchange for records he has that could be damaging to you and your enterprise."

"How very kind of Curtis. Why should I believe he would keep his end of the bargain?"

"Why shouldn't you? As you can see, he's not in much of a state to do anything other than heal," Pete said, swinging the webcam around to give Xander a shot of Curtis.

Xander smiled. "You're wasting my time. Give me one reason why I should keep this meeting going?"

"Because he'll spread your information to the press and to the authorities," Pete said, his confidence waning.

Xander laughed. "I'm sure he will. Curtis, you're a liability. You know it and I know it. We both know you aren't spending one day in jail for any job I send you on. Thank you for the offer to keep whatever information you think you have silent but I can take care of myself. Consider this meeting over."

The screen went blank. Curtis grabbed the computer and tossed it in the back seat. He started up the car for Pete, who quickly got the message that they weren't safe, even with the reinforcements they brought with them. Pete stomped on the gas and sped out of the parking lot.

A man stepped onto the road a few blocks ahead of them. The man took out what looked like a garage door opener and pressed a button. Pete and Curtis both saw a bright light before their car exploded from the explosives hidden in the computer Xander had them use.

****

Nathan reread the executive order and smiled. This will be my ticket for millions, he thought. He signed the paper and handed it to his secretary.

"How does it feel sir?" she asked him.

Nathan smiled. "Pretty damned good."

He patted her rump and she walked out with a smile. When she left, he got on the phone and called Xander.

"Hello?"

"I just signed executive order sixty-six which is effective immediately."

"Good. Should make things easier tomorrow."

"Funny how things are falling into place."

"Not so fast. I checked up on your son's claim. I think there's something to it."

"Why would your man let that damned reporter go? I thought you trusted him."

"I guess you can't trust anyone these days."

"Send this information to the state police and to any police department between here and Grand Rapids."

"Already done. I'm also having Phil McKnight monitored."

"You think this guy can be a threat?"

"Better safe than sorry. He's already learned more than he needs to."

"Then again even with what he knows how will he be able to use it? As long as we're keeping an eye on him we'll be all right. Besides, we have more important stuff to worry ourselves about. I have to get back to work here."

"Shouldn't you be sleeping?"

"I have a speech to prepare for tomorrow that I refuse to leave to my ignorant speechwriters. Have a good night."

Nathan hung up the phone. He looked at the clock. Before he was through here, he'd have to spend some time with his beautiful secretary. A Governor's work is never done, he mused.

****

Phil paced the room. Ray sat tied up on the floor, Robert and Darrell stood on either side of him.

"I thought we were buddies Ray. Why don't you tell me what I need to know?" Phil asked.

Ray kept his eyes on the floor. Phil sighed, then kicked Ray in the chest. Ray wheezed, trying his best to catch his breath. Phil knelt in front of him.

"All I want is some answers."

"You're a dead man," Ray said. "I don't have to tell you shit."

"Maybe I am. That doesn't mean I'm taking off anytime soon. Talk to me. What do you know about Leslie?"

Ray looked up, defeated. "She's my ex-girlfriend."

"Wow," Phil said. "What would you two be interested in that flash drive for?"

"We have our reasons."

"Listen to this guy. Likes to play tough even when he's beat."

Phil slapped him in the face. Ray spit on him. Phil stood up.

"I don't have time to mess around."

"Why is that? This doesn't even involve you," Ray said.

"You involved me in it when you took my son."

"You don't know the half of it."

Phil stared at Ray. "What do you mean?"

"Leslie informed me where they have Laura."

Phil paused. "My wife? Where is she?"

"Let me go and I'll tell you."

"Not gonna happen."

"Then I won't tell you."

Phil stared at him a moment then left the room. He went into the kitchen and started searching the drawers. He spotted a tool he thought might be helpful, grabbed it, and headed back into the living room. He kept it out of Ray's sight.

"Darrell, take Ray's palm and place it on the floor. Make sure he doesn't try to make a fist."

It took a moment due to Ray's struggling but Darrell finally got his hand on the ground. Phil knelt next to Ray.

"You're gonna tell me what I need to know and you'll do it now."

"Or what?"

Phil pulled the hammer from behind his back.

"Or I'll have to pound some sense into you."

****

Senator Wilson picked up the phone. "Hello?"

"It's Xander. We have to talk."

"I'm kind of busy right now."

"Then I'll be quick. Leslie is dead. She's been collecting information on our deal and that information turned up stolen. I had her taken out."

Joe grimaced. "Why did you do that without my authorization?"

"When someone in your command commits acts that affect my well being like she did, someone else has to step in. I have to ask you Joe. Are you planning something against us?"

"Why would you say that?"

"Come on. After the crap you pulled earlier today you expect me not to think that an option of yours? We have a history together. Be honest with me."

"I would never do anything to sabotage this deal or to put you and Nathan under. What happened earlier was just business. Now, when should I expect the announcement making me the new Lt. Governor?"

"Nathan will be at the Happy Child Publishing Company tomorrow morning for its grand opening. He'll make the announcement then."

"David Geraldson is still cooperating with us right?"

"Yes. He didn't even ask for a bigger cut like you."

Joe slammed his fist on the desk. "Don't blame me if I make a business decision."

"I'm not. I'm making sure your decisions won't affect me. There better not be any more mistakes from your end if you get my drift."

Joe closed his eyes and sighed. "I didn't realize Leslie was doing anything wrong. You have my word that I'm not trying to sabotage our deal."

"Good to hear. We are not enemies. I'm not doing anything to make us so."

The Senator hung up the phone. Leslie was gone. If he had known she committed such a stupid act then he should have been the one to take care of it. Xander should have consulted him before he acted. This will not happen again. He grabbed his personal organizer to look for a number. When he found the right name he smiled. She will do perfectly, Joe thought.

****

The Ganj took a drink of water from the plastic glass and tossed the cup into the trash. He stepped back into the room.

"Is she awake yet?" The Ganj asked.

"No," Roni said. "I don't want to bother her."

"That's cool. Let's head out into the hallway."

The two stepped outside. They walked in no particular direction just to relieve some stress.

"How long have you two lived together?" he asked.

"About a year and a half. We've been friends almost our whole life."

"Has Nathan tried to threaten her before?"

"To tell you the truth, a man threatening her is nothing new. If he did she never told me."

"That sucks. Pretty girl like that."

"Yeah. It does."

They walked on in silence. A commotion at the end of the hall got their attention. The Ganj held Roni back.

"Let me check this out."

He headed down to see what was going on. A man kept yelling in his room about wanting to leave. A couple nurses tried in vain to calm him down. The Ganj peeked in the room.

He almost fainted when he recognized the patient. English Bob looked unaffected by the explosion of the Spanish Moon. The two men locked eyes and smiled.

"Did Phil send you here with a stripper?" English Bob asked.

"No. He sent me to dump a forty on your grave. Looks like I can take that forty home now."

"Phil still thinks I'm gone?"

"You might want to give him a call. You two got some catching up to do."

Roni entered the room. English Bob smiled.

"All right. You left that pig Princess."

The Ganj gave him a dirty look. "No. I'm here for protection at Phil's request."

"Did he take care of that little bastard Darrell?"

"Not exactly. Like I said, call Phil. He would like nothing more than to know you're alive."

"He sure knows how to make a girl feel special," English Bob said. He pointed to the nurses.

"You two bitches go and get me released. I'm through wasting my time here."

The two women left in a huff. The Ganj handed English Bob the phone.

****

"Put some tape over his mouth," Phil said.

Darrell ran into the kitchen to find some tape. As Phil prepared to smash another of Ray's fingers, his phone rang. Phil picked it up.

"Yeah?"

"Philip T. McKnight. Thought I'd give you a call from beyond the grave."

Phil stood up, a smile beaming from his face. "Oh my God. How the hell did you make it?"

English Bob laughed. "I got lucky. The concussion from the bomb caused the termite-infested floor I was standing on to collapse and I landed in the basement in a pile of empty beer cans. Never thought I'd praise the day I procrastinated on fumigating the place."

"I'm glad you're alive."

"You had to go to The Ganj when you thought I was gone though?"

They laughed. "By the way, who's that yelling in the background?" English Bob asked.

"Remember Ray?"

"Yeah."

"It's him. I'm trying to persuade him to be cooperative."

"Nice. You mind if I drop by so we can catch up?"

"You gonna be all right and everything?"

"Amazingly so. I want to get the cocksuckers that blew up my bar. And I think I got a lead on who it may be."

"What do you mean?"

"I talked with a woman named Leslie before the bar exploded."

"Leslie?"

"Yeah. Told me that I was being punished for my curiosity. Strange woman."

"All right then. Get out of there as soon as you can and find me. We have to catch up."

"I'll get to you when these idiots let me out. See ya."

"Bye."

Phil hung up the phone and walked over to Robert. "My friend's bar was bombed by a woman named Leslie. It sounds like the Leslie you've been dealing with."

"I can tell you why Leslie bombed your friend's bar," Ray said.

The group turned to him. Ray smiled.

"Got your attention, haven't I? Untie these ropes and I'll talk."

Phil thought about it. "Darrell, get your gun ready."

He knelled down and untied Ray. He grabbed his arm and led him to the couch.

"I can be a nice guy if you tell me what I want to know."

"I don't think my body could hold out with me being stubborn anymore."

"So start talking."

Ray cleared his throat. There was a shattering of glass. Ray fell back, a spear jutted from his head. The men dived to the floor, each grabbing a weapon. Robert saw the spear had a note attached. He crawled over and took it off the spear. He read it and shook his head. He handed the note to Phil.

"I think I'm single again," Robert said.

Phil read the note. "Darrell, get upstairs and get my son. We've been here too long."

Phil crept to the window and peeked outside. He saw a car across the street drive away. He stood up.

"Was that Lydia?"

"Yeah," Robert said.

"Scary bitch ain't she."

"She can be when she wants to."

"What does she mean by this?" Phil asked, waving the note.

"We're being monitored. I don't know how but we are."

"You still have your cell phone on you?"

Robert tossed his cell phone to Phil. Phil opened it up and inspected it. Nothing seemed out of the ordinary. Phil took the battery off. There it is, he thought. He took off the tiny metallic object with the blinking red light and held it in the air for Robert to see. Robert turned away, embarrassed. Phil held it to his mouth.

"You missed. And if you think you'll get a second chance, you got another thing coming."

Phil threw it to the floor and smashed it with his foot.

****

The train station was packed despite the time of night. Passengers fighting off sleep stood or sat anywhere they could find a place. A few people used the walls for pillows and tried to catch as much rest as they could.

The door to the station opened and a woman in her late fifties walked in. She headed for the ticket counter.

"Can I help you ma'am?" the ticket attendant asked.

"I would like to purchase an open ended ticket to Grand Rapids, Michigan for the first train heading out."

"You sure ma'am? That's going to cost you."

The woman took out a wad of cash from her purse. "Money is no object. Print up that ticket."

The attendant followed orders. The woman paid him and grabbed her ticket. She found a seat and waited with the rest of the people for her train.

12:00 AM-1:00 AM

Clarissa knocked on the hospital entrance door and got her sister's attention. Roni ran over and opened the door for her. Once inside, the two sisters hugged.

"I missed you," Roni said.

"Are you all right? My goodness, I worried the whole trip here."

"Everything's fine. Mr. McKnight sent someone over so everything's cool."

"Thank goodness. What room is Melissa in?"

"Five ninety five."

"I'll meet you up there. I want to call Phil first and thank him."

The two sisters hugged again and Roni left. Clarissa took out her phone and called Phil.

"Hello?"

"Phil? It's Clarissa Day."

"Oh, hi. You all right?"

"After the day I've had I'm lucky to be alive."

"What happened?"

"Nathan Gibraltar is the most evil man I've ever known. He shot his wife."

"What?"

"You heard me. I also found out some other things about him that I couldn't quite corroborate just yet. To top it off, he's now the Governor of Michigan. What have you heard?"

"From what I understand Nathan and state Senator Joe Wilson are involved in a scheme to ship in a large shipment of cocaine for distribution."

"Why would they risk their careers to do that?"

"Why would Nathan Gibraltar kill his wife? I can't quite figure out the logic in all this. Being that he's now Governor he sure has a lot more power in his hands, that's for sure."

"What do you think that means?"

A pause. "I think I get what he's doing."

"What's that?"

"There's a guy I'm with now who has a beef with Mr. Gibraltar. We found out that Nathan and the good Senator kept someone on their payroll to be with this guy round the clock, egg him on if you will. Since you obviously saw the news yesterday, you know about the assassination attempt. This guy here was the potential assassin. With the assassination attempt yesterday, the police have stepped up their watch on Nathan Gibraltar. Now that he's Governor, he has the ability to move around the police at will. We have to assume that sometime later today Nathan will adjust things to guarantee the shipment arrives and that he'll be able to ship it back out. Completely free of police involvement. Brilliant I must say."

"Then why would he shoot his wife?"

"Unforeseen circumstances. This son of a bitch wants to clear the way for a drug delivery."

"How do we stop him?"

"I'm not sure yet. If he can kill his wife and cover it up from the public then it's safe to assume we can't just go to a TV station and tell them what we know, no offense to your chosen profession. We have to do something that would make him show the people in the state what he's doing. We have to force him to make a mistake."

"What do you suggest we do?"

"Since the drug deal is happening today, there must be some event that he'll be at which will give him the opportunity to finish his plan. When we find out what that event is then we crash it."

"I can find that out for you. Plus I have a surprise for Nathan."

"You do?"

"I won't tell you over the phone. There's no telling what he's capable of. Can you get down to the hospital?"

"Yeah. I have to get my son to a safe place. I'll be there when we can. Stay by the door."

"Let me head up and tell my sister first what I'm doing then I'll be back down."

"Sounds good. See ya."

Clarissa hung up the phone. She was elated and frightened at the same time. She didn't know what to feel. But she had one goal in mind that would keep her going. Getting rid of Nathan Gibraltar. She headed upstairs.

****

Dr. Fix It sat staring at his patient. Eva Gibraltar's breathing was steady which was a good sign. But he worried whether his breathing would be cut short for keeping her alive.

Eva stirred on the table. Dr. Fix It stood and checked on her. She opened her eyes.

"Who are you?" Eva asked.

"I'm the son of a bitch that saved your life."

"Thank you son of a bitch."

Eva smiled and closed her eyes. Dr. Fix It left the room to meet Mr. A in the kitchen.

"She's going to make it."

Mr. A sighed. "Thank goodness."

"What do we do now?"

"I'm not quite sure. I think we should leave it up to her. It's not like anyone knows she's here. Let me give Clarissa a call."

Mr. A took out his phone and dialed. He waited for her to answer.

"Hello?" Clarissa answered.

Mr. A smiled. "She just opened her eyes. She's going to make it."

A pause. "I can't believe it. This is amazing. Call me back when she's ready to be moved. I want to coordinate with her on what she wants to do next."

"Fair enough. Talk to you later."

Mr. A hung up the phone. He sighed. Why did doing the right thing feel so wrong?

****

Xander walked up the porch and rang the doorbell. He didn't want to be here. Someone had to do it though and it was better for business that he did. Besides, Onyx deserved to hear this in person. He knocked.

The lights in the house turned on. A shadow appeared from the top of the stairs heading down. Onyx approached the front door and opened it.

"Xander. What brings you by so late?"

"Tony, we gotta talk."

"Come in."

Tony Palermo escorted Xander into the house and led him to the study. Xander took a seat. Tony went to the bar and prepared himself a drink.

"You thirsty?" Tony asked.

"Scotch please."

"News that bad, huh?"

Tony prepared the drink and gave it to Xander. He took a seat across from him.

"You got me up this late. What's so important?"

Xander took a sip of the alcohol and lowered his head. "I have some news that's going to throw a wrench into our plans."

"What is it?"

Xander took a deep breath. "Nathan shot Eva. She's dead."

Tony stared at him. "What?"

"You heard me."

Tony stood and walked to the wall, taking off a picture. He stared at it.

"What was he thinking?" Tony asked.

"He wasn't."

"You know what this means Xander."

He nodded. "I do."

Tony turned and faced Xander. "You tell that son of a bitch that if I ever see him I will kill him. You mark my words. When Gibraltar goes down, a Palermo will be the one who killed him."

****

As Phil took his keys from the ignition, his cell phone rang. He cursed, taking it out and putting it to his ear.

"Hello?"

"Phil, I got your message. Just wanted to check in."

"Hey Stone. You go to that house yet?"

"Yeah. More bodies to chalk up."

"Looks like I'm onto something big."

"Who would have thought? Give me an update on where things are."

"I don't know if you'd believe me if I told you."

"Try me."

"How about our new Governor and another prominent politician in this state are behind a big time drug deal that's going down later today."

Stone laughed. "Alright, now you're talking crazy."

"I got enough proof to continue on with my investigation."

"Sounds like you got a full plate on your hands. I think you need some help."

"Oh really."

"Yeah. Where you at?"

"Do I have to tell you?"

"No. But if you don't I'll get a warrant for your arrest and we can talk then."

"Wow. Put it that way."

"Where you at?"

"I'll be heading over to Butterworth Street Hospital after I get Ty to a safe place. I'm going to visit a woman who was raped today."

"I think I know who that person is. I'll meet up with you there."

"See ya."

Phil hung up the phone and got out of the car. Robert and Darrell followed.

"Who was that?" Robert asked.

"A cop friend of mine."

"Whoa. You sure it's a good idea for him to be involved?" Robert asked.

"His being around keeps my ass out of jail. Besides, he's cool. Stone's showing up to assist. With him around maybe we could get some help in breaking this thing open that we wouldn't have otherwise."

"If you think it'll work," Darrell said.

"I have no reason not to. Now if you don't mind I have to drop Ty off with my mother. I'll be right back."

****

"Hello?"

"It's about time you picked up Nathan," Xander said.

"What have you got?"

"Just left Onyx's house. He didn't like the news he heard."

"Why does he have to throw a fit with all I've done for him?"

"Did you expect him to throw you a party?" Xander asked.

Nathan smirked. "I don't care what his reaction was. He's irrelevant now. I have the ability to send his spaghetti-eating ass to Jackson for many years. He'd be foolish to try anything."

"He's not exactly thinking rationally. Based on what I saw I think he may attempt getting back at you somehow."

"All the better for me."

"Something else. I got a lead on Mr. A's location. Mr. B's body was found about a mile from your mansion so I spread the search around the area. Eva's body is still missing."

Nathan kept silent. "Aren't you concerned a stranger may find her and report it?" Xander asked.

"Not in the least. If her body is found then we claim that she was kidnapped by some of the same people that were out to get me. In fact, we should report her missing to the state police. That should cover our rectums."

"Already been done Nathan. Point is this. What if she isn't dead?"

"I didn't miss."

"Stranger things have happened. Haven't you heard about that woman who was shot in the face and lived to tell about it? What do you think that'll do to your numbers if Eva turns up with a chest wound due to a bullet hole that you caused?"

"It's your job to make sure that doesn't happen. Now what lead do you have?"

"Remember Dr. Fix It?"

****

Mr. A peeked out the window. The street was like a ghost town. Obviously being the time of night it was it wouldn't be like Hollywood and Vine in Los Angeles but this street did get more traffic than this. The lack of traffic bothered him. He closed the curtain and headed back into the kitchen.

"You have any weapons in here?" Mr. A asked.

"Saved them for a rainy day. You'll find them in the basement. I think we have the same idea."

Mr. A opened the door to the basement and turned the light on. He walked down the stairs and glanced around for the weapons. He spotted a bunch of guns hanging on the far wall. A table sat on the side covered with enough ammunition to make a four star general happy. He stepped over and grabbed what he needed for the extended standoff he anticipated.

He headed back upstairs. Dr. Fix It wasn't in the kitchen. Mr. A put the weapons on the table.

"Where you at Doc?"

"Locking things up," came the reply.

Good idea, he thought. He grabbed a handgun, checked the ammo, and headed for Eva's room. He opened the door.

A man held a revolver to Eva's head. Eva was oblivious, lost in the throes of drug-induced sleep. Mr. A raised his gun and shot him. Eva's eyes opened with a start.

"What was that?" she gasped.

"Just some people trying to help out your husband, that's all. We gotta move you."

"I hurt so bad."

"Don't worry. This bed has wheels."

Mr. A wheeled the bed out into the hallway. Dr. Fix It was outside the door.

"Where's the best place to hole up?" Mr. A asked.

"Follow me," he said.

"Wait," Eva said. "Let me use the phone."

"Why?" asked Dr. Fix It.

"Do you want to get out of this situation or what?"

****

Laura was enveloped by the darkness. The cargo elevator plunged deeper into the ground, deeper than a human should be allowed to go. Wilson's men thought they'd be imaginative and put a blindfold on her for the drive so she couldn't guess where they were going. She also knew they'd taken the longest route they could, circling back a few times before they reached their destination in order to disorient her.

What they didn't realize was that she'd been to this place before. Grand Rapids and the outlying towns were small enough that if you lived there long enough, you'd know it by heart. Some considered that a curse. Laura thanked God now that she lived in this tiny little burg.

When they had boarded the cargo elevator, her captors took off her blindfold and put on night vision goggles for themselves. They pressed the button going down and it sank into the earth. The little light on ground level quickly disappeared and the blackness that consumed her washed over her like a wave.

The elevator came to a stop. The men forced her out.

The only lights were floor lights that guided you to your destination. She wasn't able to see much of anything in the darkness except for those lights. Her captors dragged her about a quarter mile into the mine. They stopped in front of a metal door. One of the captors opened it up. She was shoved inside. The door closed with a clang.

"Hello Laura."

Laura looked around for the source of the voice. "Who's in here?" she demanded.

"No one is in there with you. There's a speaker above your door. This is Senator

Wilson."

"What the hell do you want?"

"Just checking to see if you made it safe. I'm hoping to make your stay as pain free as possible."

"You think you can treat me like this and expect me to be all smiles?"

"Before you know it this will all be over with."

"Then I'll take your ass to court. That is if you have any intention of letting me go which I don't think you really do."

The speaker remained silent. Laura felt her way around the cell until she found a bed. A real bed, she thought. He treats his prisoners with style. She lay on the bed and tried to collect her thoughts.

****

Phil spotted Stone walking toward the hospital entrance. He walked over and opened it for him. Stone came in and shook Phil's hand.

"Thanks for coming," Phil said.

"You gotta admire the security of this place. The party's upstairs?"

"Yeah." The two men headed for the elevators. "Melissa woke up not too long ago and she's been talking."

"Really. Anything interesting to say?"

"Said she never met her attacker before but was sure he was sent by Nathan Gibraltar."

"That's an awfully big claim to make. Does she have any proof?"

"You can say that. She's pregnant with Nathan's baby. Said he probably sent the attacker cause she wouldn't have an abortion." Phil pressed the button for the elevator.

"Oh man. That's like talk show good."

"You're telling me. Sounds plausible but there's nothing you could officially do about it on your end, right?"

"Do you have any evidence for these claims?"

Phil smiled. "Of course. I'll show you later." The two men stepped into the elevator car.

"By the way, I got some more info for you on that psycho chick at the bank."

"Really? What you got?"

"Her name is Annie Walker. Turns out she's an assassin for hire. We don't know who she works for but she must have pissed someone off because her own people ratted her out. We spotted her earlier in the night but she tore through us like scissors through paper. That girl's like a pit bull in mating season."

"She just disappeared?"

"You could say that. There was a rampage in a lawyer's office a little after that. Looking at the surveillance, I saw a woman who my gut tells me looked an awful lot like her but we couldn't officially confirm it was or not."

The elevator doors opened and the two men stepped out. Phil led Stone through the hallways.

Phil found the room and stopped outside the door. "I got a surprise for you."

"What's that?" Stone asked.

Phil led him in. English Bob was sitting up in bed eating a late snack. He looked up.

"Why couldn't you bring a stripper?"

"I did. Don't you like him?"

Stone did a little dance. The men laughed.

"We need to fill in Stone on what's been going on," Phil said. "Get to the cafeteria. I'll round up The Ganj and the others."

"Oh joy," English Bob joked.

****

They locked themselves in the bathroom, the only room in the house with no windows. Mr. A and Dr. Fix It stood on either side of the door with guns ready. They heard the commotion in the house. Someone, a group of someone's, was tearing up the place looking for them. It would be only a matter of minutes before they were found.

Eva lay in the tub. Dr. Fix It had injected her with some more pain medication to make this situation as painless as possible. He turned and inspected her.

"You doing ok?"

She smiled. "As ok as I'll ever be, thanks."

"Good. Keep that smile Mrs. Gibraltar."

"I will if you never call me by that name that again."

He laughed. The noises became centralized and began coming nearer. Mr. A and Dr. Fix It readied their weapons. The noises stopped by the bathroom door.

The lights went out. At the same moment, the door was kicked in. Mr. A and Dr. Fix It fired. Two of the enemy went down. Eva covered her face in fear.

Mr. A was shot in the arm. He dropped his gun. Dr. Fix It lasted a little longer but dropped his guns after being shot in the chest. The two remaining gunmen approached Mr. A. One of them grabbed a walkie-talkie.

"Turn the lights back on."

As if from a command by God, the lights blinked on. The two men put their guns to Mr. A's head.

Shots rang out. The two gunmen fell dead. A man walked into the room, a man fast approaching old age. He looked around.

"Eva," he called out.

Eva sat up in the tub. "Daddy!"

Her father ran to his daughter and embraced her, both weeping tears of joy. Mr. A sat up on the floor.

"Who the hell are you?"

Eva turned to him. "This is my father."

"We gotta get out of here before more of Gibraltar's goons show up. You gonna be all right?" he asked Mr. A.

Mr. A stood up. "It needs to be looked at but it's not serious."

Eva's father walked over to Dr. Fix It. "You gonna make it?"

Dr. Fix It's breathing was labored. "No. I'm not gonna make it. Kill me now."

"No," Eva cried out.

"Even if an ambulance were called I'd die before I got to the hospital. Put a bullet in my head. It's the only way."

Eva's father looked at Mr. A. He nodded. Eva's father raised his gun and fired.

****

The group sat at a large round table in the cafeteria. English Bob sat back in his wheel chair and stretched.

"I have some news you may not have heard," Stone said.

"What's that?" Phil asked.

"You talked about Leslie Dubois. She's been killed."

"Killed?" Robert asked, sitting up.

"Oh yeah. Her staff too. Each was murdered with a cyanide dart."

Robert closed his eyes and shook his head. "What's the matter?" Phil asked.

"Lydia."

"You said a cyanide dart?" Darrell asked.

"Yeah," Stone replied.

"Phil, wasn't that baboon who tried to kill us today killed with a cyanide dart?"

Phil thought for a moment and nodded his head in agreement. "Now that you mention it…"

"Who's Lydia?" Stone asked.

"She was my girlfriend. She brought me into all this."

Stone leaned back in his chair. "We have to come up with a plan of action. Something terrible is going to happen today and it's up to us to stop it."

"We have to find out his itinerary for later so we can get an idea where this will go down," Clarissa said.

"Can you head to the station and find that out?" Phil asked Clarissa.

"Of course."

"Until then English Bob, Darrell, and The Ganj can stay here and protect Melissa and Roni. Robert, Phil, and I will search our way through those papers of Leslie's to try to milk that source dry. Miss Day, this ball will get rolling once we find out where Nathan Gibraltar will be today so good luck," said Stone.

"Thanks for the pressure."

"No problem. Let's get going."

The group rose. English Bob pulled Phil aside.

"Why are you letting Stone take over like that?"

"He's not taking over. He's just another mind added to the pot."

"You sure? I don't trust the guy."

"He's a cop. Calm down. There's nothin that can happen."

"Didn't Rodney King say something like that?"

****

"Are you sure this is correct?" Xander asked making sure he read the file in his hand correctly.

"Yes sir," his assistant said. "I double checked that patient list with the hospital three times. Melissa Hunter survived her surgery. To add fuel to the fire Bob Terwilliger survived the explosion at the Spanish Moon."

Xander sighed, placing the file on his desk. "Thank you. You may go."

His assistant left the room. He had to laugh at the situation. To think that he hired professionals to kill two people in ways that would normally kill a person only to have the victims end up alive and well in the same hospital would be humorous if it happened to someone else. But this would be something he'd have to laugh about later. For now, he had to clean up the mess others made. He picked up his cell phone and called the only person at the moment who could clean up the mess. Lydia.

"Hello?"

"Are you near Butterworth Street Hospital by chance?"

"I can be there soon."

"Good. I'll text you the details but long story short I need you to take out a couple people for me. Are you up for it?"

"I'd rather not get distracted from my surveillance of Robert with Phil McKnight."

"Speaking of McKnight, one of the people I need you to take out is an associate of his. By doing the job you may actually bring McKnight to you."

Lydia paused. "I think you've convinced me. I'll head there now. I'll be anticipating the text message."

Xander thanked her and hung up the phone. He hoped she'd be able to do the job successfully but with the day he'd been having, he wouldn't hold his breath.

****

Clarissa walked down the hallway towards the exit. She was eager to leave and bring an end to Nathan Gibraltar.

She opened the door and walked outside. She got to the end of the sidewalk and waited for the crosswalk signal to take her across the street to the parking garage.

Her cell phone rang. Who could be calling me this late? she thought. She took it out of her purse and answered.

"Hello?"

"I missed your voice."

Clarissa couldn't help but smile. "It's been a long time. Why haven't you called?"

"I don't want to explain it over the phone because it would probably sound facetious. I want to meet up with you tonight."

"Tonight's not good. I'm working on a project."

"Clarissa, I wouldn't ask you if it weren't important. It will only be a few minutes of your time, trust me."

The crosswalk signal changed and Clarissa crossed the street. "You said that last time and we were together close to four hours. Where do you want to meet?"

"Our place. I'll be waiting."

The line went dead. Clarissa hung up the phone and put it back in her purse. She jogged the rest of the way to her car. She knew she shouldn't be considering seeing her lover but that voice...

****

The woman gazed out the window at the lovely Illinois landscape. She loved trains. In her opinion, they gave you the luxury of a first class flight with the beauty of the scenery that you'd get on a bus. It gave you the chance to enjoy the beauty of the country.

Her cell phone rang. She took the blasted contraption out of her bag and answered it.

"Hello?"

"How's the trip?"

She smiled. "Very good Senator. At the rate the train is going I should be in Grand Rapids around five in the morning."

"I wish you didn't have to take the train. I could have sent my jet for you."

"You know my work Senator Wilson. It's well worth the wait. I'll contact you later."

She hung up the phone and put it back in her bag. She pulled out some knitting and continued her work.

1:00 AM-2:00 AM

Phil stepped into his office, Robert and Stone on his heels. Phil walked over to his desk where Pedro sat decrypting the secure flash drive.

"Got anything yet?"

"It's still not clear. Words are popping out here and there but it's still in the process of unscrambling."

"Nothing that could give us any clues?"

"Not at this point, man. Sorry."

"Not your fault. Keep up the good work."

Phil patted Pedro on the back. He grabbed the lock box off the table and joined Robert and Stone who'd grabbed seats. Phil put the lock box down.

"The papers are all here."

Stone opened it up and examined the papers inside. "She sure helped us out by keeping detailed notes," Stone said.

"What we need to do is take down any names we come across in here so we can look these people up," Phil said.

"Good idea," Stone said. His cell phone began ringing. "I have to take this call. I'll be right back."

"Go nuts," Phil said.

Stone rose and left Phil's office. He flipped open the phone and put it to his ear.

"Hello?"

"Stone, it's Randy."

"What do you need?"

"How are things in sleazy private eye land?"

"Turns out my hunch is correct again. Phil's stumbled onto something big."

"Oh really."

****

"Sir, have you considered sending someone to persuade Phil McKnight to stop his investigation?"

Senator Wilson sat back in his chair. "No, that's the first it's entered my mind," he said, the sarcasm dripping like the previous day's rain.

"No offense sir but I wouldn't call what Leslie did a legitimate plan."

"Then what do you have to suggest?"

His assistant Eric sat across from him. "I suggest a more direct approach. The people you've sent have made a half ass attempt at best at eliminating the McKnight problem. We need to find someone with no regard for his or her own personal well-being. Someone willing to take whatever steps necessary to solve the problem."

"You have someone in mind I presume?"

His assistant smiled. "Horace Spengler."

"Who the hell's that?"

"My girlfriend is an orderly over at Pine Oaks Mental Health. He's been a patient there for close to six months now. He's the definition of psychotic. Yet he's smart as a whip. I think he'd be the perfect man to help you out."

"How would you go about getting this man released?"

"I don't have the power to do that." His assistant handed over a folder. "But with this information, I think you can."

Joe took the folder and read over some of its content. He smiled.

"How come you never came forward with any ideas before?"

"I was waiting for the right time. With Leslie gone you need someone now."

The Senator smiled. "Thank you Eric. I'll be getting back to you."

Eric stood up and left the room. Joe looked over more of the papers Eric had left.

****

Eva's father led Mr. A and Eva into an empty warehouse. Set up at the far end was a makeshift living area. The man directed Mr. A to a chair and Eva to a couch.

"Someone will be along momentarily to check on you. You need something to drink?"

"I could use some water Father," Eva said.

"Got a cold beer?" Mr. A asked.

"I'll do what I can. Be right back."

He left. Mr. A looked over his injured arm.

"It's not so bad."

"A doctor will be coming soon. We'll be all right."

"I hope so."

"They'll have more equipment with them than Fix It had. Man, I can't believe he's dead."

"Deep down in his alcoholic heart, he was a good guy. He never forgot that oath they make doctor's take."

"The Hippocratic oath?"

"Whatever."

"Why did you save me?" Eva asked.

"Maybe I have twisted morals but I don't have no respect for anyone that would hurt a woman."

"Well I thank you and your twisted morals."

"Your dad's a nice guy, coming in with guns a blazing like that."

Eva cracked a smile. "That's my Daddy."

****

Clarissa approached the room. She noticed a champagne bottle in the door propping it open. She smiled, opened the door, grabbed the bottle, and stepped inside.

The room was dark. She took a few steps forward.

"Hello?" she called out.

Someone tackled her onto the bed. The person turned Clarissa around and began kissing her.

"Wait a minute," Clarissa said, laughing. "I said I don't have much time."

The person brushed their hand on Clarissa's face. "I won't be long. I've missed you so much."

They started kissing. Clarissa fought as much as she could but the pleasure she was feeling won out. They took off each other's clothes.

****

Phil passed his paper over to Stone. "This name keeps coming up in the papers I'm reading. Harvey Johnson."

"I saw it too."

"The name sounds familiar," Robert said. "Is there an address listed somewhere?"

"Let me see," Phil said, looking through the papers. "Here we go. He's in Eastown."

"That's just a hop, skip, and a jump away from Leslie's place. I think I remember him."

"What do we need to know about him?" asked Stone.

"That's just it," Robert said. "He's vice president of production at the Happy Child Publishing Company. I don't see how he could be involved in any sort of wrongdoing.

He was always a stand up guy."

"How did you know him?" Phil asked.

"I used to go to high school with him. We've kept up over the years," Robert said.

"What would make Leslie mention him in these notes?" Stone asked.

"We have to find out. You wanna come with me Robert?" Phil asked.

"Sure."

"Hopefully your history with the guy will make the job easier," Phil said.

"What's gone easy so far?" Robert commented.

"Story of my life. What about you Stone?"

"I'm not done with these papers. When I am then I'll move on to the station to work on any leads. They've obviously planned things out in order for this deal to go down at some point today. We need to focus on getting as much information as possible as to when and where this goes down before we make a move."

****

Clarissa caressed her lover. "It's been too long," she said.

"You don't know how much I've missed you."

"You didn't miss me. You missed how I make your toes curl."

They laughed. Clarissa stood up and went for her clothes.

"Do you have to go?"

"I told you I'm investigating a story. I don't have much time."

Her lover took Clarissa's hand, kissing it tenderly. "I need you now. Please stay a while longer."

Clarissa pulled her lover's face to her. They kissed.

"If it were any other day or any other story we'd be here for the rest of the night."

Her lover smiled. "I know. I also had an ulterior motive for calling you here."

"What's that?" Clarissa asked, raising an eyebrow.

"Check the dresser."

Clarissa walked over and grabbed the briefcase sitting on top of the dresser. She opened it and examined some of the files inside. Realizing what she was reading, she turned to her lover.

"Where did you get this?" Clarissa asked.

"Don't worry about where I got it. Can you use it?"

"Of course I can. The story I'm working on revolves around Nathan Gibraltar anyway so this is a gold mine."

"Good. Bring him down. Then maybe we can meet back here for a proper night of fun."

Clarissa smiled. She embraced her lover.

"I love you Annie Walker."

The two women kissed.

****

Lydia knocked on the door, getting the attention of a person inside. After a moment, the door was opened for her.

"Thanks," Lydia said. "Forgot something in the car."

She walked into the main lobby of Butterworth Street Hospital heading for the elevators. People that she passed eyed her as she walked by, uneasy but not knowing exactly why. She reached the elevators and pressed the button for the next car going up. The door opened and she got inside.

The elevator opened up on the fifth floor. Lydia got out and looked around. She took out her cell phone and read Xander's text message with the directions. She headed to her right, heading for the nurse's station.

"Can you help me?" Lydia asked the nurse at the desk.

"I'll try."

"I'm lost. My brother was in an accident and I'm looking for his room. His name is Robert Terwilliger."

"Let me check."

The nurse turned to the computer. Lydia pulled out her blowgun and blew a dart into the nurse's neck. The nurse clutched at the dart but sunk to the desk before she could make a sound. Lydia went behind the counter and looked at the computer screen. She found English Bob's room.

Another nurse appeared. Lydia placed another dart into the blowgun and shot it into the nurse's neck. The nurse collapsed to the ground, dead. She had to get this done quick before she was discovered.

****

Darrell sat next to the hospital bed watching a news channel on the hospital TV. A talking head sat blabbing about how the President's decision on stem cell research would end modern civilization as we know it. He loved watching shows like this. How the host could be worked up that the world was not running the way they wanted was beyond him. He realized that most of what he saw was theatrics but it made him wonder how much of their act they actually believed. It was a great way to be paid but the thought that the audience took these people's opinions as gold was frightening.

He heard a noise and turned his head. Darrell received a punch in the face for his efforts. He fell to the ground. The person jumped over him onto English Bob lying in the bed. The Ganj ran into the room moments later and grabbed the person off English Bob. Darrell stood up.

"Lydia," he said, surprised at her presence.

She tried in vain to escape, struggling to free herself. English Bob got off his bed.

"What the hell are you doing here?" Darrell asked.

Lydia stopped struggling. "It ain't a social call, that's for sure."

"I'll get on the phone to security," English Bob said, heading for the phone.

"I'm going to ask you one more time what you're doing here," Darrell said.

"Well, since when did you become the dominant type?" Lydia asked.

The Ganj threw Lydia in a chair. "Who sent you? Tell me now."

Lydia looked at him, smiled, and grabbed a syringe from her pocket, stabbing The Ganj before he could react. He slumped to the floor unconscious. English Bob dropped the phone and charged her. Within moments, he too fell to the floor. Darrell stood in the doorway.

"I'm not letting you out," he said.

Lydia laughed. She pulled out her blowgun and shot him with a dart. He fell to his knees. Lydia walked next to him.

"That's for fucking things up," she said.

She kicked him to the ground. He gasped his last few breaths and died.

****

Phil knocked on the door. No response. Robert stood next to him staring at the road. Phil pounded on the door again. Finally, lights went on in the house and someone answered the door.

"What the hell is going on here?"

Phil and Robert pushed their way into his house. Harvey Johnson did his best to stop them from entering.

"What the hell are you doing? Get out of my house."

Phil got in Harvey's face. "Listen pal. I'm sorry to do this. I've been up for almost twenty-four hours on an important investigation concerning Nathan Gibraltar and Joe Wilson doing some rather stupid things. The reason I'm here is because your name popped up in some papers and I want to know how you're connected to those two."

"What are you talking about? And what the hell are you doing here Robert?"

"I wouldn't be here if this wasn't important. What have you got to do with Gibraltar?" Robert asked.

Harvey stared at Robert a moment. "Follow me. We'll talk in the kitchen. And can you two please keep your mouths shut. I don't want to wake my wife up."

The three men headed for the kitchen. Phil and Robert took a seat at the kitchen table. Harvey prepared some coffee.

"So what's going on here? What does your investigation have to do with me?" Harvey asked. "I work at a children's book company for goodness sake."

"Did you have any contact with a woman named Leslie Dubois?" asked Phil.

"Sure. She's Senator Wilson's assistant."

"What was the nature of the contact?"

"We're opening a new plant in Walker later this morning. Senator Wilson was behind the effort to entice my company to build a new plant instead of moving our operation down south. He and his staff have kept an eye on things throughout the process of construction."

Phil and Robert looked at each other. "During this time were the Senator's people interested in anything strange?" Phil asked.

"Like what?"

"Anything really. Were they over attentive to details? Were they interested in things that wouldn't interest anyone but the people who work there? Stuff like that," said Robert.

"I had minimal contact with the Senator's people. The man you want to talk to would be my boss, David Geraldson."

"Why?"

"He was more involved with dealing with visitors of that magnitude. I only poked my head in if I was needed."

"You know where we can contact him?" Phil asked.

"Be right back."

Harvey left the room. Phil stood up and headed for the pot of coffee. He found a cup and poured himself some. He took a sip.

"Yuck. Can't trust a man who likes his coffee weak," Phil joked.

"I can't take caffeine. Shoots you up to high and shoots you down too quickly for my tastes."

"I'm an addict myself. Been that way since I was a kid."

Harvey walked back into the room and handed Robert a piece of paper. "There's his number and address. He lives near the Lawn Bridge apartment complex out in Comstock Park. If you know yer way around there then you should find it just fine. Just don't go barging into his place now. It's late."

Robert stood up. "Thanks Harvey. Sorry to bother you like this but it was important."

Phil finished his cup of coffee and set it on the counter. "Let's go," he said.

****

Xander burst through the doors of Nathan's new office at the capitol. Nathan looked up from his paperwork.

"Yes?"

"My crack staff just gave me an update on the Clarissa Day situation. I learned through a source at her station that earlier in the day Clarissa interviewed Phil McKnight. I checked her phone records and she's made some calls to him within the past couple hours. If you want any chance of finding your wife's body before the public finds out, we keep up our surveillance of McKnight and Miss Day will show up."

"Or we kill her and that McKnight character and not worry about any of this."

"We could do that. Then we would lose the only chance we have to find Eva. We have to find her Nathan. If we don't, either it gets out that you killed her or someone with an enterprising mind holds it over your head and blackmails you."

Nathan ignored Xander and focused on some papers. Xander slammed his fists on the desk.

"Don't you get it? Your grasp on power is thin to begin with, like any politicians. With this left unresolved your power would be nonexistent. Or worse yet, in Joe Wilson's hands. You want him running things?"

Nathan looked up. "Fine. Keep McKnight and the reporter alive. I'll order a wiretap on McKnight and Day's cell phones so we can easily monitor them. Satisfied?"

Xander smiled. "Don't you love your new power?"

****

Phil's cell phone rang. He took it out of his pocket and flipped it open.

"Hello?"

"Phil? It's Clarissa."

"Hey there," Phil said, pressing a button on his phone. "I got you on speaker. What have you got?"

"I hit the jackpot as they say. I came into contact with a secret source that gave me a lot of information concerning Nathan Gibraltar."

"Great. Where you at now?"

"I'm on my way to your office. Decided against going to the station. One more thing. I found out where Nathan Gibraltar is going to be tomorrow."

"What have you heard?"

"He'll be right here in Grand Rapids. He's giving a speech at the grand opening of the Happy Child Book Publishing Company later this morning."

Phil and Robert looked at each other. "Say that again?" Robert asked.

"He's speaking at the grand opening of the Happy Child Book Publishing Company. Why do you ask? Did you find something?"

"We just visited that company's vice president of operations," Phil said. "I'll tell you more when we meet you at the office."

"Bye."

Phil hung up the phone. "What do you think?" he asked Robert.

"He must be having the drugs shipped there. Maybe he's packaging them there too."

"That wouldn't make sense. How the hell would he be able to do that?"

"There is one thing though."

"What's that?"

Robert sat in thought for a moment. "Earlier tonight Leslie had sent me to check out this warehouse. She said Nathan had something devious there. What I ended up finding were some explosives. It wasn't much but enough to cause the owners a lot of money in damages. The place is being used by the Happy Child Publishing Company as a temporary warehouse until the new plant opens."

"Where was it at?"

"About a mile away from the Happy Child plant."

"Damn. What the hell does he have planned?"

****

The doctor injected Eva with more pain medication. She leaned back on the couch and sighed.

"When will my father be back?"

"Soon. I just spoke with him."

"Good."

The doctor packed up and left. Mr. A rubbed his hand over his bandaged wound.

"Life will throw its curve balls at you," Eva said.

"I just can't believe I'm here. If you don't mind my asking, what're your plans now after all this?"

Eva smiled. "Go out to the coast, get together with friends, have a few laughs. Nathan threw down the gauntlet. But it's going to feel painful when I smash it against his damn head."

Mr. A laughed. "Damn. You must be getting better. You're getting feisty."

"I underestimated him. I thought even he had limits. Now that I see he doesn't, I have to toss my limits aside as well."

"A nice woman like you?"

"He shot the nice out of me."

A door opened at the far end of the warehouse. They heard voices. Eva lifted her head to get a glimpse.

A group of three walked towards them. Eva looked at the man in the middle. As he got closer, Eva rose from the couch and walked toward him. She threw her arms around her father.

"Daddy," she said, tears flowing from her eyes.

Tony Palermo clutched his daughter. "Eva my dear, you need to lie back down."

He eased his daughter back on the couch. "I got some news for you," he said.

"What's that?"

"From what I heard, Nathan and Xander still think you're dead."

"You're kidding."

"I don't kid baby. You should know that by now."

"Then let's get out of here. I have an idea."

Tony smiled. "When you get ideas…"

Phil entered his office followed by Robert. Clarissa waited for them by the coffee maker.

"Looks like I beat you here. You two want a cup of coffee?" she asked.

"I'll take one," Phil said.

Clarissa poured him a cup and held it out. He took it and sat at the conference table.

"Where's Stone?"

"He had to take off," Pedro said. "Official police business."

"Oh. I thought he'd call me before he left. So what have you got Clarissa?"

Clarissa put a briefcase on the table, opened it, and passed them the papers inside. Phil and Robert looked them over. The phone rang, breaking their concentration. Phil reached to his desk and grabbed the phone.

"Hello?"

"Phil, it's The Ganj. Something terrible has happened."

"What?"

"That Lydia chick showed up. She killed Darrell and a couple nurses."

Phil went cold. Robert was already off balance. Hearing this news would send him into a place Phil didn't want to imagine. But he had to know what happened.

"Hold on. I'll put you on speaker. Robert needs to hear what you said." Phil pressed the button and put the phone back in the cradle. "Tell us what happened."

The Ganj repeated the news. Robert closed his eyes, preventing tears from coming. Without a word, he collected his things and headed for the door.

"Where are you going?" Phil asked.

Robert ignored him and walked out. Phil called after him but the door slammed shut, giving Phil all the reply he needed. Phil looked at Pedro and Clarissa.

"I think he's lost it," Phil said.

"I'm sure I'd do the same thing in his shoes," Clarissa replied.

"I thought hospitals were supposed to be safe?" Pedro asked.

Phil leaned back in his chair and sighed. "At the moment there's nothing we can do about him. Let's focus on the project at hand. These papers are good. Who was your source Clarissa?"

"A good reporter never reveals her source."

"Gotcha. I find it interesting that Dawson Layfield's name has popped up in here."

"That banker who was killed yesterday?" Clarissa asked.

"Yeah."

"What happened? I haven't seen the news since they turned off my cable," Pedro said.

"A crazy broad with some sweet equipment took him out at the bank. It appeared to be a professional hit."

Clarissa looked up from one of the papers. "What if it was?"

"Huh?" Phil asked.

"What if it was a hit? Read this."

Phil took the paper and inspected it. He read about the ex-Mr. Layfield rejecting loan after loan to Gibraltar Enterprises concerning a projected office building in downtown Grand Rapids. He read about how Nathan Gibraltar used every tool at his disposal to get Dawson Layfield fired and failed. Dawson Layfield beat Nathan Gibraltar at his game. And Layfield ended up paying the ultimate price.

Phil placed the paper back on the table and shook his hand. "If either of you want to leave and go home I'll understand."

"I already know what Nathan Gibraltar is capable of," Clarissa said. "He won't think twice to wipe out his enemies."

"This pays more than my regular job man. I ain't going nowhere," Pedro said.

"Can you use this at the station?" Phil asked Clarissa.

"I can but it's not like I can get anything on the air right now without more concrete proof."

"We might be able to get that proof if we can find the connection the gun woman has in all this. I'll give Stone a call and get to work on that. How much longer you got on decoding that flash drive Pedro?"

"I should have it decoded within an hour."

"Good. I say we get our asses in gear then," Phil said.

****

Horace Spengler walked out the front door of the Pine Oak Mental Health Facility and raised his hands in victory. Finally, freedom. He smiled, thinking of what he would do now that he was out.

A prissy little man in a suit approached him. "Horace Spengler?"

"Yeah? What do you want?"

"I'm Eric Montoya. I'm an aide to Senator Joe Wilson. You heard of him?"

"I'm not a complete imbecile. Of course I have."

"He secured your release in exchange for a little job he needs done. If you follow me I'll fill you in on the details."

This is interesting, Horace thought. He followed the kid to the limo and got in the back. Eric opened up the mini bar and offered the contents to Horace. Horace grabbed a bottle of vodka, opened it, and downed his first gulp of alcohol since before he could remember.

"So what's this job you mentioned?"

"The Senator would like you to find a local private detective named Phil McKnight." Eric handed Horace a folder with Phil's information. "We want you to find him and dispose of him quickly."

"Murder huh?"

"I don't care if you buy him a cruise to the Bahamas. He needs to disappear as quickly as possible."

"And he expects to pay me with only my freedom?"

"I'm sure the Senator would agree to a sum of money upon completion of the assignment."

"What makes you think I'll agree with that?"

"Let me…"

Horace grabbed Eric by the throat. "You don't spring me and tell me good luck. If you want me for a job, you will pay me for it. Now call your boss." He rifled through Eric's pockets until he found his cell phone. He gave it to Eric.

Horace let Eric go. Eric grabbed his cell phone, careful to keep it steady in his shaking hands. He dialed the Senator's number.

"Put it on speaker," Horace demanded.

Eric followed the order. The phone rang a couple times.

"Hello?"

"Senator, it's, uh, Eric. I, I have Mr. Spengler on the line. We're on speaker."

"Horace, glad to hear from you my boy."

"Thank you Senator. So I hear you want me to do a job for you?"

"You came with an excellent recommendation from Eric."

"Oh really."

"Now I need your help."

"Your boy tells me I'm not getting paid for this job," Horace said, leaning back in the limo's seat.

"That's right. I would think your freedom would be compensation enough under the circumstances."

"I want half a million or I won't do anything."

"Now I don't think that's fair after I helped secure your release."

"Can the driver see or hear us through the glass?" he asked Eric.

"No."

Horace lunged at Eric, jamming his fingers into Eric's eyes. Eric screamed, trying his best to get Horace off him. His body writhed. Horace shoved his fingers deeper into Eric's skull. Eric's body shuddered and went limp, sending shivers of delight through his body.

"What was that?" Senator Wilson asked.

"That was your assistant whimpering his way to death."

There was a pause. Then the Senator laughed.

"You drive a hard bargain. I won't pay the half million but I'll see you're taken care of. Do we have a deal?"

"You better keep your word."

"You don't get far in this business by breaking it."

Horace smiled. "Good."

"Take Eric's cell phone. I'll call you soon. You should have all the information you need in the folder in Eric's briefcase. Good hunting."

Horace hung up the phone. Thankfully, he didn't mess up his clothes too much. He wiped his fingers off on his shirt and checked his pockets for his wallet. He found it and looked for cash. Seven hundred forty two dollars. He found the intercom for the driver.

"Driver, take me to Mayer's on Fifty Forth Street. I have to buy some clothes."

He grabbed a bottle of whiskey from the mini bar, opened it up, and poured some in his mouth. He turned to Eric's corpse.

"Want some?"

He poured it into Eric's open mouth and laughed. This was like a fantasy come true.

****

Stone approached Phil's car. "What's up? I heard about that kid dying in the hospital. Is his brother ok?"

"He took off on his own. He didn't tell me where he was going."

"I'm looking the other way with his confession of events yesterday but we gotta make sure he doesn't try anything again."

"Unless I got like seven other people to help, the only way we're going to stop him is if we're able to stop Nathan Gibraltar first. I got something you can help me on though."

"What's that?"

"I've come across some papers that show that Nathan Gibraltar tried to get some loans through Dawson Layfield and that Dawson kept refusing him."

"With Dawson being killed today you think these allude to some sort of assassination attempts?" Stone asked.

"You got it."

"That's pretty weak and circumstantial at best."

"I realize that but I think that if we can find a connection between Annie Walker and Nathan Gibraltar, we'll be able to bring him down, at least in the media."

"What do you propose?" asked Stone.

"Find Annie Walker."

"What? You think you're going to bring her in just like that? I mean, you've got skills and everything but…"

"I'm not saying we bring her in. All I want is to find her. If what you said is true, that her bosses have left her to hang, then maybe she'll hear me out," said Phil.

"She's insane. If you do find her she'll slice you up like a paper shredder."

"After seeing her in action today, I know she'll talk with me. She'll at least give me a minute or two."

"If you find her you have to tell me her location."

"I will."

Stone looked at his friend. He pulled a piece of paper from his pocket.

"I had checked this out earlier but it came to nothing. Some old lady reported seeing a young woman fitting Annie's description go into the sewer through a manhole. Everything looked normal and no one else saw it so I figured the lady was just looking for attention. Maybe I was wrong."

He handed the paper to Phil. "Thanks. I'll keep in touch."

****

Robert lay on the hood of his car staring at the night sky. He felt numb, unable to articulate what he truly felt. The truth seemed unreal. Lydia worked for Nathan Gibraltar. She had been ordered to kill his brother. Nathan Gibraltar had destroyed everything he held dear in life. But why? Why would someone spend their energy trying to destroy someone else? What drives a person to do such evil?

But he couldn't ask that. It was all a matter at this point of deciding if he wanted to ride off into the proverbial sunset and leave things as they were or if he would do something about the evils done to him.

His cell phone rang. He answered.

"Hello?"

"Hello Robert."

Lydia. "Why are you calling me?"

"We need to talk."

"You killed my brother. Why would I want to talk to you?"

"I knew you'd be mad."

"Talk about an understatement."

"Just hear me out. Can you do that?"

He paused. "I'm listening."

"Understand one thing. I did this for you."

"You killed my brother for me. Makes perfect sense."

"Listen. You want Nathan Gibraltar dead. Ever since Darrell showed up you haven't acted right. You even joined up with Phil McKnight."

"Phil told me Leslie mentioned your name in her notes about using me to help Nathan and Wilson's plan to bring in a drug shipment into town. Is that true?"

"Yes. But that doesn't mean there's some grand conspiracy to fool you to do anything. Think about it. Why would Nathan hire someone to kill him?"

"I don't know. Maybe because he's nuts. What about me getting my gun shot out from my hands earlier?"

"You aren't even sure it was a gunshot. You gun could have jammed and it could have jerked upward because of it. You don't know."

"All I know is that you killed my brother. How can I forgive you?"

Robert turned when he heard a noise. "Please try," Lydia said, standing next to the car.

Robert turned off his phone. "How long have you been there?"

"Long enough. Please believe me. I did it for you. Look what Nathan's done to you. To us. You can't let another day pass with him living."

Lydia took Robert's hands and held them. They looked in each other's eyes. He fought in his mind to stay focused on the anger, to realize this woman killed his brother and that she worked for the enemy.

But her eyes.

****

Phil grabbed his phone, trying to turn it on without losing control of the steering wheel. "Yeah."

"It's The Ganj. Things are dull over here. English Bob wants to race wheelchairs in the hallway for cash."

"After you and English Bob getting knocked out and seeing Darrell killed I don't see how you can call things boring."

"It's boring because security has been tripled. I am not needed here. Use me."

"I'm not Princess. Quit having flashbacks."

"Dude."

"Sorry. English Bob is still there so Melissa shouldn't be in too much danger. I could use you."

"Cool. Where do we meet up?"

"Meet at my office. Pedro is still there working on the flash drive."

"What're you up to?"

"Checking out the sewer system. Gotta run."

Phil hung up the phone. He pulled his car to the curb and shut it off. He spotted the manhole cover in the middle of the road. He got out of his car and approached it.

Traffic was nil at this time of night. Phil lifted up the manhole cover and looked inside. Dark as hell. Phil took out a pocket flashlight and descended into the hole. He replaced the cover and headed down the ladder.

He reached bottom and took out his gun. He followed the footpath along the wall of the sewer. What the hell could be down here?

The smell was beyond description. He had to focus on not vomiting to keep what was in his belly down. The water dripped causing little plinks to erupt from the silence around him. His flashlight sliced through the darkness a few paces ahead of him. He had to focus to see what was ahead. He took each step slow to prevent getting an unneeded surprise.

He turned a corner. A dull light glowed ahead. It grew the nearer he got to it. It was an old sewer control room. But this wasn't like any control room he'd even seen. This place was decked out like a nice little apartment. He stepped inside. The moment he stepped through the door, someone put a gun to his temple.

"Howdy stranger."

Phil smiled, trying to hide his shock. "Nice place you got here Annie."

"How did you find out my name?"

"I have my sources. I want to talk."

"We are talking."

"I have a proposition to make."

"I'm already committed."

"Hey, I'm serious here. If I really wanted to turn you over to the police, I'd find a better way to do it than this. Hear what I have to say. Just give me a chance."

A pause, then Annie lowered the gun. She motioned for him to take a seat. He did so. She went to a lounge chair across from him.

"You look different," Phil said.

"Got tired of the old look. So what have you got to say Mr. Private Eye?"

"I assume you're familiar with Nathan Gibraltar."

"Who isn't?"

"I've come across some information that Nathan Gibraltar was having continuing troubles with Dawson Layfield, the man you killed today."

Annie smiled. "You can say that."

"Who hired you to do the job?"

"Why should I tell you?"

"Because I'm trying to stop Nathan Gibraltar."

"What did he do?"

"If I'm open with you will I get the same in return?"

"You'll know if you're still breathing. Continue."

"Nathan Gibraltar and Senator Joe Wilson have orchestrated a plan to bring in a large shipment of cocaine into town and distribute it for cash."

"Why would they do something like that?"

"For no other reason than that they can."

"What information do you have on their little scheme?"

"It all started with a rigged assassination attempt. Senator Wilson found a nut willing to kill Nathan and let him try while Nathan found someone to monitor the guy and prevent him from succeeding."

Annie laughed. "What's so funny?" Phil asked.

"Nothing. Tell me more."

"Nathan used the assassination attempt to somehow force Davis Creston out of office. Being that he's now Governor he's able to move the police force around at will, thus guaranteeing the shipment will come into town and distributed without any interference from law enforcement."

"Pretty sweet deal."

"It is if you're him. But he has to be stopped. Nathan Gibraltar attempted to kill his wife tonight and to kidnap a reporter who was there interviewing her."

"Who was the reporter?"

"Clarissa Day."

Annie stared at him. "How long has she been helping you?"

"For a few hours. We actually met earlier because of a little shindig earlier in the day."

"She saw Nathan shoot his wife?"

"Yes."

"Did he threaten Clarissa?"

"She didn't mention it to me but I have to assume she was threatened. She had to escape."

Annie folded her hands and rested the tips of her fingers on her nose. "What do you need from me?"

"Were you sent to kill Dawson by Nathan Gibraltar?"

"Not him directly but by his chief of staff. I was their assassin for hire."

"What can I use to bring Nathan down?"

"You want him dead?"

"He's come after my family. I could care less what happens to him. I just want to find my wife."

"Noble intentions. How do you propose to reach that goal?"

"Clarissa wants to get a story together linking Dawson Layfield's murder to Nathan Gibraltar. Then he can be brought down before he has any time to react."

"Again, your intentions are noble but are they realistic?" Annie asked.

"When it comes to stopping the drug deal today? Probably not."

"Thank you for being honest. Do you know where he'll be?"

"We think the deal's going down at the Happy Child Book Publishing Company."

"And you want to do what when he's there?"

"Expose the drugs. Then he'll be seen as the scum he is in front of the public and forced out of office."

"You mentioned his wife. Where is she now?"

"Back in Lansing. One of the men he used to dispose of her body discovered she was alive and brought her to get some medical attention."

"Does Nathan know she's alive?"

"From what I've heard, no. But he is aware her body's disappeared."

"Interesting. Now I'm sure you want me to agree to help you."

"I would sure like that."

"I have some items that can link Nathan with Layfield's murder. But I won't give them to you. I'll contact Clarissa Day myself and get them to her. When it comes to that drug deal today, there I can help."

"How so?" Phil asked.

"Less you know the better. I didn't get too far in my line of work without knowing a thing or two about disguise."

"This may be asking a lot but I would like us to stay in contact."

"I'll get your number and call you when the time is right. Don't ask me how, I just will. You won't get my number because I wouldn't want you letting my number slip to your police friend. Now go. We'll be in touch."

****

The aide approached Xander in the hallway. "Sir, I have some news."

"Yes, what is it?"

"That truck you asked to be tracked? We found it. It just came over the Michigan border twenty minutes ago. They'll be in Grand Rapids within the hour." He handed Xander a paper with the truck's current information.

Xander smiled. "Thank you."

Xander left and headed to find Nathan. Nathan was sleeping on the couch in the secretary's office. He headed for the phone on Nathan's desk and dialed one of his associates.

"Hello?"

"It's Xander. I have the coordinates for the truck."

Xander read the coordinates to the person on the phone. "You got it?"

"Yes sir. What would you like us to do?"

"Get that shipment no matter the cost. Kill everyone in that truck. That shipment must get to Grand Rapids in my control."

"Yes sir."

Xander hung up the phone. Finally, Joe Wilson would have to eat some crow.

****

Horace Spengler pushed his cart into the checkout lane and emptied it for the cashier to ring up.

"How you doing today sir?"

"I'm doing swell. How about yourself?"

"Can't wait to get home. Been a long night."

"I can imagine."

"So what's with all the new clothes?"

"Oh, a friend of mine had his eyes on my shirt so I thought I'd get a new one."

"That's nice."

"Just the kind of guy I am."

The cashier finished with the order. Horace paid her and grabbed his bags. He headed for the exit.

As he stepped outside, he took out Eric's cell phone and dialed. He hoped his friend was still home or at least still had the same number.

"Hello?"

"Is this Jenkins?"

"Horace? What the hell are you doing out?"

"I got a get out of the mental institution free card so I decided to use it."

"Oh man. What you up to?"

"I got a little something goin on I could use a little help with. You game?"

"Does it pay?"

Horace stepped into the limo. When the door closed, it drove off.

"Of course. Even got the fancy treatment on this one."

"Sweet. Count me in."

"Then get ready. I'll be by your place before you know it."

Horace hung up the phone. He signaled the driver and told him the new directions. This day was turning out more fun by the minute.

****

Phil took out his phone and dialed Stone's desk at GRPD. He hadn't been able to get a hold of him on his cell phone and thought he may have stopped into work. Just as Phil was about to hang up, someone picked up the phone.

"Hello?"

"Can I speak to Stone Campbell please?"

"He's not in at the moment. This is Detective Cooper. Can I help you?"

"Yes. This is Phil McKnight. I got some information for him regarding the Dawson Layfield case."

"Alright. Where are you at?"

Phil told him his location. "I'll tell Stone when he gets back in which should be soon and I'll send him out to your location ASAP."

"Uh, thanks," Phil said.

Phil hung up. He called his office.

"Hello?"

"Pedro. The Ganj there yet?"

"Yeah. He just got here. Hold on."

A pause. "Hello?"

"Ganj, it's me. I'm not able to get to the office right away so I need you to get your ass over to David Geraldson's house and find out what he knows. I have to wait for Stone to give him a report."

"He out having a donut or something?"

"Stop. He's a good guy."

"Whatever. You gonna meet me over at Geraldson's when you're done?"

"I'll try."

"There's more money for me though right?"

"Actually it's for Princess but I thought I'd humor you," Phil said.

"Funny. I'll see you."

****

Senator Wilson sat back in his chair and reflected on events. Phil McKnight. Who would have thought a failure of a private eye would be so aggressive in finding information? Nothing was making him stop. Then an idea, a crazy idea hit him. What if he called Phil? Told him the news about his wife? He looked through his notes and found Phil's number. He picked up the phone and dialed.

"Hello?"

"Mr. McKnight. This is Senator Joe Wilson."

A pause. "To what do I owe the pleasure?"

"Why are you still looking into things that don't concern you?"

"Because you people wanted to make this personal."

"It was not my intention to do so Mr. McKnight. I'm a businessman and, like any other businessman, will do what it takes to prevent any threat to my business. This you must understand."

Phil snorted. "But why would a prominent politician like you be involved in a drug deal?"

"Sometimes the most simple of tasks can reap the most reward."

"And if you get caught?"

"I won't. That reminds me, I have someone you'll want to talk to. Hold on a sec."

Joe pressed a few buttons, putting Phil on mute. He pressed another one and reached Laura in her cell.

"Mrs. McKnight?"

"What do you want?"

"I have Phil on the phone. Hold on."

Joe turned off the mute button. "Your wife is on the line. Talk to them when you're ready."

"Laura?" Phil asked.

"Phil? Is that you?" Laura responded.

"Where are you at?"

"They kidnapped me. I'm at the Gypsum mine in Wyoming. Where's Ty?"

"He's safe. I have him staying at a safe house."

"Good. Get me out of…"

Joe shut off her connection. "I hope you realize how determined I am to see this go down," Joe said.

"You hurt her I'll kill you."

"Sure you will. If you want her back in one piece, go home and go to bed. And if you're entertaining some heroic rescue at the Gypsum mine, keep in mind I have a small armada keep guard over her."

The Senator hung up the phone.

****

They pulled up alongside the truck to get confirmation it was the right one. They got what they needed. Now was the time to move.

The car moved closer and closer until the driver slammed the car into the driver's side door of the truck. The truck pulled over to the side of the road. The four men in the car pulled behind, shut off the engine, and got out.

The two men in the truck approached, looking like they were ready to pound someone or something to smithereens. But before they had a chance to react, the four men pulled out guns and shot the occupants of the truck dead. The driver of the car checked the pulses on the bodies to be sure. Once he determined they were dead, he turned to one of the men.

"It's done. Take the truck to Grand Rapids."

"Yes sir."

Two of the men ran into the truck, started it up, and drove off. The car driver got back in the car and took out his cell phone. He dialed Xander.

"Yes?"

"The shipment is secure. It's on the way to Grand Rapids."

"Good."

The driver hung up the phone. The rest of this trip would be easy. Now he'd be able to take a breather.

****

Xander smiled at the good news. Something was finally going his way.

Footsteps got his attention. He turned his head. An aide approached him.

"What is it?" he asked.

"We just found something interesting from McKnight's phone tap. Here's the text of the conversation."

Xander took the paper and read it over. The more he read the more he tried not to chuckle.

"Thanks," he said, dismissing the aide. He headed back to Nathan's office to show him the paper.

Nathan still lay snoozing on the couch. Xander nudged him.

"What?" Nathan grumbled.

"I think you want to read this."

Nathan took the paper and started reading. The more he read, the more awake he became. When he finished he sat up and handed it back to Xander.

"I think we found a way to cut Wilson out and silence McKnight," Xander said.

"I don't think that's wise in regards to Wilson."

"Why?"

"He still has things in his favor that make him useful to us. I say we renegotiate the deal he forced out of us and put him back in his place."

Xander paused. "You're right. Besides, I just got word the shipment is back in our hands anyway. He's not in any shape to argue with us."

"And McKnight?"

"That's being taken care of as we speak."

****

Phil spotted the car as it approached him and wondered who it could be. It came to a stop and two men stepped out.

"Mr. McKnight?"

"Yeah."

"I'm Detective Cooper of the GRPD. This is my partner Detective Tennant," he said, pointing to the passenger.

"Where's Stone at?"

"He couldn't make it. He asked to come in his place. Did you find Annie Walker?"

"I uh, no. I didn't."

"That's too bad. It's too bad for Stone as well. Mr. McKnight, I'm going to have to place you under arrest. Please put your hands on the hood of the car."

Phil turned around. What was this? he thought. Did Stone actually get him arrested?

3:00 AM-4:00 AM

The decryption of the flash drive was complete. Pedro opened the file and began reading its contents.

This can't be right, he thought. He read the text again. What the hell is this Blue Harvest? The more he read, the more terror he felt. He had to call Phil. He had to warn him that this whole business had nothing to do with drugs. Pedro saved the files onto Phil's computer and reached for a phone.

The door to Phil's office crashed open and a man ran in, gun in hand. He grabbed a frightened Pedro from the chair he was sitting in. The man threw Pedro to the ground. Ignoring Pedro's pleas, the man fired.

Pedro slumped to the floor. The man stepped over to the desk and took the flash drive from the computer. Without another glance, he turned and left.

Once the door closed, Pedro opened his eyes. He was going to die. But before his body shut down, he had to make sure Phil found out the truth. He crawled across the floor to the desk. He pulled on the phone cord until it fell to the ground. He picked it up and the redial button. He waited.

"Hello? Clarissa Day."

"It's Pedro… At Phil's office."

"I can barely hear you."

"I read what was on the flash drive. People came and shot me. I'm dying."

"My God. Where's Phil at?"

"I don't know. Find him and tell him things aren't what they seem. The drugs are a cover. Blue Harvest."

"What was that?"

Pedro couldn't respond. His head hit the floor. He was dead.

****

The Ganj knocked on David Geraldson's door and waited. Damned rich people and their big ass homes, he cursed. He knocked again, hoping that the force he put into knocking could be heard by someone in this mammoth house.

Success. A light turned on. The Ganj spotted someone approaching the door.

"Who is it?" a voice asked.

"I need to speak with David Geraldson."

"Do you realize what time it is?"

"What the fuck do you think this is? A makeup sales pitch? Open your goddamn door."

"Who are you?"

"All you need to know is that this concerns Nathan Gibraltar."

The man paused then opened the door. "Come in."

The Ganj stepped into the foyer and followed the man into the living room. David pointed to a chair.

"Take a seat. I'll fix you a drink." He went to the bar. "So what brings you here?"

"You are David Geraldson I presume?"

"Yeah."

"What kind of contact have you had with Nathan Gibraltar and Joe Wilson?"

"They were both a big help in bringing Happy Child to Grand Rapids. They've both monitored the entire process. Why do you ask?"

"I have reason to believe that they will be using the grand opening ceremonies tomorrow for something illegal."

David laughed, handing The Ganj his drink. "Why would two prominent people like that do something stupid?"

"Because they can."

"Hell, I can wear a dress and sing calypso music but I don't." David took a seat on the couch.

"I have enough evidence that shows Nathan Gibraltar is up to no good."

"Then why are you here? Why not go to the police?"

"Why bother them when it can be stopped before it begins?"

"Touché. How's the drink?"

The Ganj took a sip. "Very good."

"Good. So what do you think my involvement is?"

"Your name was in pa…"

The Ganj's jaw went limp. He tried to talk but his muscles wouldn't cooperate. Before he could react, he slipped to the floor.

****

David Geraldson picked up the fallen glass off the floor. He grabbed a blanket off the couch and laid it on The Ganj. That would take care of the bastard for a while.

He went over to the phone and called Xander.

"Hello?"

"It's David. I just got a visit from one of McKnight's men, just like you said."

"Where is he?"

"Passed out on my living room floor."

"Good. Any other problems give me a call."

"There better not be any more problems. Too many people know what's going down already and I'm getting uncomfortable."

"Calm down David. Things are under control. The loose elements in this equation are being taken care of as we speak. Just a few more hours and you'll be a rich man."

"Alright. This little visit has just unnerved me that's all."

"I understand. Hold McKnight's man until I send someone over to pick him up."

David hung up the phone. I hope Xander's right, he thought to himself.

****

Clarissa paced through her living room, realizing something terrible had happened to Pedro. She had to do something but what? What could she do to help?

Phil had to hear about this but he wasn't answering his phone. She felt a part of the team and everything but she sure as hell wasn't in a position to take charge and lead. She had to reach Phil in order to help fix things.

She went to her kitchen and grabbed an apple. She took a bite. What was she to do? The only thing she could do, work. At least she'd be able to bring down Nathan that way. Phil could take care of the problems at his office. She headed into her office and started up her computer.

An email alert flashed on the screen. She clicked on it and was directed to her in box. There was no name from the sender. Usually she'd delete messages like that but the subject line caught her attention.

It read 'Audio proof connecting Nathan Gibraltar to Dawson Layfield's murder.'

It couldn't be. Someone had to be playing a joke on her. She opened up the email. There was no text, just the option to download an audio file. She clicked on it and waited.

Finally, the file opened onto her audio player. She pressed play.

Nathan: 'Is your person in place?'

Xander: 'Yeah. They'll take care of Dawson Layfield tomorrow morning.'

Nathan: 'I don't want any mistakes on this one. I want that son of a bitch dead.'

Clarissa gasped. Seeing Nathan shoot his wife was one thing. This, this was the bomb she needed to derail that monster. There was another audio file. She clicked play.

Nathan: 'That son of a bitch denied me again. Who does he think he is denying me that loan?'

Xander: 'That's his job Nathan.'

Nathan: 'Refusing me that loan will cost me millions. No one costs me that kind of money.'

Xander: 'What are you saying?'

Nathan: 'I think you know what I'm saying. I want that son of a bitch's throat sliced. Got me?''

He was killed with a knife in the throat. My God, who did she have to thank for this? She had to get this to the station. If this couldn't get on the air then maybe she should consider another career.

****

Xander hung up the phone and couldn't stop smiling. What a scare today had been. And now, thanks to a detective on the payroll in the Grand Rapids Police Department, Phil McKnight was behind bars. The loose ends were tying up nicely.

The shipment had arrived in Grand Rapids. It was under guard by men whose reputations he knew, whose reputations he'd helped make. So barring any unforeseen problems, the rest of the day would go smooth.

Nathan stepped into the office, rubbing the sleep out of his eyes. "I don't know how that crotchety old man slept on that couch."

"It's what helped him stand so tall and erect."

"So what's the word?"

Xander smiled. "McKnight is in jail."

"Well I'll be."

"We're not out of the clear yet. There's been no word on Eva's whereabouts."

"Why are you so dramatic about it? Didn't you report her missing like I asked?"

"I did. But we have to consider the option that she's alive."

"Do I have to tell you again? I didn't miss."

"Many great men have been destroyed over their ego. Fine, you think you killed her? You go right ahead and continue thinking that. At least be smart enough to have a contingency plan if she is alive. You don't want to get caught with your knickers down."

Nathan paused. "What should the plan be?"

"Her father. Sure, she didn't have contact with him. She hated the life he chose to live. But she still loves the guy otherwise he'd have been in jail a long ago. I can guarantee you that if Onyx saved her, he'll be letting us know before she goes public. When that happens, we'll make them the proverbial offer they won't be able to refuse. Make them think twice about trying something stupid."

"You think that will work?"

Xander smiled. "Of course it will. Get some more rest. We're leaving at five on the button."

Nathan saluted and went back to his office. Xander didn't want him in the room for this next call. He picked up the phone and dialed.

"Hello?"

"Senator Wilson. I have some good news."

"What's that?"

"The shipment is safe in Grand Rapids under armed guard. My armed guards."

Silence. "That's right Joe," Xander continued. "Things have changed and our original deal will stand. I'm an honorable man and do what I can to keep my word. Rest assured, if you try to deceive us again, the tape I have in my possession of your conversation with Phil McKnight will reach the press. Got me?"

A pause. "I understand."

"Good. Oh, you can call your man off Phil McKnight. He's in jail. That's yet another mess I took care of for you."

Xander hung up the phone. There might even be time for a nap now for himself before heading back to Grand Rapids.

****

Annie clenched her fists in anger. Her computer showed her some news she didn't want to see. Xander had Phil put in jail. He had better not have any plans for Clarissa.

She read over Phil's arrest report again. Detective Randy Cooper, a man she'd long known to have been employed by Xander, arrested Phil for refusing to divulge the location of a known fugitive. He probably didn't have much in the way of proof but it would keep Phil locked up long enough for the drug deal to go down.

She had to act. But how? She searched through the police data systems some more looking for any more information pertaining to Phil. One name that popped up often was Stone Campbell. He was the officer assigned to her case. She'd heard of him before. He didn't have any agenda when it came to his job. He only wanted to find the bad guys. Even though in her case she was the bad guy, she still respected what he stood for. You always knew where a person like that stood. The people who preached about their high moral codes were often the ones you had to watch.

She read his number off the screen and dialed him. Her phone was secure so she had no worry about her number being traced.

"Hello?"

"Am I speaking to Detective Stone Campbell?"

"Yes?"

"Phil McKnight has been arrested by Detective Randy Cooper. Get him out of jail now if you want to stop Nathan Gibraltar."

"Who is this?"

"Maybe one day you'll find out but for now you have to get Phil. More important things are going down then the answer to my identity."

"I'll check into it and if you're right, he will be out. You have to tell me who you are though."

"Um, no."

Annie hung up the phone. She had to leave. She couldn't take the chance that Phil would tell the police her location. Not that she thought he would but anyone under duress would say things to stop the abuse. It was a damned shame too. This was a great little hiding spot.

Oh well. There were others.

****

English Bob stepped out into the hallway and saw it empty. This ain't right, he thought. He ran down to Melissa's room to check on her and Roni.

"Everything all right in here?" he asked.

"What's going on?" asked Roni.

"When someone's murdered on this floor yet security still avoids this floor like there's a plague outbreak that tells me something's going down. You have a car Roni?"

"Yeah. Across the street."

"Good. Help Melissa get dressed. We gotta get out of here."

Roni stood up. "What the hell's going on? Are we going to be all right?"

"I'm telling you my gut feeling. That feeling has kept me alive."

"It also put you in a building that was blown up."

"So it ain't perfect. Please get ready."

He left Melissa's room and headed back to his own. He reached into the closet and took out his clothes that survived the explosion. His pants were still in one piece so he put them on. His shirt was in tatters. He checked to see if his roommate was up. He wasn't. He opened the other closet and checked the size of the shirt. It was ugly as hell but it would fit. He put it on, grabbed the man's shoes, tossed them on the floor, and put them on. Once he was finished, he ran back to Melissa's room. The curtain around her bed was closed.

"Ok in there?" he asked.

"She's still getting dressed. We'll be out in a minute," Roni said.

English Bob headed back to the doorway and waited. The hallway lay deserted, eerily so. He checked the lights over the doors of the rooms. Several had their nurse's lights blinking. The nurses had not been around to turn them off. Maybe they hadn't been around yet. Or maybe they weren't around at all.

The curtain rolled back. English Bob turned and faced the two women.

"Ready?"

"Ready as I'll ever be," Melissa said.

"Hold on."

English Bob went back out into the hallway and grabbed the first wheelchair he found. He wheeled it back to the room. Roni eased Melissa onto the chair. The three walked out into the hallway and headed for the elevators.

They walked down the empty hallway, each not sure of the danger around them but nonetheless aware that the danger was there. Patients in their rooms were becoming vocal, doing what they thought necessary to get a nurse in their room to give them medication, change their bedpans, or whatever else was needed.

They reached the elevator bank. English Bob pressed the down button. They waited.

Then they heard the scream coming from one of the rooms they'd just passed. A man dressed in black walked out. He held a large knife in his hand. English Bob pressed the button repeatedly, hoping the elevator would come faster. The man spotted them and started running.

The elevator dinged and the doors opened. The three ran onto the elevator. English Bob pressed the button for the ground floor. The elevator doors were slow in closing.

The man ran to the elevator and just as the doors closed, he jammed his arm with the knife in the door. He swung it around, hoping to hit a target.

English Bob grabbed the man's arm. "My sister taught me this trick," he said to the two women.

He bit into the man's arm. The man screamed but didn't let go. The elevator doors opened and the man walked inside. With his free hand, he started punching English Bob in the head. English Bob clamped down harder on the arm, causing the knife to clatter to the ground. The doors closed and the elevator descended.

English Bob rammed his left elbow into the man's face. The second swing caused a sick cracking noise to come from the man's nose, forcing the man to his knees.

English Bob picked up the knife, turned, and jammed it into the man's chest. He twisted the blade to make sure the wound wouldn't close. The man clutched at the knife, stumbled to the back of the elevator car, and slid to the ground, dead.

The elevator reached the ground floor and the doors opened. Roni wheeled Melissa out of the elevator. English Bob was on their heels. An old couple stood waiting to get on.

"You don't want to go on there," English Bob said.

The door closed before the couple could see what was left behind. English Bob led the women through the lobby to the front door. The woman at the information desk rose.

"Where are you going with that wheelchair?" she demanded.

"We're using it for religious purposes," English Bob said, opening the door. Roni pushed Melissa outside.

English Bob scanned the area as they headed for the parking garage across the street. Everything seemed clear. This made him more nervous then he wanted to feel. They reached the crosswalk and crossed the empty street. They ran into the parking garage.

"Where's your car at?" English Bob asked.

"Second level," Roni said.

"Figures."

They hopped on the elevator and pressed the button for the second floor. It rose up and stopped. The doors opened and they walked out.

The lights of the parking garage were out. Roni directed them to where her car was parked. English Bob scanned the area, not wanting to be surprised again. They reached Roni's car.

"I think I should drive," English Bob said.

"Why? Don't you have a concussion?"

"If we're chased, and I'm more than confident we will be, I've had experience in driving a car through city streets at top speed. Have you?"

Roni paused. "Just get us out of here alive." Roni handed him her keys.

English Bob helped Melissa into the car. Roni got into the passenger seat. English Bob got behind the wheel, and started the car.

"Bye bye, bad guys."

He pulled out of the spot and headed for the exit. As they made the first turn they saw another man with a gun standing in their way, gun raised at the car's windshield. English Bob floored the gas and ran him over. He stopped the car, got out, and picked up the man's gun. Before he got back in the car, he shot the man in the head.

"What did you do that for?" Melissa asked when English Bob got back in.

English Bob raised the gun. "Insurance."

They continued to the exit. The gate was up but in its place were three gunmen with guns drawn. English Bob took out the gun, put it out the window, and started firing. The men tried to stand their ground but as the car got closer, they dove to avoid it. English Bob broke through and made his escape.

"Now that wasn't so hard was it?" English Bob laughed.

"Where are we going?" Roni asked.

"I have a friend that'll take you to his place up north in Big Rapids till this blows over. Then I gotta call Phil."

****

Stone approached Randy Cooper at his desk. "Where the hell is McKnight?"

"He's in a holding cell waiting for a ride to Kent County Correctional Facility."

"Why?"

"He knew where Annie Walker is and didn't divulge her location. So he's in for aiding and abetting."

"He told you he met her and he won't tell you where she's at?"

"Frankly, you need to stop worrying about McKnight and start worrying about your own ass. Why have you been covering up for this bumbling fool for so long?"

Stone paused. "You know what's going on don't you."

"I don't know anything and if you want a job you'll forget what you know as well."

Detective Cooper rose and walked away. Stone stood there. How can I get Phil out? he thought. Without losing my job.

He couldn't do anything but investigate the mess Nathan Gibraltar and Joe Wilson were planning. There was no use joining Phil in jail when he could actually do some good out here.

He could do one thing though. He took out his cell phone and dialed.

"Hello?"

"Clarissa?"

"Yes."

"It's Stone Campbell. Phil McKnight has been arrested."

"For what?"

"It's a BS charge to keep him in jail so the drug deal can go down. There's nothing I can do to stop this from happening on my end."

"Oh my God."

Stone checked the papers on Randy's desk. "It looks like he's going to be transported at the top of the hour to the Kent County Jail. I know there's not much you can do but as long as you have a quote from someone then maybe I've done my share."

"This isn't good."

"Look, I gotta go. I'll call you later."

****

The Ganj yawned and opened his eyes. His hands were bound to a wall. He was trapped like a prisoner back in the days of knights and dragons. What the fuck kind of twisted shit is this? he thought.

"So you're up."

The Ganj turned his head. David Geraldson sat in a chair against the wall.

"I think you answered all my questions," The Ganj said.

"Oh yeah? What questions would that be?"

"What's going down when Nathan comes to town."

"I get paid, that's what happens. And that's all you need to know."

"So you're using the book company to distribute drugs?"

"What? You think we're gonna sell a coloring book with an eight ball of coke?"

"Then what's the plan?"

"You would like to know wouldn't you?"

"If I'm trapped here then what's the point in not telling me?"

"So you want me to be like an action movie villain and tell you the whole evil, diabolical scheme?"

"Sounds about right."

"Maybe later."

David Geraldson turned and left the room. The Ganj tested the strength of his restraints. Solid metal. He walked right into this. If it wouldn't hurt, he'd have kicked himself.

****

Tony gave his daughter a glass of water and took a seat across from her. "I can't believe you're alive. Why didn't you come to me when he started beating you?"

"I had an image I wanted to keep and I guess I didn't want to be associated with you. Kind of hard for a politician to keep their job if one of their family members is a mobster."

"Well, the idea of mobsters and politicians working together is not as foreign an idea as you may think."

"What do you mean?"

"I had a hand in Nathan being made Governor."

"Why?"

"You don't need to know the gist of it. Its better that you don't actually. As to the why, I guess I felt this was a way to contribute to your well being."

"Why couldn't you..."

"Please. I made a mistake. I should have stepped in the first moment I heard of him hitting you."

"We could go at this all day. We both made mistakes when it came to trusting Nathan. For my part, I forgive you for not stepping in. Frankly neither of us knew what he was capable of."

Tony smiled. "Thank you. That means a lot."

"What I think we should be spending our time on is bring Nathan down."

"How do you propose that?"

"Give me a phone. I got someone to call."

Tony picked up a cordless phone and handed it to his daughter. She dialed.

"Hello?"

"Clarissa? It's Eva."

"You're ok. Thank goodness."

"Yes. Had a good doctor fix me up. I'm at my father's house now."

"Is it safe there?"

"You don't know my Dad. It's safe. I'm just wondering how far along on the story you are?"

"Several developments have arisen concerning Nathan. He's involved in a drug deal."

"Let me put you on speaker." Eva pressed the button. "My father is with me. Can you repeat that?"

"Nathan Gibraltar becoming Governor is no accident. It was all part of a plan to bring in a shipment of cocaine into town for the money."

"Why would he do that?" Eva asked.

"Because as Governor he'd be able to manipulate the police so he can get the most for his money and to direct them away from his little scheme," Tony said.

"You must be Eva's father. That's right," Clarissa said. "To top that off he's arrested a private detective who's been compiling evidence against him just to keep him off the streets while this goes down."

"Oh no," Eva said.

Her father rose. "I think this is something I can help with."

"How do you propose that sir?" Clarissa asked.

"You'll see. Can you give me the name of that private detective?"

"Phil McKnight."

"Good. I'll call some friends up."

"I'm glad to hear you doing well Mrs. Gibraltar. And I promise you, Nathan will pay for what he's done."

"Thank you Clarissa. One thing. Please call me by my maiden name of Palermo."

"I will."

Eva hung up the phone and tossed it to her father. "What's your plan Dad?"

Tony smiled. "Daddy knows best, right?"

****

Horace stepped out of the limo in his new threads and smiled. He headed for his friend's house. The cell phone began to ring.

"What?" he yelled.

"Don't you dare talk to me like that."

"Ahh, Senator. How can I help you?"

"There's been a complication. I have to call you off Phil's trail."

Horace frowned. "Why's that?"

"Phil McKnight has been arrested. Your purpose has ended."

"Excuse me?"

"When it comes to payment, consider your freedom payment in full."

The Senator hung up. Horace turned the phone off and put it back in his pocket. You don't promise me riches and pull back at the last minute. Who do you think you are? he thought.

He stepped onto his friend's porch and pounded on the door. The music in the house stopped and the door opened. A tall man dressed in boxer shorts answered.

"Holy shit. They let you out."

"That's right. I got me a limo and some cash too. Wanna play?"

****

Xander received the transcript from the aide and read it over. When through, he read it again. If this were true, then he'd better begin planning for the worst. He headed for Nathan's office.

"What now?" asked Nathan.

Xander handed him the paper. Nathan read it over. When he finished, he put the paper on his desk and bowed his head.

"Do you have any suggestions? Xander asked.

"You've dealt with Tony more than me. You find him and take both of them out."

"I don't think that's wise. Your wife will bring an end to you the moment her body surfaces."

Nathan grabbed a coffee cup on the desk and threw it at Xander's head. Xander ducked.

"Just do what I say or I'll find another chief of staff."

Xander turned and left the room. Under other circumstances, he'd have made sure Nathan knew who was really the boss. But the day wasn't over yet.

****

Robert finished packing the bomb back into the box. This about cleared up the mess he made earlier at the warehouse scouring for these things. He walked to the front office of the warehouse where Lydia was fixing things up nice. He wrapped his arms around her from behind.

"Are you done?" Lydia asked.

"Everything's back where it was."

"Good. That should give Nathan and Xander a surprise."

"What's your ultimate plan?"

"Nathan and Xander think I'm on their side. We use that to our advantage. When they expect the fireworks here to erupt at eight thirty, they'll be thrown off when they don't. Then at eight forty five, boom."

Robert smiled. "Yeah. That's when I'll kill him."

"No, no. Not when the police smell danger. You do it just as he's ready to leave. His security will most likely bring Nathan into the building until they feel the area is secure. When they lead him out, then pop goes the weasel."

"That's exactly what I want to hear."

"Those two have strung me along for too long. What put it over the top is what they were doing to you."

"Why didn't you try to say anything to me before?"

Lydia kissed his cheek. "I was finding the time."

He kissed her. "I'll give the warehouse one more look through before we go," he said.

He left the office. He turned his head and saw that her attention was on other things. He went to the side of the office door, knelt, and waited. After a few moments, he heard Lydia stop. She pulled out her phone and dialed.

"Hello...I've reached Robert again...The plan is back on track."

Robert lowered his head. His hunch was right. He smiled. At least he knew where things stood.

4:00 AM-5:00 AM

The officer handcuffed Phil to another prisoner and clamped the cuffs on tight. Phil winced. The officer led them out the doors into the parking garage to a waiting van. He opened up the back and shoved them inside, strapping them to their seats. He closed the doors and headed to the front, climbing into the driver's seat.

The van started and it pulled out of the garage onto the road. It took a left and headed toward the light. Phil turned to the prisoner.

"Been here long?"

The prisoner replied in Spanish. Phil nodded and turned, watching what view he could get through the grating on the window.

A bang knocked Phil into the side of the van. The van tipped over. The two in the cage tumbled around like laundry, being bumped and bruised from all the metal inside. Phil heard a crack. The Spanish prisoner went limp, causing his now lifeless body to bang into Phil more. Finally, the van came to a stop.

Gunshots rang out. Phil hid behind the dead prisoner for protection. Finally, silence. The driver's side door opened and someone grabbed the guard's keys. A moment later the back door to the van opened.

"Mr. McKnight?" a woman's voice asked.

Phil moved the prisoner's body. "Yeah."

The woman reached in and grabbed Phil's arm, unlocking the handcuffs. She pulled him out of the van.

"What the hell is going on?" Phil asked.

The woman handed Phil his bag of belongings. "A grateful man has secured your release. Just don't get caught again."

The woman started to walk off. "What? You're going to just leave me here a couple blocks away from the police station?" Phil yelled after her.

"Yer supposed to follow me silly. I'll take you to your car."

Phil shook his head and followed the woman.

****

Clarissa went into her editor's office with the CD she'd burned of Nathan Gibraltar's conversation. Stu looked up from his paper work and gave her a condescending smile.

"My star reporter. How may I serve you today?"

"I would like to do a story on Nathan Gibraltar."

"What now?"

Clarissa put the CD in his CD player and played it. He sat at the desk listening, his face non-committal. When finished, she turned to him.

"Well?" she asked.

"So Nathan talks like a brute. Nixon swore up a storm on his tapes but that didn't make him a terrible guy."

"Did you not hear what he was talking about?"

"Yeah. I talked with a guy about how a woman looked good in a red dress. That doesn't mean I'm going to go out and buy the dress for myself."

Clarissa clutched her fists. "I witnessed Nathan Gibraltar shoot his wife in the chest."

"Do you have the video or the body?"

"No but..."

"But I don't want to hear it. I've gotten a complaint from the new Governor's office concerning you anyway and your actions yesterday. Since you've shown me by your actions that your emotions will cloud your judgment, I'm going to have to suspend you."

Clarissa stood and walked over to his desk. "You fat worthless piece of trash."

"Don't try and flatter me."

She circled the desk and grabbed his hair. "Listen. You want to suspend me. Fine. You can find yourself an ignorant bimbo who can sound like she's intelligent to go to your flower shows, take your sexual advances, and pretend as if she's interested unlike me. Consider this my resignation."

Clarissa slapped him in the face, turned, and left. She wanted to clear her desk before he had a chance to call the police.

****

Laura lay on the bed, unable to sleep. How could she with what was going on? When was she going to get out of this so she could see her boy?

She should have known better. Being in security work, she should have been aware that something was wrong. With someone that paranoid, she should have sensed the danger.

Stop kicking yourself, she thought. You weren't expecting this. There's no use getting yourself down when you need to keep attentive. Her cell door opened and someone came in. They wheeled something in on a cart.

"What's going on?" Laura asked.

"Just bringing you some food, ma'am," a voice replied.

The person took some items off the cart and placed them on a table. The noise stopped. The person walked over and grabbed Laura's hand, pulling her up. She was led across the cell and set in a chair. The person laid her hands on the utensils.

"I'll be back in fifteen minutes to take these. Now eat up."

The guard left, the door shutting with a clank. She felt the cold metal of her fork and butter knife. Her hand explored the fork. She smiled, the idea popping in her mind exciting her.

****

Phil got out of the car. He thanked the woman for dropping him off then ran to his car. Once inside, he pulled out his cell phone and dialed a number.

"Hello?"

"Clarissa?"

"Phil? You got out?"

"You can say that. How are things with you?"

"I no longer have a job."

"You're kidding me."

"No. I gave everything I compiled to my editor about Nathan Gibraltar and he rejected it. He even suspended me because of my supposed harassment of the Gibraltar family."

"Oh man. That leaves us to ourselves. What are you doing now?"

"I'm heading home for the night. This has taxed me beyond belief."

"Don't do that. I could use your help. I've seen your work and you're one hell of an investigator."

"I'm just a reporter."

"A reporter is just an investigator without a gun. You just won't be on TV anymore."

"What? Are you hiring me?"

"Well if you think about it, it would make a snappy business name. McKnight and Day. You're good at what you do and damn it, any help I can get the better."

"You drive a hard bargain. How much you offering?"

"You make what you earn."

"Sounds good to me."

"Meet me at my office. We've got some things to discuss."

Phil hung up the phone. He started up the car and drove off.

****

Horace sat back in the chair and put his arm around Eric's corpse. "So buddy, got your eyes on any women? No? Oh, one of those types I guess."

Horace motioned for something from the mini bar. His friend, Jenkins, passed him some whiskey.

"Where we headed?" Jenkins asked.

"To some punk ass PI's office. The good Senator Wilson wants me to think this guy's in jail so he doesn't have to give me any cash. I say fuck that Dutch bastard; I'm earning me some money."

"What about the douche up front?"

Horace chuckled. "Slice, dice, and everything nice is what I say."

The two men raised a toast to their insanity. Horace pushed the intercom button.

"Driver."

"Yes sir."

"Take me to Riverside Park. It's just a couple blocks up on your left."

"Yes sir."

Horace turned to his friend. "I got me an idea."

"What?"

"You'll see."

After a minute or so, the limo pulled into the park's parking lot. A chained gate prevented the limo from entering the park. Horace pressed the intercom.

"Drive through the chain."

"I'm afraid I can't do that sir."

Horace grabbed one of Jenkins's toys, a handgun, and used the butt of it to smash the divider glass. He grabbed the driver by the hair.

"I didn't take my medicine today so I suggest you listen to everything I have to say. Drive though that chain. Slam that foot of yours on the gas."

The driver followed orders. The limo shattered the chain. The driver drove the car into the main parking lot and stopped it by the fishing dock, putting the limo in park.

Horace climbed through the divider. The glass that remained tore into his flesh but the pain he felt only made him more excited. He got into the passenger seat.

"Out of the car, Slappy."

The driver got out, Horace behind him. Jenkins got out of the back with his bag full of toys.

"Toss me some cuffs," Horace asked Jenkins. His friend reached into his bag and tossed them to Horace. Horace smiled and turned to the limo driver.

"Follow me."

Horace brought the driver to one of the poles by the fishing dock. He forced the driver to sit with his back against the pole and cuffed his hands. Horace turned to his friend.

"Park the limo in front of this guy. And toss me a knife, some fishing string, and some tape."

Jenkins tossed Horace the items and got into the limo, positioning the trunk in front of the pole. Horace knelt in front of the driver.

"Listen, you're a victim of circumstance. Your employer decided to stiff me on money he owed and the only way I can get his attention is by doing this. So when you come back to Earth as a ghost, haunt that son of a bitch for me so he learns not to stiff anyone else. And while you're up there, tell God I said hi."

Horace ripped off some tape and put it over the driver's mouth. He took the knife from his pocket sliced a hole in the driver's belly. The screams, though muffled from the tape, were still loud enough to demonstrate the agony the driver was going through. He slipped his hand into the hole and dug around for what he was looking for. He found it, the small intestines. He pulled out some and cut it. Horace tied the fishing string around the moist innards. He tied the other end of the fishing string to the limo's bumper.

"You see," Horace turned back to the driver, "this is a modified version of an old torture technique. As the limo slowly drives away, your small intestine will follow. Kind of like the cans they tie to limos for weddings. Only longer and more moist. The more that gets pulled out of you, the less time you have to live."

Horace stood up. He hit the trunk of the limo. "Hit the gas Jenkins. Nice and slow."

****

Laura finished her food and tried not to vomit. She knew she would need the energy for what she had planned but boy, would it have hurt the Senator to serve her some better food? She pushed the plate away.

The door clanged open. Laura grabbed the fork and palmed her hand over it. The guard grabbed her other hand and helped her up. He led her across the cell to the bed.

"Here we are."

"Thanks," said Laura.

She swung her arm up and jammed the fork into the guard's neck, covering his mouth to prevent his scream from getting past his lips. She ripped off the man's infrared goggles and put them on her head. The cell appeared to her as if a hallucination clouded in emeralds. She checked the person for any weapons and found a gun. She took out the clip, saw it was full, and headed out of the cell.

Someone spotted her and yelled. She turned toward the direction of the elevator and ran. She fired off a shot behind her. Shots came back in return. She weaved, trying to make the chance of her being a clear shot slim.

She rounded a corner and spotted the elevator. The elation she felt made her feel like a balloon ready to pop. She sprinted for the elevator entrance.

Someone tripped her, sending her sprawling to the ground. They tried ripping the goggles off her head to bring her back into darkness. She punched the person's side, causing them to let go. She used her strength to force him off her.

They both rose. Laura ran toward the man, and kicked him in the groin. When she went for another kick, he swept her legs out from under her causing her to fall. She rolled out of the man's way as he tried to force his knee into her back. She looked for her gun. Nowhere to be found. She saw the next best thing on the ground by her foot.

A big fucking rock.

She picked it up and hurled it at the man's head. He ducked. The rock smashed against the wall. She ran and punched him, forcing him to the ground. She heard more people coming. She turned to the right and saw her gun on the ground. She dove for it. The man jumped on top of her. She turned the gun and blew the man's head away. She pushed him off her and ran into the elevator. The doors closed. She saw the guards running toward the elevator through the gate as the elevator went up.

The trip up would take longer than she wanted. The guards below would have enough time to alert the men up top she was coming. She shivered.

About halfway up, something terrible happened. The elevator stopped. She was right where they wanted her. Trapped in a cage.

"You aren't going to do this to me," she yelled.

She looked up and spotted the opening in the elevator ceiling. She would have to jump to reach it. She put the gun in the waist of her pants and jumped. The first try wasn't successful. The second try also yielded no results. The third time she got a hand up. She pulled herself to the top of the elevator.

A ladder was on her right. She tried not to think of the mess she'd make if she lost her grip and fell down the elevator shaft. She took a breath and started to climb.

****

A knock on the door interrupted them. Tony stood up and opened it. A man whispered a message to him. He thanked them and closed the door. He turned to his daughter.

"We have to leave."

"Why?" Eva asked.

"Xander's sending some people over to kindly put us out of our misery."

"How did they find out I was here?"

"It has to be that either Clarissa is working with them or her phone is tapped. I'd say the latter."

"We have to tell her. We have to warn her."

Tony pondered this. He picked up the phone and handed it to his daughter.

"Call her. Tell her only that her phone is tapped and that she should throw it away. Then we move out and head to Grand Rapids."

****

Clarissa stood in the entrance of Phil's office and tried not to vomit. Pedro's body lay in the middle of the floor, his bullet-ridden body a message of brutality from the people they were investigating.

Phil stood by his desk. "The flash drive is gone."

Clarissa's cell phone rang. She fished it out of her purse and answered.

"Hello?"

"It's Eva. Your phone is tapped. Get rid of it."

She hung up. Clarissa looked at her phone as if it had just emitted a foul smell.

"What's the matter?" Phil asked.

"Eva called. Said my phone is tapped."

"What?"

"My phone is tapped."

The sound of sirens made them turn. Phil grabbed her by the arm and ran out of the office.   Phil got to his car and started it up. Clarissa got in the passenger side and buckled up.

"You sure it's safe to drive this car?" Clarissa asked.

"They're looking for me, not my car. Everything's legal so we should be all right."

"I'm just saying, we can take my car. It'll drive faster than this bucket of bolts."

Phil kept the car in idle for a moment. Then he shut it off.

"Where's it at?"

"It's a block away," Clarissa said.

They got out and ran over to Clarissa's car. She tossed him the keys.

"I'm sure they've trained you in driving at high speeds when you got your license," she said.

"Shit, I learned all my driving from video games."

They got in the car. Phil started it up and pulled away.

****

Laura reached the top of the ladder and faced a dilemma. The elevator door was on her left. To get to it she'd have to jump across the shaft to get to it. If she failed, she'd have a long drop before she went splat.

She heard voices on the other side of the elevator door. The wall muted it so all she heard was a low mumble but she knew she'd have people waiting for her.

She had to do this. She positioned herself on the ladder. Laura said a little prayer and jumped.

She grabbed the door, clutching the lever that opened it. Safe. The noises on the other side stopped. Laura took out her gun and opened the door.

"Howdy boys," she said.

A guard stood on the other side of the door. She grabbed his arm and yanked him into the shaft, sending him plummeting to the bottom. She ran out of the elevator shaft and fired at the remaining guards. She took the two close to her out first. She dived for cover. More shots came her way. She spotted a cell phone attached to one of the dead guard's belts. She crawled over and took it off. She dialed Phil.

"Hello?"

Laura fired off a couple shots. "Hi Phil."

"Where are you? What's going on?"

"I'm currently in a gun battle with some of the Senator's men. The moment I get a chance I'm making a break for it."

"Tell me where you're at so I can get you."

Laura fired off some more shots. "The old gypsum mines."

"I can be there in a few minutes."

"No. I'll be out of here before then. Your office ok?"

"No. Long story. Meet me where we first met."

"Is it still open?"

"Yeah. And it's close by anyway."

"I know where it's at idiot. I'll be there."

She fired off a shot and hung up the phone. The area was clear. She made a break for the door.

****

Mr. A stepped out of the limo and stretched as much as his injured arm would let him. He turned around and knelt back into the limo.

"Thanks again Mr. Palermo for all your help."

"Call me Tony. Are you sure you don't want to stay with us? You'll be much safer that way."

"I'll be fine. I just want to hop on the bus and go as far away from here as possible."

"What are you going to do?" Eva asked.

"Don't worry about me ma'am. Think of me as a slightly flawed guardian angel who found you at the right time."

"What's your name?" Eva asked.

Mr. A smiled. "What's in a name?"

"I will contact you," Tony said.

Mr. A waved and walked to the building. It was a bus station. Eva saw him walk to the ticket counter.

Eva held her head in her hands. "I am so lucky."

"That you are. But then again, good things happen to good people."

Tony hugged his daughter. "It's going to be ok. We'll be in Grand Rapids before you know it. And then this will all be over with."

Eva embraced her father and burst into tears. Tony held her, ashamed that his actions, or lack of, caused his daughter so much pain. He committed so much evil in his life. This was as close to seeing all the misery he caused anyone he'd ever seen. He hung his head. After seeing this, he would do what he could to make it up to her.

****

The convertible Laura stole burst onto the road. She turned the wheel to the left. The car roared, speeding through the streets. Two cars sped out of the gypsum mine parking lot after her.

The wind whipped back her hair. Though the day would probably be a warm one, the weather now was bitterly cold. She wondered why they even had convertibles with the weather as temperamental as it was in Michigan.

She knew this side of town like the back of her hand. Up ahead she'd have to turn left. She eased the car into the turn as much as she could. The car felt like it was holding onto the road with all the strength it had. She made the turn and headed down the road. About a mile up the road was the entrance to the highway. If she could get on that, she was confident she could lose these guys.

She reached the highway in no time and sped onto the entrance. She darted south through the light highway traffic. She looked in the rearview mirror. The cars were still on her tail. She took out her cell phone and dialed.

"Hello?"

"Phil. I'm on the highway. I need your help."

"Where you at?"

"I'm heading south towards Kalamazoo. The entrance I used was about a mile from where we first met."

"What's your car look like?"

"It's a red convertible. There are two black cars on my tail."

"Gotcha. I should see you in a few minutes. I'll call when I spot you."

Laura hung up the phone. She prayed nothing would prevent her escape.

5:00 AM-6:00 AM

Nathan and Xander walked down the steps of the capitol and waved to the press. The reporters clamored for any comments from the new Governor. Security held the reporters off as Nathan and Xander walked past them to the limo. The two men got in.

"Is Alex coming?" Xander asked.

"Yeah. The nanny is bringing him. He'll be in Grand Rapids by the start of the ceremony. Is everything in place?" Nathan asked.

"Yes. I still have men out there trying to clean up the mess you created but that should be resolved soon. Speaking of that," Xander said, pulling something from his pocket. "We have the flash drive back."

"Good. Any word on Eva and Onyx?"

"They split town. We don't know their location."

Nathan shook his head. "They're coming to Grand Rapids."

"If they do there's not much I can do to stop them, whatever they have planned."

"Why not?"

"Imagine the footage. Armed guards beating down your wife who has scars from a gunshot wound in her chest. You think that'll go down well with the public?"

"Enough with the lectures."

"If what I think is going to happen happens, you'll be praying for these lectures. I don't think you want to be the first Governor to be a prisoner in Jackson."

"That won't happen. Try to get her out of the way, anyway you can."

"Consider it done. If you didn't have me you'd be fending off suitors in the prison showers."

****

Phil spotted Laura's car up ahead and the two cars on her tail. He took out his phone and dialed Laura.

"Yes?" Laura yelled.

"I'm right behind you."

"Come on Philip. Take them bitches out. Show me you still got it."

Phil smiled and hung up the phone.

"What do you plan on doing?" Clarissa asked.

"Improvise like a motherfucker. We gotta switch sides."

"How are we going to do that?"

"Grab the wheel and put your foot on the gas. You'll sit on my lap and I'll slide out from underneath you."

"I don't know if I'm comfortable with that."

"Look, the only woman whose attention I want is in that car over there. And besides, if I were hitting on you I'd be a little smoother than that."

Clarissa smiled despite herself. She grabbed the wheel and put her foot on the gas. She slid onto his lap. When she was secure, he let go and slid out from under her. He rolled down the passenger window.

"Nice perfume by the way."

He glanced in the back seat for something that could help him. He rummaged through the junk in the back until he spotted something. A crowbar. He grabbed it.

"Sorry about the mess. Haven't had the chance to clean this up since I had a flat last week," Clarissa said.

"Don't worry about it. You should see my car."

He rolled down the window. "Bring us close to that car," he yelled.

Clarissa drove the car as close to the other vehicle as she could. Phil hung out the window, extending his arm with the crowbar out. The man in the car turned and faced Phil, surprised. Phil smiled, throwing the crowbar at the man's head. The crowbar smashed onto the man's temple, causing the car to swerve off the road. It flipped, crushing the driver. Phil leaned back into the car.

"Nice shot," Clarissa said.

"Congratulate me when we get the other guy."

The other motorist turned and stared at Phil. How am I going to get this guy? he thought. Phil didn't have much of an option. Unless...

Phil started to crawl out the window. "What are you doing?" Clarissa screamed.

"Something I shouldn't."

Phil climbed out of the car onto the hood. He held on for dear life as the car barreled down the highway. He inched across the hood until he got as close to the other car as he could. He pulled out his gun, knelt for a moment, and prayed.

He jumped, landing in the passenger seat. Phil put the gun to the man's head.

"Time to pull this stallion over pal. Don't try anything funny."

The driver pulled the convertible to the shoulder and followed Phil's instructions. Clarissa pulled over in front of them. Further down the road Laura pulled over on the shoulder as well and backed her car up to meet them.

"Step out the car," Phil said.

The driver obeyed. Laura ran up to them with her gun drawn. Clarissa stood by her car.

"Nice to see you, baby," Phil said.

"Why were you following me?" Laura asked the guard.

"You forgot your purse. What do you think?"

"I don't appreciate you talking to my wife like that," Phil said. "Answer her questions and I won't feel the need to bash your head in."

"Senator Wilson wanted to keep you confined until later today."

"Why?" Laura asked.

"I know why," Phil said. "You done with this guy?"

"Yeah."

Phil slammed the butt of his gun in the back of the man's head. He fell to the ground in a heap.

"Follow us back to town," Phil said. "We'll fill you in when we get there. Meet at the safe house."

"Is Ty there?"

"Yeah."

"Remind me to hug you later."

Laura headed off to her car. Phil and Clarissa went back to her car and got in.

****

The woman stepped off the train and breathed in the crisp morning air. There was something about the air in Michigan that revitalized her every time she breathed it in. She walked off the platform and into the parking lot. A limo sat, its engine idling. The driver held a sign with her name on it. She approached him.

"I see the Senator arranged for my transportation."

"The Senator is inside ma'am."

The woman stepped into the limo. Senator Wilson sat across from her holding a glass of wine. He raised it in toast.

"Thank you for coming on short notice."

"We'll talk pleasantries later. What brings me here?"

"Nathan Gibraltar and his chief of staff, Steven Alexander Falcone."

The woman smiled. "Xander causing you trouble?"

"You can say that. I want you to take Xander out."

"Why only Xander?"

"With him gone, Nathan's lost. The puppet has no power if the puppet master's gone."

"I see. I assume you're looking to control a situation."

"Exactly. They're going to be in Grand Rapids around six thirty, seven o'clock this morning. I want Xander gone while Nathan's giving his speech at the Happy Child Book Publishing Company."

"When does the speech start?"

"Eight o'clock on the dot."

"Then by eight thirty Xander will be dead."

The Senator smiled. "One more thing. I want you to get in contact with your daughters and straighten them out."

"What's going on?"

"It's too much to get into here. You need to get them in control though."

"They will be taken care of."

"Good. Until then, would you care for a drink?"

"Not this early in the morning. I'd prefer to knit."

****

"Hello?"

"English Bob, its Phil. Where you at?"

"Things got a little hairy at the hospital so I took Roni and Melissa to the safe house."

"Cool. You hear from The Ganj?"

"Not since you sent him off to see David Geraldson."

"I'll have to give him a ring. It's not like him to just disappear."

"You wanna meet?"

"Yeah but the office is off limits. Someone killed Pedro."

"Oh man. We've gotten ourselves in a big ass mess here."

"Uh huh. We have to meet up. Remember where you were chased by your friends?"

"Yeah."

"Meet me there."

"All right. See ya."

Phil hung up the phone. "Where are we going?" Clarissa asked.

"A cemetery. He tripped on a big dose of acid once and his friends brought him to the cemetery when he was passed out. They stripped him to his underwear and when he woke up, they started chasing him back home in their car."

"My God."

"So he hasn't always been the brightest."

"Should you call Laura?"

"Good idea."

****

Robert drove the car past the Happy Child Publishing Company inspecting the building and the area around it. People were already at work preparing the stage and setting up the sound system. He turned his car in the parking lot across the street.

"Looks like I'll have to camp out up there to get a clear shot," he said, pointing to the roof of a building across the street from the stage.

"Should I drop you off now?" Lydia asked.

Robert thought about it. "No. It'll be better to see the security precautions before we make any commitments on shooting locations."

"You know best."

Robert smiled. God, he wanted to kill her. That insipid smile that tried to hypnotize him every chance she could. She did one hell of a job at convincing him she was on his side he had to admit. He did everything he could to let her show through her actions that she made a mistake. That she still loved him. But the truth couldn't be hidden. The film had lifted from his eyes and what he saw sickened him. Lydia was a sad, pathetic individual who wouldn't know what love was from a hole in the wall.

"Let's go get some breakfast. I thought I saw a diner a few blocks away," Robert said.

Lydia rubbed up against him. "We could spend some time alone."

He grinned. Maybe he could postpone his hate for at least fifteen minutes. Lydia's phone rang interrupting his response. She answered it.

"Hello?"

She listened to the person on the other line. Her face paled. "Yes Mother...Sure...I'll meet you there."

She hung up the phone. "What's the matter?" Robert asked.

"Head downtown to the 1920 Room at the Brisbane. My mother is in town."

****

Horace threw the match on the limo and ran a safe distance away. The flame caught, spreading over the entire limo in seconds. Once it was hot enough, it ignited the stick of dynamite Jenkins had left inside. The limo lifted off the ground about a foot after the explosion and crashed back to the ground.

He walked over to a new car that Jenkins had stolen and got in the passenger seat. He tilted the seat back.

"We ready to find this McKnight?" Jenkins asked.

"Where there's a will there's a way. Anyone can be found if you look hard enough."

"Where do you want me to drive?"

"The file has a bunch of places listed that he's known to frequent. We keep our eyes open and we're bound to run into him."

"Can I kill him?"

"We'll see."

****

The Senator leaned back and sighed. Laura McKnight had escaped. Escaped with ease to make things worse.

With Leslie gone, he really didn't have anyone that could help make this problem go away. He had to think of something.

Then it hit him. He knew from the report that Laura had taken one of the guard's cell phones. If she still had it on her then she may be reachable. What could it hurt if he tried to call her? The worst that could happen would be a dial tone. He picked up the phone.

It went for a couple rings with no answer. Finally...

"Hello?"

"Laura McKnight?"

A pause. "Senator, why are you calling?"

"I would like to call a truce."

"You've got to be kidding."

"I would like us to meet and discuss a financial settlement to make this unfortunate incident go away."

"Again, you've got to be kidding."

"No. And to prove I'm not using this as a ploy to kidnap you again, I will agree to meet at a place of your choosing."

Laura thought about it. "Let me call you back."

****

She hung up the phone. He goes through all the trouble to keep me hidden and now he wants to give me money to shut me up, she thought. Interesting. Laura called Phil.

"Yeah?"

"Guess who just called me?"

"Who?"

"Senator Joe Wilson. He called to say he wants to throw some cash my way to shut me up."

"Oh really."

"Yeah. Even offered meeting at a place I suggest."

"What's your feeling?"

"It may be a ploy but I think the old jackass is serious. He realized how this could affect him if I talk and he wants to shut me up. For as much as I want to see him burn, I wouldn't mind compromising my morals for a couple million."

"Set up the meeting. But give no indication that we've spoken. When you meet him, I want to ask him a few questions myself."

"Where do you suggest I set it up at?"

"Remember that park about a quarter mile from where we first met?"

"Of course."

"Use that place. It's open enough where you won't get surprised if he tries something and it has enough hiding spots to keep me hidden."

"You want to go alone?"

"Don't really have a choice."

"What have we always talked about?"

Phil sighed. "There are always choices. Even choices we don't want to take."

"Exactly. I'll give Gomez a call.

"You know I don't like that bastard."

"I know. You've told me many, many times."

"Will he do it?"

"For you? No. For me? Yes."

"Then call him. When do you want this meeting?"

"I would like to get it over with so the sooner the better."

"I'll drop off Clarissa at the safe house, pick up English Bob, and head to the park."

"I'll pick up Gomez and meet you by those benches in the middle of the park. See you later."

Laura hung up the phone. She veered the car in the right lane and got off the highway. On the way to see Gomez, she'd call the Senator back and tell him her decision. She didn't know exactly what was going on with Phil wanting to interrogate this guy but after today, it would feel good to slap someone around a little bit.

****

Robert and Lydia entered the fancy restaurant. Lydia eyed the place, finding her mother motioning to them in the back. They reached her table and took a seat.

"Hello Lydia."

"Mother."

"Who is your male friend?"

"I'm Robert Sampson."

Her mother looked at him as if he were a diseased dog. Robert sank back in the chair.

"I've heard some bad reports from people about your behavior recently. Do you have a response?"

"What have you heard?"

"Enough."

"Well I would like to know what is being said about me before I respond."

Her mother leaned over the table and slapped her across the face. "I thought you learned your lesson a long time ago that you never talk cross to me. Do you understand missy?"

Lydia sat back in her chair. Robert sat frozen, not sure whether to love this woman or be afraid of her. Lydia's mother glared at her.

"I don't like hearing stories of your misbehavior. It almost makes me want to move back home so I can keep an eye on you."

Lydia's eyes became as big as saucers. "But I won't," her mother smiled.

Lydia breathed a sigh but did her best not to show it. Her mother glared at her and smiled.

"Did you miss me?"

"I did," Lydia squeaked.

The woman smiled. "I missed you too. I have a surprise."

"What's that?"

Her mother stood. Robert and Lydia turned their head. Annie Walker strode across the floor toward their table. Robert stared at her. He turned to Lydia, stumped.

"Meet my twin sister," Lydia said.

Annie took a seat across from Lydia. The two sisters stared at each other, fake smiles plastered on their faces.

"Well, well sis. I hear you've been looking for me," Annie said.

****

Stone Campbell walked into Captain Aaronson's office. The Captain sat at his desk looking over a file. He motioned for Stone to take a seat without looking up. He took a few more moments to read than set the file on his desk.

"We have a problem here."

"We do?"

"You're aware Phil McKnight escaped."

"Allegedly."

"Knowing this guy's record and his associates, I'd say it was a fact. I don't think you've heard about the recent incident on the highway though which resulted in a crash with a fatality and left another person unconscious."

Stone laughed. "Let me guess who was there."

"According to eyewitnesses they saw a man in his late twenties, early thirties cause one car to flip resulting in the driver of that car to be crushed in the wreckage. He proceeded to crawl out the vehicle he was in, crawl across the hood, and dive over to another vehicle which he promptly brought to the shoulder."

"Sounds exciting."

"I'd be laughing myself if this weren't true."

He handed the file to Stone. He opened it up and read.

"Who gave you the information?" Stone asked.

"The person who called it in asked to remain anonymous but it all checks out. Can you get a hold of Phil?"

"I can try."

"You'll have to do better than try."

"Is he still in trouble with us?"

"Officially yes. Unofficially, as long as he cooperates we're willing to let things slide. Besides, Detective Cooper has a lot to answer. Make sure you keep this to yourself. You're dismissed."

Stone rose and left the office, taking the file with him. He had to do what he could to find Phil and tell him the good news.

****

Laura knocked on the door and waited. It had been a while since she'd seen Gomez. They used to work together at a local security firm until Laura went into business on her own. They'd drifted apart as some friends do. They knew how to contact each other but didn't find the time to connect. The chain went off the door and Gomez opened it. He smiled when he saw Laura.

"And I was going to shoot the person knocking on my door this early."

"Give me a hug."

The two embraced. "What brings you here? Is there a problem?"

"Yeah, I do have a problem. I was kidnapped today by Senator Joe Wilson. Now that scumbag wants to meet so he can buy my silence."

"You have been busy. What's the plan?"

"You may not like it but it needs to be this way. I need you to hide out with Phil so you can sneak up on Wilson and interrogate him."

"What the hell is Phil involved for?"

"This actually has to do with a case he's been working on."

"So his case got you kidnapped?"

"Yeah, but he's not to blame. Trust me. If he was I would have stapled his genitals to a tree."

They laughed. "I need you with me to nail this bastard," Laura said. "At least to slap the Senator around a little. Imagine. You get to live the American dream. Kicking the shit out of a politician."

Gomez smiled. "I can live with that. Phil better not fuck up."

"Phil's not a bad guy."

"I have no respect for him."

"Then respect the fact that I do."

Gomez smiled. "Girl, I'll get my coat."

****

Senator Wilson gazed out the limo window. His whole world felt as if it was crumbling like a cracker. That it happened in a matter of hours didn't massage his bruised ego. And now he sat waiting for Laura McKnight to call him back. If she didn't and decided to go to the police, he would be ruined. Hell, she could walk out of their meeting with his money and still tell people what he did. His life was in her hands.

His phone rang startling him. He held it in his hands, judging the right time to answer so he didn't appear to be too desperate. He finally answered.

"Yes?"

"Meet me at the benches in Truman Park off Grandville Ave," Laura replied.

"When?"

"Whenever you can get there."

Laura hung up the phone. At least with Mrs. Walker out there ready to kill Xander he wouldn't be going down alone.

****

"So what did Xander offer to pay you to kill your sister?"

"Mother," Lydia said.

"I want an answer."

"We never talked about a price."

Her mother gave her a disapproving look. "You know better than that. I don't care if you're hired to take me out, you never agree until you hear a price."

"Mother," Annie said.

"Don't try and fool me with that false sense of modesty, Annie. I raised you two right. And I will take whatever action necessary to keep you two on the right path. Now Lydia. Apologize to your sister."

Lydia gave her mother a quizzical look. "I am not a child Mother."

"Do it."

Lydia lowered her head and sighed. She looked up at her sister.

"I'm sorry I tried to kill you."

"Annie, tell your sister you forgive you."

Annie gave her sister an evil glare. "I forgive you."

"There. Didn't that clear the air?"

"Changing the subject," Lydia said, "what brings you into town?"

"I have been employed by Senator Wilson to take care of a problem."

"What's that?"

"Your ex-employer."

"Oh really," Annie said, smiling.

"Yes. Seems like the Senator wishes to rule the roost and Xander is in his way."

"Interesting. Can I help you Mother?" Annie asked.

"No. I work alone."

"I would like to be involved in Xander's demise," Annie said.

"Annie, never take revenge out on anyone. When you're emotional you don't think properly."

"That's rich, coming from you."

Her mother gave her an icy stare. The smile on her face could melt paint off a car, Robert thought.

"What makes you say that dear?"

"Remember what brought you to the Windy City?"

"Don't you dare bring that up."

"I think I should. When the Presidential Museum had its twentieth anniversary, you were hired to assassinate the three former Presidents who came to commemorate the occasion. And as I recall you failed miserably."

"Annie, keep quiet."

"You failed to assassinate three old men and you dare give me instruction on how to do my job? I don't think so."

"Annie, don't," Lydia said.

Their mother stood and stepped next to her daughter. She raised Annie to her feet and slapped her. Mrs. Walker smiled.

"Annie my dear, I'm afraid I didn't do that to you enough growing up. Maybe you would have turned out more civilized, more straight if you will."

"Go to hell."

"That's where you'll be if I see you again. Go. Make the most out of the rest of your life. Because if I see you again, you'll rue the day you crossed your Mother."

****

Phil spotted Laura's car and pulled into a parking spot. Laura stood next to her car along with her annoying friend Gomez. He knew the guy's reputation when it came to work but he wondered if Gomez's opinion of him would get in the way of doing the job. Phil shut off the car and got out.

"Hey Phil," Laura said.

"When did the Senator say he'd come?"

"He should be here any minute. I'd get to your position as soon as you can."

"Follow me," Phil motioned for Gomez.

The two men ran into a wooded area behind the benches. They found hiding spots that gave them a good vantage point.

"So what's happening here Phil?"

"Senator Wilson and the new Governor Nathan Gibraltar are involved in a drug deal."

"What? That's ridiculous."

"It may be but you have to ask yourself, why would Senator Wilson meet with Laura in a park this time of day?"

Gomez was silent.

"Listen, I like you about as much as you like me. But you can get the job done. And I'm sure you wouldn't be here if you didn't realize this benefited Laura and Ty."

"You're right about that. Someone's coming."

The two men quieted down as an older gentleman approached Laura at the benches. He walked up and offered his hand for a shake. Laura refused to touch him. The man sat down. Phil recognized the face from the six o'clock news. Phil listened in.

"Hello Laura."

"Senator."

"Thank you for meeting with me."

"This better be worth my time."

"I wish to offer you a cash settlement in return for your silence."

"Why should I accept?"

"Nothing is stopping you from walking away. But if you accept, you'll receive a cool sum that'll allow you to never work again."

"Quit talking to me like I'm about to win a contest. Why did you kidnap me in the first place?"

The Senator sighed. "I'd rather not get into that."

Phil motioned for Gomez to follow him. They sneaked up to the bench. Phil grabbed the Senator.

"Why don't you go into it for me?" Phil asked.

The Senator's face turned pale. He began stammering. Laura stood up and slapped the Senator in the face.

"Now I think it's time you start talking Senator."

Joe glared at all three of them. Then he burst into tears.

"Everything had been planned out to the smallest detail. I should have been more careful."

"Tell us what's going on," Phil said.

The Senator didn't get a chance to respond. A hatchet flew out of nowhere and landed in the Senator's chest. He fell to the ground dead.

Phil and Gomez took out their guns and shot at the hatchet throwers. After a couple shots, Phil heard screams and saw two men go down. Phil ran toward the bodies.

Both men were dead. Phil checked for a wallet on the first man, found it, and checked his ID. The dead man's name was Horace Spengler. Phil turned to Gomez and Laura.

"This is pretty fucked up right here."

6:00 AM-7:00 AM

The crate was loaded onto a forklift. The forklift driver put the vehicle in gear and drove back to the production room. A select pair of workers was set up to package this special product. They were told when they were first given the job that they shouldn't ask any questions. This was a special job for the new Governor so they should be happy to be involved in such a project. They had their instructions and were eager to follow them.

Their job was simple. Fill tiny hourglasses used in board games with the white powder in the crate.

The new Governor himself would pick up the delivery later today after his speech. Word had it that he would be delivering these to an elementary school in Lansing in order to promote an education bill he was supporting. But if that were the case, why all the secrecy?

Harvey Johnson set up the box and the empty hourglasses. "Simple job here guys. Put the tube under the funnel, press the button, wait until it dispenses the appropriate amount, and then put the cap on. Simple as that. This should keep you busy for most of the day. And remember to keep a mask on at all times. You wouldn't want to inhale the dust."

****

Stone Campbell got out of his car and ran to the group waiting by the benches. Phil met up with him.

"Damn. Just when I thought you couldn't top yourself," Stone said.

"This is different from those thugs I left on the highway."

"Yeah, a prominent state official getting whacked with a hatchet is a little different."

"What's your plan then?" Phil asked.

"Well, my Captain seems to think you're not a threat. He didn't get into it but he made it clear that there wouldn't be any effort made to get you back into custody. All that's asked is that you finish your job."

"What does that mean?"

"That means you get your ass moving if you don't want to head back to jail. I heard the food is terrible there."

"You gonna be by your phone?"

"Where the hell else am I going to be?"

"Then do what you can to remove the tap that's on my phone. It's on Clarissa Day's phone as well."

"Will do."

Phil walked over to Laura and Gomez. "We gotta get out of here. Follow me in the car and meet me at the safe house."

"Why should we?" Gomez said.

"Listen pal. Enough. I could care less about your opinion of me. What you need to do now is follow my lead so we can properly resolve this. I appreciate your help and will appreciate it if you stay longer. But if you're going to be on my ass then go home. The only person who has a right to be on my ass right now is Laura."

Gomez stared at him. "This had better result in you taking better care of Laura and Ty. Because if it doesn't..."

Phil smiled. "You've seen how Laura works. You think I want her pissed off at me?"

****

The Ganj shook the drowsiness from his head. Someone was coming down the stairs. Probably that coward SOB, he thought. David Geraldson opened the door and walked inside. He was dressed in the best suit money could buy.

"Is there anything I can get you?" he asked.

"A bathroom break would be nice."

"I'm afraid I can't allow it. I wouldn't want you escaping after all."

"This is insane."

"Maybe it is. But it'll be worth it at the end of the day when I'm paid. See you later."

"What are you going to do with me when this is over?"

David turned and walked out the door. "You'll see," he said, closing the door.

That sounds hopeful, The Ganj thought. Phil and the gang had better get here or I'll haunt the fuck out of them for the rest of their lives.

****

Xander's phone rang. "Yes?"

He heard what the person had to say and smiled.

"Thank you."

He hung up the phone and turned to Nathan. "Guess what?"

"What's that?"

"A report just came in from Grand Rapids that Senator Joe Wilson has been assassinated."

"What? Where was he?"

"That's the strange thing. He was sitting on a park bench alone. Someone killed him with a hatchet."

"A hatchet? Should this be something that worries us?"

"This could actually be our ticket to making out quite nice."

"Explain."

"Imagine the headlines. Late Senator Joe Wilson killed by nut case in Grand Rapids park. Think about it. You got the police out tenfold looking for your attempted assassin. Now there'll be even more cops coming in looking for these goofballs. The more cops that come and look for these people, the fewer cops that'll be around when we're ready to pick up the shipment."

"Let's not start patting each other on the back just yet. We don't know if that kook Sampson could have done this since your girl couldn't keep her reins on him."

"That's not true. She got him back. They're going to be at the event on schedule."

"I don't like it. I have a bad feeling about this."

"You have a reason to have a bad feeling. If you hadn't screwed up and shot your wife, we'd be doing much better. What do you think will happen if Eva shows up?" asked Xander.

"She won't."

"You sure about that? I think you gave her a big shot full of courage."

"You said yourself. She's a mentally disturbed woman who would go to any lengths to destroy the one man who loves her," said Nathan.

"And what do you suggest we do with that reporter?"

"I didn't tell you. I had her fired."

"Excuse me?" Xander asked.

"I called her station manager and complained about her harassing my family. One thing led to another and she's no longer employed at that station. She's blacklisted."

Xander smiled. "One step ahead of me. That's good thinking. What about Eva's father?"

"What about him? You think he wants to be exposed? Sure, he's pissed. He may even try something sometime. But he won't do it today. His business sense will rule out his anger."

"Are you sure?"

"Of course I am. He'd be foolish to do otherwise."

"You sure that's how you want to handle it?"

"But of course."

Xander leaned back in the seat and smiled. Nathan did have some brains. He would have to work on using them more often.

****

Clarissa turned her head when she heard the front door open. Before she could go downstairs, her cell phone rang. She picked it up. She read the number off the caller ID. Annie. She smiled and answered.

"Hello?"

"Hello Clarissa."

"You're up early."

"I couldn't get to sleep thanks to you."

"You didn't exactly make me drowsy either."

"Where are you at?"

"I, uh, can't really say."

"Why is that?"

"Long story."

"You all right?"

"Yeah. I've had better days though."

"Did that information I give you help?"

"Not really. I had to quit my job because they weren't going to go with the story."

"Oh no. This ain't good."

"Why does it matter to you anyway if I may ask?"

"Personal reasons. Are you still going to try and do something with it?"

"I'm going to help Eva tell her story. But with no cameras, I don't know what all I can do. At least I have a new job."

"Really? You're quite the enterprising woman."

"I'm working with this investigator I interviewed yesterday."

"What's his name?"

"Phil McKnight."

Annie laughed. "You know him?" Clarissa asked.

"Yeah, we met. He's a good guy."

"Is that a recommendation?"

"You could say that," Annie said.

"He's the only reason I'm still working on this. I found out that Nathan had my sister's roommate attacked and raped."

"I'm sorry."

"Be sorry if Nathan gets away with it."

"He won't."

"Don't be so sure."

"Call it arrogance but this girl's got a feeling. Word of advice, call Eva now. Find out where she's at. You need her to appear in Grand Rapids like clockwork."

"I can't. My phone's tapped. Same as Phil's."

"Really? Let me help you two out. I'll call you back in fifteen minutes."

"What are you going to do?"

"Work some magic."

****

Laura and Gomez headed into the kitchen of the safe house and met Phil and English Bob inside. Laura looked around.

"Is Ty here?"

"He's upstairs."

She ran for the stairs heading to her son's room. Gomez took a seat.

"Tell me what's going down."

English Bob looked at Phil. "You want I should tell him?"

"Go nuts. I gotta get some coffee in my system."

Phil went to the cupboard to grab some coffee. English Bob found a seat.

"Nathan Gibraltar and the now late Senator Joe Wilson have a plan to bring in a large shipment of cocaine into town and distribute it for cash."

"Phil mentioned that. Why the hell would they do that?"

"Because they're arrogant bastards."

"How have they executed the plan so far?"

"For one, they got Davis Creston out of office giving Nathan Gibraltar the reins of the state. Remember the assassination attempt yesterday?"

"Yeah."

"It was staged. They had some kook make the shot in order to get things rolling, with someone else monitoring this guy to make sure he wasn't successful. With Nathan being Governor and with that attempt on his life so fresh in people's minds, he's able to manipulate the police force..."

"So he can keep them out of the way when the drug deal goes down. Great idea."

"It's not the best plan but it's working for them. They just seem to have too many people involved."

"So what brought this ragtag group together?"

"We're trying to stop him. We're going to the Happy Child Book Publishing Company where this is going down today and crash the party."

"Is there any organized plan?"

English Bob thought a moment. "Not really. No."

"Great. Sounds like a Phil plan all the way."

"Love him or hate him, he gets the job done."

"Not with his wife and child."

"You can't always judge a person on their actions. Phil needed a kick in the ass a long time ago when it came to Laura and Ty. For that, we'll all agree. Hell, I'm not the first to tell you that Laura was the best thing that ever happened to him. He'd be a loser playing video games for the rest of his damn life. But I know Phil. He'd die for those two."

"I can't proclaim to know him too well. When you only see one side of a person, you tend to judge them based on what you see. And I haven't seen much that I like. For Laura's sake, I hope I see something more."

Phil sat at the kitchen table with a cup of coffee. Clarissa came down the stairs and joined them.

"I heard you come in," Clarissa said. "I was on the phone."

"Boyfriend?" he asked.

"Not exactly."

Phil turned to English Bob. "You heard from The Ganj?"

"No. Haven't heard from him since he went to David Geraldson's."

"Then he still has to be there. There's no two ways about it."

"Do we want to go get him?" English Bob asked.

"In a minute. Clarissa, you heard from Eva?"

"I was going to call her."

"Let's call her now."

"I'm getting someone to take care of that tap on my phone."

"Think you can have them get the tap off my phone too?"

"I already did. They're working on removing the tap on your phone too."

"Cool. Stay here and call up Eva when you can. Find out what her plan is. If she's coming to Grand Rapids then we can try and find out what she's doing."

"You have something planned she can be involved in?"

Phil smiled. "No. I just want to keep her whereabouts known so when we go to the authorities we'll be able to show them what Nathan did to her. For now though, off to find The Ganj."

****

Annie opened the bedroom window of Judge Benjamin Cross and crept inside. The old man lay sleeping on his bed, his chest fighting for each breath. Annie smiled. The old man looked cute lying there in a beige satin slip with lace trim. She took out her camera phone, made sure the volume was on high, and took a picture.

Judge Cross woke with a start. He turned and saw Annie staring at him with the camera phone in hand. He attempted to cover himself but seeing that she saw what he had on, he stopped.

"What are you doing in my house?" he bellowed.

"Nice outfit. I have one just like it."

"What do you want? I don't carry any money in the house so if you're here to rob me you won't get much of anything."

"I know. I'm not here to rob you. I'm here to ask a favor."

"Why should I do anything but call the cops?"

"Because I'd have to send this picture of you in that cute little outfit to my friends at the newspaper. I think they'd love to print a picture of the judge that's been using his bench to make life terrible for them."

"That's..., you can't do that."

"I can and I will if you don't do what I say."

The Judge glared at her. "What do you want?"

"You signed a subpoena authorizing two wire taps against Phil McKnight and Clarissa Day. Rescind them."

"I just can't..."

Annie pressed a button on the phone making the Judge stop mid-sentence. She turned the phone in his direction and showed him the photograph.

"Looks cute don't it. Tough conservative judge like you dressed up like an old French whore. You think that'll go down well with the conservatives in this town? You think any defendant will be scared of the man who sleeps in satin and lace?"

The Judge's face turned crimson red. He tried his best to control his fury, causing his hands to shake.

"How dare you come in my home and blackmail me."

"How dare you give me clichés for a response. You got three seconds to decide."

Annie held up three fingers. She lowered one finger. She lowered another. Just as her last finger was about to hit the send button on her phone, the Judge held up his hand.

"Wait. I'll do it."

He reached over and grabbed the phone off his side table. He dialed a number. He spoke to his assistant and got the phone taps rescinded. When he hung up the phone, he looked up at Annie.

"You satisfied? Now delete that picture."

Annie smiled. And pressed the send button. The Judge leaped out of the bed and charged her. One kick in the gut sent him to the ground. She put her foot on his chest and smiled.

"I only sent it to my email address. I like to keep insurance for rainy days if you know what I mean. Now in the future, please make it a point to be a little more respectable to your defendants. If you use your bench to humiliate people who haven't made the best choices in life, I may have to leak this picture just so you know your place. We square?"

The Judge nodded. Annie took her foot off his chest and exited through the window.

****

Clarissa paced the floor waiting for Annie to call. Just to hear her voice would be worth the wait alone but the promise of having the phone taps lifted would be heaven indeed.

She wondered about Annie. She was so mysterious. She'd never mentioned where she worked. She never mentioned what type of work she was in for that matter. This wasn't a typical relationship for sure but she felt a closeness with Annie that she hadn't felt with anyone before.

Her phone rang. "Hello?" she replied.

"I called the exterminator and the bugs are gone."

"Oh bless you."

"I have to go now. I'll talk you later."

"Thank you Annie."

"I love you."

Clarissa smiled. "I love you too."

She said she loves me, Clarissa thought. She dialed Eva.

"Hello?"

"It's Clarissa. I got the bugs out."

"Great," Eva said.

"Where are you at?"

"In Grand Rapids. My father doesn't want me to give my location over the phone."

"I understand. The man I'm working with on this was curious what your plans are."

"It's best you don't know as of yet. But keep the lines of communication open so we don't step on each other's toes."

"All right. How are you doing?"

"The Vicodin is making me feel like a million bucks. I'll be heading to the hospital when this is over with."

"What happened to Mr. A?"

"He's ok. He was treated by a doctor and took a bus out of town to stay low."

"I hope he's ok. He did a brave thing."

"He did. And he'll get compensated for it," Eva said.

"Will I see you again today?"

"I guarantee it. And I'll introduce you to my father."

"Who is he?"

"He owns a small restaurant. Does some other work on the side."

"Can't wait to meet him. My line will be open so keep in touch."

"I will. And thank you."

Clarissa hung up. Now she had to wait until Phil got back. She'd have time to relax…and to think.

****

The limo pulled up to the front entrance of the Happy Child Book Publishing Company. Nathan and Xander got out, stretched, and entered the building. Nathan's security detail followed on his heels. David Geraldson met them inside. He shook each man's hand.

"Thank you Governor for coming to our grand opening today."

"Consider it my pleasure. I worked long and hard along with my chief of staff to help bring this company to Grand Rapids and I'm proud to be here under the circumstances."

"We do appreciate it. Now if your security staff is hungry we have set up a breakfast bar in our main conference room. It's the least we can do."

David led the men through the hallway and directed the people to the buffet. He pulled Xander aside.

"Everything is running without a hitch. The package should be ready when you leave."

Xander smiled. "Very good. Now please leave. The Governor wants to eat."

Xander entered the main conference room and grabbed a plate of his own. Just as Nathan was about to put a couple pancakes on his plate, Xander leaned in next to him.

"Want him gone when the day is done?"

Nathan nodded. "He's a big mouth." He put a couple pieces of bacon next to his pancakes.

****

"What are we waiting for?" Gomez asked.

"Stone said he'd be here in a minute. It's better to do a B and E with an officer of the law around," Phil said.

"I can't believe that bastard is clean," English Bob said.

Phil smiled. "You gotta learn to trust a brother on this one."

A car turned the corner and came in their direction. Despite the newly rising sun, the car still had its lights on.

"There's Stone," English Bob said. "Always obeying the traffic laws."

The car pulled over and Stone got out of the car. Phil flashed his lights to get his attention. Stone saw the car and walked over. Phil rolled down his window.

"Howdy."

"Enjoying your freedom McKnight?"

"What little of it I can. That's the house over there."

Stone turned and looked at the house Phil pointed at. "I can only imagine his mortgage payments."

"English Bob staked it out. He saw four guards outside. Who knows how many are inside."

"You sure your friend is in there?"

"This is the last place I knew he was at. There's no way he would leave here with contacting me," Phil said.

"Then let's get going."

The three men in the car got out and followed Stone to the gate. "You all packing?" Stone asked.

"Made sure of it," Phil said.

"Follow my lead folks."

Stone went to the front gate and pressed the intercom button. They waited.

"Can I help you?" a voice replied from the intercom.

"I'm Officer Stone Campbell of the Grand Rapids Police Department. I have a couple questions to ask the man of the house."

"Sir, the man of the house is not here right now. If you call and ask for an appointment I'm sure you'll find a time that's agreeable for both of you."

"You see, that's where you're wrong. This is concerning the security of Governor Nathan Gibraltar. So I suggest you open these gates up and have someone ready to answer some questions."

There was no answer. Stone turned to the others and smiled.

"No problem."

Still no answer. Stone shook the gate. Nothing.

"They don't believe us," Gomez said.

Stone rubbed his chin in thought. "Let's scale the walls and pretend we're commandos."

The men climbed the gate. Once over, they made a run for the house. A guard ran towards them from the right. Gomez took him out with a shot to the knee. Another guard ran at them from the left. English Bob leveled a shot in his stomach. They reached the front door. Stone kicked it in.

"Police! Everyone come out with your hands up."

Gunshots came in reply. "Does that ever work?" Phil asked.

"Not really, no."

Stone fired some cover shots. The other men ran into the house firing their weapons. "The two of you check upstairs. Phil, follow me," Stone yelled.

English Bob and Gomez ran upstairs. Phil and Stone headed into the main part of the house. The living room was quiet. The guards seemed to have followed Gomez and English Bob upstairs. They headed into the dining room where they met with more silence. The gunshots in the other part of the house stopped.

"We clear?" Phil whispered.

"Probably not. Find the way to the basement."

They walked into the kitchen. A maid who had been making food lay on the floor. She looked up when the two men entered the room.

"Who are you?" she cried.

"Amway salesmen. Where's the basement?" Phil asked.

She pointed the way. Phil thanked her and the two men headed toward the basement entrance. Stone opened the door and turned on the light. The two men looked down.

"Just a regular basement," Phil said.

"That's usually where you'll find the most trouble."

They heard a noise behind them and turned with guns drawn. English Bob and Gomez entered the room.

"All clear," English Bob said.

"Follow us," Phil commanded.

All four men headed downstairs into the basement. It appeared to be a regular, ordinary finished basement. It was carpeted with a pool table, a flat screen television hanging on the wall, and a refrigerator at the far end. The men lowered their guns.

"You could watch football down here, not store a prisoner," English Bob said.

"Start exploring," Stone said.

The men began inspecting the basement. English Bob turned on the television and turned it to a sports channel. The others turned to him.

"What? I want to hear how the Lions are doing."

"Turn that off," Phil demanded.

English Bob complied. Each went back to their particular areas. Phil went to the fridge.

"Anyone care for something to drink?" he asked.

"Oh, and you tell me to turn off the TV," English Bob mocked.

Phil opened the fridge door and gasped. "I think you all might want to check this out."

The other three walked over. It was not a fridge at all. It was an entrance to an underground bunker.

"Is this the part where Roger Moore comes walking out with a martini?" asked Gomez.

"Shall we?" said Stone.

The men headed downstairs. They couldn't find a light switch so they had to go slow, taking each step with care.

When they reached the bottom, Phil searched the walls for a light. He found a switch and turned it on. They were in a small room. A metal door was next to English Bob. Stone reached for it and shook the handle. Locked. Phil walked over and shot the lock on the door. There was a yell inside the room. Phil put his ear against the door. He could hear The Ganj yelling inside.

"He's in there all right."

The men continued to kick at the door. After three or four good kicks, the door swung open. They ran inside.

The Ganj hung on the wall from metal shackles. "Get these damn things off me," he yelled. "And try not to shoot me."

Stone looked at the shackles. He turned and inspected the room. He spotted something. Stone walked to the other end of the wall and rubbed his hand against it. He found what he was looking for and pressed it. The shackles released. The Ganj lowered his arms and rubbed his wrists.

"How did you know that?" he asked.

"There was no lock on your shackles. It had to be an electrical device."

"You're the best cop I've ever met."

"Aww, you're sweet. Now I think this is the time we make our leave and head to the publishing company."

That's when the power went out.

7:00 AM–8:00 AM

Davis Creston opened the door of the hotel room and stared inside. He saw her body lying nude on the bed. It was Audrey. She was dead. He stepped inside and closed the door.

He'd gotten the call about a half hour ago. He was at Gerald R. Ford International Airport in Grand Rapids waiting for a plane to nowhere when he was paged with the news. How anyone knew he was there was beyond him.

He approached her body. She still radiated beauty even in death. He sat on the bed next to her and picked up her hand, caressing it. He held back the tears. He saw a note on the side table. He picked it up and read.

'Davis, I'm so sorry I hurt you. You were always good to me. Too good in fact. I hope you can find yourself someone you deserve.'

He hung his head. His life was in ruins.

Someone opened the door causing Davis to turn. He quickly covered Eva in a sheet before the person walked in. The door closed. Davis balled his hands into fists.

"What do you want Tony? You want to desecrate my wife even more now that she's dead?"

"No. I came to apologize."

"Of all the nerve."

"Davis, I only ask that you hear me out. When I'm done, you have my permission to do what you want with me."

Davis glared at him. Tony walked over to a recliner and took a seat.

"You've known for a long time that I have a daughter and that we haven't spoken for years. Well I got back into contact with her tonight. Her husband attempted to kill her."

"What does your daughter have to do with anything?"

"My daughter's Eva Gibraltar."

Davis couldn't hide his shock. "My God. I can't believe Nathan would do that."

"My daughter has disapproved of my profession ever since she was in high school. When she went away to college, she broke off all contact with me. I was hurt but she has a mind of her own. I did what I could to support her yet respect her wishes.

"She met Nathan Gibraltar when she first became a lawyer. I didn't meet him while they courted. I never even got the chance to be there for her wedding. I paid for it though. Was glad to.

"Nathan found out what I do. He confronted me about it and I had to confess. And he laid down an ultimatum. I either follow his commands whenever he gave them or he exposes my history and get my daughter disbarred for having a disreputable father. I had no choice. I couldn't hurt my baby girl.

"Throughout the years I had many commands to follow, too numerous to list. But I also spent this time monitoring him. I heard all about his extramarital affairs. But I couldn't do anything because I knew it would hurt my daughter."

"But you had to have heard about her getting beat by him by someone else other than me."

"I was boxed in a corner Davis. I wanted nothing more than to put a bullet in that son of a bitches head. But Eva would have been hurt by it. She would be publicly humiliated with him by default thanks to the great journalists in this country, blood sucking leeches that they are."

He spit on the ground. "My daughter was left for dead, her son made to put a tarp over her lifeless body."

"Why did you force me to resign?"

"Nathan's doing. He has something going down today that's going to make him a lot of money."

"What is that?"

"It's a large shipment of cocaine being delivered to Grand Rapids which he's planning to distribute around the state."

"What? He's a mad man. Did you alert his chief of staff?"

"His chief of staff initiated the deal. You've heard of a man named Xander I presume?"

"His name has popped up in various crime reports I've read."

"Steven Falcone's middle name is Alexander from which my grandson takes his name."

"We have to tell someone about this."

"No one is listening. My daughter contacted a reporter, Clarissa Day, and gave her all the information she had. Miss Day has since been let go from that station. There has also been a private detective in town here that's been on the case for a while and he's been put in jail. I had to use some of my people to secure his release."

"We've both been played for fools."

"Davis, my daughter was almost killed by that uncaring fuck. I know I did something terrible to you, something which I'm sure you'll never forgive me for. But I need your help to stop him. He not only tried to hurt my daughter, he's trying to hurt many others with this drug shipment."

Davis stared at Tony. "You were my friend for many years. I've known your daughter for many more. You ripped the life out of me yesterday. But if what you said is true, a very evil man was pulling your strings. All I ask of you is that when this is over, you purge yourself of this evil lifestyle and be the type of man your daughter wants you to be. The type of man I saw everyday when I entered your restaurant."

Tony smiled. "I'll be like Al Pacino. Maybe we can both go to the Bahamas and retire."

"Maybe."

Davis and Tony stood. Davis walked over to Tony and shook his hand. Then he socked him in the jaw. Tony hit the floor hard.

"If you ever try to screw me again I'll kill you myself. That's a fact," Davis said.

Tony looked up at Davis a moment…and began to laugh. "You deserved to hit me worse." Tony rose. "I'm in room 1413. When you're done here come on up. Eva would love to see you."

"Thank you. And you're right. I was holding back."

****

The darkness enveloped them. Phil felt along the wall of the cell, hoping to feel anything that might turn on a light, open a door, anything.

"Anyone find a light switch, anything?" he yelled.

"Find your way over here private eye," Gomez yelled from the hallway.

Phil felt his way along the wall finding his way to the exit. He left, bumping into English Bob, Stone, and The Ganj along the way. He reached Gomez.

"The doors to the exits have been sealed off but I think I've come across something here. Feel this."

Gomez took Phil's hand and tapped it against the metal wall. An echo came back in reply.

"What's back there?"

"Hell if I know. But that wall is pretty hallow so I think we should try and see what's behind it."

"English Bob, Stone, Ganj, get over here. We have a project," Phil yelled.

The other three felt their way around until they joined them. They began kicking at the wall. Kicking, ramming their shoulders into it, anything they could do to force it open.

The metal bended, a light bursting through from the other side. Seeing the light, the men attacked the wall harder. Gomez stopped them.

"Hold on. I used to play football in high school."

The men cleared a path for Gomez. He stepped back about a foot and knelt down in a football stance. Then he ran, jamming his shoulder into the wall forcing it down.

The room, if you could call it that, housed electrical wires and a fuse box. There were more wires than a house this size needed.

"What are we, in a submarine?" Stone asked.

Stone walked over and inspected it. "I have no idea what these wires are for but we can screw around with them to see what they'll do."

Stone opened the fuse box and began flipping switches. Lights flicked off and on. The door leading upstairs slid open as well. The men bolted for the entrance, running upstairs with guns drawn. They burst through the fridge door.

Four men waited for them. They fired at the gunmen, taking them down fast. Stone ran to the fallen man nearest him and picked up his gun.

"We're getting low on ammo. Grab their guns."

They each grabbed a weapon. Phil checked his ammo and handed the extra gun to The Ganj.

Stone motioned for them to go upstairs. They walked up slow, trying to keep an ear out for anyone. Stone opened the door to the kitchen and peeked out. All clear. The men walked into the kitchen.

Phil walked up to Stone. "Where we headed?" he whispered.

Stone looked around. He spotted doors that led out to a patio. He motioned for the others to follow. They burst out, the sun filling the sky over an expansive backyard. The men jumped the railing and made a break for the fence, to freedom.

Stone took the lead, Gomez the rear. They ran for all they had, wanting to get out of this ridiculous place and bring down the true monster waiting for them at the Happy Child Book Publishing Company. The men reached the fence. Stone grabbed the top and leaped over. The others followed. Just as Gomez reached the fence, gunshots rang out. Gomez fell to the ground, clutching his leg. Phil climbed back over and checked on him. The others provided cover fire.

"I got shot in the leg," Gomez said. "Get out of here."

"You ain't playing hero today."

Phil picked him up in a fireman's carry and climbed back over the fence. The men put away their guns and ran for their cars. When Phil put Gomez in the car, he ran over to Stone.

"Let's get Gomez to the hospital. Then we'll confer at a place of your choosing and end this thing. Today."

****

"Is the press asking any questions they shouldn't?" Nathan asked.

"Nothing out of the ordinary. A few have asked if there have been any leads on your wife's whereabouts."

"And you told them?"

"That you killed your wife."

Nathan glared at him. Xander laughed.

"Quit being paranoid. Everything's covered."

"How is everything out on the floor?"

"Just watch."

Xander opened up a laptop and clicked on a program. The security camera's for the building popped up on the screen. Xander clicked on the camera for the production room. Nathan peered at the image.

"Do they have any idea of what they're dealing with?" Nathan asked.

"No. But they have commented that the powder is too fine to actually make the hourglass's work."

"They won't be around when the products out on the streets so no worries there.

Are the trucks ready for the shipment?"

"They'll be here around noon to pick up the first batch. It'll take the workers most of the day to complete the job."

"Then we sit back and wait for the profits to roll in. What should we do about the Lt. Governorship now that Wilson is out of the equation?"

Xander rubbed his chin in thought. "I think with the election coming up that it would be wise to leave that position vacant until after the election. Besides, history says you have a rat's chance in hell of winning anyway so what's the point of going through all that effort for nothing."

"True. Let me finish prepping my speech. It's almost show time."

Xander left the room. As he walked down the hallway, he took out his cell phone and dialed a number.

"Hello?"

"This is Sylvester Banks. Is the plane going to be ready at nine thirty?"

"Yes sir."

"Very good."

Xander hung up the phone and smiled. This would almost be over. And it was about time.

****

Robert climbed the ladder to the top of the building. He walked across the roof, taking off his backpack, setting it down. He unzipped it, taking out the pieces for his gun. He sat down and assembled it. When he finished, he took a walkie-talkie out of the backpack.

"Lydia, you there?"

"Yes honey."

"I'm in place. Everything's assembled."

"Good. The ceremony is going to start at the top of the hour."

"I can see everyone getting ready now. Where is the big press contingent?"

"Guess Nathan's reputation for long boring speeches precedes him. The big networks will probably be tapping into local feeds."

"True. Find out when the big ones tap into the feed. Would be nice to give them some ratings."

Lydia laughed. "Always thinking. I'll get back to you. Over and out."

Robert switched off the walkie-talkie. He had enough of her voice. It was bad enough she was trying to double cross him and that she made him sit through that bizarre visit with her mother. But this was almost over. She'd find out what a mistake it was deceiving him.

****

Laura sat next to Ty's bed and watched him as he slept. It made her feel warm inside watching him lying there in peace, his little chest going up and down. Clarissa came to the door.

"Laura, we need you down stairs."

"I'll be down in a second."

Clarissa left the room. Laura brushed her hand across her son's cheek and left. She met Clarissa downstairs by the front window.

"What's going on?"

Clarissa pointed out the window. Laura stared out. A shiny black car sat across the street, its window's darkened. She looked to the left and saw another one about a hundred yards down. There was another one a hundred yards down on the right.

Laura shut the curtains. "You know how to use a gun?" Laura asked.

"No."

"Good time to learn. Follow me."

Clarissa followed Laura to the study. Laura ran to the bookshelf and grabbed a Robert Ludlum novel on the bottom shelf. The bookcase slid aside revealing an arsenal of weapons. Laura grabbed a handgun and handed it to Clarissa.

"It's simple really. Aim and shoot."

"I'm not sure…"

"Listen, if you're interested in doing this type of work, you're going to have to learn to use a gun. You ain't gonna use it often but when you do, use it well."

Clarissa nodded her head. Laura took a few extra weapons for them both. She led Clarissa out of the study and into the living room. Breaking glass from upstairs stopped them.

"Oh my God," Laura yelled.

The two women ran upstairs to Ty's room. The door was locked. Laura kicked it in and the two women ran in with guns drawn.

A man held Ty on his shoulders like a sack of potatoes. Ty for his part gave the guy as much trouble as he could. He stepped out the window onto a waiting ladder.

"What are you doing with my son? Put him down," Laura yelled.

"He's insurance. Drop the gun."

Laura made a run for the window. Before she reached it however, she was tripped by someone she didn't see. She fell, her head hitting the hardwood floor, knocking her out. Clarissa tried helping but was knocked out as well. The second man followed the man holding Ty out the window.

****

The woman walked into the growing crowd and made her way to the front of the building. Guards blocked the way to the entrance. She approached one and put on her best smile.

"Excuse me sir. My name is Gwendolyn Falcone and my son is chief of staff for Nathan Gibraltar. He told me he wanted to meet here today. I have the appropriate identification if you wish to see it."

"I'm sorry ma'am. Mr. Falcone is busy and is not seeing visitors."

"Can I have a message sent in to him? I'm afraid I forgot my cell phone at home."

The guard looked over at his partner who offered no help. "Sure. I'll get a note to him."

"Thank you. You're such a dear."

The woman took a note pad and a pen from her purse and wrote a note. She folded it up and gave it to the guard.

"Tell him I'll be here all day and will call on him later. Thank you again."

The woman turned and walked back into the crowd. She smiled. That should throw him off guard, she thought. Now to find a way into the building.

****

Xander gave some directions to an aide when a guard approached. Xander dismissed the aide.

"Yes?"

"Sir, I have a note for you."

Xander cocked his head in curiosity. He took the note and thanked the guard. He opened it up and read.

His blood went cold. Looks like Senator Wilson was getting one last shot in from beyond the grave. This changed things. He had to confer with security to change some things around to plug up any possible holes.

His cell phone rang. "Yes?"

"We've got McKnight's kid."

"Report to the publishing company service entrance. I'll be waiting for you."

Xander hung up the phone. He stood for a moment, thinking of his options. McKnight was a nuisance but not a big enough threat to kill. He just had to keep him busy and out of his business. He went into the security room and pulled the head of security aside.

"Hank, I need you to post some of your men inside the factory with me."

"We hardly have enough men to properly protect the Governor much less you."

"I told you that the Governor's personal security staff would be working with your people today so don't give me that short staffed bull. Just do what I say and I'll make it worth your time."

Hank paused. "A little extra money in the stocking at the end of the year would be nice. Give me ten minutes and you'll see the men."

"Good. I just need three."

"You got it."

****

Phil answered his cell phone. "Yes?"

"Phil, they've kidnapped Ty," Laura said, sounding groggy.

Phil felt empty, like he was floating. "What?"

"They took him and attacked Clarissa and me. I can't believe this is happening."

"We're just pulling up to the house now. Gomez was shot in the leg."

"Just get back here as soon as you can."

Phil hung up the phone. English Bob looked at him.

"Everything all right?"

"The safe house was hit. They took Ty."

The rest in the car were silent. As they drove, Phil felt a hand on his shoulder. He turned. It was Gomez.

"That was cold what they did. Let's bandage this leg up and get them sons of bitches."

Phil smiled and patted his hand. "Thanks."

Phil pulled up to the curb. He shut off the car and ran to the house. Stone pulled up behind Phil's car. English Bob pulled Stone aside to fill him in on the recent developments. Phil burst through the doors and found Laura on the couch crying. He sat next to her and took her in his arms.

"What are we going to do?" Laura sobbed.

"I've sat back and let things happen once too often. I say we get down to that publishing company with guns blazing."

"But they have Ty. They could kill him."

Stone approached Laura. "Listen. In all my years of police work, I've gained some experience when it comes to the criminal mind. This is nothing but a scare tactic. They've already bungled too many things. They wouldn't want to have a child's blood to add to everything else."

"Look what they've done so far. You think they'll care about a child?" Clarissa asked.

"They're not the average criminals," Stone said.

Phil stood up. "We're not the average good guys. We know where these bastards are going to be. Instead of sitting here crying about it, let's go to that place and make them shed some tears."

"Eloquently put," said The Ganj. "Now how do you propose we do that?"

Laura and Phil looked at each other. "Let's go," Laura said.

Laura led everyone into the study. She took out the book revealing the weapons collection on the other side.

"Dude, you've been holding out on me," The Ganj said. Phil took out various weapons and passed them around. He turned to Laura.

"Get Gomez into the kitchen. He was shot in the leg."

"I'm all right," Gomez said, limping into the room.

"Come on tough guy," Laura said, taking him by the arm. Stone walked up to Phil.

"These are all legal right?"

"Would I lie to you?" Phil smiled.

Stone laughed. "What do you have planned?"

Phil put his hand on Stone's shoulder. "I don't know man. I don't know."

8:00 AM-9:00 AM

David Geraldson approached the podium, taking in the applause from the audience. He took a sip of water and waited for the crowd to calm. He smiled.

"Thank you ladies and gentlemen for coming here so early in the morning to the grand opening of the first Happy Child Publishing Company plant in Michigan."

The audience applauded. "We have a number of dignitaries with us today. Joining us from Washington D.C. are Ambassador Earl Simmons and Senator Carl Woodrow. The mayor of Grand Rapids, Ronald King is here as well. And our new Governor, Nathan Gibraltar is here to join us in the festivities. We'd especially like to thank the new Governor for joining us at the last minute after Davis Creston's sudden resignation last night. But before we begin, I think it would be appropriate if we take a moment of silence for someone who had just as big a part as anyone in bringing this company to Grand Rapids, the late Senator Joseph Wilson."

The crowd went silent. David bowed his head. After waiting an appropriate amount of time, he raised his head. "Thank you. Without further ado, here is Ambassador Simmons to give us a few words."

****

Xander met the guards at the service entrance. They brought in the boy, tied up with tape over his mouth. Xander grabbed him and took the tape off his face. Ty screamed.

"Why did you do this?" Xander asked the guards.

"I think it's kinda obvious," the first guard said.

"I told you not to do anything to the kid but bring him here. I didn't want this."

"The kid was going nuts sir," the second guard said.

Xander put the kid down. He turned to the guard, grabbed him by the throat, and rammed him against the wall.

"Don't mess with the kid, understand?"

He threw the guard to the ground. He turned to the first one.

"Take care of him."

The first guard grabbed the second one by the arm knowing what the order meant. Xander turned his attention back to the child. He took off the ropes.

"There you go Ty. Were those men mean to you?"

Ty held back tears, not responding. Xander smiled.

"It's ok. I know you saw some scary things and I'm sorry you had to see it. We're going to have some fun here today."

"I want my Mommy."

"She'll be by later. You and I are going to have some fun."

The boy started to shiver. "Have you eaten breakfast yet?" Xander asked.

The boy shook his head. Xander took his hand.

"Come on. We'll get you something good to eat."

****

Before Clarissa started her car, her phone rang. She took it out of her purse.

"Hello?"

"Clarissa, its Eva."

"Oh hi."

"I have someone here who wishes to speak with you."

A pause. "Clarissa?"

"Governor Creston. This is a surprise. How are you sir?"

"We have to meet."

"Why? I'm not sure I could help you with anything. I no longer work for the station."

"I'm not looking for an interview. I've been filled in on everything that's been going on concerning Nathan Gibraltar. I want to help bring Nathan down."

"Join the club."

"Where can we meet?"

"Let me call you back. I have to consult my partner."

Clarissa hung up the phone. She dialed Phil.

"Yeah?"

"Just got a call from Davis Creston. He wants to join the gang."

"By George, let the man join."

"He wants a meeting. Should I go or should we make it a party?"

"Set up the meeting and call back with the destination. I want to hear what he has to say."

****

Robert stared out the scope at the Ambassador on stage. He felt calm. All the emotions he felt yesterday at the statue ceremony were gone, replaced by cold, hard determination. The only emotions left in him were for Lydia, and they weren't happy ones.

He heard a noise behind him but dismissed it as the breeze. He kept his attention on the stage. So when someone placed a gun on his skull, it caught him off guard.

"You work for Gibraltar?" a woman asked.

"No. I'm self employed," Robert said.

Robert turned. It was Annie, Lydia's sister. Robert stood up.

"To what do I owe the pleasure?"

Annie kept her gun leveled at him. "I want to talk."

Robert turned to the crowd across the street. "I got some time. There's no reason to keep that gun leveled at me. I got nothing against you."

"You are my sister's boyfriend so I think I'll decline."

"Appearances are deceiving."

"Having a rift with her are we?"

"She killed my brother and is working with Nathan Gibraltar and Xander, using me as their pawn."

"Than what are you doing with her now?"

"Finding the right time to bring her down, if you get my drift."

"Why are you telling me this?"

"After everything that's happened today, I could care less what happens to me."

Annie grinned and lowered her gun. "Good answer."

"So what would you like to discuss?"

"Actually, I have a question for you? What are your plans here today?"

"Killing everyone involved in destroying my life."

"Ahh, a revenge play. Simple yet effective."

"You stick with what works I guess," Robert said.

"Yet it won't work. You may get off a shot against Nathan and you may even get my sister but you won't leave here alive."

"Didn't plan to."

"What's the point of a revenge play if you can't live to enjoy it?"

Robert eyed her. "What do you propose?"

****

The woman turned the corner and walked down the sidewalk, her bag flopping off her shoulder. She headed for the end of the block. The parking lot to a bottling company appeared ahead. She entered the parking lot. Men and women were pulling in for work, getting out of their cars with the energy of someone on their way to an execution. She passed each of them, getting curious glances along the way.

She reached the back of the parking lot. She looked back. All clear. She reached for the fence.

"Can I help you ma'am?"

The woman turned, grinning. "How are you sir? I'm head of security for the Governor. I was checking out how secure the back of the publishing company was."

"Do you have any identification?"

The woman pulled out a badge and showed it to the man. "Are you the security man here?" she asked.

"No ma'am. I'm the shift supervisor."

"Ahh. Diligent fellow I see. Can I get back to work?"

"I would like to call your supervisor. Someone representing the state police checked us out yesterday. I'd like to ask why they sent someone here again without notifying us."

The woman smiled, looking around the parking lot. No one was around. She pulled something out of her pocket and flung it at the man. It hit the mark. The man rubbed his neck. He tried talking but suddenly felt weak.

"You're starting to feel a poison I concocted myself. What it essentially does is turn your insides to mush in a matter of minutes. It dissolves bones, tissue, major organs. You'll end up a DNA puddle the maintenance crew will have to clean up. And all because you didn't respect your elders. You have to ask yourself, was it worth it?"

She turned and scaled the fence. The shift supervisor fell to the ground in convulsions. She trudged through the trees that divided the two buildings until she reached the other side and headed for the back of the publishing company. She hid behind a tree and eyed the area. Three guards were on patrol. This should be easy, she thought. She picked up a rock and threw it at a window on her far left. It shattered. The three guards ran to the source of the noise. She bolted for the door and ran inside.

An empty office lay directly ahead of her. She ran and tried the knob. Locked. She pulled a barrette out of her hair and picked the lock. She entered the office, locking the door. She went to a dark corner away from a window and sat down. She took a laptop out of her purse and turned it on. The woman inserted an earpiece into her ear. She grabbed a USB cord and plugged it into the security camera on the wall above her. The monitor turned on. The woman clicked on a program and the security system of the publishing company came on screen. Now she had time to sit and wait. Wait for the right time.

****

The audience applauded as the Ambassador took his seat. The mayor, Ronald King rose and approached the podium.

"Being the low man on the political totem pole and a Democrat to boot, I get to be hero for you the audience because I don't get to give a speech."

The audience laughed, giving the mayor a chance to take a sip of water. "It gives me great pleasure to introduce a good friend of mine. Though he comes from Lansing, through his years in political office he has been a great friend of the West Michigan area. Though I'm sure he would have liked to take office under better circumstances, he comes to you today as Governor of the state of Michigan. Ladies and gentlemen, Governor Nathan Gibraltar."

The audience rose to its feet, cheering the new Governor as he shook the mayor's hand and took the podium.

"Thank you. It's great to be back in the wonderful town of Grand Rapids again. I'm sure each of you has heard of the terrible events that have happened in the last twenty-four hours, everything from the attempt on my life, Davis Creston's sudden resignation, the disappearance of my lovely wife Eva, and the murder of my good friend Senator Joe Wilson. These events have saddened me beyond words.

"But the work of the state does not rest and neither will I. The only way I can honor the tragedies of yesterday is to do the work of my office to the best of my ability today."

The audience cheered.

****

The group entered the old diner and found the former Governor at the counter. The place used to be an old train station many years ago. It was converted to a diner in the fifties. The current owners were well off and kept it open so they could keep in touch with their friends. One of those friends was Davis Creston. The closed sign was in the window guaranteeing they wouldn't be interrupted.

Davis rose and hugged Clarissa. "It's been a long time. How have you been doing?"

"I've had better day's sir."

"Call me Davis."

"This is my new partner Phil McKnight. These are his friends that are helping out."

Davis shook everyone's hand, learning each one's names. They took a seat at a table. The waitress came out with a pot of coffee and began pouring cups for the group.

"So what brings us here Governor?" Phil asked.

"Well, you all heard the news about my resigning yesterday. I'm sure you didn't hear the details."

"I can guess it wasn't a long, thought out decision," English Bob said.

"Nathan had a well known criminal figure named Onyx force me out of office."

"How would he have contact with him?" Clarissa asked.

"Onyx has a day job. He runs a nice little Italian restaurant a couple miles from the capitol. His name is Tony Palermo and he has been a friend of mine for close to thirty-five years. I had no idea of his criminal activity. I knew through our conversations through the years that he had a daughter that he was estranged from. Tony met up with me a couple hours ago and told me that his daughter was shot by her husband. Tony's daughter is Eva Gibraltar."

The group's jaws collectively dropped. "Why would Nathan shoot the daughter of a crime lord?" Phil asked.

"Because he had that crime lord in a corner where he couldn't act. He's been Nathan's lap dog whenever Nathan needed something dirty done. That's over now. He wants revenge."

"You're still talking to this guy?" The Ganj asked.

"We won't be poker buddies anytime soon but he's doing this for his daughter. I'd do anything for her."

Phil took a sip of coffee. "Like what?"

"We have the seed of an idea. What we need is some help to make that seed grow."

****

Nathan took a sip of water. "This state stands on the threshold of greatness. But corporations have been avoiding our state because of the antiquated policies of the failed previous administrations. I promise you that starting with the Happy Child Publishing Company, this state's economy will explode with a bang."

Nathan raised his arms for dramatic effect. Yet the only explosion he received was from the audience. He started sweating. He turned his head hoping to see Xander. He didn't. He had to go on. He cleared his throat.

"I admit. I have been put in a difficult position due to Davis Creston's untimely decision. History is not on my side when it comes to job security. But I have been in difficult positions before. And all I ask of you great people is to give me a chance. I have worked hard at maintaining the economic security of this state. The record will show how my involvement helped cause this event today. Give me the chance and I will bring this state to the economic heights it deserves."

Applause. The best salve for the nervous heart.

****

Xander looked at the security monitors. The bomb hadn't gone off as Nathan had expected. Many things hadn't gone as Nathan had expected today but here they were.

His cell phone rang. "Hello?"

"It's Lydia."

"Seems that it worked."

"Should be going off in about fifteen minutes. Hopefully the timers won't fail on us."

"As long as they do the job I'm happy. Nathan's beginning to float in flop sweat out there. When is your boy going to make his move?"

"Around the time Nathan is dragged into the building after the bombs go off."

"Timing it just nice."

"When are you planning on leaving?"

"The top of the hour. I have the rest of the dominoes laid out. All Nathan has to do is knock over the first one. When will I see you?"

"I'll be in the building soon. Then we can have that bottle of champagne you've been promising me."

Xander smiled. "Sounds about right. Talk to you soon."

He hung up the phone. He walked over to the man standing guard over the room where Ty was having breakfast.

"Keep this between us. You tell anyone, I'll find out."

"I understand sir."

Xander took two pictures from his pocket. "This boy's parents will be arriving within the hour to pick up their son. Whatever happens, make sure this boy reunites with them without incident. Do not harm a hair on the boy or the parent's head. There are plans in place for them. That's an order."

"Yes sir."

Xander gave the pictures to the man.

****

"This fills in some of the dots," Stone said.

"Why would he take such extreme measures like this?" Phil asked.

"I don't know. With all that's gone down, this doesn't make much sense," Davis said.

"Why are we talking sense with these people? None of what they're doing makes sense," English Bob said.

"But kidnapping the boy compared to their other actions doesn't fit," The Ganj said.

"How much danger is my son in?" asked Laura.

"Sitting here musing about it isn't helping things," Davis replied.

"This is a desperate move," Stone said. "Compared to Annie Walker killing Dawson Layfield today and…"

"What did you say?" Clarissa interrupted.

"Compared to Annie Walker killing Dawson Layfield today…"

Clarissa rose and ran out of the diner. Phil stood up but Laura held her hand out.

"Stay. I got this."

She ran out to join Clarissa. Clarissa held onto a street sign, crying. Laura put her hand on Clarissa's shoulder.

"What's the matter?"

"I know Annie Walker."

"What?"

"I didn't know she was involved in all this. Heck, I even did a story on her yesterday without knowing it was her. She's my lover."

Laura gulped. "Your lover?"

"Yes. I'm gay. God, I haven't even come out of the proverbial closet yet and the one woman I choose to be my lover is a crazy killer."

"It's all right. We all don't pick gems. Hell, look at Phil."

The two women laughed. Laura took Clarissa and embraced her.

"It's going to be all right."

"How can you be so comforting when your son is kidnapped?"

"I'm trying not to think of it. Besides, we will get him back. Let's get back inside. We'll stop these monsters."

"Can we keep it quiet? You know, about me?"

"There's no reason those boys need to know."

The two women walked back into the diner. They took their places at the table.

"Everything all right Laura?" Phil asked.

"Yeah. It is. When are we leaving?"

"We're taking off now."

"Are you joining us Governor?"

"I'll be at the plant later. Got something special planned."

"Then let's get our asses rolling. Excuse my French Governor," The Ganj said.

****

Xander picked up the phone. "Yes?"

"Sir, we think there may have been a breach back by the service entrance. We need you back here."

"I'll be there in a minute."

Xander hung up the phone. He left the office and headed back toward the main factory passing a couple janitors wearing baseball caps along the way. He reached the service entrance, opened it up, and looked outside.

No one around. Strange. Who would call him and then disappear like that? He closed the door and turned.

A woman stood in his path, a smile on her face. Xander smiled.

"Hello there. What brings you here today?"

The woman smiled. "Why ask when you already know the answer?"

"Who hired you?"

"Senator Joe Wilson."

"I'm sure you've heard of his passing. He won't be able to pay you."

"You're wrong. I always take payment in advance, unlike my daughters. And I never quit a job without finishing." The woman pulled out a small dart. "You know what this is?"

"I can see where Lydia gets her ideas."

"She may not be original but she knows what's effective. You will not leave here alive."

A janitor came near mopping the floor. The woman turned in annoyance.

"What about your daughters?" Xander asked.

"What about them?"

"You know if I die there won't be a place on Earth you can go to be safe. You think my people won't hesitate to have your daughter's killed?"

"Go ahead. Lydia knows how to talk a good game to stay on my good side but I know where she'd stand if pushed. And Annie. She can't control her immoral urges, associating with that homosexual…"

The mop hit the woman in the head like a spear causing the woman to tumble to the ground. The janitor walked up. The woman's face paled in shock.

"Annie."

"That's right Mother," Annie said, pulling off her hat. She pulled out a gun. "Welcome to the twenty first century."

She pulled the trigger. Her mother's head cracked open like a broken watermelon. Annie turned to Xander, lowering the gun.

"So."

"So."

"Where does this leave us?" Annie asked.

"In a much better place than ten minutes ago."

"I have a proposition to make."

"I'm in no position to argue."

"I know my sister is here. In exchange for her life, I'll let you live and you leave me alone."

"Why should I do that?"

Annie raised the gun. "I don't think I have to explain. I don't care what you have planned today. I'm not here to stop it. All I want is to settle our score peacefully."

Xander stared at her. "What a bargain. I'm heading to the production room in a few minutes. Your sister will be meeting me at that time. You can kill her then."

Annie walked over to Xander and kissed him on the cheek. She smiled. "Thank you."

She turned and walked into the heart of the factory, the other janitor following her. That is one messed up family, Xander thought.

****

"Ladies and gentlemen, the state of Michigan is making head ways in the areas of education. While our record is nothing to be ashamed of, we can certainly do more in regards to funding and testing to guarantee that our young ones will get the most from their school years. In return, the rewards the state of Michigan will receive in return will be priceless.

"As your new Governor, I will make it my mission to make the state of Michigan the top state in the nation. The top in education. The top in business. Either I will succeed or I will end my career in disgrace."

The bombs went off. Nathan dove to the ground. Security ran up on stage and grabbed him, dragging him into the building. The audience went nuts, people running back and forth in panic. Cameramen swiveled their cameras around to get a glimpse of the explosion.

****

Lydia watched as Nathan was dragged into the building. No gunshots followed. Robert failed. What was going on? She ran across the street to the building he was on and circled around to the ladder. She climbed to the top.

The roof was empty. The bastard chickened out, she thought. What was he trying to pull?

She ran to the ladder and climbed down. She took out her phone and dialed.

"Hello?"

"Xander. Robert disappeared. He didn't get a shot off."

"Great. Get in here as soon as you can. We'll leave sooner than expected."

Lydia smiled. "Good."

She hung up the phone and put it back in her pocket. She took out a badge from her pocket and clipped it onto her blouse. She headed back across the street, weaving her way through the fleeing crowd. She reached the door. The guards saw the badge and opened it for her. She entered.

The place was nuts. Guards were running up and down the hallways, each trying to look as if their involvement in all this was crucial to the Governor's survival. She walked through the mass, found the door to the main floor, and entered.

The main floor was empty. She ran to the back of the building to the production room where Xander said he would be waiting. She rounded a corner.

A broom tripped her, causing her to fall. She looked up. Standing there, in a janitor's suit, was Robert.

"What are you doing?" she asked.

"Sweeping up my mess."

"You should have been taking care of business on the roof. Why did you leave?"

"I don't know. Maybe us fish can't follow orders as well as you think."

Realization dawned on Lydia's face. She reached for her blowgun. Robert pulled out his gun first.

"Don't try it."

"I can still get in a shot Robert."

Robert smirked. "I don't care."

They stared at each other, testing to see who would be the first to budge. Robert kept the gun on her, his body as stiff as a statue. Lydia quavered, and lowered the blowgun.

"On your knees. You should know how to do that by now."

She complied. "What are you going to do to me Robert?"

"What I was planning to do to Nathan Gibraltar."

"You gonna forget him now and take your frustrations out on me?"

"No. But it will be fun to kill you."

Robert pulled the trigger. Lydia fell to the floor, dead.

****

Phil pulled the car to a stop and shut off the engine. Everyone in the car got out and met the others in front of the entrance to the parking lot.

"Why did we come here?" Phil asked Stone.

"We are not going to be able to walk into the Happy Child factory. The only way in is through the back entrance."

"You know the place?"

"That building used to be an automotive parts factory. I worked here just after high school."

The group headed into the empty parking lot. They passed by the cars. At the back of the parking lot, they avoided a strange gelatinous puddle with clothes on top. They reached the fence.

"Before we go in, we need to break into teams," Phil said. "English Bob, Ganj, you two go together, Laura, Clarissa, you're a team. Stone, you come with me. Gomez, I want you to swing the car around to the front entrance and stay on the radio telling us if there's any trouble."

"But..."

"You're injured. You'll do us better being a lookout, not limping around in there holding us back."

Phil tossed him a radio. "Just think of yourself as a designated driver."

"You son of a bitch," Gomez laughed. He limped back to the car.

Phil turned back to the group. "Let's get this over with."

****

Xander walked into the production room. The workers inside turned in surprise when he walked in.

"What are you doing?" one of the men yelled. "Get a mask on."

Xander pulled out a gun and shot each of them. He walked over to the box of what everyone thought was cocaine. He stuck his hand inside and let the baby powder spill through his fingers. When it seeped back into the box, he pushed it to the ground, spilling the contents onto the floor.

An object poked out of the pile of powder. Xander knelt down and pulled out a metal box wrapped in plastic and brushed it off. He ripped open the plastic and took out the box. He opened it up.

Xander pulled out a pair of vials with a dark blue liquid inside. He smiled. Blue Harvest. The vials were safe. He put the precious vials back into the metal box, closed it, and left the room.

9:00 AM-10:00 AM

Annie spotted Clarissa with another woman and almost fell off the scaffolding. What was she thinking being here? And with a gun no less? She had to see what Clarissa was up to. She scaled down the scaffolding and reached the ground. Looking left and right she ran forward, making sure to keep hidden from anyone, much less the two women.

Two guards appeared out of nowhere spotting the women who didn't notice them. They pulled out their weapons. Annie pulled out two knives and threw them. They landed in the guard's backs. They fell to the floor with a yelp, one of them firing a shot in the air. Clarissa and Laura turned, spotting Annie. Annie approached.

"You killed them," Clarissa squeaked.

"I had to. They were going to kill you."

"You sure about that?" Laura asked.

"I don't kill for fun. And you are?"

"Laura McKnight."

"Ahh. I've had the pleasure of meeting your husband."

"Hope that's not a bad thing."

"Believe me, it's not. Follow me. Your son is in the building."

"Where?"

"That's why I said follow me."

Annie ran off, the two women on her tail.

****

Nathan picked up a glass of water and threw it against the wall. "What do you mean you can't find him? Turn on the damn security cameras and get me Xander."

"That's just it sir," David mumbled. "I can't. The security cameras have been disabled."

Nathan glared at David. "What do you mean?"

"Xander is gone. Without the aid of the security system, we have no way of tracking him."

Nathan paused. "I have to go out on the floor."

"We don't know what's out there sir. Is that wise?"

"If those drugs aren't delivered on time, I'm a dead man. I couldn't use my own money to finance this. I had to borrow it. And if the people I borrowed it from don't get a return for their investment…" Nathan left it at that.

"What should we do now sir?"

Nathan thought it over. "We have to go into the main plant and check the shipment ourselves."

"What about the police?"

"We'll have them secure the exits, preventing anyone from coming or going. That way we'll be in the clear to do what we need to do. My personal guards will be with us on the inside."

"Should we bring anyone else in with us?"

"Bring in that ignorant load Harvey Johnson. He's knee deep in this with us and if we're going down, he's going down with us. And get word to my guards to shoot any stranger on site. We don't know who he could have brought in."

"Yes sir."

David left the room. Nathan walked over to the window and looked outside. Xander had played him for a fool. He fed him everything he wanted to hear and Nathan ate it up like a hungry newborn. *My God, what has he done to me?*

****

Phil and Stone looked at the GPS readout on the cell phone. "Damn. I can't see a thing," Phil said.

"Did they tell you that you could read a newspaper from space with this?"

"Shut up. Every place we've checked so far has had nothing."

"You know, you would be a terrible cop."

"I'm a terrible private eye but I get the job done. With style."

Gunshots spoiled Stone's reply. The two men dove under a bookshelf, taking out their guns.

"Looks like they're at our one o'clock. I see two of them," Stone said. "You spot anymore?"

"There. Nine o'clock. You ready?"

"Whenever you are."

The battle ensued. Stone took out one of the men. Phil's shot missed, but caused a stack of books to fall over causing his man to move out of position. Phil fired again, nailing him. The guard ran off. He turned to Stone.

"I meant to do that."

"Uh huh."

Phil left the bookshelf and ran after his man. Stone gave him cover fire. The man ran down an aisle as fast he could. The warehouse being huge, it would take him a long time to reach the other end. Phil leveled his gun and fired off a shot. Miss. The guard reached the end of the bookshelf and took a right. Phil followed. He spotted the guard circling back. He was heading somewhere. Thinking that he may be heading for back up, Phil fired again. The guard's leg flew out from beneath him. Phi caught up to him with gun drawn.

"Where the hell are the drugs?" Phil yelled.

Phil noticed the man chewing on something. His mouth began foaming and he started convulsing. Phil grabbed the man's head, tilted it, and forced open his mouth. Tiny pieces of glass fell out. This guy popped a cyanide capsule, Phil thought. Why the hell would he do that?

More gunshots broke his concentration. He circled back to join Stone. He slid under the bookshelf.

Stone wasn't there. Only a puddle of blood waited for his return.

****

Eva gave Davis a hug. "You are an angel. You've always been good to me."

"Are you sure you want to do this?"

"Believe me Davis. I'll find the energy to get this done. Then I'll go to the hospital."

Davis kissed her on the forehead. "Good. I'll see you later."

Davis turned and left the room. Eva sat on the bed. She turned to her father.

"I don't like lying to him."

"Neither do I. But he wouldn't have agreed to help if he knew what we had planned. Are you going to be all right? This can be done a different way."

"No. It's going down my way. It's time for Nathan to pay for his sins."

****

Nathan locked the door, preventing anyone in the office from coming into the main plant. David Geraldson and Harvey Johnson stood at his side. Each had a radio.

"Keep radio contact always. I want to reach you two at a moment's notice."

"Yes sir," they replied.

"Search for any intruders Xander may have let in. I'll check out the production room."

The two men walked off. Nathan turned right and headed down the walkway. He reached the end and took a left. The production room was dead ahead. Nathan already knew something was wrong. The production room door lay opened. He went to the door and stepped inside.

Powder filled the air. Nathan covered his nose. He spotted the bodies of the workers splayed in various positions on the ground. The box of cocaine was tipped over, piled in a heap. A ripped piece of plastic sat on top. Nathan grabbed and inspected it. This couldn't be. Why would Xander do this? He held the plastic up. Something else was in this container. And from the smell of things, this powder was about as illegal as baking powder.

He heard gunshots. He ran out of the room, closing and locking it behind him. He spotted one of his guards running in his direction. Nathan stopped him.

"What's going on?"

"We have some intruders."

"Give me a gun."

Nathan grabbed the gun and ran toward the source of the gunshots.

****

Annie grabbed the guard and sliced his throat. His blood spewed like a sprinkler on the floor. Annie shoved him forward and motioned for Laura and Clarissa to follow. They entered the room. Ty looked up, smiled, and ran into his mother's open arms. "Mommy."

"Oh my God. I can't believe you're all right."

"We have to get out of here," Clarissa said.

"Follow me. I think I know a quick way out of here," Annie said.

The women followed. They side stepped the blood and ran down the walkway.

When they reached the end, they took a right. A group of guards appeared about a hundred yards down and started firing. Clarissa and Annie returned the fire. The women quickly ran behind a bookshelf for cover.

"There are too many of them," Laura said. "I don't want Ty getting hurt."

"He won't," Annie said. "I didn't get this far in life without having evaded a few ignorant men."

She led them down the walkway, being quiet so they could hear if guards were following them. They arrived at the entrance to the cafeteria. Annie opened the door and escorted them in.

"Laura, head over to the bathroom and lock the doors. There are too many guards out here. Hide out in there with your son until everything is safe. You have a radio with you so your man on the outside can tell you when it's clear."

Laura looked at her, hating to be put into the position of the damsel in distress. But Annie was right. She couldn't risk Ty getting hurt. Laura walked over to a vending machine and broke the glass with her gun. She grabbed a handful of snacks and went into the bathroom. She turned to Annie.

"I don't know if I'll see you again. Thanks for everything."

Annie smiled. "My pleasure."

Laura walked into the bathroom and locked the door. Clarissa and Annie looked at each other.

"How did you become this?" Clarissa asked.

Annie turned her head. "I didn't ask for you to love me."

"But I do. Why didn't you tell me about all this?"

"Would you have wanted to date a hired killer?"

"All right, you got me there. But now we're here and I can't change my feelings. I'm in love with you. A killer."

Annie laughed. "I only kill bad people. We have to get out of here. Let's go."

Annie and Clarissa left the cafeteria. As they ran down the walkway in the main plant, they held each other's hand.

****

Tony looked at his watch. "Davis should be getting there in a few minutes."

"Good. That will give the reporters something to feed on. It's something Nathan isn't expecting either. Should ruffle his feathers a little."

"What about you? Are you ready?"

Eva rose from the bed. "Yes Daddy. My moment with destiny."

She took her father's arm as they walked out of the hotel room. She had on a long jacket that covered her body. A hat and sunglasses hid her features from curious bystanders. She radiated happiness.

****

Robert spotted Nathan on the ground floor. He almost didn't see him, not thinking Nathan would ever walk around in the open with a gun. His body hummed in excitement. He crept down the stairs, making sure this would be done right. He reached the ground floor and followed Nathan. Each step brought him closer to his prey, closer to his fulfillment, closer to his destiny. An insane sort of happiness filled him like a good Sunday dinner. He followed Nathan around the corner.

No one was around. Nathan was alone in the walkway. If there ever was a time now would be it. Robert crept toward Nathan until he was close enough to touch him. He raised his gun.

"Nice to see you again Nathan."

Nathan stopped and turned. He dropped his gun.

"Robert."

"Hello. It's been too long."

"So. You're going to kill me?"

"Not just yet. I want to ask you a question. Why me? Why did you see fit to ruin my life?"

Nathan shook his head in confusion. "What are you talking about?"

"Why did you have to ruin my marriage? Why did you have to set me up in this scheme of yours? Why me?"

"Because you were there. It's nothing personal."

Robert shook with fury. "You did it because you could?"

"Concerning your wife, she came after me. I had no choice in the matter."

Robert hit Nathan in the head with the butt of his gun. "You could have said no."

"If you want to know whether I killed your wife, I didn't. Her death was a coincidence. When it happened, I took advantage of it so I'd get you off my back. You wife's killer is still out there."

"That's not true."

Nathan smiled. "Then kill me."

Robert raised his gun and put it on Nathan's forehead. His finger quivered on the trigger. He put pressure on it. He wanted this scum to die so bad. Then he thought of his wife. Despite her imperfections, she was a good woman. He loved her and he knew deep down she loved him.

And she wouldn't want this. He lowered his gun. That's when someone behind him knocked him out.

****

Davis Creston approached the mob of reporters and smiled. They took pictures of the now former Governor. They yelled out any question they could think of. Davis held up his hands.

"People, I would love to talk but we need to organize this. I have something I want to say and I want each and every one of you to hear it."

The reporters calmed down. "What brings you hear today?" a reporter asked.

"It concerns my removal from office."

"Removal? You resigned."

"You don't know the whole story."

****

Phil tried the doorknob. It was locked. He looked around. All clear. Phil kicked the door in. A cloud of dust bellowed out of the room. Phil started coughing, covered his mouth, and walked inside. He spotted the bodies on the floor. Along with the tipped over box of cocaine. But the smell. He took a whiff. He couldn't believe it. The powder on the floor was not cocaine. It smelled like baby powder.

Phil took out the radio. "Gomez."

"Yeah?"

"Found the cocaine. Guess what?"

"What?"

"It ain't cocaine. It looks like a package might have been hidden in this powder." Phil took out his keys and picked up the plastic bag.

"What do you think could have been in there?" Gomez asked.

"I don't know. There is an empty plastic bag here. Don't know what was in it. But why would they go to all this trouble for baby powder?"

"Maybe that's it. The story of the drugs could have been a diversion."

"Let me get back to you. I gotta find English Bob and The Ganj."

Phil turned and stepped out the door. When he turned the corner, he ran right into a guard. The guard swung, hitting Phil in the belly. Phil kicked the guard. The guard side stepped him and slugged him in the face. Phil fell to the floor.

"That's what you get for sneaking around," the guard said.

****

Annie kicked the guard in the belly. Clarissa raised her gun and shot him in the chest. Annie kicked the man to the ground.

"Nice shot. Let's go."

Annie and Clarissa reached the door. Annie kicked it open. The two women ran outside and ran for the fence. They scaled it. They ran through the parking lot of the bottling company to the road.

"Wait," Clarissa said.

"What? We have to go."

"No. I can't go with you."

"Why? Please come away with me. We can escape all this."

"But I have nothing to escape."

Annie took Clarissa's hands. "I didn't try to love you. I did everything I could to distance myself from you but I couldn't. You've done something to me no one's ever done before."

"What's that?" Clarissa asked, choking back tears.

"You loved me."

The two women looked into each other's eyes. They embraced.

"I love you Clarissa."

"I love you Annie. I just can't leave with you."

Annie paused, closing her eyes. "I understand."

Annie brushed her hand across Clarissa's cheek. "I'll always love you. I'll always be there for you when you need me. Consider me your guardian angel."

The two women kissed. Annie pulled away and got into her car. She started the engine. She looked out the window at Clarissa. She blew her a kiss. Annie put the car in gear and pulled away. She looked in the rearview mirror at Clarissa. Clarissa stood in the road waving. Annie smiled.

Phil was shoved into a room, tumbling onto the floor. The guard closed the door and locked it. Phil stood up. A moan made him turn his head. Stone sat by the far wall, clutching his shoulder. Phil ran over to him.

"You ok? What the hell happened?"

"Hit in the shoulder. When you took off they grabbed me and dragged me here."

"You hurt bad?"

"I'll live. Just won't be able to play softball for a while."

They laughed. "I found the room with the drugs," Phil said. "Guess what?"

"What?"

"It was baby powder. They were hiding something inside it. I'm thinking that maybe Nathan was kept in the dark about what was really in the shipment. He's running around that warehouse like a chicken with its head cut off."

Stone paused, and started to laugh. "He got played? It makes this all worth it."

"It'll be worth it if we can get our asses out of here. I hope English Bob and The Ganj find us."

English Bob turned and fired the gun at the guards. The Ganj knelt down, reloading his gun.

"This is all I got," he yelled.

"Then let's do it like the movies and go out in style."

The Ganj stood and started firing. A guard fell from the second story to the ground below. Both men's guns clicked. Empty. They ducked.

"Where do we go?" The Ganj asked.

"Follow me."

The two men crawled along the ground toward a bookshelf. Once they were in the clear, they stood up and started running. Between the shelves, a guard popped in their path. English Bob grabbed a book off the shelf.

"Here's a good book about the Iron Curtain bitch," he said.

He swung the book, hitting the guard in the head. The guard fell to the ground. English Bob took his gun.

"Let's get to the stairs. I saw some guards standing by a door," The Ganj said.

They arrived at the stairs and ran up. A guard waited for them up top. English Bob shot him in the leg. The Ganj ran over and grabbed his gun.

"Thanks. What's in the room here?" The Ganj asked.

"A couple prisoners."

"Thanks again."

The Ganj kicked him in the head. They ran to the door, English Bob kicking it in. The two men ran inside. Phil and Stone were waiting for them.

"Bout time you fuckers got here," Phil said. "Got your radio?"

English Bob tossed him his. Phil turned it on.

"Gomez?"

"Phil. Where you been at?"

"Where's Laura?"

"She's locked inside a cafeteria bathroom with Ty. She's waiting till this blows over."

Phil sighed. "Thank God. Clarissa?"

"She radioed me. She got out and went home. Sounded pretty choked up about something."

"As long as she's safe. What's it like out there?"

"Davis showed up. He's having a chat with the reporters. They seem real interested in what he has to say."

"Hopefully they listen. Rev the engines my man. We're blasting our way out of here."

"Adios, amigo."

Phil smiled. He turned off the radio. "We ready to rumble?"

The Ganj smiled. "I don't care if we were ready to play Gin. This is better than being with Princess."

****

Gomez put the radio down and turned to the man seated to his right. "I did what you asked. Can I go?"

The man smiled. "That was a fine job. Your friends will walk right into our trap. Your job is done. There's just one more thing…"

The man pulled out a taser and jammed it into Gomez's side. Gomez writhed from all the electricity surging through his body. In moments, he went limp in unconsciousness. The man smiled, pulling out a cell phone. He dialed.

"Yes?"

"The job is done. The bait is set and our subjects will be captured soon."

"Very good. Drive the vehicle you're in back to the church."

The man hung up the phone. He pulled Gomez over to the passenger side before stepping out of the car and heading to the driver's side. Phil McKnight may have visions of his quest reaching a happy ending. Those visions would change after he met the Elder.

****

Alex sat against the wall staring out into nothing. He felt numb, cold. He couldn't believe his mother was dead. By his own father's gun. Why did he feel this way? After everything his mother did today, he thought he would feel different. But seeing her dead on the lawn…

His father walked into the conference room. Two men came behind him dragging an unconscious man behind them.

"Put Sampson over there," Nathan said, pointing to the corner.

The men shoved the body to the ground. Nathan stood by the door.

"Did you find anything?"

"No sir."

Nathan shook his head. "I can see why Xander involved you two. You two ignorant fuck ups were meant to sink me. You've done a good job."

"What are you talking about?" Harvey yelled.

"I'm talking about cleaning up his trash. There's no chance in hell this shit will be pinned on me."

Nathan took a gun he had hidden and shot both men in the head. He walked over and placed the gun in the hands of the unconscious man. He turned to his son.

"Follow me. We're have to find the security room before the authorities decide to review the tapes."

****

Xander sat in the back of the limo staring at his laptop. He watched Nathan kick the dead bodies of David Geraldson and Harvey Johnson. You rascal, he thought. After all this time, you're finally getting it.

He closed the screen and brought up another. Before he left the publishing company, he'd worked it so that the security cameras seemed as if they weren't working. Not so. He'd just rigged the monitors to appear as if they weren't recording when in actuality they were. With a few key strokes, the glitch was fixed. Xander picked up his cell phone. He dialed a number.

"Hello? News 8 tip line. Can I help you?"

"Yes. I have some video here that I think you people are really going to find interesting."

"If it's an animal rescue we have enough of those."

"Oh no. It's better than that. Are you by your computer?"

"Yes. You know the email address here?"

"I wouldn't be calling if I didn't. I'm sending it now."

Xander pressed enter, sending the video to the station. He waited for a reaction. It took a minute.

"You gotta be kidding me."

Xander smiled. "I wish I were. If you go to the publishing company and check their security system, you'll find footage better than this. I'll also email you some interesting information concerning Nathan's involvement in the rape of Melissa Hunter and the death of Dawson Layfield."

"Thank you. What is your name?"

"Sylvester Willis."

Xander hung up the phone. That should just about do it.

****

"We took care of the guards Phil. What else do you want to accomplish here?" Stone asked.

"I want to bring down Nathan Gibraltar."

"Trust me. You and your rag tag gang of hoodlums already have. He's fucked up enough. We have to get out of here."

Phil paused, taking a breath. This was over. Stone was right. It wasn't as if he could find Nathan, slap him around, and make him confess. Besides, that room full of baby powder would make him look silly enough. He had to leave. But first…

"I'll be right back."

Phil ran over to the cafeteria and went inside. He tried the men's room door. It was unlocked. He went to the ladies' room door and tried it. Locked.

"Laura, it's me. Everything is clear. We're leaving."

A pause. He heard a click. The door opened. A man stood on the other side, a gun aimed at Phil.

"Good morning Mr. McKnight."

The man pulled the trigger. A cloud of dust emanated from the gun barrel, spraying Phil in the face. Phil inhaled and fell to the ground unconscious.

****

Nathan took his son by the arm and dragged him out of the conference room. As they walked, Alex gazed into the rooms he passed. Empty room after empty room. The guards behind him dragged Robert Sampson, who was just waking up. Nathan burst through the door outside with an air of victory. He clutched the hand of his son. Behind him, two of his guards dragged Robert Sampson to show the press. Xander wouldn't win this round. The press turned their attention to him and ran towards the door. Nathan looked to the back of the crowd. A man stood at the back of the crowd, staring at him. Is that...? The press began taking pictures and shouting their questions all at once. They were so noisy Nathan couldn't hear a word they said. He raised his hand and waved.

Then he saw her.

Eva stepped through the parting crowd like a ghost. Alex pulled himself from Nathan's grasp and ran to his mother. She hugged him.

"I'm sorry Mom."

Eva smiled. "It's ok baby. I have to talk to your father. Go over to those police men there."

She watched as Alex walked away. She turned to her husband, opening her coat, revealing her bloody dress.

"Nathan, surprised I'm here?"

"Where have you been?" he asked, voice quavering.

She smiled. "Oh I think you know. Wanna tell the good folks here what you did?"

Nathan stammered. "Eva, I love you."

Eva looked at him, a tear falling down her cheek. "Yeah? Well love hurts."

Eva pulled out the gun she had hidden in her coat and fired. Nathan fell to the ground, the hole in his forehead gushing blood. Alex screamed. Eva dropped the gun and walked over to embrace her son.

"It's going to be all right. I promise you, we're going to be all right."

Alex clutched his mother. She sensed the hesitation, but the longer she held him, the more his grip tightened. Eva smiled.

****

Sylvester Willis boarded the plane, briefcase in one hand, metal box in the other. He found his seat. A steward came up and offered him a glass of champagne. He thanked him and took the glass. He took a long sip of the cold alcohol and sighed. Xander set the champagne glass down and put the metal box on his lap. He opened it up and took out one of the vials. The blue liquid swirled inside, making designs with the light reflection. He smiled. He'd waited a long time for this day and it was finally here. And Grand Rapids would never know what hit it.

Epilogue

Phil shook his head, opening his eyes. There was darkness, a small light waving to and fro from the ceiling. Where am I? he thought. He rose from the cot he was laying on and stood up.

Wherever he was, it was moving. He assumed he was in the back of a semi. The last he remembered he was in the Happy Child Book Publishing Company trying to find his wife and son when a man sprayed a chemical in his face, knocking him out. How did he get here? What was going on?

He heard a cell phone ring. He headed over to where he heard the sound, his hands investigating the ground. He found the phone and turned it on.

"I see you're up Mr. McKnight."

"Who are you? Where is my family?"

The man on the other line laughed. "All in due time. First off, I wanted to congratulate you on your efforts to bring down Nathan Gibraltar."

"Cut the crap. Why am I here?"

"Well Mr. McKnight, you've made quite a mess today that's for sure. You and your friends have made my life quite difficult."

"Who is this? Are you Nathan? Or are you Xander?"

The man laughed. "I'm neither. Nathan is dead, killed by his own wife. And Xander is out of the country. You can call me the Deacon."

"Well Mr. Deacon, where is my family?"

"They're safe. For now. But that's all depending on you. See, you've been unconscious for about a week now. And during that time, your wife and child have been taken to a safe location waiting for you to wake up."

"Well I'm up. Where are they?"

"That's just it. It'll be up to you to find out. You have exactly forty-eight hours to find your wife and child. Otherwise, the explosions I have set up in the building where they're at will kill them. I don't take kindly to people interfering in my affairs. So you and you're friends will go on a little treasure hunt. When the semi stops, the driver will hand you your first clue. Happy hunting."

THE END 10/2002-04/06/2009

Phil McKnight will return in Master of Puppets

AUTHOR'S NOTE

Thank you for your purchase of my novel, Time to Play the Game. Since the day I first put pen to paper, this novel has been quite an experience to finish. While it may not go down in the history books alongside other classic adventure novels like The Bourne Identity or Goldfinger, my hope is that your time reading my story has been fun and encourages you to want to read more of my work.

I have to say, this story was fun to write. Many aspects of the novel were pulled from other works of mine that have never, and probably should never, see the light of day. Being able to take certain ideas and scenes from other stories that didn't quite work and add them to this novel was a great feeling. It felt like I was able to add all my lovelies into a story while still creating something new. I also had fun with little homage's I placed throughout the story. I had a lot of influences that helped inspire this novel and as a thank you, I wanted to show my appreciation to some fine work by crafting certain scenes as an homage to the items that influenced me. Much like Robert Rodriguez and Quentin Tarantino have done with their amazing films, ideally, someone reading this will put two and two together, find the source of my homage, and discover what great work is out there.

Once you've reached this point, it's safe to assume you're finished reading the book (If not, what the hell are you waiting for? Get back to page 1.). Now that you're finished, I ask a favor of you. If you liked this book, pass it along to a friend or family member to share the excitement you had with them. Also, feel free to stop by your local book store and request that they stack of couple of copies of this book on their shelves.

As a first time author, my goal is not to make cash; my goal is to get my story into as many hands as possible. That can only happen if you, kind reader, will pass this story along when you're finished. The more folks that read and enjoy this novel, the more audience I will have for the sequel and any future work I create. Then, and only then, can I start raking in the bucks and buy myself a diamond cane, a cape, and a pimp hat and fulfill my dream of being a 1970's pimp.

Till then, thank you for your purchase of my novel and I hope you'll keep your eyes out for my future work. For more information about that, head to my website, TimJousma.com. See you next time.

www.ingramcontent.com/pod-product-compliance
Lightning Source LLC
Chambersburg PA
CBHW020251030726
47499CB00001B/152